Praise for internationally bestselling author Julie Kagawa and The Iron Fey series

"Fans will revel in the reappearance of familiar characters and new readers will be drawn deep into a new and dangerous world. The final pages will leave readers breathlessly awaiting the next volume."

—*School Library Journal* on *The Iron Traitor*

"Kagawa never loses the pace or character development of her imaginative tale, and readers will be both absorbed and satisfied with the twists, turns, and gender politics of this latest episode."

—*Booklist* on *The Iron Traitor*

"Strong world building and character development—of both fey and humans—continues to abound...Kagawa cleverly balances Ethan's complex emotional life, the humorous antics of misbehaving gremlins, Kenzie's jocular but authentic bravery, and the frightening powers held by historic fey."

—*Booklist* on *The Lost Prince*

"Kagawa's fans will enjoy this expansion of her world."

—*Kirkus Reviews* on *The Lost Prince*

"This is a true quest story...one that anyone looking for great action and inventive worldbuilding should be sure to check out."

—*RT Book Reviews* on *The Iron Knight*

"Kagawa pulls her readers into a unique world of make-believe with her fantastic storytelling, and ultimately leaves them wanting more by the end of each book."

—*Times Record News* on *The Iron Knight*

"Fans of Melissa Marr—and of Kagawa—will enjoy the ride, with Meghan's increased agency and growing power showing the series' maturity."

—*Kirkus Reviews* on *The Iron Queen*

"This third installment in the series is just as compelling and complex as its predecessors, and wholly satisfying."

—*Realms of Fantasy* on *The Iron Queen*

"A book that will keep its readers glued to the pages until the very end."

—*New York Journal of Books* on *The Iron Daughter*

"Fraught with danger and adventure. The action never stops."

—*School Library Journal* on *The Iron King*

Books by Julie Kagawa
available from Harlequin TEEN

The Talon Saga

Talon
Rogue

Blood of Eden series
(in reading order)

The Immortal Rules
The Eternity Cure
The Forever Song

The Iron Fey series
(in reading order)

The Iron King*
"Winter's Passage" (ebook novella)**
The Iron Daughter*
The Iron Queen
"Summer's Crossing" (ebook novella)**
The Iron Knight
"Iron's Prophecy" (ebook novella)**
The Lost Prince
The Iron Traitor
The Iron Warrior

*Also available in *The Iron Fey Volume One* anthology
**Also available in print in *The Iron Legends* anthology
along with the exclusive *Guide to the Iron Fey*

JULIE KAGAWA

THE IRON WARRIOR

THE IRON FEY

CALL OF THE FORGOTTEN

HARLEQUIN® TEEN
www.HarlequinTEEN.com

If you purchased this book without a cover you should be aware that this book is stolen property. It was reported as "unsold and destroyed" to the publisher, and neither the author nor the publisher has received any payment for this "stripped book."

Recycling programs
for this product may
not exist in your area.

ISBN-13: 978-0-373-21135-7

The Iron Warrior

Copyright © 2015 by Julie Kagawa

All rights reserved. Except for use in any review, the reproduction or utilization of this work in whole or in part in any form by any electronic, mechanical or other means, now known or hereinafter invented, including xerography, photocopying and recording, or in any information storage or retrieval system, is forbidden without the written permission of the publisher, Harlequin Enterprises Limited, 225 Duncan Mill Road, Don Mills, Ontario M3B 3K9, Canada.

This is a work of fiction. Names, characters, places and incidents are either the product of the author's imagination or are used fictitiously, and any resemblance to actual persons, living or dead, business establishments, events or locales is entirely coincidental.

This edition published by arrangement with Harlequin Books S.A.

For questions and comments about the quality of this book, please contact us at CustomerService@Harlequin.com.

® and TM are trademarks of Harlequin Enterprises Limited or its corporate affiliates. Trademarks indicated with ® are registered in the United States Patent and Trademark Office, the Canadian Intellectual Property Office and in other countries.

Printed in U.S.A.

To Laurie and Tashya, who began this crazy journey with me.

PART 1

CHAPTER ONE
FLOATING

My name is Ethan Chase.

And I can't be certain, but I think I might have died.

CHAPTER TWO

WAKING UP

The dream always ends the same.

I'm in my room again. Or, maybe it's my sister's room or a stranger's. I can't tell. There are photos on the wall I don't recognize, pictures of a family that isn't mine. But the desk is mine, I think. The bed and the chair and the computer are mine. There's a figure sleeping on the bed, long chestnut hair spilling over the pillow. I'm trying to move about silently, so that I don't wake her, though I can't remember why she's here, in my room. If this *is* my room.

Whoever's room this is, it's dark. I can hear rain pattering on the tin roof overhead, and the distant squeals of the pigs in the shed outside. Dad wanted me to feed them today; it's going to suck tromping out there in the rain and mud. I told him I would feed them when the rain lets up. Truthfully, I don't want to go outside in the dark. I know *it* is out there, lurking in the shadows, waiting for me. I've seen it in the mirror, reflected in the glass: a tall, thin silhouette at my bedroom window, peering in. Sometimes, from the corner of my eye, I think I see long black fingers reaching out from under the bed. But when I turn and look, there's nothing there.

My phone buzzes on the desk. I let it ring, feeling my stomach knot and twist as the phone vibrates on the surface.

"Why don't you answer?" the brown-haired girl asks, now sitting up on my bed. Her green eyes seem to glow in the darkness.

"Because she'll be angry with me," I reply. "I left her. I promised to come back, but I left her alone. She won't let me get away with that."

The phone falls silent. Voices echo from downstairs—my parents, telling me it's time for dinner. I look at the chestnut-haired girl again, only it's not her any longer, but Meghan, sitting on her bed, her long hair pale and silvery in the shadows of the room. She's smiling down at me, and I'm four years old, hugging my stuffed rabbit to my chest.

"Go get dinner, squirt," Meghan says gently. She's still smiling, though I can see the tears on her face, creeping down her cheeks. "Tell Mom and Luke I don't feel well right now. But come back when you're done, and I'll read to you, okay?"

"'Kay," I answer, and pad to the door while clutching Floppy tightly in one arm. I wonder why she's crying, and if there's anything I can do to make her happy again; I hate it when my sister is sad.

"She's lost someone," Floppy whispers to me, as he does sometimes when we're alone. "Someone has gone away, that's why she's sad."

Outside my room, the hallway is dark, and the rest of the house is cloaked in shadow. A single light flickers from our tiny kitchen, and I make my way down the stairs toward it, trying to ignore the dark things that move and writhe around me, just out of sight. A boy, shaggy-haired and ragged, waits for me at the foot of the stairs. "Can you help me?" Todd Wyndham asks, eyes pleading. The shadows curl around him, clinging to his thin frame, drawing him back into the darkness. I shiver and hurry past, squeezing Floppy to my face, trying not to see. "Ethan, wait," Todd whispers as the shadows suck him in. "Don't go. Please, come back. I think I've lost something."

Darkness swallows him, and he's vanished from sight.

"There you are," Mom announces when I finally step into the kitchen. "Where's your sister? Dinner is ready. Isn't she coming down?"

I blink, no longer four years old, and bitterness settles on me like a second skin. "She doesn't live here anymore, Mom," I say, sullen and angry. "Not for a long time, remember?"

"Oh, that's right." Mom takes a stack of plates from the cupboard and hands it to me. "Well, if you do see her again, will you tell her I'm keeping a plate warm for her?"

There's a knock on the front door before I can reply. It echoes through the house, a hollow thud that makes the shadows writhing at the edge of the light draw back in terror.

"Oh, good. Right on time." Mom opens the oven door and pulls out a pie, steaming and oozing red. "Ethan, would you get that, please? Don't leave your guest standing out in the rain."

I set the plates on the table, walk through the living room and open the front door.

Keirran stares at me over the threshold.

He's dripping wet, his silver hair plastered to his neck and forehead, his clothes also drenched from the rain. Water puddles at his feet, only the puddle is much too dark to be water.

Below his shirt, something pulses, dark and menacing, like a twisted heartbeat. I can feel it, suddenly, right under his sternum, a twin to the weight around my own neck, the cold circle of steel hanging from a chain.

The storm rages behind him; lightning streaks across the sky, illuminating the red streaks on his face, the icy gleam of his eyes. For a split second, gazing over his shoulder, I see someone else out there in the darkness. Tall and pale, with hair like writhing mist. But the light quickly fades, and the figure is gone.

I look back at Keirran, a chill creeping through me as I see his hands. They're soaked in blood, wet and gleaming, all the way past his elbow. One hand holds a curved blade, glimmering between us.

I meet those icy blue eyes. He smiles sadly.

"I'm sorry, Ethan," he whispers, always the same.

And rams that blade through my stomach.

I gave a soundless gasp and opened my eyes.

Darkness surrounded me. I lay perfectly still, gazing up at what appeared to be a normal ceiling, wondering where I was. There were cracks running through the plaster, forming odd shapes and faces, but they didn't swirl together and laugh at me as they had several times in the past. In fact, this was the first time…in I didn't know how long…that my mind was clear. Before, I would tear myself out of one dark, surreal dreamscape, only to fall right into another, where everything was twisted and frightening and screwed up, but you didn't know it because you were in a dream. There were a few lucid moments where, if I thought hard enough, I recalled faces hovering over me, eyes bright with worry. One face in particular showed up in my dreams a lot, her cheeks wet with tears. She spoke to me sometimes, telling me to hold on, whispering how sorry she was. I desperately wanted to talk to her, to let her know I was all right. But I could never hold on to reality for very long, and quickly slipped back into the twisted nightmares of my mind.

I couldn't remember how I'd gotten here, but I finally had a conscious hold on my brain. I was awake, and alert, and determined to stay that way this time.

Cautiously, I probed my shaky thoughts, gathering fractured shards of memory as I tried to piece together what had happened. First things, first.

Where am I?

Slowly, I turned my head, scanning my surroundings. I lay in a large bed, the covers pulled up to my chest and my arms at my side. The room looked like a normal bedroom, or maybe an office, though I didn't recognize it and had never been here before. A desk sat in one corner, computer screen glowing blue, and a dresser stood beside it. To my right, a partially open window let in the cool night air, and silvery light cast a hazy glow through the room. A full moon shone through the glass, huge and round and closer than I'd ever seen before.

Blinking, I turned my head toward the other wall, and my breath caught in my throat.

A chair sat in the corner closest to my bed. Slumped in that chair, with her arms crossed and her head resting against the back, was a girl with pale hair and slender pointed ears.

My sister. Meghan Chase, the Iron Queen.

I watched her for a second, my newly woken mind trying to make sense of it all. Meghan stirred, shifting to another position, a queen trying to get comfortable. A blanket had been draped over her, and a book lay on the ground beneath the armrest. My throat felt suddenly tight. Had she been watching me, keeping vigil at my bedside? How long had I been here, anyway? And what the hell had happened, during the time I was out?

I tried sitting up to call to her. But the movement sent the room into a sickening tailspin, and my voice came out as a choked rasp. Grimacing, I sank back, feeling frail and horribly weak, like I'd been sick for a long time. Still, Meghan must've been barely asleep, for her eyes shot open, piercing blue in the gloom, and immediately fell to me.

"Ethan." Her voice was a breathless whisper, and in an instant, she was at my side. One slender hand gripped mine as she knelt beside me, the other reached out and brushed my face, soft fingers sliding over my cheek. Her eyes were suspiciously bright as they met my gaze. "You're awake," she said, her voice faint with relief. "How do you feel?"

I swallowed. My throat was like sandpaper; talking felt like tiny razor blades being dragged through my windpipe, but I managed a hoarse "Okay, I guess." And then my throat exploded in a coughing fit that brought tears to my eyes.

"Hang on," Meghan said, and left my side. A minute later she was back with a cup, handing it to me with a stern "Drink it slowly."

I took a tiny, cautious sip, wondering if it was spiked with faery glamour. It turned out to be water—normal, nonmagical water, as far as I could tell. Suddenly parched, I had to force myself to swallow slowly, knowing it would probably come right back up if I gulped too fast. Meghan waited patiently until I was done, then dragged the chair to the side of the bed.

"Better?"

I nodded. "Yeah," I breathed, testing out my voice. It still sounded raspy, but at least I could talk without coughing. "Where am I?"

"The Iron Realm," Meghan replied softly. "You're in Mag Tuiredh."

The Iron Realm's capital. Meghan's court, right in the center of the Nevernever. I'd ended up in Faeryland yet again.

I shifted against the pillow, and the room tilted a bit, making me clench my teeth. Meghan's expression grew concerned, but I set my jaw, hoping she wouldn't leave to fetch the doctor or healer or whatever faery creature took care of such things. I was awake and alert, and I still had no idea what was going on. I needed answers.

"How long have I been out?" I asked, gazing at my sister.

She didn't respond immediately, watching me with concerned blue eyes, and something on her face made my stomach twist. "Meghan?" I prodded. "How long have I been here, in the Nevernever?"

"A little over a month," Meghan finally answered. "As far as we could tell, you've been in a coma, until today. No one was certain you would wake up. We found you…at the faery ring in Ireland and brought you here."

"A month?" I choked out. A month in the Nevernever meant an indefinite amount of time had passed in the real world. A year could've flown by while I lay here, oblivious. "Why here?" I asked faintly. "Why didn't you bring me back to the human world?"

Again, Meghan didn't answer, gazing down solemnly, her eyes bleak.

"What about Mom and Dad?" I demanded. Right before I left, I'd promised I wouldn't disappear into Faery for God knew how long. Another promise broken, another lie I'd told the people I loved. Mom was likely freaking out. "Do they know where I've been?" I asked. "Has anyone told them? Do they know I'm okay?"

"Ethan," Meghan whispered, and her voice trembled. And, looking into my sister's face, my insides went cold with fear. Her expression was haggard, and she stared at me as if I were a ghost. Flickers of raw anguish glimmered behind that composed mask she wore, the guise of the Iron Queen. My memory was fuzzy, but I knew, in the back of my mind, that something terrible had happened.

Closing her eyes, Meghan took a deep breath before facing me again.

"When we found you," she went on, her voice growing a little stronger, "you were close to death. Your blood was everywhere, and you had already stopped breathing. We did everything we could to save your life, but…" She swallowed, and I could see she was barely keeping herself from bursting into tears. "But, in the end, we lost you."

My heart seemed to stop. I stared at her, incredulous, my mind refusing to accept the concept. "What…what do you mean?"

"Ethan…you died. For a few minutes, you were dead."

Reeling, I slumped back against the pillow. Bits of that night came back to me, untangling from the mess of dreams and nightmares. Some of it had been real. "But I'm still here," I reasoned out, glancing at Meghan. "I'm still alive. How?"

"I don't know," Meghan said. "But the healers found this on your body."

She leaned close and handed me something that clinked in my palm. Cold metal pressed against my skin as I stared at the two pieces of copper in my hand. They fit together perfectly, forming a round, flat disk with a triangle etched into the very center.

An amulet. It had been a gift to me from…my mentor, Guro Javier, for protection against the dangers of the Never-never. But I hadn't always had it… My brain spun, trying to remember. I had worn it when I'd gone with Keirran to meet the Lady of the Forgotten in Ireland. And standing in the faery ring, surrounded by dozens of Forgotten, the Lady had told Keirran that the way to tear open the Veil—the magic barrier that kept normal humans from seeing the fey—was a sacrifice. A sacrifice of one whose blood tied him to all three courts, who had family in Summer, Winter and Iron. For the exiled fey to live, for the Forgotten to be remembered by humans once more, I had to die.

And then, Keirran had stabbed me. And I had died.

"My healers tell me there was powerful magic surrounding that amulet," Meghan continued, her tone unnaturally calm. "And when you…died, it shattered. I thought I'd lost you."

Her voice shook, but she composed herself again. "But just as we stopped trying to revive you, your heart started beating. Very, very slowly, and we couldn't wake you up, but you were alive." She looked at the broken amulet in my palm, wonder and relief laced through her voice. "Whatever this was, it probably saved your life."

I stared at the glittering pieces, not knowing what to feel. My emotions were so jumbled up, it was hard to focus on just one. It's not every day your older sister informs you that you were dead, even if it was for just a few minutes. And that you had been killed, stabbed in the back, by your own family member.

Keirran.

I forced my thoughts away from my traitor nephew. "Mom and Dad?" I asked hoarsely, glancing at Meghan. "Do they know?"

A pained look crossed her face. "They've been told where you are," she replied. "They know you're with me, in the Nevernever. I told them something happened to you, and that you have to stay here for a while, for your own protection." She took a shaky breath. "I couldn't tell them the truth, not yet. It would've killed Mom. I was hoping you would wake up before I had to explain what really happened. Why I couldn't send you home."

And then, in that dark bedroom, with the shards of the amulet that saved my life glittering between us, Meghan broke down. The mask of the Iron Queen disappeared, and she covered her face with one hand. Her shoulders trembled, and short, quiet sobs escaped her hunched frame, as my heart and stomach twisted themselves into a painful knot. Meghan had always been the strong one; before she'd disappeared into Faery, I could always look to her for everything. True, I was just a little kid back then and worshiped the ground my older sister walked on, but whenever I was tormented by nightmares or terrors or monsters only I could see, Meghan was the one I went to. She was the one who could make me feel safe. Even now, years later, I still couldn't stand the sight of her unhappy. After she left, I'd spent the greater part of my life resenting her, angry that she'd chosen Them over family and hating the world that had taken her away. But even through all that, I'd still missed my sister like crazy and wished she could come home.

"Hey." Not knowing what else to do, I leaned over, ignoring the brief moment of vertigo, and took her hand. Her fingers wrapped around mine and squeezed tight, as if to convince her that I was still there. Still alive. "I'm all right," I told her. "Meghan, it's okay. I'm still here. I'm not going to die anytime soon."

"No," she whispered back. "It's not okay. It hasn't been for a while now." She took a breath, trying to compose herself, though tears continued to stream through her fingers. "I'm sorry, Ethan," she went on. "I'm so sorry. I wanted to protect you from all of this. I tried so hard to stop it, distancing myself, never visiting, keeping you and K-Keirran apart..." Her voice broke on Keirran's name, and I felt a rush of grief, anger, guilt and despair surge between us, so strong it made my skin prickle. "I've kept so many secrets, hurt so many people, to keep this from happening. Now Keirran is out there, and you almost died..." She shook her head, her grip tightening almost painfully around my fingers. "I'm sorry," she whispered again. "This is my fault. I knew this was coming. I should have kept a better eye on you both, but I *never* thought Keirran would... That he was capable of..."

A shudder racked her frame, and she gave another quiet sob. Abruptly, I remembered that, that night, right after Keirran had stabbed me and I had passed out, I'd heard the sound of hoofbeats getting closer. Had that been Meghan and her knights, come to save me? Had she seen Keirran, her only son, run a sword through my body and leave me to die?

And then, I remembered something else.

"That was the prophecy," I said, feeling like an idiot for not seeing it, for *never* guessing it. Of course, how could I? How could I have guessed that Keirran, my nephew, and, in all honesty, one of my only friends, would stab me in the back? "The one that had everyone so worried. You, Ash, Puck, even Titania. You all nearly had a heart attack when you saw me and Keirran together. Because of the prophecy."

Meghan nodded wearily. "I guess I shouldn't be surprised that you found out," she said, wiping her eyes as she sat up straighter, facing me. "Who told you?"

"The Oracle," I said, remembering the dusty old hag with empty holes for eyes, the stabbing pain as she'd touched my head and seemed to sink her talons right into my brain. I remembered the vision flashing through my head: Keirran, covered in blood and with sword in hand, standing over my lifeless body. "Right before she died," I added, seeing Meghan's eyes widen. "She was killed by the Forgotten."

A pained look crossed Meghan's face. "So, the rumors were true," she said, almost to herself. "I'm sorry to hear it. We didn't part on the best terms, but I'll always be grateful for the help she gave." She closed her eyes briefly in a moment of silence for the ancient faery, then fixed them on me again. "Did she tell you anything else?" she asked. "What the prophecy meant? How it would come about, and your part in it?"

I shook my head. "She didn't have time to explain before the Forgotten killed her," I replied. "All I saw was me on the ground, and Keirran standing there. I mean, I knew I was dead, that she was showing me my death..." I shivered, and I saw Meghan's jaw tighten, too. "It looked like something had killed me. But, I never thought...that it would be *Keirran*."

Anger flared once more, dissolving the last of the shock, and I clenched my fist in the blankets. "But you knew about it," I told Meghan, and it was hard not to make it sound like an accusation. My sister regarded me sadly as I tried to control my emotions, the feeling of betrayal from all sides. "You knew about the prophecy," I said again. "That's why you kept Keirran and me apart. That's why you never came back." She didn't answer, and I leaned forward, determined to get to the bottom of this, once and for all. "How long did you know?"

"Since before Keirran was born," Meghan replied, her gaze going distant. "The Oracle came to me not long after I became the Iron Queen and told me that my firstborn child would bring nothing but grief. That Keirran was destined to either unite the courts or destroy them." She looked down at our hands, still held together. "And that the catalyst…was your death, Ethan. If Keirran killed you, that would be the trigger, the start of the destruction."

I stared at her in disbelief. Before Keirran was even born. That was *years* of knowing, years of that dark cloud hanging over her head. She had carried the knowledge that her son might do something horrible for his entire life.

"And now, it's happened," Meghan said, her voice flat. "The prophecy has come to pass. Keirran has started something he can never undo, and I must respond, as queen of this land."

I felt a cold lump settle in my gut, and I swallowed the dryness in my throat. "What's going on?" I asked, my voice coming out faint. I was almost afraid of the answer. "Where is Keirran, anyway?"

"No one has seen him since that night," Meghan replied. "But we have reason to believe he is with the Forgotten."

The Forgotten. The fey who were slowly fading from existence because no one remembered them anymore. The blood froze in my veins. If I had "died," then the Veil—the thing that had kept Faery hidden and invisible to humans—was gone. Keirran believed that destroying it would save the Forgotten, providing them with the human belief that they desperately needed to survive, as they had no glamour of their own. But I could only imagine the worldwide terror, chaos and madness that would have ensued if all humankind had suddenly discovered the fey were real.

"What happened?" I asked, looking up at Meghan. She closed her eyes, making dread settle in my stomach. Had Keirran really started a Faery apocalypse? "Was the Veil destroyed?" I choked out. "Can everyone see the fey now?"

"No," Meghan whispered, making me slump in relief. "It's not possible to permanently destroy the Veil," she went on. "Even if the ritual had worked the way it was supposed to, the Veil would have eventually re-formed. But…" She hesitated, her voice going grave. "When you died, the entire Nevernever felt it. There was this surge, this ripple of emotion from the mortal world, the likes of which Faery has never felt before. It went through the courts, the wyldwood, Mag Tuiredh, everywhere. We didn't know what it was at first, then reports started coming in from the human world. For a few minutes after your death, Ethan, the Veil *was* gone. For a few minutes…"

"People could see the fey," I finished in a whisper.

Meghan nodded. "Thankfully, after you revived, the Veil came back quickly, and minutes afterward, everyone forgot what they'd seen. But, in that short time, the human world was in chaos. Many people were injured trying to escape, kill or capture the faeries they came across. Some went mad, or thought they had gone mad. A great many half-breeds were hurt, some even killed, when the humans saw them for what they were. It was only a few minutes, but the event still left its mark. Both our worlds are still recovering, even if one doesn't know from what."

I felt sick and tried not to think of what I knew could have happened the night I had died. "Mom and Dad?" I asked in a strangled voice. I never thought I'd have to worry about the ones I left behind in the mortal realm, the normal world, but all bets were off, it seemed. "Where were they that night?"

"They're fine," Meghan assured me, sounding relieved herself. "They were both asleep when it happened, and your anti-faery charms kept their house safe. By the time they woke up, everything was mostly back to normal. Though there was a lot of confusion, fear and anger in the days that followed."

I breathed deep, dispelling the knot of panic in my stomach. At least my family was all right, safe from the faery madness that had apparently swept the world. Though something else nagged at me. Frowning, I raked my fuzzy memories of that night, trying to recall what was real and what was nightmare. There was something I was forgetting…or someone. Keirran and I had gone to Ireland together to meet the Forgotten Queen, but we had left someone else behind…

"Kenzie!" I gasped, feeling my gut knot once more. *Kenzie* had had the amulet—it had saved her life a few times while we were in the Nevernever—but she'd given it back to me when I'd left her in the hospital that last night. My mind swirled with memories of a slight, defiant girl with dark brown eyes and blue streaks in her hair. Mackenzie St. James had been the third part of our little trio, a girl who bargained with faery queens to gain the Sight, argued with obnoxious talking cats and blatantly refused to stay safely behind in the mortal world. Cheerful, stubborn, relentless, she had followed me into Faery, ignoring all my attempts to keep her at arm's length, and I had, against all my better judgment, fallen completely in love with her.

I'd told her as much, the night Keirran and I had gone to Ireland to meet the Forgotten Queen. We'd had to leave her behind because Keirran had picked a fight—with *Titania*, of all faeries, the freaking queen of the Summer Court—and Kenzie had gotten caught in the middle. I remembered my whispered confession that night in her hospital room, remembered my promise to return, and felt like throwing up. How much time had passed in the real world? Was Kenzie all right? Was she still waiting for me?

Or had she moved on, convinced that Faery had swallowed me whole once more, and I wasn't coming back this time?

"Where's Kenzie?" I asked Meghan, who gave me a concerned look. "She was in the hospital the night I left with Keirran. Is she all right? Where is she now?"

Meghan sighed. "I don't know, Ethan," she said, making my pulse spike with worry. "I wasn't aware the girl was injured. Had I known, I would have sent someone to check up on her. But between you and Keirran and the upcoming war, I haven't had time to think of much else. I'm sorry."

"War? What war?"

For a moment, Meghan seemed to stare right through me, her expression one of guilt, anger and grief. But then she rose, and the persona of the Iron Queen filled the room, composed and resolved, making the air crackle with power.

"The Forgotten Queen has grown strong enough to invade the Nevernever." Meghan answered calmly, though her eyes were hard. "Her army of Forgotten have left the mortal realm and have crossed into the wyldwood. There is to be a council tomorrow night in Tir Na Nog to decide what must be done. If it is to be war, we are at a disadvantage."

"Why?"

She paused, a thread of anguish creeping into her voice as she answered, turning my stomach inside out.

"Because Keirran is leading them."

CHAPTER THREE

CRASHING THE UNSEELIE COUNCIL

I stared out the window as the carriage rattled through the streets of Mag Tuiredh, the Victorian steampunk city of the Iron fey. The wide cobblestone streets teemed with faeries, and the dying evening sun glinted off bright metal, copper, wire and clockwork, mostly from the fey themselves. Gremlins skittered over the walls and towers, flashing neon blue grins. A trio of wraiths made of rags and iron cables fluttered across the street, leaving the smell of battery acid in their wake. A green-skinned faery in coattails and a top hat paused at a corner and bowed his head as we passed, a rusty clockwork hound sitting patiently beside him.

Glitch, Meghan's first lieutenant, sat across from me, the strands of neon lightning in his hair making the walls of the carriage flicker like a strobe light. It was giving me a headache, and I'd already been feeling kinda sick. Between Meghan's news last night and the nagging dread about where we were going now, I could probably puke with very little effort.

Also, I was still recovering from being run through with a sword. That might've had something to do with it.

"Are you well, Prince Ethan?" Glitch asked, regarding me with concern.

I glanced his way, trying not to be sullen. The slight faery lounged in the opposite corner, watching my every move. Like all Gentry, Glitch looked young, no older than me, though I knew he'd been in the Iron Realm since before Meghan became queen. I also knew Meghan put him here to baby-sit me, and, though it wasn't his fault, I resented being under the watch of some punky-looking faery with purple plasma-globe hair.

"Yeah." I sighed, staring out the window again. "I'm fine." I wanted to tell him not to call me *prince*, but it would do no good. I was the queen's brother. Therefore, at least to the fa-eries of Mag Tuiredh, I was a prince.

Although, where we were headed, I doubted even being the Iron Queen's brother would do me any good.

Tir Na Nog. The Winter Court, home of Queen Mab and the Unseelie fey. And the last place I wanted to find myself in the Nevernever. All of Faery was dangerous, of course; even Meghan's kingdom was not completely safe, but it paled in comparison to Mab's realm. The Iron fey were a weird, quirky, eccentric bunch; They could be annoying, They could be deadly, but from what I'd seen, They wouldn't rip your face off just for the fun of it. The same could not be said for the Unseelie Court, which boasted entertaining things like goblins, redcaps and ogres. And all the dark, twisted creatures you did not want to meet in a dark alley or under your bed.

You wanted this, I reminded myself. *You insisted on coming. You argued with Meghan to be here. This is your own damn fault.*

A lump settled in my stomach as I remembered the heated words from this morning and the hasty actions that led to this trip.

"Sire, you're not supposed to be up."

I glared at the faery in the long white coat, wondering if he had been lurking outside my door, waiting to pounce as soon as I got out of bed. It was early afternoon, and I'd already been poked, prodded and fussed over far longer than I thought was necessary. Meghan was off ruling the Iron Realm, so I had been left to the mercy of several attentive but annoying healer fey, who swarmed around me with needles and thermometers, asking multiple times if I was in any pain. My repeated assurances that I was fine seemed only to convince them that I was not. Finally, after deciding for themselves that I was in no danger of dying a second time, the swarm had left me, with firm instructions to stay in bed and not push myself.

Yeah, like that was going to happen.

"I'm fine," I told this new healer, who arched his bushy eyebrows at me, making me wince. *I'm fine* seemed to be their code for *I'm really feeling quite awful and need immediate medical attention.* "Where are my clothes?" I went on, hoping to stall him from calling the rest of the swarm. "I don't need to rest— I need to talk to my sister. Where is she?"

He gave me a dubious look. I glowered back. Truthfully, I wasn't feeling the greatest. My legs were shaking, and just standing up was making the room sway, a side effect from being horizontal the past several weeks, I guessed. But I couldn't lie there like a vegetable while so many things were happening around me. Last night, after Meghan had dropped that bombshell about Keirran, the healer swarm had arrived, preventing me from asking the ten thousand questions swirling through my head. I'd tried waiting until they left to resume talking to my sister, but whatever faery concoction they made me drink must've been a sleeping potion of some kind, because the next thing I knew, I was waking up.

I didn't need more sleep. I needed to know what was going on, with Keirran, the Forgotten and the entire Nevernever. I needed to contact my parents, let them know I was all right.

And Kenzie. My insides churned. Where was she now?

What had happened to her in the time I'd been gone? Was she still waiting for me? Or had she given me up for dead and moved on, returning to her old, normal life, one without dangerous faeries and deadly magic?

A chill crept up my spine, and I almost dropped onto the bed again. One month in Faery likely meant several had passed in the real world. How long had it been since I last saw Kenzie, lying in that hospital room? Her illness...

The cold spread to all parts of my body, and I was suddenly torn between curling into a ball on the bed and punching the walls until my knuckles were bloody. What if...what if she'd never left that hospital? What if I went back home, and Mackenzie St. James was no longer there?

"Sire." The healer stepped forward, a note of concern in his voice. "You really should lie down. You've gone quite pale."

"No," I rasped, waving him off. I'd done enough sleeping, and I couldn't get home to see Kenzie now. I had to get out and do something before I drove myself nuts. "I'm fine. I just...need to find my sister."

He blinked. "Her Majesty is in the war room with the prince consort and her advisers. But they're in a private meeting and have ordered that no one disturb them. Are you sure you don't want to lie down, rest a bit?"

I left him sputtering protests and walked into the hallway, pausing a moment to get my bearings. I had no idea where the war room was and didn't think the healer would give me directions. An Iron knight, tall and imposing in full plate armor, shot me a sideways look from where he stood at the end of the hall, but the stern face and large sword made me nervous. A gremlin, bat-eared and razor-toothed, peered down from a chandelier and gave me a sharklike grin, but I was not going to waste time trying to have a sane conversation with a gremlin. Two packrats—short, hunched faeries carrying enormous mounds of junk on their backs—waddled down the hall, chittering in their strange, squeaky language, and I pushed myself off the frame.

"Hey," I called. "Wait a second." They stopped and blinked up at me as I stepped in front of them. "I need to find my sister. Where's the war room?"

They cocked their heads, and I wondered if this had been a good idea after all. I knew they could understand *me*, but I didn't speak packrat and didn't have time for a game of charades in the middle of the Iron Palace. "I don't need a detailed map," I went on. "Just point me in the right direction."

They held a short, squeaky conversation with many head bobs and hand gestures, before turning and beckoning me to follow. Relieved, I trailed the faeries down several long, winding hallways, passing knights, gremlins and countless other Iron fey. They stared at me with varying degrees of curiosity, wariness and awe. As if I was the monster, the thing out of place.

I supposed I was.

Finally, they took me through a wide-open doorway into an antechamber I'd seen once before, large and airy, with a massive iron chair at the end of a long carpet. Meghan's throne room. It was mostly empty now, only a few Iron knights standing in corners and one wire nymph polishing the steps of the dais. The packrats hung back in the doorway but pointed across the chamber to another door on the far wall, guarded by a single Iron knight. I smiled and nodded, letting them know I was grateful without thanking them outright. I didn't know the particular rules of the Iron Court, but saying the words *thank you* in Faery was generally a no-no. The packrats smiled back, chittered something I didn't understand and waddled away.

I took a deep breath, clearing the faint light-headedness,

and walked across the throne room to the door on the other side. The Iron knight watched me approach, narrow face impassive, and didn't move. I raised my chin and tried to sound authoritative, like I was supposed to be here.

"I need to see my sister. It's important."

He stared at me long enough to make me wonder if I was going to be escorted back to my room "for my own protection," before he bowed his head and calmly stepped aside. Trying not to shake with relief, I walked through the door and followed a short hall until it ended at another door, this one unguarded. Carefully, I tested the handle, expecting it to be locked, but it turned easily in my palm, and familiar voices drifted through the crack as I eased the door open.

"And you are certain it was him?" said a low voice that I recognized instantly, making my hackles rise. *Of course, he would be here.* I caught myself, trying to banish the feelings of anger and resentment toward that particular faery. They were just habit now, part of the lingering grief from when I'd thought he had stolen my sister from me. It wasn't Ash's fault that Meghan never came home. She loved him, and she had chosen to stay in the Nevernever, to become the Iron Queen. I was tired of being angry, tired of the bitterness that ate at me from the inside. I didn't like the thought that I had died hating part of my family.

"Yes, sire." This second voice shook a bit, as if its owner would rather be anywhere else. "I saw him myself. He was with a small contingent of Forgotten, in the wyldwood. Right outside Arcadia's borders."

"Scouting the area."

"I believe so, sire. Though, when we tried following them, they disappeared. It's as if they vanished into thin air."

"So, it's true." This from Meghan, her voice grief-stricken, resigned, furious and terrifying all at once. "The Forgotten in-

tend to attack the courts. I'll have to tell Oberon that the Forgotten are practically on their doorstep, and that Keirran…"
She trailed off, took a deep breath. "Glitch, send patrols to all
our borders. Tell them to be on the lookout for Keirran and to
report any sightings immediately. If they do see Keirran, do
not attempt to talk to him. Until we know his intentions and
why he remains with the Forgotten, we have to treat Keirran
as a potential threat. Is that understood?"

There was a general murmur of consent, though Glitch's
voice, angry and frustrated, chimed in a moment later. "Why
is he doing this?" the first lieutenant almost snarled. "This is
his home. Why is he throwing everything away to side with
the enemy?"

"Because he thinks he's saving them," I answered, stepping into the room.

Instantly, a table of about ten faeries straightened and turned
toward me. Meghan was standing at the head with a tall faery
in black close beside her. His silver eyes met mine across the
room, cool and assessing, and I gave a small nod.

"Ethan," Meghan said, a note of weary disapproval in her
voice. "You are not supposed to be up right now."

"Yeah, so everyone keeps telling me." I walked to the table,
clenching my jaw to keep the pain from my face, to appear
perfectly normal. The fey watched me curiously, but it was
Meghan's gaze I sought, meeting her blue eyes as I reached
the table and put a hand against the surface to steady myself.

"I know Keirran," I said, speaking to Meghan but address-
ing them all. "I was with him when he went to the Lady.
The Forgotten Queen. He…he really wanted to save them,
the exiles and the Forgotten, from ceasing to exist." My gaze
went to Ash, standing quietly beside the queen, and for a moment, I wondered if I should reveal the *other* reason Keirran
had wanted to help. That, long ago, Ash had gone through

the place where all the Forgotten went to die, and unknowingly woke up the Lady.

I decided against it. The damage was already done, and accusing Ash of this whole mess wouldn't help anything. Besides, it didn't excuse Keirran's actions. I was done helping him; even this, explaining why the prince was with the Forgotten, was to help my sister understand her son's douchy behavior. Keirran was family, but he was not my friend. I'd tried to help, I had stuck my neck out for him, and he had literally stabbed me in the back. I could excuse a lot, but not that. If I ever saw my nephew again, I was going to kick his ass.

"Save them?" Glitch shook his head, making the lightning in his hair flicker. "By waging war on the other courts? By threatening his own kingdom, his own family? Why? How will that accomplish anything?"

"It doesn't matter." Meghan's voice was steely and resigned at the same time. "What matters is that Keirran and an army of Forgotten are moving on the Nevernever. We must take this news to Tir Na Nog, to the war council of Summer and Winter. If the Forgotten do intend to attack, we must be prepared." Her gaze went around the table and fastened on Glitch. "Make ready the army," she ordered, and Glitch snapped to attention. "We depart for the Winter Court first thing tomorrow. Dismissed."

The crowd of fey bowed and departed the room, leaving me alone with the rulers of Mag Tuiredh.

When the door closed, Meghan put both hands on the table and bowed her head with a shaky sigh. "So, it really is happening," she murmured. "The prophecy has come to pass. I really am going to wage war against my son."

I didn't know what to say, if I should even say anything, but Ash moved close, putting a hand on her shoulder. "We don't know that yet," he said gently. Meghan's hand came up to clutch his, as if he was a lifeline keeping her from drowning. "We don't know how far gone he is," Ash continued, "or what he might have promised. Perhaps there is still time to talk to him."

"He killed Ethan, Ash!" Meghan spun on him, as if she'd forgotten I was standing right there. "In cold blood. He stabbed him, *sacrificed* him, to make way for these Forgotten. I never thought..." She covered her face with one hand. "Even after the prophecy, and the Oracle's warning, I never thought he would do it. What's happened to him, Ash? We did everything we could to prevent this, and now..."

Ash held Meghan's shoulders and peered down at her with intense silver eyes. "Nothing is certain yet," he told her. "Ethan is alive, and neither Keirran nor the Forgotten have attacked. We can fix this, Meghan, I swear it. There is still time."

"Um..." I ventured, reminding them that I was still in the room. They turned, giving me somber looks, and I swallowed hard. "I might have an idea," I said, wondering if they thought of me as an intruder, a human pest who had no stake in this war. I thought Meghan might order me back to my room to "rest," but she only nodded for me to go on.

"Keirran is trying to save the Forgotten and the exiles," I continued. "Tearing away the Veil was supposed to stop them from Fading into nothingness. For some reason, he thinks he's responsible for the Forgotten. And...he's trying to save Annwyl, too." Annwyl, his exiled love from the Summer Court, had been Fading away, as well. In fact, this whole stupid mess started because Keirran was trying to find a cure for her. "We even went to Arcadia to ask Titania to lift her exile," I went on, and noted Meghan's and Ash's grave looks as they probably guessed how that little endeavor had gone. "When she refused, Keirran flipped out and attacked her. He was pretty desperate at that point, I think. But, maybe if the courts can come to some kind of accord with the Forgotten and let Annwyl come home, Keirran will back down."

I wondered what the hell I was doing, defending Keirran like this. If he was with the Forgotten and marching to wage war on the courts, let him deal with the mess he had caused. Let him see the consequences of his actions.

It's not for Keirran, I thought fiercely. I'm not defending him; I'm trying to help my sister prevent a faery war from breaking out. Keirran, the Forgotten and the Lady can go to hell, but if Meghan has to fight her own son, it will destroy her.

Meghan nodded and seemed to regain some of her composure. "The council tomorrow is to decide if Keirran and the Forgotten are truly a threat," she said, sounding thoughtful. "If we can keep Summer and Winter from declaring war, perhaps that will allow us enough time to find Keirran. We still don't know what the Lady really wants. If all she wishes is for her people to survive, then maybe we can work something out. Something that will allow the Forgotten to exist within Faery and not Fade away."

Relief washed through me, but I couldn't relax yet. "There is…one more thing," I continued. "Keirran was looking for a cure to stop Annwyl from Fading. Right before we went to see Titania, he convinced Guro—my kali instructor— to make an amulet for her. The amulet connected him and Annwyl and…uh…drained Keirran's magic and life force and gave it to her. It allowed Annwyl to live but…it was probably going to kill Keirran."

For a few heartbeats, there was silence.

"But…Keirran is still alive," Ash said, as Meghan's face went as pale as a sheet. "We've seen him with the Forgotten. Could Annwyl have taken the amulet off, destroyed it?"

"I don't know." I leaned against the table to steady myself.

"But that amulet was the only thing keeping Annwyl from Fading. I don't think Keirran would do anything to jeopardize that." *Unless he's changed so much that I don't recognize him anymore.*

Meghan straightened, becoming the Iron Queen once more. "This will need to be addressed at the war council," she said.

"I'm coming, too," I said, and Meghan gave me a sharp look. "I was with Keirran when all this started," I continued, holding my ground. "I know what happened, and I think the other courts will want to hear it. I want to help, Meghan," I added as she hesitated. "I can't hide from this any longer. This has become my fight, as well."

Meghan sighed. "I'll have someone send a message to Mom and Luke," she muttered, rubbing her eyes. "Let them know you're all right, at least. You just have to promise me one thing, Ethan. If the worst happens, and war does break out between the courts and the Forgotten, you *cannot* get involved. I don't want you on the front lines—I don't want you anywhere near the battle or the fighting. If it comes to that, I want you to go home. Please, I need to know you'll be safe, that one part of my family is far away from this mess. Will you promise me that?"

I swallowed hard and nodded. "Yeah," I rasped, "I promise."

Gazing out the carriage window, I shivered, both from the chill coming through the glass, and the pristine white palace looming at the end of the walk. I knew Mab, Queen of Winter and one of the scariest fey in existence, held court in a massive underground city filled with Unseelie nightmares. I knew it was going to be cold and had borrowed some warmer attire from Meghan's court in preparation: long wool coat, gloves and hat. But there was cold, and then there was *cold*. As in, hurts-to-breathe cold. As in there were colored ice crystals, bristling from the ground and dangling from rooftops, that were taller than me. As in unnatural, Winter Court cold. The door opened with a swirl of frigid, stinging air, making me grit my teeth as I slid out of the carriage. Grimacing, I stepped onto the ice-covered path, turning up my coat collar and wishing I had a scarf to wrap around my face. Jeez, it was freezing! What I wouldn't give for a couple flamefruits right now.

Whoa, wait a second, Ethan. Crossing my arms, I followed Glitch up the path through the pristine, snow-covered courtyard toward the palace steps. *When did you start wishing for magical solutions? You hate faery glamour, remember?*

Oh, shut up, I told myself, annoyed. Obviously I wasn't going to make any dangerous bargains or drink a bottle of faery wine, and I was going to be extremely paranoid of any strange glamour cast my way, but the entire Nevernever was one giant, magical place. I couldn't avoid magic if I wanted to. I would admit, very reluctantly, that *some* faery magic could be useful.

Like keeping me from freezing to death in the freaking Winter Court.

Meghan and Ash were waiting at the top of the steps when Glitch and I came up. Meghan wore a dark blue cloak, but below that, a coat of glimmering silver scales rustled metallically as she turned to us. A sword hung at her waist, and her hair had been pinned up, making her look older, regal, almost intimidating. Beside her, Ash was dressed in jet-black armor with the silhouette of a great tree on the breastplate. Seeing them like that caused a lump of dread to settle in my gut. This wasn't a faery ball or a fancy party. This was a meeting to determine if the courts of Summer, Winter and Iron would go to war with the Forgotten, the Lady…and my former best friend.

We strode through the halls of the Winter Palace, and I stayed very close to Glitch and the retinue of Iron knights accompanying us. I wasn't afraid…well, no, screw that, I *was* afraid. The twin swords at my waist were a necessity; no way I was walking through Tir Na Nog unarmed. But I was mostly nervous for Meghan. Iron Queen or not, Keirran was her son; I couldn't imagine what it would be like to have to declare war against your own family. I hoped the faery courts could find a peaceful solution to the Forgotten and the Lady. I would do my damnedest to help make that happen.

Redcaps, ogres, goblins and other Winter fey stared at us, eyes and fangs gleaming, as we made our way through the frozen halls. At the end of a long corridor lit with blue ice chandeliers, a pair of Winter knights pulled back huge double doors and bowed to Meghan as we swept through.

Oh, crap.

An enormous round table made entirely of ice stood in the center of the room, throwing off tendrils of mist that writhed along the floor. Surrounding it were scores of fey, both Seelie and Unseelie, most of them dressed in battle gear. My skin prickled. For a council that was supposedly about "discussing" the Forgotten menace, everyone here seemed more than ready to fight.

The rulers of Summer and Winter stood at the head of the table, watching us as we came in. I'd never seen either of them before, but they were instantly recognizable. Oberon, the King of Summer, stood tall and proud at the table edge, silver hair falling down his back, his antlered crown casting jagged shadows over the surface. A pale, beautiful woman stood a few feet away, dark hair cascading around her shoulders, a high-collared cloak draping her armor of red and black. Piercing dark eyes stabbed me over the table, and my insides curled with fear. Mab, the Queen of Winter, was just as dangerous and terrifying as I'd imagined she would be. The only good thing was that Titania, the Summer Queen, appeared to be absent today. The queens' hatred for each other was well-known, and the situation was volatile enough without two immortal faery rulers having a spat in the middle of the war council.

There *was* one faery in the room who could, unintentionally, cause a lot of trouble, just by being himself. Robin Goodfellow lounged against one wall, hands laced behind his head, watching everything with bright green eyes. When he saw me, one eyebrow arched, and he shot me a knowing smirk. I sighed and sidled around the table to stand beside him, not wanting to be too close to the Winter Queen and her retinue. Even though I was the Iron Queen's brother, I was still fully human, something that was viewed as "lesser" here. Or even quite tasty. At least I didn't have to worry about some goblin attacking me if I was with the Great Prankster.

"Hey, Ethan Chase," Puck greeted softly as I settled beside him, crossing my arms. "Back from the dead, I see. Were there choirs of angels and twinkling lights? I've always wondered about that."

"Couldn't tell you," I muttered. "I don't remember being dead."

"Aw, well, that's disappointing." Puck shook his head with a grin. "Dying sounds terribly dull. I was hoping you would prove me wrong." He sniffed and turned his attention back to the meeting. "Anyway, speaking of dull, these war councils are such a bore. Let's see if I can guess exactly how this is going to go. First off, Mab will be all cold and threatening, because well, that's Mab…"

"Iron Queen," Mab stated in a cold voice as Meghan and Ash stepped forward. "How good of you to join us. Perhaps you would like to hear the reports of what your son has been doing of late?"

"I am aware that Keirran is with the Forgotten," Meghan replied, far more calmly than I would have expected. "I know they have been scouting the borders of Arcadia and Tir Na Nog. They have not, to my knowledge, harmed anyone or made any hostile overtures toward the courts."

"Yet," Mab seethed. "It is obvious they plan to attack, and I refuse to be besieged in my own kingdom. I propose we take the fight to the Forgotten now, before they and their mysterious Lady set upon us en masse."

"And now Lord Pointy Ears will jump in with his eternal logic," Puck went on.

"How do you plan to do that, Lady Mab?" Oberon asked, his voice like a mountain spring, quiet yet frigid. "We do not know where the Forgotten *are*, where the rest of this army is hiding. Whenever anyone tries to follow them, they disappear, both from the mortal realm and the Nevernever. How do you propose we find something that does not exist?"

Puck yawned. "Right on the money," he mused. "And now we'll have to endure several minutes of arguing as they try to solve the mystery of where the Forgotten have vanished to."

"I know where they are," I muttered, and he arched a brow at me.

"Well, maybe you should get in there, human."

"Yeah, but I don't really want to."

Mab glared at Oberon. "They cannot simply vanish into thin air," she snapped. "An entire race of fey cannot simply will themselves into nothingness. It is impossible. They have to be somewhere."

Puck raised both brows at me, and I groaned. "They are," I answered, and shoved myself off the wall. "They're in the Between."

All eyes turned to me. My heart stuttered, but I took a furtive breath and stepped forward, meeting the inhuman stares of a couple dozen fey.

"King Oberon is right," I said, moving beside Meghan, feeling the chill of a Winter knight to my left. "The Forgotten can't be found in the mortal world or the Nevernever because they're *not* here. They're slipping in and out of both worlds, from a place called the Between. It's—"

"I know what the Between is, Ethan Chase," Mab stated coolly, narrowing her eyes. "Most call it the Veil, the curtain between Faery and the mortal realm, the barrier that keeps our world hidden from mortal sight. But the ability for fey to go Between has been lost for centuries. I know of only one who has accomplished it in the past hundred years, and she has not seen fit to share her knowledge with the rest of Faery."

Leanansidhe. I knew from Keirran that those who went into the Between were often trapped there, wandering for eternity. The Exile Queen was the only one who had managed to create permanent trods to her mansion in the Between, allowing her network of exiles and half-breeds to come and go as they pleased. But they still needed to use a trod. Not even Leanansidhe could part the Veil and slip between worlds whenever she chose. "Well, it might've been lost to the courts, but the Lady, the Forgotten Queen, remembers how," I said. "And she taught the rest of the Forgotten, too. You haven't been able to find them because they're all hanging out in the Between."

Mab's icy black gaze lingered on my face, and I feared she was seeing far too much. "And the Iron Prince?" she asked in a soft, lethal voice, making Meghan stiffen beside me. "He has also been vanishing into thin air whenever we approach. Does he have this special talent? Has the Lady taught him to go Between, as well?"

I swallowed.

"Yes," Ash confirmed before I could say anything. "We

have seen it. Whatever old knowledge the Lady brought with her when she awoke, she has taught Keirran, as well. He can move through the Between like the rest of the Forgotten."

Oberon raised his head. "Then it seems the Lady has chosen her champion," he stated in a grave voice. "And so the prophecy comes to pass. Keirran will destroy the courts unless we can stop him. Iron Queen…" He gave Meghan an almost sympathetic look. "You know what you must do. Declare Keirran a traitor and cast him from your court. Only then may we stand united against the Forgotten and the Lady."

"What? Whoa, wait a second." I leaned forward, feeling the frigid edge of the table bite into my hands. "You don't know what they want. Keirran is only trying to help the Forgotten survive. Yeah, he did it in the most ass-backwards way possible, but maybe you should try talking to them before declaring all-out war."

"And what do you know of war, Ethan Chase?" Mab inquired, as her cold, scary gaze settling on me again. "You are the reason we are here, the reason the prophecy has come to pass. It was your presence that allowed the Forgotten to invade, your blood that tore away the Veil, even if it was for but a moment. You and the Iron Prince have brought utter chaos to Faery, and now you dare to tell us that we should be merciful?" Her eyes narrowed, and her lips curled in a terrifying smile. "I have not forgotten your hand in the destruction of my Frozen Wood," she said, making my blood chill at the memory. I tried to back away, but I suddenly couldn't move. My hands burned on the edge of the table, and I looked down to see that ice had crept up and sealed my fingers to the surface. "You are lucky that the impending war demands my attention for now," Mab hissed, "but do not think for a moment that I will let that slide. You and the Iron Prince have much to answer for."

"Lady Mab." Meghan's steady voice broke through the rising fury. "Please stop terrorizing my brother before I take offense." My hands were suddenly free, and I yanked them back, rubbing them furiously to start circulation. "I am aware of the prophecy," Meghan went on, as I stuck my frozen fingers under my arms. "I am aware that, misguided or not, Keirran has done terrible things. But I beg you all to consider whom we are dealing with. This is my son, and your kin. Both of you," she added, looking to the Summer King and the Winter Queen in turn. "Are we going to declare war on our own blood without knowing the details? We are still uncertain as to what the Forgotten and the Lady really want."

"I can tell you what she wants," said a new, familiar voice behind us.

I spun, as did the rest of the table, to face the entrance of the room. The double doors had been pushed back, and a figure stood in the entryway with a pair of shadowy sidhe knights flanking him.

Keirran.

CHAPTER FOUR

THE LADY'S DEMAND

I stared at the Iron Prince, a chill sliding up my spine as our eyes met. Keirran's flat gaze held no emotion, no spark of regret or remorse, nothing but blank apathy. His silver hair was longer now, tied behind him in a loose tail that made him look older and showed off his pointed ears. A tattered cloak draped his shoulders, trailing wisps of shadow that writhed into the air. His shadowy entourage stood rigid behind him, four silhouettes in ghostly gray armor with the glowing yellow eyes of the Forgotten.

I saw a shiver go through Meghan, saw her lips breathe Keirran's name, though no sound came out of her mouth.

"Iron Prince." Mab's voice was glacial and lethally soft. "What is the meaning of this? How dare you come into my home uninvited?"

"Apologies, Queen Mab." Keirran's tone could match the Winter monarch's for chilliness. "But is this not a war council? You have gathered to speak of the Forgotten, what they want, if you should prepare for war. I am here to tell you exactly what you wish to know. Be warned," he continued, with a quick glance at Meghan and Ash's side of the table, "I came here in good faith, under the banner of peace. The ancient law states that you may not attack a messenger of war. I trust you all to uphold that policy."

"Speak, then," Oberon said, his voice hard. "Deliver your news, Iron Prince, and be done with it."

Keirran bowed, but it was a short, mocking bow, and his eyes remained cold as he straightened. "I come on behalf of the Lady," he continued in a low, terrible voice. "The Forgotten goddess, the First Queen of Faery. She demands that the Summer and Winter courts be annulled, and that the Nevernever exist as one realm, without borders or boundaries. There will be no Seelie or Unseelie lands, no Arcadia or Tir Na Nog. There will be only Faery, and she will rule the Nevernever as she did in the ancient times, before the courts came to be. Only the Iron Realm will remain as it is." He glanced at Meghan, whose face had gone pale with horror. "The Lady understands that the Iron fey are integral to Faery, but wants no part of them. Mag Tuiredh will become a separate seat of the Nevernever, and the Iron Realm may still have its queen, if she swears fealty to the Lady and recognizes her as the true monarch of Faery.

"If these terms are not met," Keirran went on, "the Lady will declare war on the Nevernever, and she will descend on the courts with her army of Forgotten, to take back what has been stolen, and to restore Faery to what it was."

A brittle silence fell over the room, broken only by the frantic thud of my pulse in my ears. Meghan stared at Keirran, and the look on her face made my insides hurt. It was one of complete devastation, shock and denial, and it made me want to smash the prince's head through the wall. The Iron Queen gazed at her son like she didn't know him anymore, like the person standing before her was a stranger.

Then Mab's laughter rang out, harsh and mocking, making me jump. "You dare, Iron Prince?" she hissed, as the temperature in the room dropped. As if it wasn't cold enough. "You dare stand with this Lady, this forgotten pretender, and demand that I give up my kingdom? Annul the Winter Court? Blasphemy!" She spat the word at him, and icicles made sharp crinkling sounds as they grew from the walls and floor. "You can tell the Lady that the Winter Court will never bow to usurpers, that she can expect to face the full might of Tir Na Nog on the field of battle."

"And the full might of Arcadia," Oberon chimed in, his own voice making the icicles tremble. "The Summer Court stands with Winter in rejecting your Lady's claims. If she wants the Seelie Court destroyed, she will have to take it herself."

Silence fell once more. Keirran regarded us all without emotion, then looked to Meghan. "And you, Iron Queen?" he asked, when the silence had stretched to a breaking point. "What is your answer?"

"Keirran." A lump caught in my throat at the sound of Meghan's voice, broken and desperate. Almost immediately, however, the queen straightened, regaining her composure and standing with her back tall as she faced the Iron Prince. "Why are you doing this?" she asked in a quiet, yet calm voice. "What can you possibly hope to gain?"

"Nothing." Keirran's answer was completely without emotion. "It's not for me," he continued in that same steely tone. "This is for the exiles, and the Forgotten. For too long, they have been ignored. For too long, the exiles have suffered the cruelty of the human world, and the courts have done nothing. It is time to change that, even if I must clear away the old to make room for the new."

"This is not your responsibility, Keirran," came Ash's voice, deep and controlled, though I could hear the bridled fury beneath. "There are other ways for the Forgotten and the exiles to live. Stop this madness and come home."

For the briefest of moments, a tiny, agonized furrow creased Keirran's brow. But the Iron Prince blinked, and it was gone. "I've made my choice," he said serenely. "I cannot turn from it now." His cold gaze went to Meghan and narrowed. "It seems I was prophesied to bring destruction to the courts, long before I was born," he said, making her flinch. "Everyone knew of this. Everyone, except myself. I am only walking the path that has been destined for me all along."

"Dammit, Keirran," I snarled, unable to hold back any longer. "You know that isn't true. Get your head out of your ass and wake up!"

He gave me a frigid smile. "You're very loud for a ghost," he remarked, making me want to step forward and drive a fist through his teeth. "I guess I shouldn't be surprised that you lived. You're too stubborn to stay down for good." His smile faded then, as his eyes glittered with icy malice. "I am glad that you survived after all, Ethan, but know this. If you get in my way, if you try to stop us, I *will* kill you. And this time, I'll make certain that you stay dead and gone."

I clenched my fists, but Meghan's voice rose up before I could do anything. The Iron Queen's power filled the chamber, sharp and crackling, like the air before a storm. "If you do this, Keirran," she said, "if you declare war on all of Faery, I will have no choice but to cast you from the Iron Court. You will no longer be welcome, or safe, in Mag Tuiredh, or anywhere in the Nevernever. So, please..." She wavered, very slightly, though her voice remained strong. "Think of what you are doing. There's still time, to stop this, to find another way."

Keirran gazed at her, a faint, sad smile crossing his face, before his eyes hardened and he took a step back. "It's too late for me, Iron Queen," he whispered as the knights closed in, surrounding him. "The prophecy has been set in motion, and

I must follow it to the end. I will return to the Lady and inform her of your decision."

"Really?" Puck had pushed himself off the wall, his green eyes glittering with a dangerous light. "And what makes you think we're going to let you walk out, princeling?" he asked, smirking in a way that made my skin prickle with fear.

Keirran didn't move, though the Forgotten knights stiffened, hands dropping to their sword hilts. "I came here in good faith," the Iron Prince said calmly, looking not at Puck but at the other rulers. "According to ancient Faery law, a messenger of war may deliver his news without fear of repercussion. I have presented my Lady's demands, and I have harmed no one while I was here. You must honor tradition and let me go, or the Nevernever itself will rise against you."

I glanced at the table, wondering if this was bullshit, but the grim looks on everyone's faces told me it was not.

"Go, then," Mab said, her voice icy. "Return to your Lady. Tell her that the courts will not bow. We will not submit to her, or the Forgotten. If she rises against us, we will send her and all her followers back to the oblivion from whence they came."

Keirran bowed. "As you wish," he murmured, with one final glance at the rulers of Mag Tuiredh. There might've been a hint of regret in his eyes, or I might've imagined it. "When next we meet, it will be on the field."

And then, he turned and walked away, the knights flanking him once more. No one stopped them. No one said anything as the Iron Prince slipped into the hall without looking back, and the doors creaked shut behind him.

"It seems," Oberon's voice echoed into the deathly stillness that followed, "that the Iron Prince has made his choice." His tone didn't change, though you could practically hear the barb, pointed and accusing, as he glanced at Meghan across the table. "What is *yours*, Iron Queen?"

Meghan closed her eyes. Her back was turned to the other rulers, but I saw a tear slip down her face. Chilled, I looked at Ash, saw the grim resignation in his eyes, and wanted to kill Keirran for what he had done.

"I have no choice," Meghan whispered. Opening her eyes, she took a deep breath, her voice growing stronger, though the heart-wrenching pain on her face never disappeared. "I hereby declare Prince Keirran a traitor to Faery," she announced in clear, firm tones, "and exile him from the Iron Court. He is no longer under the protection of Mag Tuiredh, and all titles and privileges of rank have been stripped. Let this be made known to all—Keirran is now the enemy of Mag Tuiredh, the Iron Court and the Nevernever."

The ride back to Mag Tuiredh was tense. Glitch didn't say anything, though the strands in his hair snapped and flared an angry red, filling the air with a furious buzzing energy. He glowered out the window, surrounded by a miniature lightning storm, his eyes distant and dark. I sat as far away as I could get in the corner.

So, Keirran had really done it. Sided with the Lady and the Forgotten, marched right into the heart of Tir Na Nog and declared war on the entire Nevernever. I clenched my jaw, remembering Meghan's face, the look in her eyes when she was forced to exile her own son.

Dammit, Keirran! What the hell was he doing? How had he fallen so far, to switch sides and declare war against his own family? I truly did not understand him, why he thought he had no other choice. What did he think he was saving? Had he reached the *screw it* point, where he thought nothing he did would matter anymore, or was there something else?

I was certain of one thing: if Keirran and I did cross paths again, all bets were off. I couldn't think of him as family. He was my enemy, and I couldn't hold back or I'd find myself with another sword through my insides.

When the carriages finally stopped, I glanced out the window, surprised to find myself in Mag Tuiredh. I'd half expected Meghan to send me back to the mortal world straight from Tir Na Nog. Now that war with the Forgotten was a sure thing, I wondered how much time would pass before she ordered me to go home.

Slowly, I climbed out of the carriage and made my way into the palace. Meghan and Ash stood in the vestibule, the Iron Queen deep in conversation with Fix, the packrat. I tiptoed past, hoping she wouldn't notice me, but she straightened quickly and turned.

"Ethan."

I winced. This was it; Meghan was sending me back to the mortal world. And, for the first time in my life, I didn't want to go back. Not now. I knew my parents were probably frantic. I couldn't even think of Kenzie for fear of breaking down. But this was my fight, too. I was partially responsible for everything that happened with Keirran. I couldn't go home to one family knowing I had abandoned the other.

I turned, ready to protest, to find the words to convince my sister that I was in this, too. But Meghan had a strange look of resignation and amusement on her face as she gave me a faint smile.

"There is…someone waiting in your room," she said, making me frown in confusion. And before I could ask what she meant, she took Ash's arm and turned away, though the shadow of a smile lingered on her face. "Go see what they want, and I'll speak to you later tonight. Try to take it easy for the rest of the evening."

She tugged Ash's arm, and they walked down the hall, though Ash gave her a brief, questioning look. I saw Meghan lean up and whisper something in his ear, and he pulled back, raising his eyebrows. They turned a corner and were out of sight before I could see more of his reaction, leaving me alone in the corridor.

With a shrug, I made my way back to my quarters, hoping my guest wasn't another healer fey, waiting to pounce the second I walked through the door. My middle *was* aching again, a low, constant throb, but it wasn't too bad. I could walk, at least. Still, the thought of lying down for a few minutes became more tempting with every step. If there was a healer faery lurking in my room right now, I wouldn't say no to a painkiller.

Wearily, I pushed back the door, bracing myself to be set upon by a swarm of small faeries in long white coats.

And Mackenzie St. James looked up from my bed.

"Hey, tough guy."

I stared at the girl on my bed, unable to do more than blink. That was her voice, her straight black hair and brown eyes, her smile breaking across her face. She was here. How she'd accomplished it, given how impossible it was to travel through the Nevernever alone, I couldn't comprehend. Just that she had, completely unexpectedly and unexplained, shown up in my room in the middle of the Iron Realm.

"Kenzie?"

Kenzie leaped off the mattress and, in the two seconds it took for my brain to unfreeze from shock, crossed the room and threw herself at me.

Pain shot through my stomach as the girl collided with my chest, throwing her arms around me and squeezing tight. The stab through my gut was instant and breathtaking. I yelped and staggered back, and she immediately let go.

"Oh, God! I'm so sorry, Ethan, I didn't realize—"

Recovering, I grabbed her wrist, yanked her forward, and covered her mouth with mine.

She gasped, before kissing me back with just as much fervor. Her hands clutched the front of my shirt, though she kept her touch light, probably not wanting to hurt me again. But I wrapped my arms around her waist and pulled her close, wanting to feel her body against mine, the heart beating wildly in her chest. Her hands climbed my shoulders and buried themselves in my hair, and I held her tighter, not caring about the pain. Kenzie was alive, and...*here*. In the Iron Realm, though, truthfully, I shouldn't have been surprised. Of course Mackenzie St. James had made her way through the Nevernever to find me. Once she set her mind to something, there was no force on earth that could stop her.

Her eyes were suspiciously bright as we pulled back, though she gazed up at me with a wry smile. "Well," she whispered, "I was wondering if you'd be happy to see me when I finally got here. Guess that answers my question."

I stroked her cheek, just taking her in. Her straight black hair was shorter now, just brushing the tops of her shoulders, and the neon blue streaks were gone. Crazily enough, I missed them; they'd seemed part of her, part of who she was. But other than that, she was the same small, stubborn, brown-eyed girl I'd fallen head over heels for. "How did you get here?" I finally asked.

"Razor showed me the way," Kenzie replied, nodding to the far corner. I looked up, and the spindly, bat-eared gremlin buzzed and waved maniacally from the dresser. Unable to help myself, I grinned back, absurdly happy to see the hyper thing.

"Hey, Razor. Good to see you, too. Have you been taking care of Kenzie?"

He nodded vigorously. "Razor help," he stated, more serious than I'd ever heard him before. "Razor here. Take care of pretty girl." His glowing eyes narrowed sharply. "Funny boy died," he accused, making my heart skip a beat. "Funny boy made pretty girl sad. Razor take care of her. Bring her here. Not sad anymore, right, pretty girl?"

I swallowed hard. Abruptly, Kenzie shivered and ran her hands down my chest, making my stomach knot. "You're here," she whispered, her voice catching a little. "You're really okay. I wasn't sure if... I thought—"

She shuddered, and my heart gave a violent lurch as the girl leaned forward, pressing her face to my shirt, and began to shake with sobs. Not knowing what to say, I wrapped my arms around her, while Razor flattened his ears and glared at me from the dresser.

"I thought you were dead," Kenzie whispered. "I waited for you in the hospital, and when you didn't come back, I was afraid something awful had happened. I tried to convince myself that it was nothing, but I knew deep down that something had gone really wrong. So I sent Razor to find you. When he came back..." She shivered again. "He told me you were dead. That you had been killed in Ireland."

"I'm okay," I told her, because that was all I could think to say. "I'm fine, Kenzie. I'm not going anywhere."

She sniffed and took a deep breath, trying to regain her composure. "What...*happened* in Ireland, Ethan?" she asked, gazing up at me with tear-glazed eyes. "I tried to get the whole story out of Razor, but he kept saying that *Keirran* stabbed you." She blinked, looking grief stricken, incredulous and furious all at once. "Keirran was the one? Is that true?"

I hesitated, then nodded slowly. "Yeah," I muttered. "Yeah, he did."

"*Why?*"

"Because I was a sacrifice," I went on. "The Lady told him as much. My blood was supposed to tear away the Veil, so that the human world could see the fey, and all the Forgotten and exiles would be saved. That's what Keirran wanted, more than anything else, I guess." My eyes narrowed. "So he stabbed me and left me there to die."

Kenzie's face went white. "Oh, my God," she whispered. "That's where it started. Why everything went crazy that night."

My blood chilled. "What happened?"

She licked her lips. "I knew something was up when the nurse came in and started screaming at Razor like she could really see him. So I turned on the news, and there were all these live reports about weird creatures and crazy circumstances. People were talking about ghosts, vampires, aliens, you name it. That's when I knew something big had happened in Faery." Her brow furrowed, and she wiped her eyes. "It was weird, though. Maybe ten, fifteen minutes after it started, it just…stopped. I couldn't find any more information, the news reports stopped talking about it, and it was never mentioned again. Everyone just forgot about it."

"Yeah." I nodded. "When the Veil re-formed, the fey became invisible again, so people forgot they ever saw them."

"Re-formed?"

"When I…um…revived, it came back." At her incredulous look, I shrugged. "I wasn't quite as dead as Keirran thought."

Kenzie blinked rapidly, laying her head on my chest again. "I thought I lost you," she whispered. "When Razor said you had died, the only thing I could think was…that I had killed you. I told you to go with Keirran. I insisted, and the next thing I knew, you were dead."

I pressed my forehead to hers. "I'm so sorry."

She choked a tiny laugh through the tears. "Don't...apologize for dying, tough guy," she whispered. "I'm sure you didn't plan it that way." She took a ragged breath, ducking her head. "If anything, you should be angry with me. I was the one who sent you to the Lady. If you hadn't left with Keirran—"

"Kenzie." I put a hand on her cheek. She blinked and peered up at me, and I shook my head. "You couldn't have known what would happen," I told her softly. "None of us could. Maybe if we'd known about the prophecy or what was really going on—but no one was telling us anything." I raised one shoulder helplessly. "This whole thing with Keirran just... spiraled out of control, and we got caught in the middle. I don't blame you for what he did." I ran my fingers through her now shorter hair. "In fact, you probably saved my life." She blinked, frowning in confusion, and I smiled. "The amulet you gave me right before Keirran and I went to see the Lady—I think it protected me one last time."

"Guro's amulet?"

I nodded. "Sadly, I won't be able to return it like I said I would. When Keirran stabbed me, it broke. Snapped right in two. I think it's safe to say the magic is completely gone now."

She gave a soft chuckle and pressed closer. "I'd rather have you than a magic necklace any day of the week," she murmured, winding her arms around my waist. Holding her tight, I closed my eyes, just feeling her heartbeat against mine, and Kenzie sighed, relaxing into me. "I missed you, tough guy," she whispered. "It's been a pretty sucky four months."

Four months. Had I really been gone that long? And what had Kenzie been going through in that time? "Are you all right?" I asked, gazing down in concern. The last time I'd seen my girlfriend, she had been in the hospital. "You know I don't want to bring it up, but...what about your illness? Have you recovered? Is it okay for you to be here now?"

She smirked. "No, Ethan, I'm on Death's doorstep as we speak, having gone through Faeryland on a wish and a prayer." Her grin was wicked, but a flicker of something dark went through her eyes, though it was gone in the next heartbeat. "I just trekked across the wyldwood and Mag Tuiredh to find you, tough guy. Do I look like I'm gonna keel over?"

"Okay, okay." I held up my hands. "Point taken. I was going to say that I can't believe you traveled all the way to Mag Tuiredh by yourself, but...it's you, after all." She gazed up at me warily, and I smiled. "I'm glad you came, Kenzie," I told her, lowering my head. "I missed you, too."

Our lips met, and I let my eyes slide shut. Razor buzzed something from the dresser, probably mocking us, but I didn't care. All I could think about was Kenzie, that she was all right, that she had found a way to Mag Tuiredh, and that suddenly, I wasn't so alone anymore.

A sharp rap on the door made us pause. Irritated, I waited a few heartbeats, and when nothing happened, leaned forward to kiss Kenzie again. The knocking resumed immediately, accompanied by a squeaky "Prince Ethan? Are you awake, sire?"

Sighing, Kenzie drew back and gave the door a half annoyed, half resigned look. "Guess you'd better see who that is," she said, smiling ruefully as she wiped her eyes. "If I remember anything about the Nevernever, it's that the fey don't understand the concept of privacy. And they have the worst timing possible."

Yes, they do. Stalking to the door, I yanked it open and glowered at the wire nymph on the other side. "What?"

The small faery cringed. "Forgive me, Prince Ethan," it

squeaked, looking so cowed I felt guilty for snarling at it, "but I was instructed to give this to you posthaste."

It held up a note between long, glimmering fingers. I took it, and the nymph instantly scampered off before I could say anything else, skittering around a corner and vanishing in a flash of wire and steel. Vowing to be a little nicer to Meghan's subjects in the future, I closed the door and turned around, meeting Kenzie's curious gaze.

"Who is that from?"

"I don't know." I looked down at the note and flipped it open. The handwriting was simple and elegant, but I didn't know if it was Meghan's. The message was also short, direct and to the point.

Come to the library, it read. That was it.

"That's weird," I muttered and handed the paper to Kenzie. She skimmed the note with a frown, then looked back at me.

"Do you think it's from your sister?"

"I don't know. Maybe."

"Well." Kenzie shrugged and handed it back. "Whoever it is, I guess we should go see what they want. Come on, Razor."

She raised her arm, and the gremlin leaped from the dresser with a cackle to land on her back. Turning, Kenzie bent down and picked up a full backpack from the floor, then swung it to her shoulders. It rattled as it settled into place, and the gremlin hopped to perch on top of it.

I blinked. "What do you have in there?"

She grinned. "Remember a while back, when I mentioned something about putting together a survival kit for the Nevernever? This time, I came prepared."

"I'm almost afraid to see what's in there."

She laughed, walked up to me and took my hand. "Don't worry about it, tough guy. I got us covered." Lacing our fingers together, she squeezed once and bumped her arm against mine, as Razor snickered at us from her shoulder. "You just worry about stabbing things, and I'll take care of everything else."

"Really."

"Yup."

I pulled open the door of my room, gazed down one of the many, many hallways of the Iron Palace and sighed. "Well, if that's the case, then maybe you can find us a map," I said, "because I have no idea where the library is."

Kenzie grinned. "Oh, I've got something better than a map," she returned, and raised her head. "Razor," she called, and the gremlin bounced upright, huge ears perked and quivering. Kenzie smiled at him pointed with a finger. "To the library, Razor, stat!"

The gremlin gave a buzz of excitement. Leaping off her shoulders, he scurried up the wall and to the ceiling, where he hung upside down like a huge spider. Beckoning us with a claw, he scampered away, then paused and glanced back to see if we were coming. Kenzie gave me a smug grin.

"You were saying?"

"You're cute when you're bossy," I told her, and grunted when she poked me in the ribs. Raising my free hand, I pushed her hair back from her cheek. "I'm really glad you're here."

An annoyed crackle came from the ceiling, and Razor skittered a few feet toward us. "Funny boy!" the gremlin called, bouncing in impatience. "Pretty girl, this way! Library this way, follow Razor!"

Kenzie rolled her eyes. "Come on," she sighed, tugging me forward. "We'd better hurry, before Razor gets bored and leaves us. Then we *would* need a map."

Keeping an eye on the gremlin, we walked down a long corridor, through several chambers, up a spiraling set of stairs and down another hall until we came to a pair of large double doors. Razor crawled up to Kenzie's shoulder and pointed with a claw.

"Quiet room! Lots of books, *bleck*. Gremlins not allowed."

"Good boy," Kenzie said, and the gremlin grinned manically. We pushed open the doors with a faint creak and stepped through.

Inside, it looked like a normal library, albeit bigger than the ones I had seen before. Rows of books lined the walls to the ceiling, and more shelves were arranged in narrow aisles throughout the room. It was quieter here than in the rest of the Iron Palace, the air musty and cool. Warily, I gazed around, searching for the one who'd called us here, but with the maze of aisles and the shadows that clung to the corners of the room, it was difficult to see if we were alone or not.

Kenzie turned in a slow circle, the glow from Razor's teeth piercing some of the gloom. "I don't see anyone," she murmured. "Do you think your sister is here?"

"No," said a deep voice from the shadows. I spun as Ash stepped out of the darkness, his expression grave as he came into the light. "Meghan didn't call you here," the dark faery explained, fixing us with his piercing silver glare. "I did."

CHAPTER FIVE
ASH'S REQUEST

I stiffened, fighting the urge to step in front of Kenzie and drop a hand to my sword. Old resentment bubbled up, filling me with a long-familiar hate, I shoved it down. Ash was not my enemy, I reminded myself. He was not responsible for my sister's disappearance, all those years ago. Meghan had chosen to be with him, to become a queen of Faery, and from the small interactions I'd seen between them, if my sister ever decided to return to the mortal world, Ash wouldn't stop her. *Follow* her, sure; I doubted anything short of an act of God would keep him away, and maybe not even that. But I couldn't keep blaming Ash for my sister's decisions, my abandonment hang-ups or for Meghan falling in love. Like it or not, he was family, too. It was time I grew up and accepted that.

"Ash," I greeted, as the faery regarded us solemnly. "You sent that message? Why?"

"I want to talk to you about Keirran." Ash settled against one of the shelves, long black coat falling around him. "There are some things I need to understand. And I..." For the first time I'd ever known him, his voice faltered. "I have a favor to ask of you, Ethan."

Stunned, I could only stare and try to keep my mouth from dropping open. Ash sighed, looking away for a moment, his gaze distant. For just a heartbeat, he wasn't the cold, emotionless Winter faery I had always seen. He was, like Meghan, someone whose world had been torn apart by Keirran's betrayal, and was struggling to understand what had happened.

"You were with Keirran at the very end," Ash finally said. "You knew him, before and after he met the Forgotten Queen. Both of you fought side by side, and I know he considered you a friend—one of his only friends." His expression darkened, and he shook his head. "The Keirran at the war council today...I didn't recognize him. He's changed so much, nothing about him made sense. I refuse to believe that was my son."

I swallowed at the underlying pain in Ash's voice. The faery paused, a flicker of anguish breaking his perfect composure, before he was himself again. "Keirran didn't just change into that overnight," the dark faery went on, looking at me. "Something must have happened to him, someone must have done something, to turn him against his own court. Ethan, you mentioned an amulet. Can you tell me what it does, what type of magic we're dealing with?"

The amulet.

The bottom dropped out of my stomach. Dammit, how could I have forgotten? Maybe the shock of being killed and the worry for Kenzie, my parents and the war with the Forgotten had driven it from my brain, but I felt like an idiot for just remembering it now.

You do not know, do you? He is mostly human. It is taking his soul.

Ash noticed my reaction, and his eyes narrowed. "Tell me," he said, and pushed himself away from the shelf. "Everything, Ethan. Everything that led up to that night. What happened to you and Keirran before you went to see the Lady?"

Reluctantly, I nodded. I didn't want to, didn't want to reveal my part in all this, but Ash deserved to know. "When Keirran disappeared that first time," I began, thinking back to that night and the chain of events leading up to it, "Ann-

wyl came to me at home. She was Fading. Whatever the Forgotten did to her had accelerated the process. Keirran was
desperate to stop it. We—Annwyl, Kenzie and I—tracked
him to a goblin market, where he was trying to find a cure
for the Fade. That's when you caught up to us," I added, remembering that night, following the Iron Prince through
the New Orleans streets, trying to outrun the faery before us
now. "We got away because Keirran had figured out how to
go Between—that's why you couldn't find us. The Lady had
taught him how to open the Veil."

Ash didn't give any indication of surprise, just nodded for
me to go on. I hesitated, steeling myself for what came next.
For the decision that had cost me a friend, a family member
and, ultimately, my life.

"I decided to take him to Guro," I said quietly. "My kali
instructor, back in the real world. He's…I guess he's kind of a
shaman, a faith healer, though I didn't know that part of him
until recently. Guro was the one who crafted that protection
amulet, the one I was wearing when Keirran…" I trailed off,
not wanting to say it, and Ash gave a stiff nod of understanding.

"We went to see him," I continued, "because it was the only
thing left I could think of. Annwyl was dying; she didn't have
much time left. It was our last hope. But, when we explained
what was happening, Guro said that he couldn't save her. That
there was nothing in the light arts that would help." I paused,
then added, "That's when Keirran…asked about the dark arts."

"Black magic," Ash muttered, sounding grim. "I know
there are still those in the mortal realm that are capable of real
power. It is not something to be trifled with, Ethan."

"Yeah," I said. "I sort of got that. But Keirran wouldn't let
it go. He begged Guro to save Annwyl, no matter the cost.
Guro told him what would happen. He told him the dangers
of black magic, laid it out word for word. But Keirran was

determined to do it anyway. And I…agreed to let him do it. I knew it was a bad idea, and I didn't stop him."

Ash shook his head with a weary smile. "I don't think you could have," he murmured. "Once Keirran puts his mind to something, he won't let it go. He's always been that way. Too much of his father in him." He sighed, all traces of amusement fading as he nodded for me to go on. "What happened after that?"

"There was a ritual," I continued. "Dark magic, blood magic, whatever you want to call it. It got pretty intense." I repressed a shiver, remembering that night. The drums, the chanting, the rage and hatred surging up in me. Rage toward Keirran, for taking my sister away, for being the cause of her abandonment. "Keirran and I both had to participate," I confessed, wishing I had never agreed to do it. I still didn't like what had been revealed, what I'd discovered about myself that night. "And when it was done, we had this amulet that would steal Keirran's strength and his glamour and give it to Annwyl. It would keep her alive, keep her from Fading, but at the cost of Keirran's own life. Eventually…it would kill them both."

There was a moment of grim silence. I felt the chill emanating from Ash's direction and shivered, wondering if he would blame me for the ultimate death of his son. If he did, he would be right. I had nothing to say in my defense.

"You mentioned this before," Ash said, frowning. "But Keirran is still alive. How?"

"I don't know," I answered. "Annwyl went back to Leanansidhe's when we crossed into the Nevernever. I haven't seen her since. But…" I took a furtive breath. This was going to be the hardest part to explain. "There is…one more thing you should know, about the amulet. When Titania refused to let Annwyl return to Arcadia, Keirran lost it. He attacked the queen, she tried to kill us, and we had to run." I couldn't stop my gaze from straying to Kenzie at that point, reliving the terror of that moment. Keirran and the Summer Queen had been hurling deadly magical projectiles at each other, and Kenzie, caught in the middle, had been struck by a stray lightning bolt and been badly hurt. She eased behind me and laced our fingers together, as if to let me know she was still here, that she was fine. I squeezed her hand and continued.

"After that," I told Ash, "Keirran didn't know what to do. Titania was our last resort. He was going to go home, but then, the Forgotten Queen called for him. And since he'd promised to speak with her one last time, he had to go. To Ireland—that's where she was waiting."

"And you went with him," Ash guessed.

I nodded. "I couldn't let him go alone." Keirran was family, and he'd been trying to save Annwyl, despite all the stupid stunts he'd pulled. He couldn't go by himself.

I did not mention that I'd nearly let him do just that. It was only Kenzie's insistence that I help Keirran out, one more time, that had made me relent. Even lying in a hospital bed, recovering from the latest catastrophe he had caused, she was far more forgiving than I.

Ash was quiet. He knew, as I did, what came next.

"So, we went to see the Lady," I continued. "And right before…Keirran stabbed me, the Lady mentioned something. She told him that my sacrifice would lift the Veil, that if I died, all exiles and Forgotten would be saved, because humans would be able to see them. And that belief would let them exist again. But, there was…one other thing she told us. About Keirran, and the amulet. She said that not only was the amulet draining Keirran's strength and magic, it was also…" I hesitated. Ash was going to hate me after this.

"What?" Ash prodded gently. I swallowed.

"Stealing his soul."

"It was just supposed to be a temporary solution," Kenzie broke in, as Ash went very still, looking dangerous now. "It was supposed to keep Annwyl alive until we could convince Titania to lift her banishment. Once she went back to the Nevernever, Keirran promised he would destroy that thing. It wasn't…" Her voice shook, very slightly, and dropped to a whisper. "It wasn't supposed to end like this."

Silence filled the room. Memories, regret and what-ifs tore at me. So much waste, lost friendships, broken promises and families torn apart. The Nevernever was going to war. Meghan was going to have to fight her own son. All because Keirran had tried to save someone he loved from dying. It didn't seem fair.

"*Can* the amulet be destroyed?" Ash questioned at last, his voice lethally soft.

"I—I don't know," I stammered helplessly. "We would have to find Annwyl, see if she still has it." *If she's still alive.* "But even if we do destroy it, Guro said the damage it causes might be permanent. I'd have to talk to him, see if there's anything we can do, some way to reverse whatever's happened to Keirran."

Ash nodded slowly. "I think that's all we can hope for now," he mused, almost too faint to hear. Closing his eyes, he took a breath, and then his gaze sliced into me again. "I will not lose my son," he said in a terrifying yet almost desperate voice. "Meghan is queen—her hands are tied in this matter—but I will do whatever it takes to see him returned to us. Ethan, you were his friend, once. You stood with him when no one else would. I know that what Keirran has done can never be forgiven, but…would you be willing to do this one final thing? For Meghan, if for no one else. Go to your Guro. Ask him about the amulet. See if there's anything we can do to return Keirran to himself. If it's not too late to save him."

I swallowed hard. "Yeah," I rasped, nodding. "I'll do it. For Meghan." *For everyone.*

Ash turned away, gesturing for us to follow, and we trailed him to the end of an aisle. Reaching up to a shelf, Ash hooked a finger atop a book spine and pulled it down. There was a creak, and a section of shelf swung back, revealing a narrow stone tunnel snaking away into darkness.

"This will take you out of the city," Ash said, turning back. "There is a trod at the end of the tunnel that will return you to the mortal realm, very close to your own house, Ethan." I blinked in surprise, and Ash smiled sadly. "Keirran used this passage all the time to sneak out of the palace, until I finally locked it down."

A pained look crossed his face, but he shook his head, and it was gone. "I would go with you myself," he continued, "but...my place is here, with Meghan. Too much is at stake in the Nevernever right now. We must prepare the Iron Realm for war, so I am counting on you—both of you—" he added, looking at Kenzie "—to save Keirran. Bring him home, so we can end this madness for good."

"I can't promise anything, Ash," I said, thinking that my attempts to do the right thing had gotten us into this mess in the first place. "But I'll try. If there's a way to destroy that amulet without killing Keirran and Annwyl, I'll find it."

Ash nodded once, then turned away. I watched his lean, dark form fading into the shadows, and took one step after him.

"Hey," I called. "Ash, wait."

He turned back toward us, and the words caught in my throat. What did I want to tell him? *I don't hate you anymore? I no longer blame you for keeping Meghan from us?* It sounded stupid and childish, even though it was true.

Ash, in that surreal, eerie way of his, seemed to know exactly what I was thinking. "We all have regrets, Ethan," he said. "Things we wish we could change. Events we wish had never happened. I myself have too many to count, but there is one thing that I have never regretted, and that is meeting your sister." He said it calmly, like he was stating the obvious. "I would not change anything when it comes to Meghan," Ash went on, "but I do know that our decisions have made your life very hard. She wished it could have been otherwise, but I think we both know why she chose what she did. Just remember that she was always thinking of her family, and you especially, Ethan."

I blinked rapidly and swallowed the lump in my throat. "I know," I husked out, and said something that I had never spoken out loud before in Faery, had never thought I would. "Thanks."

Ash spun and vanished into the darkness, leaving me and Kenzie alone. I stood there a moment, waiting for my eyes to clear, before I felt Kenzie's warm hand on my back. "You okay, tough guy?"

I dragged in a deep breath. "Yeah," I rasped, turning to face her. "I'm fine. You ready for this?"

She smiled, slipped both arms around my waist and hugged me. For a moment, I just held her, my brain looping in dark, endless circles. Find Guro, destroy the amulet. Or at least, reverse whatever soul-sucking juju was at work here. That was it. And, hopefully, once that was done, Keirran would stop being an unforgivable douche and go home. Of course, there was still the Lady and the Forgotten to worry about, but one problem at a time.

Kenzie let me go and stepped forward, peering into the tunnel. Razor leaped from a shelf and landed on her shoulder, buzzing happily, and the blue-white glow from his fangs threw strange flickering lights over the walls. "Do you think Annwyl is all right?" Kenzie whispered. "And that Keirran will really come to his senses once we kill the amulet?"

I stepped up beside her and took her hand. "Let's find out."

Together, we walked into the darkness.

PART II

CHAPTER SIX
RETURN TO GURO

We followed the passage for a while as, I suspected, it took us beneath the palace and then below the streets of Mag Tui-redh. The stone tunnel soon dumped us into a large copper tube, where I had to bend slightly to keep my head from hitting the ceiling. Smaller pipes and tubes broke off from the main passageway, dripping water, oil and, occasionally, some strange, bright green substance that sizzled when it touched anything but the copper piping. I was careful to avoid it and kept a sharp eye on Kenzie, hoping she would not get curious and poke a stick into the caustic green puddles just to see what happened.

Small metal cockroaches crawled along the walls and ceiling, waving bright, hair-thin antennae at us, pinprick eyes glowing the same poison green as the puddles. Razor's arm shot out once, faster than thought, snatching one of the metal bugs from the roof and stuffing it in his mouth with sharp crinkling sounds. Kenzie *"Eww-ed,"* handed me the gremlin and refused to let him sit on her shoulder again until we got outside. Despondent, Razor pouted on my back, muttering nonsense and making my teeth vibrate with his constant buzzing.

Finally, the tube came to a dead end, with a steel ladder leading up to a square trapdoor. Pushing back the lid, I squinted as bright sunlight flooded the air above me. Crawling out of the tube, I felt a tingle of magic against my skin, like walking into a spiderweb. Ignoring the urge to wipe at my face, I heaved myself onto a patch of cool, dry grass, leaving one realm behind and entering another.

The real world. Home.

I turned to help Kenzie through the hole, grabbing her wrist and pulling her up beside me. Razor immediately leaped to her shoulder, as I gazed around to get our bearings.

"Where are we?" Kenzie asked, dusting off her hands. I blinked, shaking my head in amazement.

"I don't believe it," I muttered, staring around at the overgrown lot. "We are literally three blocks from my house. When Ash had said it was close, he wasn't kidding."

"Really?"

I nodded and gazed through the trees, spotting the road a few yards away. An old gray truck rumbled past, tossing branches, and a knot formed in my stomach. *So close.* My parents, Mom especially, were probably frantic to see me.

And…I couldn't go home yet. Three short blocks from my house…and I couldn't see them. Because they wouldn't let me go back, and Meghan still needed my help. I couldn't abandon one half of my family for the other.

Kenzie's eyes were sympathetic as she put a hand on my arm. "Missing home?"

"Yeah, but there's nothing I can do about it now." I turned and forced a smile. "Come on. Guro's house is clear across town. We're going to have to call a taxi."

Thankfully, Kenzie had enough cash for the taxi ride, and the cab eventually dropped us off at a curb in a small suburban neighborhood. Across the street, Guro Javier's simple brick house waited at the end of the sidewalk, though the driveway was empty. After piling out of the cab, I looked at Kenzie.

"What day is it?"

"Um." Kenzie pulled out her phone and frowned at the screen. "Ugh, the battery is already almost dead. Stupid faery time differences. It's Thursday, according to this."

Thursday. Kali class was on Thursday evenings. "He'll be at the dojo tonight, teaching," I told Kenzie, peering over her shoulder at the phone. "We probably have an hour until he gets back."

She nodded, and we sat together on a ledge to wait. Cars trundled by, and a couple of joggers passed us without pausing, not seeing the gremlin hissing at them from Kenzie's shoulder. I hid my swords behind the ledge, just in case someone saw a pair of strange teenagers loitering around the neighborhood and noticed that one of them was armed.

Finally, a single white car pulled into the driveway and shuddered to a halt. The driver's side door opened, and Guro stepped out, carrying his gear bag over his shoulder. Slowly, I stood up, wondering if I should walk forward, suddenly uncertain as to what my mentor thought of me now. I'd been gone for months. The last time he'd seen me, I'd brought a pair of fey into his home, performed a dark ritual and vanished into the Nevernever. That was a lot of weird crap for anyone to handle.

Guro froze when he saw me hovering at the edge of the sidewalk. I swallowed and stayed where I was, waiting. If Guro didn't want to see me again, if he turned, walked away without looking back and slammed the door behind him, I wouldn't blame him.

"Are you just going to stand there, Ethan, or are you going to come inside?"

My legs nearly gave out with relief. Numb, I followed Guro

up the driveway to the front door of his house, where a series of wild barks could be heard beyond the door. Razor hissed and hid in Kenzie's hair, and she grimaced.

"I'll wait outside, if you need me to," she offered.

But Guro shook his head. "One moment," he said, unlocking the door and pushing it open a crack. "I will return shortly."

He slid through the opening, and I heard him calling to the dogs, leading them away from the door. Kenzie and I stood on the step and waited, the gremlin muttering nonsense beneath her hair. A few minutes later, Guro appeared in the doorway again, motioning us inside.

We followed him into the same living room where, not so very long ago, it seemed, Keirran, Kenzie and I had gathered with a dying Annwyl, and Keirran had begged Guro to save her. Even if it meant turning to the dark arts. And Guro had agreed. And Keirran had lost his soul.

Dammit, why did we ever come here in the first place? Why did I agree to let Keirran do it?

Guro sat down in the armchair and faced us, his dark eyes unreadable. My heart was pounding again. I breathed deep to calm it down, not knowing why I was suddenly afraid. This was Guro, who believed in the unseen, who had always helped us before.

Who could perform black, bloody magic and create an amulet that sucked out your best friend's soul.

"Much has happened since I saw you last," Guro said, his dark gaze solely on me. "Ethan, before you say anything else, answer me this—where have you been for the past four months?"

My stomach dropped. "I...uh...I've been in the Nevernever, Guro," I said, knowing I couldn't deny it, not with him. "I couldn't really come back."

"And your parents?"

"They knew where I was. I told them…before I left."

"Do they know you are here now?"

"No, Guro." My voice came out a little choked, and I willed my gut to stop turning. "I'm not…quite finished, with what I have to do." He continued to watch me, and I stared at my hands. "I…made a mistake a while ago, and a lot of people were hurt. I'm trying to fix it."

"I see." Guro laced his fingers under his chin, his expression grave. "Does it have anything to do with what happened four months ago, the night the Hidden World became visible?"

Kenzie and I both jerked. "You know?" Kenzie gasped. "You remember! Can you…" She glanced at Razor, buzzing on her shoulder. "Can you see Them now?"

"No," Guro said calmly. "When the spirits faded from sight once more, I lost the ability to see Them. But I do remember what happened that night, though everyone else seems to have forgotten."

"What happened?" I asked. He frowned.

"Chaos," he said, and his tone sent shivers up my back. "I was teaching class that night," Guro went on, "when suddenly we heard screaming in the parking lot. When we went to see what was going on, there was a body lying in the road with a strange creature perched atop it."

"What kind of creature?" I asked, feeling sick. "What did it look like?"

"It was very small, with sharp teeth and pointed ears. It carried a dagger in one claw, and its skin was green."

"A goblin," Kenzie muttered, as I felt a stab of dread for where this story was going. Kenzie's eyes widened, too. "Oh, no," she said, also guessing this wasn't going to end well. "What happened to the students? Did they try to catch it?"

"I warned them to leave it alone," Guro said, "but by the

time I reached them, it was too late. The creature became angry, and several more of its kind appeared, right before they attacked. Most of the students escaped with minor cuts to their legs, but..." His eyes darkened. "One boy tripped trying to run, and they swarmed him before I could get there. He was taken to the hospital with multiple stab wounds, but thankfully, they were able to save his life."

"Oh, God," I said, and ran both hands through my hair, sick and furious all at once. *Was this what you wanted, Keirran? Is this what your perfect faery world looks like?* How many more had been hurt? How many had died when the Veil went down? And it was partially my fault. Because I'd been stupid enough to trust Keirran, to believe that he wouldn't stab me in the back.

Guro's voice was low with regret as he continued. "By the time the police arrived," he went on, "the students had already forgotten what they had seen. They could not tell the officers what had attacked them. I knew the truth, but what could I say? They would not believe me. So I told them there were several attackers, that they were small, and they were carrying knives. No one could explain the events of that night or even remember what had happened, but it haunts me every day. I will never forget that boy's screams as those creatures brought him down."

"Dammit," I muttered, and covered my eyes with one hand. "I'm sorry, Guro. I caused this. This is my fault—"

"No," Guro interrupted. "It is mine. Black magic always leaves its mark. This is the price I must pay for using it."

I blinked in surprise. For a moment, Guro was silent, brooding as he stared past us with troubled eyes. Finally, he said, in a sorrowful voice, "Your other friend is not here. I assume... you have come to know about the *anting-anting*?"

I could only nod, though Guro still wasn't looking at me.

He stared at the floor over his folded hands. "Did it kill him?" he asked softly.

"No," I answered. "It...took his soul."

Guro sighed, his expression tightening, but he didn't seem at all surprised. I watched him, my teacher, my mentor, the only other human who truly knew what was going on with my life. I'd thought I knew Guro Javier. I couldn't have been more wrong.

"Did you know?" I asked, my voice rough. "When you created that thing. Did you know what the amulet would do?"

"I suspected," Guro said calmly, and lowered his arms to his knees. "I had not performed black magic before, Ethan," he went on. "Nor have I ever worked my craft for spirits, or creatures of the Hidden World. I was not sure your friend even had a soul."

"Would you have told us if you were?" I wasn't trying to be accusatory; I just needed to understand. Keirran was gone, and I had seen firsthand the demon that was left behind. A true fey; no emotion, no regret or remorse or conscience to slow him down. Without his soul, Keirran had become the kind of faery I had always loathed and feared.

"If I did," Guro returned in a quiet voice, "would that have stopped him?"

I slumped, shaking my head. "No," I muttered. Nothing would have stopped Keirran. He was bound and determined to save Annwyl, and now, he was well on his way to destroying the courts. Just like the prophecy had said.

And I had helped make it happen.

"Can it be reversed?" Kenzie asked, as Razor crawled up her back to peek out of her hair. "Or, is there a way to destroy the amulet without hurting Keirran and Annwyl?"

"The *anting-anting* cannot be destroyed," Guro said gravely, making my stomach drop. "Not by normal means. Nor can it be given away or lost. It will always find its way back to its bearer. If you want your friend's soul to be saved, there is only one solution." Guro raised his dark eyes to me and held my gaze. "*He* must destroy it, of his own free will. He must make that choice."

The air left my lungs in a rush. Keirran had to destroy the amulet himself. How impossible was *that* going to be?

"If Keirran does destroy it," Kenzie asked, "what will happen to Annwyl?"

"She will die," Guro said simply. "Or, she will return to how she was before the *anting-anting* was created. There is nothing I can do for her. I am sorry."

Kenzie slumped against the couch, her face tightening with grief. Razor crawled onto her shoulder and made worried buzzing sounds, patting her hair, and Kenzie clutched his tiny body close. She didn't contradict Guro's statement or insist that he might be able to do something else. No more magic. No more spells. We both knew better than to ask.

"I wish I could give you better news," Guro continued, his own voice subdued, full of regret. "But, if you want your friend's soul returned to him, the *anting-anting* must be destroyed, and he must be the one to do it. There is no other way."

I nodded numbly. "I understand," I said, feeling the impossibility of it all weighing me down. How would we ever get Keirran to destroy the amulet, especially if it would kill Annwyl in return? Even if we managed to talk to Keirran without him attacking us, he would never agree to that. "Thanks, Guro."

"One more thing," Guro added as I prepared to stand. "A few months ago, someone came to my house. I could not see it, but I could feel it. I knew someone was there."

"What did it want?"

"I do not know." Guro shook his head. "It never said anything. But I do not believe it wished me harm, whomever it was. It left soon after, and has not been back since."

Kenzie looked at me. "Annwyl?"

I shrugged. "Why would she come here and not say anything?"

"I don't know," Kenzie murmured, as Razor bobbed on her shoulder, muttering, "Pretty elf, pretty elf." Her face darkened. "But I think it's safe to say we have to find her now."

I nodded, already thinking about where we had to go next when, somewhere behind closed doors, the dogs exploded in a frenzy of barking. And not the excited *people are here* barks I'd heard dogs make before. This was a snarling, guttural racket, the kind with bared teeth and raised hackles, and it made the hair on my neck stand up.

Razor gave a hiss of alarm and crouched low on Kenzie's shoulder. Guro rose swiftly, eyes narrowed to dangerous black slits. I leaped to my feet, watching Guro and wondering if I should pull my swords.

"Something is coming," Guro said, just as a dark shadow slid across the window outside, peering in. It was lean, too lean for a human, with long thin arms and a featureless black body like a spill of living ink. Two bulbous glowing eyes stared out of the dark mass, pupil-less gaze fixed on us all. It raked long fingers down the glass, and my blood turned to ice.

The Forgotten were here.

CHAPTER SEVEN

AGAINST THE FORGOTTEN

With a curse, I drew my blades, as a second Forgotten moved across the window, a black blur against the glass. Panic fluttered inside, and I shoved it down. Guro didn't have the Sight; he couldn't see the Forgotten like Kenzie and I could. If these were human invaders, I'd almost feel sorry for them, but how could you fight something you couldn't see?

"Guro," I said, as he glanced at me sharply, "the Forgotten are here. Er, faeries that are after Kenzie and me. Do you have a back door? If we leave now, we might be able to lead them away."

His eyes narrowed. "How many?" he asked in a lethal voice.

"Uh…" I glanced at the window. Three Forgotten pressed against the glass now, and another two scuttled past the window beside it. "I don't know, exactly. At least five, maybe more."

A high-pitched screech interrupted us, setting my teeth on edge. A Forgotten glaring in the window raked its claws down the glass, leaving four long, thin gashes behind. Razor screeched in return, baring his fangs, and Kenzie cringed back in fear. Guro shot a look at the window, at the white scratches made by invisible claws, and whirled from the room.

"This way," he ordered. "Follow me."

We followed Guro through the kitchen and paused as he opened a single wooden door on the opposite wall. A set of stairs led down into what I assumed was a basement, and Guro motioned us through. "In here, quickly."

I went down the steps, Kenzie close behind. The bottom of the stairwell opened into a large room with cement walls and floors. It was dark down here, the shadows clinging to the walls and hiding everything from view, until Guro flipped on the light.

My eyes widened. The space in the center of the floor was clear, but the walls were covered with weapons. Crossed swords, knives, clubs, wooden rattan sticks, a couple machetes and tomahawks, all hung in pairs around the room, glimmering wickedly in the fluorescent lights. A tire dummy sat in one corner of the room, a heavy bag in the other, and a couple wooden stands with padded coats and helmets stood at the back. One entire wall had pairs of traditional Filipino short swords—the kris, gayang and kalis were a few I knew by name— hanging beneath a crest that read *Weapons of Moroland.*

"Okay," I almost gasped, "I'll admit it. I'm a little terrified."

Guro stalked to the back wall, where a pair of swords hung, isolated from everything else. I recognized them as his personal blades, his family's swords, passed down from his father and grandfather before him. They were shorter than mine but no less lethal, a pair of razor-edged *barong* that were probably several decades older than I was.

"Ethan!"

Kenzie's frightened cry rang behind me. I whirled to see a solid flood of Forgotten stream through the door and scuttle down the stairs, climbing along the walls and ceiling like huge black spiders.

"Guro!" I called, as one spindly shadow dropped from the ceiling and lunged at me. "They're here!"

I dodged back as the faery's long, thin claws barely missed my shirt, and lashed out with one of my blades. It struck the thing's neck, biting deep, and the Forgotten didn't make a sound as it writhed into tendrils of darkness and disappeared. Another leaped in, slashing at me, and I hacked through its arm before backing away.

The Forgotten hissed and drew back, melting into a crowd of its brethren. As I raised my swords, a chill crawled up my spine. The Forgotten had surrounded three sides of the room. Guro, Kenzie and I stood near the back wall, a semicircle of solid black glaring at us with baleful yellow eyes.

"Kenzie," I panted, "get back. Try to stay between me and Guro." Though I didn't know how my mentor was going to fight them. There were an awful lot of Forgotten down here, and they were invisible to normal eyes. Unless Guro had somehow gotten the Sight, which I doubted, most of the fighting was going to be up to me. "If you see an opening," I continued, not daring to look back at the girl, "run. Get out however you can, and don't wait for me. I'll catch up."

"Screw that," Kenzie snapped, and I heard the frantic zip of her bag opening. "I'm sure as hell not leaving you, Ethan. you should know that by now. Just keep them back for a few seconds."

The Forgotten edged forward, silent and deadly, preparing to attack. Guro stood next to me, the *barongs* held loosely at his sides. I snuck a glance at him and saw that his eyes were closed.

Like a flood of black water, the Forgotten surged forward.

Before I could react, Guro leaped past me into the midst of the attackers, both swords spinning through the air. They moved like helicopter blades, blurred and almost too fast to see, whirling and slashing around him. They cut through the ranks of fey like a thresher through wheat, and clouds of darkness erupted around Guro as the Forgotten fell before the relentless assault.

Hissing, they drew back, rallied and lunged forward again, claws and talons raking the air. I kicked myself out of my shocked trance and threw myself into the chaos, lunging beside the whirling dervish of death, adding my own swords to the fray. Forgotten shrieked in fury, falling back to avoid the steel, trying to pounce on me from behind. I stood back to back with Guro, fending off attacks, not thinking of anything but keeping my arms moving, reacting to the dark blurs of shadow clawing at me from every side.

"Ethan, above you!" Kenzie's voice rang out from somewhere beyond the mass of Forgotten. I stepped back, whipping my sword up, and sliced through a Forgotten dropping toward me from the ceiling. I caught a split-second glance of Guro, surrounded by Forgotten, his swords moving so fast they were a blur. His eyes were still closed as he spun and whirled his blades around him, driving the faeries back.

"Ethan, Guro!" Kenzie called out again. "This way! Back to the corner, hurry!"

I didn't dare look back to see what she was doing. Glancing at Guro, I started edging toward her voice, falling back before the relentless press of Forgotten. They hissed and slashed at us, still crowding in from all sides, and my arms started to burn from constantly swinging my blades. One of the Forgotten hit my arm, claws tearing through my forearm and sending a spatter of blood to the cement floor. I barely felt the wound, though I knew it was going to hurt like hell when this was done. If they didn't tear me to pieces before then.

And then, as we backed into the corner with Kenzie, still fending them off with our blades, the press of Forgotten just... stopped. Like we had crossed some invisible barrier the Forgotten couldn't pass. Panting, I looked down at my feet to see that a thick line of salt had been poured across the floor, boxing us in. The Forgotten hissed and crowded the other side of the salt line, glaring with sinister yellow eyes, but they couldn't come any farther.

Slumping in relief, I looked at Kenzie. Her backpack sat open in the corner, and she held a huge canister of salt in both hands. Catching my gaze, she offered a wry grin.

"Part of the survival pack for the Nevernever," she said, her voice shaking only slightly. "Item number one on the list—iron. Item number two—salt." She gave a small shrug and put the canister on the floor by her pack. "I might not be able to swing a sword, but I can sling salt around like nobody's business."

Still keeping an eye on the Forgotten, I reached out with my uninjured arm and hugged her. She squeezed back, her heart thudding rapidly against mine. The black wall of Forgotten had gone silent again, standing motionless outside the circle. They didn't look like they would move or go away anytime soon, but I'd worry about getting us out of here after I'd caught my breath.

Guro turned to us, dark eyes searching. "You are injured," he said, and of course at that point, my arm started to throb with the reminder. I gritted my teeth and pulled back from Kenzie with a hiss of pain, looking at my arm. Four long, straight gashes were raked across my forearm, oozing blood down my skin and dripping to the floor.

Kenzie winced in sympathy. "Oh, Ethan. Hang on," she said, and knelt by her pack, rummaging through the pockets. "Item number three," she sighed, and pulled out a red-and-white plastic box, setting it on the ground. "First-aid kit."

Guro loomed over us, sword in each hand, watching patiently, as I sat in the corner and Kenzie took care of my shredded arm. His dark eyes scanned the room beyond the salt barrier, and my heart leaped.

"Guro? Can you see them?"

"No," Guro replied calmly, not taking his eyes from the room. "Not completely. I can see...flashes. Glimpses from the corner of my eye, like dark shadows. But they disappear when I look at them directly."

"Is that why you closed your eyes?"

He glanced down at me. "What have I told you before, Ethan?" he asked softly. "Your eyes are not your only senses in a fight. I do not need to see my opponent to know where he is."

"Damn," I breathed, shaking my head. My respect for my instructor had just turned into terrified awe. If I ever got out of here, I would never miss a class again.

"How many are left?" Guro asked, going back to scanning the room.

"Um." I clenched my jaw as Kenzie tightened the gauze around my arm and clinched it shut. I stared at the Forgotten, trying to get a head count. It was hard. They were just black blobs of shadow that melted into each other. If it wasn't for their glowing yellow eyes, it would be impossible. "Hard to say. Maybe a dozen?"

"Fourteen," Kenzie said quietly. Snapping the first-aid kit shut, she slid it into her pack and hefted the bag to her shoulders. Razor bounced to her shoulder as she stood, holding a hand out to me. "So, the question is," she continued, as I grabbed her wrist, and she pulled me upright, "how do we get out of here?"

I eyed the Forgotten over the salt line and narrowed my eyes. "I could always smack them from this side of the barrier, I guess."

As one, the Forgotten drew back. Just a few steps, but just out of reach of my swords. Kenzie grimaced.

"They do understand us, Ethan. Maybe you could try talking to them?"

I glared at the Forgotten, and as I did, one of the shadowy forms eased closer to the edge of the salt barrier. I raised my sword and stepped in front of Kenzie, as the Forgotten stared back with its empty gold eyes.

"What do you want?" I asked.

"You," the Forgotten whispered, its raspy voice making my skin crawl. "We want you, Ethan Chase. Your life. Your blood. You."

"Sorry, you already got both a few months ago." I sneered at the Forgotten, as if dying was something I did every day. No big deal. "And I don't really feel like doing that again. You can go back and tell the Lady she only gets to kill me once."

"Not the Lady," the Forgotten hissed. "She did not send us here."

Not the Lady? "Then, who—"

The answer hit me like a slap, and I stared at the Forgotten in growing rage and horror. "Keirran," I said, as Kenzie gasped and Razor gave a disbelieving *"Master?"* from beneath her hair. "Keirran sent you after me?"

"Yes," whispered the Forgotten, and pointed at me with a long, sharp finger. "He wants you, Ethan Chase. You have the disturbing habit of not dying when you are supposed to, and the Iron Prince will take no more chances. You will not interfere with the Lady's plans. Surrender now, and the others may go. We have no interest in the other mortals. But you must come with us."

My arms shook, and I didn't know if it was from shock or a blinding, absolute fury. Not that Keirran really wanted me dead, but that he'd sent minions to finish the job. He couldn't even be bothered to face me himself. Just further proof that the Iron Prince, the Keirran I used to know, was gone. "Yeah?" I challenged, feeling the cold spread through my whole body. "And how do you expect to do that, with us on this side of the barrier?"

"You cannot stay there forever," hissed the Forgotten. "Sooner or later, you must come out. You are only mortal." It eased back, into the crowd of its brethren. "We can be patient, Ethan Chase."

"Dammit," I muttered, and turned away from the Forgotten, feeling desperation rise up to mingle with the fear and rage. They were right; we couldn't stay here forever, especially with Guro's family still out there. His wife and little girl could come home at any minute, and my blood chilled at what might happen to them. "Fine," I growled, raising both my swords again. "You really want me that bad, huh?" The Forgotten shifted eagerly, ready to attack as soon as I crossed the barrier, and I smiled grimly.

"Kenzie, stay back," I said, stepping to the edge of the circle. She made an angry, impatient sound, but at least she didn't protest. "Guro," I went on without turning around, "I'm sorry for the trouble this has brought you. You don't have to do anything. They're here for me." Though I doubted my master would stay back and let me face the Forgotten alone.

As expected, Guro silently moved beside me, raising his swords, and it might've been my imagination, but the crowd of Forgotten seemed to flinch as he came close.

"Wait!" And Kenzie lunged beside us, glaring fiercely as the Forgotten pressed close. She raised both hands, the large, now open canister of salt between them, and flung the contents in a wide arc before us.

The Forgotten screamed as the salt hit them, flinching back and covering their eyes and faces. They staggered away, tendrils of black curling from their bodies like smoke, and a hole opened up through the mob.

"Go!" Kenzie cried, and darted forward, slinging more salt and forcing the faeries back. Jolted into action, I raced after her, Guro right behind me. We hit the steps without being clawed to pieces, bounded up the stairwell into the kitchen, and slammed the door behind us.

Heart racing, I whirled, ready for the dark flood that would come from below, but Kenzie was already pouring the last grains of the salt over the threshold. As she did, a long black arm slid beneath the crack in the door, slashing at her and making my stomach lodge in my throat. Kenzie flinched back but finished dumping the last of the salt across the door frame, and the arm dissolved into black mist and writhed away into nothingness.

"There." Shaking, Kenzie rose and quickly stepped back, while Razor buzzed and hissed from her shoulder, shaking a tiny fist at the door. "That should buy us some time, at least. Everyone okay?"

"Yeah," I gasped, looking at Guro. "We should go," I told him, backing toward the door. I wished I could've stayed, talked to him a little more. I still had so many questions and so many things I wanted to explain. Who knew if I'd get another chance? But as usual, when involved with Faery madness, the best thing I could do for anyone was to stay far, far away. "Thank you again, Guro. For everything."

"Wait," Guro ordered, and stalked to the kitchen table, grabbing a pair of keys and a cell phone off the surface. "I'll drive you somewhere safe," he said, turning back to us. "Do you have somewhere you can go, somewhere these creatures won't follow?"

"Guro." I hesitated, grateful but reluctant to drag him in even further. "What about your family?"

He held up the phone. "I'll call Maria, tell her and Sadie not to come home tonight. They can stay with her grandparents until it is safe to return. They will be fine. But you two need to put some distance between yourself and those hunting for you."

"But…"

A blow rattled the door to the basement, making me jump, and Guro's eyes narrowed. "We can talk about it in the car, Ethan," he said briskly, striding across the room. "Let us go now."

With no choice, I followed Guro out the door and into the driveway, sliding into the backseat of his car with Kenzie and Razor on the other side.

A yellow-eyed silhouette appeared in the window of the house, and Razor hissed, his glowing blue teeth throwing flickering lights over the cab, giving me a slight headache. But Guro didn't seem to notice the gremlin or the shadow as he backed onto the road, put the car in Drive and sped off into the coming dusk.

CHAPTER EIGHT

CALLING ON FAERY

"They're not following us," Kenzie murmured, peering out the back window. "At least, I don't see them."

I relaxed, finally loosening my death grip on my swords, and leaned them upright against the seat in front of me. Kenzie turned from the window, sliding close, and Razor crawled into her lap and curled up like a naked mutant Chihuahua.

Guro watched us from the rearview mirror, dark eyes appraising. "Where will you go now?" he asked.

"Um." I raked my hair back, trying to think. "Back to the Nevernever, I guess," I said, knowing full well that Guro couldn't take us there in his car. The impossibility of what we had to do descended on me again: get the amulet, find Keirran and convince the Iron Prince to destroy it himself. The Iron Prince who had just tried to kill me using his horde of Forgotten minions. It seemed pretty hopeless, but one step at a time. "We'll need to get that amulet first," I mused, planning the next course of action, "so that means we have to find Annwyl. Any idea where she is?"

"Leanansidhe," Kenzie said, making Razor hiss and flatten his ears to his skull. "Last time we saw her, she had gone back to Leanansidhe's. We have to find a trod to the Between."

"Easier said than done," I muttered, trying to remember

the few instances we'd gone to Leanansidhe's. Keirran had taken us there both times, and of course that wasn't an option now. "We have to *find* a trod to Leanansidhe's first. There *was* one just a few blocks from my house," I said, scowling as I remembered, "but then Keirran went and destroyed it from this side, so that's out. Dammit, where's Grimalkin when you need him?"

Huh, never thought I'd ever say that.

There was a buzz from Kenzie's lap, and Razor suddenly poked his head up, blinking at us with huge green eyes. "Razor knows," he said, glancing up at Kenzie. "Don't need bad evil kitty. Razor knows trod to Scary Lady's house."

"What?" Kenzie looked down, and the gremlin watched her like an adoring dog. "Razor, you know how to get to Leanansidhe's from here?"

The gremlin shook his head, ears flapping. "Not here," he said. "Not from human world. Go to wyldwood, find trod to Scary Lady. But Razor knows. Razor show pretty girl and funny boy the way."

"So, just to be certain," I said, attempting to follow the gremlin's strange way of speaking, "you're saying, if we go back to the Nevernever, you can get us to Leanansidhe's, right?"

The gremlin blinked at me, as if *I* was the thick one, and nodded.

"Okay." I sighed, leaning back in the seat. "That sounds just about right. So now all we need is a trod back to the Nevernever."

"What about the one at the abandoned house?" Kenzie mused. "That one should work if Razor is with us. And the local bogeys don't chase us away."

I nodded wearily. "That's our best option, I guess. Do you remember how to get there?"

"I think so."

Throughout this whole conversation, Guro hadn't said a word, though I could still feel him watching us from the mirror. If he thought we were both out of our minds, having a conversation about faeries with something he could neither see nor hear, he didn't say anything. "Where do you need to go?" he asked, and Kenzie scooted forward to give him directions.

A few minutes later, we pulled up in front of a familiar abandoned house surrounded by chain link and rotting in the middle of an overgrown lot. I swallowed hard, remembering. The last time we'd come here had been with Keirran.

Guro rolled down the window as we piled out, his dark gaze fixing on me. I hesitated, knowing how suspicious this would look to anyone else, two kids walking toward an abandoned house, one of them wearing a pair of swords at his waist. "Guro," I began, not really knowing what to say. "I…"

"It's all right, Ethan." As always, Guro was far calmer than anyone I'd ever seen. "I have always known, from the very beginning, that you were different. From the moment I saw you in my class, I knew that your destiny would be unlike any I have seen before. I understand, and I want you to know I don't blame you for anything." A lump caught in my throat, as Guro smiled faintly and nodded toward the abandoned house. "Now go," he ordered. "Do what you have to do. We will see each other again, and you can tell me everything."

I glanced at Kenzie and backed away, toward the fence. "I'll come back," I said, my voice thick. "When this is all over, I promise I'll come back." Guro didn't answer, and I turned away, walking to the padlocked gate with Kenzie and Razor. I felt him watching us as we slipped through the fence, felt his dark eyes on me all the way across the yard, up the rotten steps and into the shadows of the house.

Inside, the room smelled of dust, mold and rotten wood.

Razor buzzed and stood up on Kenzie's shoulders, flashing his glowing smile along the walls to pierce the darkness. No movement, no creepy fey or boogeymen lurking in the shadows as far as I could see. This place was rumored to be haunted, but I knew that was because a pair of bogeys used to live here, feeding off fear and suspicion. That was before Keirran, Kenzie and I had come through on our way to the Nevernever only to find a group of Forgotten waiting for us, having scared away the current residents.

"I don't see any bogeys." Kenzie gazed around. "Maybe they never came back after the Forgotten chased them off."

"Maybe. Let's hope the trod still works," I muttered, picking my way across the shaky floor. She followed, lighting the way with Razor. Carefully, we eased across the room, climbed the creaky, groaning staircase and ducked into the kid's bedroom on the upper floor. Walking to the closet, I grabbed the knob and pulled open the door.

It jerked out of my hand, slamming shut with a bang, making me jump. Razor yelped, making the light dance wildly, and I scowled. "What the hell?"

"Go away!" rasped a harsh voice from the other side of the door. "My closet! Mine!"

"Well," Kenzie said, sounding amused, "looks like the bogeys are back."

"Yeah." I frowned, then tried opening the door again. It didn't budge, and I pounded on the wood with my fist. "Move!" I bellowed through the wood. "We need to use the trod. Get out of the way."

"My closet!" the voice screeched back. "Not yours! Mine! You go away."

"Dammit, I am not in the mood for games! If you're not out of there in five seconds, I'm coming through this door with steel."

"Ethan," Kenzie said, and shrugged off her pack, "hang on."

Pulling out a bear-shaped golden bottle, she set the honey on a bookshelf and turned back to the closet. "You know the drill," she said, pulling her backpack over her shoulders once more. "One bottle of honey. That's what we can trade for using the trod. You have five seconds to make a decision. Four. Three. Two…"

No answer from the other side. Kenzie waited a moment longer, than nodded at me. Carefully, I reached out, grabbed the knob and pulled.

There was no resistance this time. The door swung back without a creak, and a cold breeze fluttered in from the thick, gray forest through the frame.

I smiled, shaking my head. "All right," I said, glancing at the girl beside me. "I can take a hint. I'm going to let you and Razor lead this excursion from now on. Just call if you need something stabbed."

Razor took the lead when we crossed into the wyldwood, sometimes leaping through the branches ahead of us, sometimes scurrying along the ground like a huge spider. In the eternal gloom of the wyldwood, the gremlin made a bright yet difficult to follow guide. His huge eyes and neon teeth were clearly visible in the murk, but he was easily distracted by every small thing that moved through the branches or undergrowth. He also left a faint but definite trail of corruption behind him—withered grass, dying leaves, yellowed vegetation—as Iron fey still had an adverse effect on the rest of the Nevernever. Thankfully, Razor was small enough for the damage to be minimal, though this worked against us, too. Once, something large moved through the trees ahead of us, causing the gremlin to flee back to Kenzie and not budge from her shoulder for several minutes.

So we hadn't traveled very far into the Nevernever when

night began to fall, making me nervous as the shadows length-
ened around us. Though I wanted to keep moving, I knew
we probably shouldn't press our luck. Traveling through the
wyldwood in the dark was never a good idea; the things that
stalked the woods at night were things you generally wanted
to avoid.

"We should stop soon," I told Kenzie, who was watching
Razor scamper along an overhead branch, green eyes bob-
bing in the darkness. "The wyldwood gets pretty dangerous
at night. We should find a place to hole up until morning.
Unless we're really close to the trod."

"Well, Razor says we are, but I'm not entirely sure about his
definition of *close*," Kenzie replied. "Anyway, I think stopping
soon is a good idea. I'll see if he can find us somewhere safe."

A few minutes later, when the wyldwood was almost at full
dark, we trailed the gremlin to a stand of massive trees so huge,
a ring of six people wouldn't be able to fit their arms around
the trunks. They soared overhead until they were lost to the
canopy and the darkness, so high I couldn't see the tops of the
branches. Luminescent blue moss hung in curtains from the
trunks and lower branches, fluttering in the wind like glowing lace curtains.

I crossed my arms, looking at Kenzie. "Here? How is this
considered a safe place to stop? We'll be right out in the open.
Unless your gremlin thinks we're going to climb the trees."

Razor wrinkled his nose at me, then buzzed quietly in Kenzie's ear. She nodded, then stepped forward and pushed back
the moss like a pair of drapes, revealing a large, dry, hollowed-
out space in the enormous trunk.

"Okay." I nodded, as Razor shot me a look of triumph.
"That'll work."

The strange moss bathed the inside of the trunk with an
eerie glow, as Kenzie knelt and unzipped her backpack. The

night was warm, and the trunk blocked the wind, so it wasn't cold enough for a fire. Which was good, because I didn't think open flames in a large wooden room was the best idea.

"Here," Kenzie said, handing me a power bar and a bottled water. "That's dinner for tonight, sorry. I only have a couple each. There was lot of stuff to pack, so I had to make some sacrifices for space."

"No complaints here." I settled against the wall and tore open the wrapper. "That magic bag of yours has already saved our hides a couple times now. At this point, I keep expecting you to pull out a car or something."

She chuckled. "I'm gonna have to stock up on salt, it seems. I had no idea it would be so effective. I wonder if there's a way to make salt grenades." She took a sip of water and leaned close, her slender arm brushing mine. Razor crawled up the wall until he found a small ledge jutting from the trunk, and perched there like a tiny gargoyle. "Do you think Guro is all right?" Kenzie asked after a moment.

"I hope so," I muttered, crumpling the wrapper in my fist. "The Forgotten were after me, not him. I just hope they keep looking for us and leave him and his family alone."

Kenzie went quiet, chewing on her bar. I fell silent, too, thinking, and in the stillness, the questions rose up, taunting me. Now that we weren't running for our lives or trying to find a way through the Nevernever, a thousand uncertainties crowded my mind, slipping past my defenses. Annwyl. Was she alive? Could we find her and the amulet before it was too late? My parents. Was Mom crying herself to sleep every night, waiting for me? Would I ever get to go home?

And Keirran. My stupid, stubborn, infuriating nephew. How were we going to deal with him? To get his soul back, Guro said he had to destroy the amulet himself. Willingly. I remembered the Keirran at the war council, the faery with flat, cold eyes, and the impossibility of the task seemed overwhelming. That Keirran was not going to do anything we asked of him. That Keirran would probably shove another sword through my guts and then cut off my head to make sure he killed me this time.

"Ethan?" Kenzie asked in a hesitant voice, staring straight ahead. "Can I ask you something?"

Apparently, I wasn't the only one with questions. "Sure."

"You were gone for over four months." Turning, she gazed at me, not angry, just puzzled. And maybe a little hurt. "Why didn't you tell me you were still alive? All that time, back in the human world, I thought you were dead. Why didn't you send word, let me know you were okay?"

I swallowed hard. Oh, yeah. She hadn't known I was asleep that whole time. Maybe I should've explained that little fact earlier. "I couldn't," I murmured back. "After Keirran stabbed me, I was in a coma for a long time. I've really only been awake a few days now, and when I woke up, everything was crazy, with Keirran and the war. I didn't have time to do anything." She blinked, looking relieved that there was an explanation, that I hadn't just forgotten about her. I could see it in her eyes, the fear that I'd left her behind again.

Reaching out, I tugged her toward me, and she relented without hesitation, sliding over my leg and sitting down between my knees. I wrapped my arms around her stomach and leaned in, resting my chin on her shoulder. "I didn't mean to worry you," I said quietly, as she relaxed against me. "I would've sent word if I could."

She sighed, reaching back and burying her fingers in my hair. I half closed my eyes, just holding her, feeling the rise and fall of her breath. In this small pocket of reality, everything was peaceful. Overhead, fireflies bobbed through the air like stars, and luminescent moths floated lazily past, attracted to the glowing curtain of moss. I let myself relax a bit, feeling content, at least for the moment. Kenzie was here, and nothing had attempted to eat my face off. Pretty good day in the Nevernever so far.

Kenzie sighed. "I wish we could stay here, sometimes," she whispered, sounding wistful all of a sudden. "In the Nevernever. I wish we didn't have to go home."

Mildly alarmed, I raised my head. "We have to go back, Kenzie," I said, and she didn't answer, raising my concern. "We can't stay here," I insisted. "What about your family? And school? If we stay here too long, everything in the real world will pass us by. There won't be anything left that we remember."

"Yeah," Kenzie muttered, but she didn't sound convinced. "I know. I wasn't being serious. It's just…" Her voice faltered. "I'm scared, Ethan. The past few months have been…rough." She sighed again, her gaze dark and far away. "I didn't mean to complain. Sometimes it just gets to me, that's all. Sometimes I wish I had the same chance as everyone else."

My stomach prickled, even as the girl shook herself, as if coming out of her dark mood. "Anyway, it doesn't matter," she said brightly. "I know we can't stay here, tough guy. Don't freak out on me." She tilted her head back, resting it on my shoulder. "When we finish this thing with Keirran and Annwyl, I fully intend to go home and face whatever nuclear explosion my dad has in store when he sees us again."

I frowned. There was something else, something she wasn't telling me. Normally, Kenzie didn't let anything get to her, but ever since she'd come back to Faery, she seemed slightly different. "What happened?" I asked, making her stiffen. "Those months where I was gone, you said they were bad. What happened to you?"

"Nothing," Kenzie answered quickly, hunching her shoulders. "Don't worry about it, Ethan. It's over now. There's nothing you can do."

"Kenzie." She slumped, and I lowered my voice, pleading. "Please. I want to know. Was it...your sickness?"

She sighed. "Yeah," she finally whispered. "I...um... Dammit, I didn't want to explain it here, but I guess you should know."

She hesitated, took a deep breath. I sat perfectly still, waiting for her to go on, reminding myself that it couldn't be too terrible. Kenzie was here, after all. That's what mattered now.

"After I heard you...died," she began in a faltering voice, "I got sick. Really sick. I was transferred back to my home hospital, and I didn't leave for a long time. They...they were afraid that this might be it, that I wasn't going to get better this time. It was kind of touch and go for a while." She swallowed, and I held her tighter, feeling my stomach twisting in on itself. "Of course, I wasn't helping anything," she went on. "I thought you were dead, and that I had killed you when I sent you off with Keirran. I was...well, I was pretty depressed. I wasn't even trying to get better."

I closed my eyes, pressing my forehead to the back of her skull. Kenzie wove her fingers through mine and squeezed.

"I did, eventually," she finally whispered. "I rallied, pulled out of it, and they finally sent me home. At that point, I couldn't even bear to look at the fey again. Razor hadn't left my side the whole time I was in the hospital. But when I got home, I sent him back to the Iron Realm. I told him to go home, too."

On the wall, Razor looked up from a ledge jutting out of the trunk, his eyes solemn and knowing. I remembered his stubborn insistence, remembered the way Keirran had struggled to make him do anything. "Did he really leave?" I asked.

"He didn't want to." Kenzie sounded remorseful and a little guilty. "But, I made him, in the end. I thought it would be better that way." She sighed, bowing her head. "I was in a pretty bad place, Ethan. Everyone assumed you had run off, or had gotten yourself thrown in prison. And, of course, I couldn't talk to anyone about what really happened. My dad wanted me to go to therapy. I refused, and we fought about it for a while.

"And then, one night, Razor came back." Kenzie glanced at the gremlin perched on the ledge. "I was surprised. I never expected to see him again. But he said you were still alive and in the Iron Realm. I didn't believe it at first, but Razor was absolutely certain." She paused, trailing her fingers down my arm, making my skin prickle. "So, naturally, I decided to come find you. I made plans with Razor, put together everything I would need and had him take me into the Nevernever. So, yeah. Here we are."

I shook my head, imagining Kenzie trekking through the Nevernever, alone, following a gremlin toward Mag Tuiredh. "What about your dad?"

"He doesn't know where I am," Kenzie said without hesitation or remorse. "And, after everything that's happened, he'll probably think I ran away. Again. But, whatever. I'll deal with him when I get back, when this thing with Keirran and the amulet and the Forgotten is done. I couldn't stay home. Once I heard you were still alive…" She shivered, her voice breaking a little, before she composed herself again. "I had to be certain."

"Kenzie…" I didn't want to ask, didn't really want to know, but… "What's your condition now?" I asked, and felt her tense. The lump in my gut got bigger, and I closed my eyes. "You're not really better, are you?"

"No," Kenzie replied calmly. "The prognosis the same as before. I'm…supposed to go in for more tests next month. Provided I get out of Faeryland in time." She squeezed my arm before I could protest. "But I don't regret this, Ethan. And I wouldn't have changed anything, so don't tell me I should be home. There's no way I could stay there, wondering if you were alive."

I strengthened my hold on her, my throat suddenly tight. "I'm sorry," I murmured, thinking of those long, awful months where Kenzie had been left behind. I'd been unconscious or insensible through most of it; Mackenzie had had to live through it all, dealing with the aftermath, thinking I was dead. Battling her sickness alone. "I wish I could have been there."

Kenzie shifted in my arms so that she was kneeling in front of me. Soft fingers brushed my cheek, making my breath catch, as she gazed down with solemn brown eyes.

"You're here now," she whispered. "I'm just grateful for that. It's not every day your boyfriend comes back from the dead." A wry smile tugged at one corner of her lips, before she sobered once more. "I guess we both dodged that bullet."

I gently pulled her down and kissed her. She instantly pressed forward, sliding her arms around my neck, her fingers in my hair. Wrapping my arms around her waist, I leaned back, drawing us both down until I was on my back, and Kenzie was perched above me. She didn't hesitate, pressing her lips to mine, sliding her hands over my chest and shoulders. When her fingers slipped below my shirt, tracing my skin, I groaned. Pulling her close, I kissed her neck, trailing my mouth down her jaw, and Kenzie sighed against me.

"Kissy," buzzed Razor's voice from the ledge, dousing me with figurative ice water. "Kissy kissy, funny boy! Ha-ha!"

I groaned, letting my arms drop to the ground, and gave Kenzie a defeated look. She shook her head and sat up, a resigned smile on her lips.

"I suppose we should wait until we have a little more privacy," she whispered, resting her palms on my chest. "Where gremlins and nosy faeries aren't hovering around, watching our every move."

"If that's even possible," I grumbled, sliding my hands up her arms. Her body felt good against mine, and I didn't want to stop. But there was no way I would keep going while Razor was here, cackling at us from the ledge, seeing everything. The mortification would be too much. "Just remember, you wanted the Sight," I said in a teasing voice. "And all the faery madness that came with it. Sometimes ignorance really is bliss."

Kenzie sighed. "It *would* be nice to take a bath without putting salt around the windowsill all the time."

"Saint-John's-wort," I told her. "It works wonders. The flower, not the pill. I started buying it wholesale online just to keep faeries out of my room. Just make sure you replace it when it wilts or goes bad. Nothing like having a pisky pop into your bathroom when you're in the shower."

Kenzie laughed, then trailed her fingers down my cheek, her eyes suddenly intense. "I love you, Ethan," she said softly, making my heart skip a beat. "You know that, right?"

"I love you, too," I rasped, feeling my stomach twist with the understanding. "But, Kenzie, we're still alive. We're not going anywhere yet. It was close, we both got really lucky, but—" I reached up and smoothed a strand of hair from her eyes "—we're still here. We have a little time."

"I hope so." Kenzie shifted again and settled into me, laying her head on my chest. I wrapped my arms around her and held her close, feeling her heart beat, basking in the warmth. "There are still things I want to do."

She was asleep a few minutes later, curled against me with her cheek on my shoulder, her breaths deep and slow. That was another thing I'd learned about Kenzie: she could fall asleep just about anywhere. Unlike me. I was way too paranoid to sleep in the wyldwood, particularly when we were out in the open. I was scared of waking up in a cage, or a pot, or halfway down some monster's throat. If something did attack us in the Nevernever, I wanted to see it coming.

The night went on. On the ledge, Razor curled up and fell asleep as well, tiny buzzing snores coming from his fanged mouth. I shifted carefully, pillowing Kenzie's head on my leg, letting her stretch out beside me. She mumbled something that included the words *greyhound* and *tacos* but didn't wake up.

Crossing my arms, I leaned back and waited for morning, listening to the soft snores of my companions. Inside our shelter, everything was quiet, though I could hear things moving around outside, rustling branches and crunching leaves. Sometimes, a cry or a guttural snarl would echo somewhere in the forest, and at one point, I thought I heard singing, but it was too faint to make out the words.

"Ethan Chase."

I jerked up. *That* was perfectly clear, a whisper filtering through the mossy curtain, coming from outside. It knew me, whatever it was, and it knew I was here.

Silently, I reached for my swords and drew them from their sheaths. Careful not to disturb Kenzie, I gently eased away from her, resting her head on her backpack before facing the opening, holding my blades at the ready. If something came lunging through the hole, it would get a sharp length of steel jammed through its teeth before I let it touch my girlfriend.

"We mean you no harm, Ethan Chase." The whisper came again, sounding a few yards outside the trunk. "We only wish to talk. Please, come out and face us."

Oh, great. There was more than one of them. I sighed, looking down at the girl. Sleep was precious in the Nevernever, and Kenzie needed to rest. I didn't want to disturb her, though I was reluctant to leave her alone, too. But better that I go out and see what they wanted, rather than wait until they shoved their way into the trunk after me.

I debated for a minute, then rose quietly and looked at Razor, snoozing soundly on his ledge.

"Razor," I whispered. "Can you hear me? Wake up."

No answer. I stepped forward, raised my arm and prodded him with the flat of the blade. "Hey, wake up."

He buzzed, twitched, and then glowing green eyes cracked open, peering blearily over the edge. "Quit it, funny boy," he muttered, drawing farther back, away from my sword tip. "Go 'way. Stop poking Razor."

Oh, that's hilarious. The gremlin is telling me to stop bugging him. "I have to go outside," I said quietly, and he frowned down at me. "Something is out there, calling my name. I have to see what it is and what it wants." I cast a quick glance over my shoulder at the still-sleeping girl. "Keep an eye on Kenzie until I get back, okay? Make sure nothing happens to her. If something comes in, or the instant something weird starts happening, let me know. Can you do that, Razor?"

Suddenly wide-awake, the gremlin bounced to his feet, nodding furiously. "Razor help!" he exclaimed, thankfully in a buzzing whisper. "Razor guard pretty girl, not let anything happen to her."

"Good," I whispered, sheathing my sword. Not perfect, but the screeching of an alarmed gremlin would certainly let me know if anything went wrong. "I'll be back as soon as I can."

I walked past the gremlin, pushed myself through the curtain of glowing moss and stepped into a moonlit grove full of fey.

Dryads. Dozens of them, as far as I could tell. Tall and willowy, with bark-like skin and huge black eyes, their slender bodies resembling the trees they were attached to. My heart beat faster, and I forced my hands away from my swords. Dryads had never harmed me in the past; the tree spirits usually kept themselves aloof and distant from the politics of the courts, only intervening when something big was at stake. Seeing so many of them here, staring at me with shiny black eyes, filled me with dread.

Especially when I drew closer and realized not all of them were dryads. Mixed in with the Summer tree spirits were several tall, pale faeries with long white hair and ice-blue eyes. Similar to the dryads, perhaps, but definitely Winter fey. Which made this even more disturbing. I couldn't think of anything that would bring a bunch of Summer and Winter faeries together unless it was huge.

"Okay," I said, warily gazing around the clearing. "You called me, and I assume this little gathering isn't to discuss the weather. What do you want?"

One of the dryads stepped forward. Her hair was short and spiky, bristling atop her head like pine needles. The smell of sap and pinecones drifted through the air as she regarded me with dark, unblinking eyes.

"The Forgotten hunt for you, Ethan Chase," she said, her voice like the whisper of wind through the pines. "Even now, they scour the Nevernever, the tangled corners of the wyldwood, even the human realm, looking for you. It is dangerous for you to be here, alone. Why do you not stay in the Iron Queen's realm, where they dare not venture?"

"I'm looking for something," I said evenly. "Something that might put an end to this stupid war. I can't sit back in Meghan's realm and hide. This is my fight, too."

One of the Winter faeries came forward. Its hair was as fine as spiderwebs, drifting around its sharp, pale face, and tiny flurries fluttered from its skin as it moved. The dryad shivered, leaning away as the other faery stepped toward me, but did not retreat.

"The wind whispers to us," the Winter faery said, her voice sharper than the dryad's, reminding me of ice crinkling in a glass. "Tells us things, hints of events beyond our knowing. You search for something that will bring you close to the soulless one. The prince who commands the magic of all three courts. Who leads the Forgotten, and is never far from the Lady's side."

Keirran. I felt a lump of ice settle in my gut, and swallowed hard. "Yeah." I nodded. "I am. What about it?"

"If you go to the Iron Prince now," the dryad said softly, "you will die."

I stared at her. She shook her head sadly. "He is not the same, Ethan Chase. Nothing remains of the Iron Prince you once knew. The loss of his human soul has unleashed the demon of prophecy, and he will not stop until the Lady, the First Queen of the Nevernever, regains what she believes has been stolen from her."

"He has grown infinitely more powerful," the Winter faery added. "Even as an outside force drains his glamour, his sense of self, the Lady's magic—and her anger against the courts—sustains him. He has become her champion, and she has become a force to rival that of Oberon, Mab and the courts she wishes to destroy."

"I don't get it," I said, frowning as I tried to follow along. "The last time Keirran and I saw the Lady, she was barely hanging on to existence. She was hardly more than a Forgotten herself. How'd she get so powerful, so quickly?"

"The ritual, Ethan Chase," the dryad whispered. "The sacrifice, *your* sacrifice. When your blood was spilled in the Faery Ring that night, the Veil lifted. For a few minutes, the world could see us. All that power—all that fear, panic, wonder, *belief*—flowed directly into the Lady, restoring her completely. She is now as she was before. Before the Summer and Winter courts ever came to be, before Oberon and Mab, when there was but one queen who ruled the entire Nevernever."

"The wind remembers," the Winter faery said, its voice low and grave. "Even if we do not, the wind remembers those days of blood and fear. The Lady will destroy us, remake the Nevernever in her own image, bring back the terror and bloodshed of those early days, before the land rose up to overthrow her. She must be stopped, but the Iron Prince stands between her and anyone who would try."

"Well, I'm certainly going to try," I growled, ignoring the shivers crawling up and down my spine. "And I'll do it by talking, pounding or beating some sense into Keirran. I don't care if he's become her champion or whatever. We'll make him see, somehow." Both faeries gave me a very solemn, dubious look, and I crossed my arms. "I have to try. I promised Meghan, and Ash, and everyone, that I would bring Keirran back."

"You are no match for him," the Winter faery insisted. "He will blast you apart before you get within twenty feet of him. But," it added, as I took a breath to argue, "if you insist upon this course of action, if you truly intend to face the Iron Prince, there is something we can do for you."

I instinctively recoiled, fighting the urge to back away. *Never make bargains with faeries*, that was my number one rule. I'd lived my life by that code, refusing to compromise, knowing faery bargains never turned out the way you wanted.

But this was bigger than me now; an entire world ready to plunge into chaos and destruction. Could I really let fear stop me? Even if it screwed me royally, if it meant I had a chance to save the ones I loved...

A chill crept over me. That was exactly what Keirran had

been thinking when he started down this path. "No," I rasped, and now I did back away. "No bargains. No contracts. I can't promise anything, I'm sorry."

"Not a bargain, Ethan Chase," the dryad said, holding out a twig-thin hand. "An agreement. An understanding. We will hold you to nothing, except the promise that you will find the Iron Prince and do your best to stop him, whatever that might mean."

"This war affects us all," the Winter faery added. "And the Iron Prince is the piece that determines which direction the balance of power will sway. As the prophecy says, he will either unite the courts or destroy them. And you, a mere mortal with no magic or power of your own, might hold the fate of the Nevernever in your hands."

I blew out a shaky breath and pressed my forehead into my steepled fingers, thinking. *Dammit, this isn't about me anymore. This is for Meghan, and Kenzie, and everyone. I need all the help I can get. I just hope I'm not making the same mistakes he did.* "What are you offering?" I asked without looking up.

A pause, as if the two faeries were sharing a glance with one another, and then one of them stepped close again. "The Iron Prince commands the magic of Summer, Winter and Iron," the dryad said. "Before, his human side tempered his power a bit. Now, as a full-blooded fey, nothing is holding him back. If you are to face him, Ethan Chase, you must prepare for him to bring his full might against you. Summer lightning, winter's death chill, turning the very land against you—Keirran can control it all."

"No normal human will be able to stand against that barrage of magic," the Winter faery said, as my insides shriveled a bit. I'd seen Keirran truly lose control only once, when he attacked Titania, the Summer Queen. And though the Seelie monarch was clearly stronger, especially in her own court, the magical throw down between the Iron Prince and the Summer Queen had ripped the ground apart and shredded the forest around us. "However," the Winter faery continued, "though we are unable to do anything about his Iron glamour, we can make it so that the magic of Summer and Winter will not be able to affect you."

I straightened. "What? Really?"

It nodded. "It can only be granted to mortals, and only if the Nevernever itself chooses to bestow the gift. It is not something we can grant on our own. But all magic comes from Faery. Humans generate glamour, but it is through the Nevernever that we are able to use our power. Faery sustains us, and in the same way, Faery can render a mortal completely invisible to glamour. Magic will pass right by them, or slide around them without touching, because they are no longer 'there.' They are an empty space, a hole, where glamour simply cannot exist."

"This does come with a price," the dryad added, as I stared at them, imagining what could've happened if I'd had this knowledge sooner. What would my life have been like if I was completely invisible to faery magic? "If we complete this ritual and the Nevernever grants you immunity to magic, you will ignore *all* glamour. Including beneficial effects, like healing, or invisibility. Nor will it stop physical harm in any way. This will not save you from an arrow to the chest, or from something's jaws biting your head off."

"But it will stop magical attacks," I repeated, just to be sure. "Say, like a lightning bolt. Or a bunch of ice daggers."

"Yes." The Winter faery nodded again. "Anything that is produced by the glamour of Summer or Winter will slide right off you. The Iron Realm, however, and its poisoned magic, is beyond our understanding. Immunity to Summer and Winter magic will have to be enough."

"Can you give this ability to someone else? Like Kenzie?"

"We do not yet know if we can grant it to *you*," the dryad said, narrowing her eyes. "Like we said before, this ability does not come from us, but from Faery itself. You are part of the prophecy, and you are the Iron Queen's kin. The Nevernever knows you. It does not know her."

"If I say yes, how long is this going to take?"

"Not long," the Winter faery said. "But we must begin the ritual soon, while the moon is high overhead. So, the question remains, Ethan Chase. Are you willing? Is this something you wish to do?"

I hesitated, thinking. Not long ago, I would've jumped at the chance. Being immune to magic and glamour and all the nasty spells the fey could throw at me? Seemed like a no-brainer. But after I'd met Keirran, magic had saved my life and Kenzie's life, on more than one occasion. It had gotten me out of trouble, kept me from freezing to death, and allowed us to avoid some very unpleasant circumstances. I had just gotten to a point where I would, begrudgingly, admit that not all fey magic was pure evil and was actually very helpful in some situations. Glamour itself wasn't the problem; it was really just a tool. An extremely dangerous tool where you had to be on guard the whole time or risk it blowing up in your face, but the real threat came from the creature using it, not the magic itself. To never experience it again…was I ready for that?

I sighed. Again, this wasn't about me. As much as I hated to admit it, I knew the dryad was right. I was no match for Keirran if he decided to use magic against me. I wasn't even certain I could defend myself from his sword; we'd "fought" once before, and were pretty evenly matched when it came to swordplay. But if Keirran used any of that power I'd seen only glimpses of in the past, I'd be blown apart with a thought.

"Yeah," I answered, slumping. "I'm willing. I want to do this. What do you need from me?"

The ring of faeries closed in, gliding across the grove with a rustling of leaves and branches. "Not much," the dryad whispered, as I tensed and forced my hands to remain still, off my swords. "Only stand in the middle of the circle as we commune with the Nevernever. If it chooses to bestow the gift, you need only spill a few drops of your blood to the ground to accept. There is nothing you can do beyond that. This decision is Faery's alone. Are you ready, Ethan Chase?"

"Yes."

"Then we will begin."

The faeries closed their eyes, and each one, both Summer and Winter, took the hand of its neighbor, forming a ring around me. Crossing my arms, I stood uncomfortably in the center as they began to sway, moving like saplings in a strong wind. The forest around us was silent and still, but I suddenly felt like something was approaching, coming closer through the trees, from the very ground itself. Something...huge.

The dryad I'd been speaking to opened its eyes, its stark black gaze fixed on me. "It accepts," she whispered in a low, inhuman voice, and a chill raced up my spine. Though from terror or excitement, I couldn't tell. "Spill your blood onto the ground, Ethan Chase," the faery went on, holding my gaze as the others continued to sway, "and the ritual will be complete."

I drew my sword, hesitated for half a breath, then sliced the edge across the meat of my thumb. Blood welled, pooling in my palm, before I tipped it over and let the liquid stream to the dirt.

A collective sigh seemed to go through the ring of fey as my blood hit the ground, and a gust of wind swirled around us, tossing leaves into a cyclone, whipping at my hair and clothes.

The branches overhead rattled, trees bouncing up and down, as if the entire forest was coming alive.

The land under my feet gave a violent lurch, like a giant drawing in a deep breath. I lost my footing and dropped to my knees, the earth cold beneath my palms, and felt something sucking at me, like it was trying to pull me under. I gasped and tried to fight it, but it was like trying to drag a car out of a hole with your bare hands. My hands disappeared into the earth, held in place by the massive force, and I couldn't budge an inch as something, whatever it was, continued to pull me down. My legs vanished into the dirt, and the ground continued to slide up my arms, past my elbows, toward my shoulders and head.

Trying not to panic, I looked up at the circle and saw they were still swaying in the same place, fingers interlaced, eyes closed, as I continued to be sucked into the earth.

"Hey!" I yelled, looking at the dryad who'd spoken to me earlier. Her eyes were shut again, and she didn't stop swaying. "Sort of being swallowed whole by the Nevernever, here! Is this a normal part of the ritual, or should I just start panicking about now?"

Of course, there was no answer. I had now sunk in nearly to my shoulders, with no signs of slowing down. I thrashed again, trying to free my arms at least, to grab my swords, futile as that was, but I couldn't move a finger. Cold earth tickled my neck and slipped down the collar of my shirt, and my stomach writhed in fear. *Dammit, why do faeries never tell you all the details?* I thought, furious with myself for agreeing to this. *Why am I even surprised?*

Dirt pressed against my jaw, oozing up my cheekbones. Panting, I craned my head back, feeling it cover my ears, muffling all sound. As it inched up my face, I took several deep, final breaths and closed my eyes as the force finally dragged me under, covering my head and plunging everything into darkness.

I couldn't breathe. I couldn't move. I could feel the weight of the earth, crushing me from all sides, and my own rapid heartbeat, thudding frantically in my chest. *I'm going to die here,* I thought numbly. *Buried alive by the Nevernever, and Kenzie and Meghan and my parents will never know what happened. How could you be so stupid, Ethan?*

And then, as I waited in the suffocating darkness, wondering when my breath would give out, I felt a presence. One that tied my stomach in a knot and made my heart nearly stop with fright. *Massive* wouldn't quite cover it. *Ancient* didn't even begin to scratch the surface. I was underground; I could feel cold earth against my skin, my closed eyelids, filling my ears and nose. But this consciousness surrounded me, engulfed me like the ocean or the sky, eternal and depthless. I was like a grain of sand, a speck of dust. I felt if I dared open my eyes, I could be floating in the vastness of space, surrounded by galaxies and planets and stars, and this presence encompassed all of it.

Was this...Faery itself? The Nevernever, come to kill me in person? I didn't know, but my ability to hold my breath was rapidly giving out. My lungs were starting to scream for air, and I was getting light-headed.

Ethan Chase.

There were no words. No booming voice, speaking to me from across galaxies. No echo of voices in my head. But the message was as clear as if someone had shouted it in my face. *Stop the Lady,* it continued. *Stop the Iron Prince. Restore the balance and save this world.*

Abruptly, my arms were free. The force holding me immobile vanished. I flailed, thrashing in my dark grave, hoping I wasn't six feet underground.

My head broke the surface of the earth, and I gasped, sucking blessed oxygen into my starving lungs. Coughing, I clawed my way out of the dirt, ignoring the circle of fey that had stopped chanting and were now watching me, and collapsed to my back on the ground.

"Ethan!"

Kenzie pushed her way through the crowd and sank down beside me, her face pale as she leaned in. Razor bounded up, gibbering nonsense and waving his arms, and the ring of faeries shrank away from him.

"Ethan," Kenzie gasped, pressing a palm to my chest. "Are you all right? What the hell is going on? There was this freaky wind, you weren't there when I woke up, and Razor said a bunch of faeries were calling for you." She glared at the dryads surrounding us, and I groped for her hand, trying to find my voice. "What happened? What did they do to you?"

"I'm okay," I rasped out, hoping to stop her in case she leaped up and started yelling at the dryads. "It's all right, Kenzie, I'm fine. They didn't do anything to me."

She gave me a dubious look. "I just saw you claw your way out of the ground, while a circle of faeries stood there and watched. It sure looked to me like they were doing something."

The ring of dryads and Winter fey were dispersing, fading into the woods without a sound. The two that had spoken gave me one last solemn glance, before they, too, glided back and vanished into the trees. I struggled into a sitting position, leaning against Kenzie's arm, and gazed around. The grove was quiet now. The wind had died, and nothing moved except the ghostly forms of dryads melting into the forest.

"You okay, tough guy?" Kenzie asked once more, gazing at me in concern. I nodded, drawing in one last, deep breath, and she frowned. "What happened?"

"Oh, not much." I looked down at the patch of disturbed earth, where I'd clawed my way out of the ground. My hands were still shaking, and I didn't make any attempt to stop it. "Just…I think the Nevernever itself told me to stop Keirran."

CHAPTER NINE

OLD ENEMIES, OLD FRIENDS

We reached the trod to Leanansidhe's a few hours later.

"Here!" Razor announced, leaping atop a broken pillar that marked the entrance of an old ruin, stone columns and broken statues littered about the glen. "Trod to Scary Lady's house! Through here!"

I gazed around warily. Old ruins in the Nevernever were usually occupied and were often filled with massive spiders, marauding goblin tribes, hungry giants and other fun things. "Are you sure this place is empty?"

He cocked his head at me, as if I was being deliberately thick. "Not want to see Scary Lady?"

"Well, yeah we do, but..." I sighed. "Fine. Let's get this over with, but be careful." Drawing my swords, I began walking toward the crumbling entrance of the ruin, Kenzie at my back and Razor scuttling over the walls. Creeping up the steps, listening for any sounds of movement, I felt strangely torn. On the one hand, I certainly didn't want to fight my way through a horde of nasties to get to the trod, and I especially didn't want to risk Kenzie getting hurt. On the other, I was curious to see if this new resistance to glamour would really work. I didn't *feel* any different. Unless you counted feeling filthier than normal from being buried alive. If I was to go up against

Keirran, and he casually tossed a lightning bolt in my direction, I would kind of like to know if I was really immune to magic *before* I was fried to a crisp.

But, it did seem the ruin was mostly uninhabited as we ventured farther in. Shafts of sunlight pierced the canopy overhead, spilling into an ancient courtyard with a rectangular pool in the center, shimmering in the sun. A pair of spotted deer raised their heads to watch as we came down the steps, and two piskies hovered over the water, blinking huge purple eyes at us, before zipping away with high-pitched giggles Razor leaped onto a stone railing and bared his teeth at their retreating forms.

"Where to now?" I asked, as Kenzie gazed around the courtyard with large eyes. The gremlin didn't answer, suddenly distracted by a large green and yellow spider crawling along a shimmering line of web. "Razor?" I prodded, and he jerked up. "The trod? Where is it?"

The gremlin blinked, then leaped down and scurried to where a pillar had broken in two, half the column resting against the upright part, forming an arch between them. "Here!" he exclaimed, pointing and bouncing up and down. "Trod through here!"

I glanced at Kenzie, and she smiled. "All right." She shrugged and started across the yard, stepping over rocks and broken columns. "Back to Leanansidhe's. Hopefully we'll catch her on a good day."

But when I followed Kenzie beneath the arch, nothing happened. I'd been bracing for instant darkness, for that clammy, spiderweb feeling of passing through the Veil into the Between. But there was no blackness, no tingle of magic as we went through the arch. We both came out on the other side, and Kenzie blinked in confusion, looking back at me.

"Huh, that's weird. What happened?"

"Uh, Razor?" I stared at the gremlin, who looked almost as confused as we did. "I don't think this is the right place. Did you forget where the trod actually is?"

"Noooo!" Razor flattened his ears and scurried forward, ducking through the arch. He appeared on the other side, same way as we had, blinked and scuttled through again. To the same effect. "Is trod!" the gremlin cried, leaping to the top of the pillars, glaring down at them. "Razor not forget! Is trod to Scary Lady's house!"

"I am afraid the Iron abomination is correct," said a new, sibilant voice, seeming to come from nowhere. I spun, raising my swords, as a tall, slender form *turned* out of thin air, smiling at me from across the pool. "That *was* the trod to Leanansidhe's," the Thin Man said, observing us from profile, his spiderlike hands folded before him. "Unfortunately, due to certain events, the roads to the Exile Queen no longer exist."

"Hello, Ethan Chase," the Thin Man greeted, raising one pale hand to wave at me. "We meet yet again."

"Kenzie, get back," I growled, as Razor bared his fangs with a hiss and leaped to her shoulder. "Grab your knife and any iron you may have. Razor, stay with her. Don't leave her side for a second, understand?" The gremlin buzzed an affirmative, and I heard her scramble away, shrugging out of her pack, but didn't dare take my eyes off the faery in front of us.

The tall fey blinked calmly, a faint smile on his narrow face, as if he thought I was being unreasonable. "You can relax, Ethan Chase," he said in a cool, serene voice. "I am not here to fight you."

"Yeah? Then you can leave." I jabbed a sword toward the entrance of the ruins. "Right now. And don't pull your damn disappearing act, either. I want to see you go."

He sighed. "Well, you said he would be unreasonable," he

stated, to the empty air, apparently. I scowled in bewilderment. "I suppose I should have listened and let you explain things from the start."

"A common lament," purred another, familiar voice, coming from the top of the arch where Razor had been a moment before. "And one that nobody realizes until it is too late."

I grimaced. *Well, you did wish he was here earlier, Ethan. This is probably your own damn fault. And the gremlin is going to start screeching right about...*

"Bad kitty!" Razor wailed as I turned back. "Evil, bad kitty! Drown in lake! Shave off fur! Burn, burn!" Kenzie, wincing at the shrill gremlin voice two inches from her ear, pried Razor off her shoulder and told him to shush. Grimalkin blinked at us lazily, bushy gray tail curled around himself, looking smug. I eyed him and the Thin Man in turn, feeling utterly confused.

"What the hell is going on?"

Grimalkin twitched his tail. "I knew you would come here eventually," he said, as Kenzie finally got the gremlin to calm down. "It was only a matter of time before you sought out the Exile Queen, and, as you have discovered, the trods to the Between no longer work."

"Why is that?" Kenzie asked, coming forward as she frowned up at the cat. Razor mumbled something that sounded nasty and vanished into her hair. "Does it have anything to do with the Veil disappearing a few months ago?"

"We are uncertain," the Thin Man said from across the pool. I glared at him; he wasn't moving any closer, but all he had to do was turn his paper-thin body to face me head-on, and I would lose sight of him. And he knew how to move around so that it stayed that way, essentially becoming invisible. I'd been stabbed enough times with a crazy thin sword that appeared out of nowhere; I really didn't want to go through that again. "We do not know what has happened to the Between, exactly," the Thin Man went on, "but I suspect that is the case. You will not be able to reach the Exile Queen by trod. If you want to get to Leanansidhe, you must travel through the Between itself. But I don't recommend you go alone." He steepled long fingers in front of his face. "The Between is…not friendly to those who do not know the way. If you are unsure as to where you are going, you will quickly become lost and wander for eternity."

"Let me guess," I said flatly. "You can take us there."

Atop the arch, Grimalkin yawned. "Do you have a better idea, human?" he asked, slitting his eyes at me.

"I'm not letting him take us through the Between," I snapped, gesturing sharply with my blade. "We're going there to find Annwyl, and last I checked, he was trying to drag her back to his creepy Forgotten town. Oh, yeah, *and* kill the rest of us." I fixed him with a hard glare. "What's to stop him from leaving us in the Between and then going to Leanansidhe's himself for Annwyl?"

"No, Ethan Chase." The Thin Man's voice was suddenly quiet, lethal. "It is far too late for that. The damage is done. Taking the Summer girl would have no effect on the Iron Prince now. The prophecy has been set into motion."

"What does that have to do with anything? You still tried to kill us."

"I never personally wished you harm, Ethan Chase," the Thin Man almost hissed at me. "I was simply trying to restore the balance, to prevent the rise of the First Queen. But you have started something that could tear the fabric of this world apart. Because of you, the prophecy came to pass. Because of you, the Veil is now weak, unstable. And after the First Queen eliminates the courts and takes control of the Nevernever, she will attempt to destroy it again. *Permanently.*"

A chill spread through my insides. Destroy the Veil, allowing all humans to see the fey. Forever this time. Meghan said it wasn't possible to permanently rip it apart, but I'd heard enough to know we could never let that happen again.

"Could she really do that?" Kenzie whispered. The Thin Man raised his wiry shoulders in a shrug.

"I do not wish to find out," he said solemnly. "I simply want the balance restored, the First Queen stopped and the Forgotten put to rest once more. But I cannot face the First Queen alone, not with the power she wields now. The Iron Prince is at the heart of the prophecy. He will be the one to unleash hell upon both worlds. He is the one who must be stopped."

"And Annwyl?" Kenzie asked. "What do you plan to do, once we find her?"

"The Summer girl is the key to the Iron Prince," the Thin Man replied. "She may be his only weakness. But worry not," he added, holding up a hand as Kenzie glared at him. "I do not intend to threaten, kidnap, put her in harm's way, or drag her back to Phaed. She is in no danger from me. Quite the opposite, in fact. I will not allow anything to damage the girl before we reach the Iron Prince."

Kenzie crossed her arms. "I want a promise," she announced. "Can you swear to me that you mean Annwyl no harm?"

I smiled at her, surprised. Getting a faery to promise anything was a big deal, as They absolutely could not break Their vows, even if They wanted to. I was amazed at how fast she had learned Faery's many quirks and idiosyncrasies; navigating the fey world was tricky to say the least, but Kenzie had pulled it off all on her own in a matter of months. She would, I realized with a flicker of both pride and regret, be just fine when it came to the invisible world. She didn't need me to handle Faery for her; she was more than capable of dealing with it herself. Put a sword in her hands and teach her how to fight, and she would be unstoppable.

The Thin Man made an annoyed gesture with his hand. "Oh, very well." He sighed. "Stubborn humans. If this is what it takes." He straightened, putting both spiderlike hands on his chest. "I, elected mayor of Phaed and caretaker of the Forgotten, do swear to aid Ethan Chase and...friends—" he eyed Razor, peeking out of Kenzie's hair, and curled a lip "—in the search to find Annwyl, the former handmaiden of Queen Titania. I also do swear not to threaten, kidnap or physically harm the Summer girl in any way. This I swear, on pain of death, unraveling and nonexistence." He paused and stared at Kenzie in defiance. "Is that sufficient enough for you, my girl?"

Kenzie glanced at me. I shrugged. There was probably some hidden faery loophole in that promise, some funny turn of phrase I wasn't seeing, but it sounded good enough for now. "Okay." Kenzie nodded, looking back at the Thin Man. "I guess we can accept that."

"Finally." Grimalkin sat up and stretched, arching his back. "Then, if we are quite finished babbling at each other, perhaps we can get on with saving the Nevernever?" His half-lidded eyes fixed on me. "There is a group of Forgotten converging on this area right now. I suggest we hurry, unless you think you can talk them to death."

I straightened. "The Forgotten are coming? Now?"

"I do find that human habit of repeating everything they are told *so* very endearing." Grimalkin scratched an ear and looked to the Thin Man. "But perhaps we can speed things up a little? I assume you can get to the Between from here."

"Yes," the Thin Man said, and disappeared. I jumped, looking around for the sneaky faery, but he reappeared on the other side of the pool, walking toward us. "Though the trod to the Exile Queen no longer exists here, the Veil between it and the Nevernever is still quite thin. So we should be able to enter the Between fairly easily."

Reaching out, he stuck an arm between the pillars, and his fingers vanished into empty space as I'd seen Keirran's do several times before, parting the curtain between worlds. The Thin Man eased the Veil aside, and a dark tear appeared through the archway, mist boiling out of the opening. The Thin Man smiled. "After you, humans. Oh, but a word of warning." He held out his remaining arm, stopping us. "The Between, much like the Forgotten, is an empty space that can be shaped and re-formed into whatever it needs to be. Mansions, towns, even whole kingdoms—all can be created out of nothing, if one has a strong enough will and desire to see it born. Of course, without some kind of anchor, these embodiments of will simply vanish into nothingness again, but many things have been created in the dark spaces between worlds. And at the moment, the Between is quite sensitive, unstable even. Do not let your emotions get the better of you, or you could will something into existence that might prove…problematic."

Well, that sounded awesome. Sheathing one of my swords, I reached out and took Kenzie's hand. She laced our fingers together, squeezing hard, while Razor peeked out of her hair and bared his teeth at the cat peering down at us.

"Bad kitty," he growled, as Grimalkin yawned and very deliberately raised a paw to lick it. "Evil bad kitty. No like. Go 'way."

Kenzie looked up, as well. "Are you coming with us, Grimalkin?"

The cat gave a slow blink. "I am curious as to what has happened to Leanansidhe's mansion," he replied. "She has proven most elusive to track down, and it is uncertain if she and her minions are even alive after the destruction of the Veil. So, yes, humans. I will be accompanying you. That was part of the bargain." Grimalkin sniffed and curled his whiskers at me. "If you ever get started, that is."

"Oh, shut up. We're going." Taking a deep breath, I raised my weapon, tightened my grip on Kenzie's hand and stepped through the tear, feeling that cold, spidery tickle that was absent before. The Thin Man stepped behind us, holding open the curtain, and Grimalkin trotted through the crack, tail held high. Then the Thin Man dropped his arm, the tear swooshed shut, and we were trapped between the real world and the Nevernever.

And it was just as creepy and uninviting as before. There was no light, no sky, no shadows. Everything was a flat, muted gray, the fog so thick you couldn't see ten feet in front of you. There were no sounds or smells. Or any signs of life. Nothing but mist and fog and emptiness.

Pretty damn depressing, actually.

A nearby patch of fog suddenly roiled and curled back, revealing a gnarled, withered tree, drooping branches bent under the weight of large, pulpy fruit. I frowned, certain nothing had been there a moment before. The tree looked…angry, somehow. Maybe it was because the fruit, hanging from the limbs, looked eerily similar to human heads. Scowling human heads.

I felt a jolt and stumbled back, nearly bumping into the Thin Man. One of the ugly fruits had shifted a bit, and I saw that it was *me*. My head, my face, twisted into a grotesque scowl as it dangled there on the branch. The Thin Man looked over and let out a sigh.

"I told you, boy. Don't let your emotions get the better of you." He waved a hand at the tree and the mist beyond. "The Between is quite sensitive right now. It will latch on to any strong emotion and turn it into an embodiment of will, and you might not like the results. So let's try to keep those nasty negative feelings to a minimum, shall we?"

I'll show you a nasty negative feeling, I thought, but behind me, the tree branches rattled, shaking the fruit, and I took a deep breath, trying to control myself. The Thin Man sniffed.

"This way, please," he stated, turning in a seemingly random direction. "I have a general idea where Leanansidhe's mansion is located, but I'm not entirely certain how long it will take to get there. I advise you to stay close. Wouldn't want any of you getting lost."

I'm sure you wouldn't…no, stop it Ethan! Happy thoughts, remember? I looked at Kenzie, who made an exaggerated scowling face, as if she knew what I was thinking. I rolled my eyes, and she grinned.

With the Thin Man leading and Grimalkin's tail poking up from the mist like a fuzzy periscope, we started into the fog.

CHAPTER TEN

CARNIVAL OF HORRORS

I lost track of how long we walked. Maybe minutes, maybe hours or days, it was impossible to tell. It was bad enough in the wyldwood or the Nevernever, where time was completely screwy and you had no way of knowing how much had passed. At least the wyldwood still had a day and a night. Here in the Between, there was nothing. I felt like I'd been dropped into a vacuum, with no way of knowing if we were still on track or walking in circles. If I'd been alone, if I hadn't had Kenzie, Grimalkin, even Razor's disturbed mutterings from Kenzie's shoulder, I'd probably have started to go completely nuts.

As I strode through knee-high mist, my foot hit something solid and unyielding, hidden in the fog, and I tumbled forward with a yelp, barely catching myself.

When I looked up, the world had changed.

The nothingness had disappeared, as had the dull gray light that muted everything, though the mist was still there, drifting in ragged shreds along the ground. Straightening slowly, a chill crawling up my spine, I wished I had the foggy emptiness back.

I stood at the edge of a carnival, abandoned and silent, red-and-white tents flapping limply in the breeze. The area was muddy and littered with trash, popcorn containers, deflated balloons and empty paper cups rolling along the ground or floating in puddles. The silhouette of a Ferris wheel loomed in the distance, and the entire scene looked like it could've come straight out of a horror movie.

"Oh, blast it all," the Thin Man said, stepping up beside me. "Someone has found an anchor."

I frowned at him. "A what?"

"An anchor," the Thin Man repeated, gesturing impatiently. "Something that exists simultaneously in the Between and the real world. Generally, nothing lasts in the Between. You could will an entire town into existence, only to have it fade away and vanish within the hour. Nothing created here is permanent unless you have an anchor, a tie to the real world. It is how Leanansidhe built her mansion, how she forged her own realm in the Between when there should be nothing." He looked around the creepy carnival and shook his head. "How very annoying."

Kenzie edged up, peering over my shoulder. I felt her shudder. "*Annoying* isn't quite the word I would use," she said, as Razor gave a soft buzz of agreement. "Creepy, disturbing, absolutely terrifying—those all come to mind before *annoying*. I vote we get out of here before the killer clowns show up."

"We can't."

Kenzie and I both stared at the Thin Man in horror. He sighed. "The places Between are intangible, eternal. They do not conform to regular space, nor do they have boundaries. Once you stumble upon these pockets of reality, you are trapped in them. Unless there is a trod that leads outside— very unlikely—or unless you find and destroy the anchor."

"Great." I glared into the fairgrounds, feeling my skin crawl. I did *not* want to venture through this B-rated horror set; I absolutely hated clowns. But I certainly wasn't going to stand here and wait for them to pop up with balloon animals and carving knives. "So where can we find this anchor?"

"In the center," the Thin Man said, nodding toward the carnival. "The land changes, spreads out and is conformed around the anchor, so it is always in the very middle."

"Of course it is," Kenzie said, echoing my thoughts. "So that means we have to go into the creepy-ass carnival that probably has a bunch of creepy-ass killer clowns, because creepy carnivals *always* have killer clowns, and look for this anchor that could probably be anything..." She paused, gazing around a moment, then sighed. "And of course, Grimalkin has disappeared."

I shook my head. "Come on," I muttered, and drew my swords. "Nothing we can do now except find this anchor thing and destroy it. The cat will show up when we get out of here, I'm sure. Let's get this over with."

Warily, we started toward the carnival grounds.

The earth sucked at my shoes, making squelching noises as I walked through mud and puddles, watching for any signs of movement between the tents. I didn't spot any indications of life. I *did* spot a lot of weird, disturbing shit—bumper cars that had long spikes bristling from the hoods, roller-coaster tracks that twisted in crazy, unnatural patterns, even tying themselves into knots, teddy bears with skulls for faces, and so on. There was a popcorn stand where I was sure I saw a tentacle vanish beneath the kernels, one whole wall of porcelain dolls with shrunken heads, and a bright red balloon that hovered in midair, except it wasn't attached to anything.

"Who *lives* here?" Kenzie muttered, eyeing a poster that advertised some sort of freak show in the main tent. Come See the Bearded Lady, it read, only the "bearded lady" had a gaping mouth that could easily swallow you whole and huge barracuda-like fangs. "Did someone actually conjure this entire place *on purpose*? What kind of crazy would do such a thing?"

"I believe you have just answered your own question, my dear," the Thin Man said, his long legs easily carrying him over puddles and patches of mud. "The Forgotten know how to move between worlds, sliding through the Veil like fish through water, but there are cases of fey and even a few mortals who have become lost in the Between. No one knows how it happens. It could be that a trod is unstable, or sometimes, though very rarely, it just vanishes on one end, and the traveler never makes it to his destination. And he is never seen again. Because once you are lost in the Between, you wander for eternity. After so long, their minds simply...snap." He snapped his thin fingers for emphasis, making a sharp, quick sound that echoed through the silence. I winced at the noise, hoping it wouldn't attract attention, though it probably sounded louder than it really was.

The Thin Man continued to address Kenzie, waving a hand at our thankfully still silent surroundings. "What you see now are the remnants of a fractured mind," he stated. "If we do stumble upon the owner of this place, there will be no reasoning with them. Whether they be mortal or fey, their world has become as dark and twisted as they are, and they do not realize that it traps them as much as it does outsiders. Thankfully, this world appears to be rather new. I suspect it has not been here long, which is why it seems deserted. Still, whoever lives here will not be happy with us trying to destroy the anchor. I suspect we will see the worst of this place when we try."

"Oh, well, that's something to look forward to," I remarked. "Haunted carnival that sprang from the head of an insane faery, what could be better?"

Razor poked his head out of Kenzie's hair, enormous ears

twitching back and forth. "Razor hears music," he said solemnly.

We all froze. I gripped my swords and moved closer to Kenzie, holding my breath as I listened hard. A faint, barely audible melody drifted through the aisles and the fluttering tent flaps. It sounded bright and cheerful, reminding me of the tune the ice-cream truck would play as it cruised down the street, luring kids out of their homes like a modern day Pied Piper.

Yep, I was definitely creeped out.

"This way," the Thin Man whispered, and turned down a tent aisle. We trailed him through the narrow cloth corridor, following the elusive sound of music as it faded in and out through the tents. Of course, the tents didn't conform to logic, either, and we soon found ourselves in a maze of red-and-white cloth, trying to find the one path that would lead us out.

"All right, this is ridiculous," I growled, as we turned another corner and found ourselves in yet another narrow hallway of candy cane stripes and canvas walls. "I say we stop now, and I start hacking through tents. Who's up for that?"

Abruptly, the Thin Man came to a halt in the center of the aisle, causing Kenzie to pull up sharply. I slid in the mud to avoid running into her, grabbing one of the poles to steady myself.

"What the hell—"

The Thin Man raised an arm, silencing me. Edging forward, I peered over Kenzie's shoulder, gazing between Razor's huge ears, to see the rest of the aisle.

A body stood at the end of the corridor, its back to us. It was very broad, especially its shoulders and girth, and long brown hair fell in waves down its back. It wore a purple spangled dress that glittered in the dim light, and just as I was thinking that I'd seen that same dress somewhere before…it turned around.

"The Bearded Lady," Kenzie whispered in horror, as the woman, a thick brown ruff sprouting from her jowls and chin, opened a fang-filled mouth wide enough to swallow a basketball and screamed.

"Run!" said the Thin Man, whirling around, and we did, scrambling down narrow, twisted aisles, hearing the heavy footsteps of the Bearded Lady splash through the mud after us.

Tearing around a corner, I skidded to a stop. Somehow, we'd come to a dead end, the looming tent walls flanking us on every side. I turned, but there was no time to go back; the gasping snorts of the Bearded Lady were coming closer, and her shadow fell over the striped red-and-white walls.

"Dammit," I growled, and slashed at one of the tents. My blade sank easily into the canvas and sliced a long gash in the wall, parting the fabric. Orange light spilled through the crack, and I gestured to the others. "Kenzie, through here, hurry!"

She ducked through the opening, and the Thin Man followed, vanishing briefly as he turned from sight. I had just enough time to see the Bearded Lady lurch around the corner, gasping, the fangs gleaming in her huge mouth, before I dived through the tear after my companions.

Music greeted me as I looked up, panting. We now stood beneath a large, open tent, shadowy and dark except for the middle. Bleachers lined the perimeter of the room, facing an enormous open circle in the center, and the smell of sawdust, manure and cotton candy hung thick on the air, making me gag a little. The bleachers were empty, as was the open circle, though it had been set up for some kind of show. Colorful hoops, stools and barrels sat in the sawdust, awaiting performers, though there was no one here but us.

A snorting shuffle echoed through the tear from outside,

and we quickly headed deeper into the room. Sliding behind a set of bleachers, I watched to see if the Bearded Lady monster would follow us into the tent, but a purple spangled dress passed briefly by the opening in the tent wall and continued down the corridor.

"Okay, I officially don't like this place," Kenzie whispered, and Razor nodded vigorously in agreement. "If that was the Bearded Lady, I don't even want to think about the clowns. Let's find this anchor thing, kill it and get the hell out of here."

That sounded good to me, and I was about to say so when the lights beneath the tent clicked out, plunging everything into darkness.

I swore and pressed closer to Kenzie, raising my sword. "Dammit, now what?"

A spotlight flickered on in the center of the ring, which was no longer empty. A lone figure perched on a stool, gazing out over the "crowds." It wore a bright red coat and tails, black trousers, and shiny knee-high boots. Which were abnormally long, because the figure's legs were twice the length of a normal person's and as thin as a broomstick, making him tower over everything else. His face was not just pale, but white, with painted black lips and dark triangles beneath his eyes. Reaching up, he plucked the top hat off his head and flashed a toothy smile that stretched, quite literally, from ear to ear.

"I know you're out there," he called in a shockingly high-pitched voice. "Come forward, visitors, don't be shy. Welcome to the greatest show on earth!"

The Thin Man shook his head.

"Poor lost creature," he murmured, his mouth set into a grim line. "You've built your world, and you don't even know you're a prisoner here. Now you are trapped in this role forever."

"Yeah, well, I'd kind of like to make sure *we* don't get trapped here forever," I whispered. The walls of the tent were only a few yards away, and I took a step toward them. "Come on, we can sneak out through here."

"Come, come now!" the ringmaster called as I reached the wall. "No need for that, honored guest. This is my circus, and I know exactly where you and your little friends are. If you do not step forward to see the show, I will have to convince you another way."

Crap. I raised the sword and sliced down the fabric, tearing through the wall like before.

A massive white hand shot through the opening and grabbed my arm. I yelped and tried jerking back, but the fingers on my wrist didn't budge as an enormous clown stepped through the tear. It was thick and broad-shouldered, with a bloated belly and curved yellow nails that dug into my skin. Its painted mouth stretched into a wide, toothy smile as it lumbered forward, reaching for my shirt.

Shit! Well, there are the clowns. I lashed out with my second blade, swinging at its thick neck, but a second one appeared, identical to the first, and grabbed my arm, squeezing tightly. Snarling, I kicked one of them in the gut, but it felt like my foot hit a wall of Jell-O, and the clown actually chuckled.

Grunting at each other, the two clowns turned, put their hands under my arms and lifted me off my feet to dangle in the air. Helpless, I looked up to see Kenzie in the grip of another clown, while Razor buzzed furiously and gnawed on its gloved hand. It frowned at the curls of smoke rising from its fingers, seemingly too thick to realize it was being hurt, and flicked the gremlin away like a bug. Razor bounced to his feet again, hissing, and tensed to attack once more.

"Razor, don't!" Kenzie ordered. He froze, looking up at her, and she jerked her head. "Just run! Get out of here! Go!"

With a despondent wail, the gremlin bounded away, scuttled up a pole and disappeared. Desperate, I looked around for the Thin Man, but he, too, had vanished. I did notice a fourth clown walking around the bleachers scratching his head, as if he was sure he'd seen something a second ago, and it was no longer there.

Dammit, I'm tired of faeries disappearing on us when there's trouble, I thought, as the fourth clown lurched up and stripped my swords from my grasp. *Grimalkin, the Thin Man; hell, the only one that ever sticks around is the freaking gremlin.* I had no idea what the Thin Man could've done against four giant mutant clowns, especially when Kenzie and I were captured. But he could've done something. *At least he didn't get caught. But I swear, those two had better be doing something to get us out of this.*

"Excellent, excellent!" The ringmaster's voice echoed from the center of the tent. "Come forward, lovely visitors! Please, don't be shy! Come forward and see what we have for you."

Still carrying me by the arms, the two clowns lumbered toward the front, while the third trailed behind holding Kenzie by the wrist. I tried craning my head back to look at her, hoping she wasn't freaking out, but my gorilla-like captors gave me a shake that made the world go blurry for a second. By the time my vision cleared, we were at the edge of the circle, and the ringmaster was beaming down at me.

"Hello, little ones!" he said, raising his arms as if to welcome us all. "So happy to have you at the show! And it's your lucky day. We have front-row seats just for you."

He pointed with a skull topped cane, and the clowns turned to a row of seats at the edge of the ring. Unlike like the wooden bleachers surrounding the tent, they looked like theater seats. Though the leather was cracked and rotting, and I saw a few suspicious dark smears that I hoped weren't what had become of the *last* visitors to this crazy hellhole.

The clowns plopped me onto a seat and, before I could react, tied my wrists to the armrests with strips of red-and-yellow cloth. They did the same to Kenzie a couple seats down. When they left, I flexed my arms, trying to loosen the bonds holding me to the chair. But the knots had been tightened by gorilla clowns with melon-sized hands. I wouldn't be going anywhere for a while.

The ringmaster did a strange little dance, grinning like a demonic Cheshire cat. "Ladies and gentlemen!" he called, as if speaking to a room of hundreds instead of two very reluctant teens. "Welcome to the show! Welcome, one and all, to the circus! Let me tell you of the wonders you will see tonight!"

"Kenzie," I muttered, as the ringmaster rambled on, "do you know where they put my swords?"

"I saw the clown drop them on that barrel over there," Kenzie replied, nodding to a bright blue barrel with a yellow star painted on it. My swords gleamed atop it, and I narrowed my eyes. "Do you have a plan?" Kenzie asked, sounding hopeful. "They took my backpack, too. I really don't want to stick around for the show. I'd feel a lot better if you told me you had a plan."

"Working on it," I muttered. "If I can get to my swords, I think I have a chance. Still struggling with phase one, though."

"What's phase one?"

"Not being tied to a chair."

The ringmaster suddenly stopped his speech, giving me and Kenzie a very exaggerated pout. "Oh, dear, I think we have someone who isn't entertained," he stated. "We can't have that, now, can we? We want everyone to have fun tonight!" He flung out his arms, speaking to his imaginary audience. "What can we do to make the show more entertaining? Ah, I have it! For this first act, I think we need...a volunteer."

Oh, no. Panic shot through me as the ringmaster turned his head back and forth, as if scanning the audience. "Anyone?" he called, raising a hand. "Come now, it'll be fun! One brave volunteer is all we need. No reason to be shy." His eyes traveled down, toward the row where Kenzie and I were sitting. "Nobody? There must be some brave soul willing to step forward."

"Me," I rasped, as his gaze finally reached us. "I volunteer. Take me."

"Ethan, no," Kenzie whispered, looking at me sharply. I ignored her, holding the gaze of the ringmaster. He blinked at me, then deliberately turned his head to smile at Kenzie.

"Ladies and gentlemen," he said, as my heart tightened in horror. "I believe we have our volunteer. Let's all give the young lady a hand!"

"No!" I yanked on the ropes, struggling to free myself, as the clowns closed on Kenzie. "Leave her alone!" I yelled to the ringmaster. "I'll volunteer. Take me instead!" All of them ignored me, as the clowns cut Kenzie's restraints, grabbed her by the arms and pulled her into the ring. I yanked harder on the ropes. "Hey!" I called, refusing to give up. "Look at me! I'm talking to you, dammit. I know you can hear me!"

The ringmaster snapped his fingers, and a bright red cloth was suddenly forced into my mouth from behind. "Ladies and gentlemen, please restrain your enthusiasm," he said calmly, as the clown tied the gag around my neck. "I realize this could be frightening for younger children, but if that is the case, please respect your neighbors and take them outside. We do not want anyone ruining the show now, do we?"

Sickened, I watched them drag Kenzie to a large wooden disk sitting upright in the sand like a giant bull's-eye, push her back against the surface and fasten her wrists to the leather straps near the top. Grunting, they stepped away, leaving her bound to the center of an enormous target. My heart seized up with the realization.

I moaned and doubled my efforts with the ropes, as a bony

creature stepped into the ring, facing Kenzie. It wore a black-and-red vest that showed off its sunken rib cage, and copper throwing knives were strapped everywhere to its skeletal body. Its head was a mummified bird's skull, empty eye sockets blank and dark as it regarded the girl several yards away.

"Ladies and gentlemen, I need your complete silence for this act," the ringmaster said in a dramatic voice. "Absolute concentration is necessary for Bull's Eye Pete not to impale our lovely volunteer through the heart, or worse. We don't want her to end up like his *last* assistant, do we?" He laughed, and it made my skin crawl. "Remember, Pete, you're supposed to hit the bull's-eye, not the girl's eye. Make sure you remember the difference."

The skeletal creature never took its gaze from Kenzie. "Don't flinch," I heard it whisper as it drew one of the knives on its belt. "I don't see very well, anymore." Slowly, it raised its arm, the knife gleaming between its talons, and my stomach twisted so hard I felt nauseous.

Oh, God, I can't watch this. I'm so sorry, Kenzie.

"Wait!"

Kenzie's voice cut through the tense silence, making the knife thrower pause. Surprised, the ringmaster turned, a slight frown on his face, as Kenzie looked over at him. "I'll make you a deal," she said clearly. "One that will be even more entertaining than what you're having Bull's Eye Pete do."

The knife thrower glared at Kenzie as if offended, but the ringmaster raised his gloved hand, halting him. "A deal, you say?" he repeated. "Well, this is an interesting twist. What are you proposing, young lady?"

My heart pounded. I hated making bargains with faeries, but in this case, if Kenzie came out unharmed, I wouldn't complain. Making any kind of deal, even one to save your life, was risky, but Kenzie knew that just as well as me. She knew what she was doing.

I trust you, Kenzie, I thought, relieved that I wasn't watching a creepy knife-throwing faery impale my girlfriend. *I know you can handle this. Just…be careful.*

Kenzie took a deep breath. "Let Ethan do this," she said, making me start in surprise. "If he can hit the target three times without hitting me, you let us go. If he misses, then we'll stay and watch the rest of the show, for however long you want us to."

"Intriguing," the ringmaster said slowly. "And if you get hit?"

Kenzie shrugged. "Then I get hit. And there will probably be a lot of blood and screaming from me, and a lot of angst and guilt from Ethan. Either way, it'll be entertaining, right?"

The ringmaster scratched his chin for a moment, thinking, then beamed a smile and whirled, holding out his hands. "Ladies and gentlemen!" he called. "We have a new participant! Please, give a warm welcome to our wonderful volunteer who will take Pete's place."

My mind was spinning as the clowns cut me loose, dragged me to my feet and shoved me toward the circle. Yanking out the gag, I stumbled forward, trying to think, to form some sort of plan. I was good at knife fighting, sure; kali taught us how to be proficient with all blades, not just swords. But my knife skills were more defensive, focused on disarming a person trying to stab you, not hurling the blade like a ninja star. Guro didn't advocate throwing knives, because even if you didn't miss, you were now weaponless. I'd never thrown a knife at a target before, certainly not at a real person. I didn't know what Kenzie expected me to do, but my hands were shaking as I stepped into the ring.

The ringmaster loomed over me, grinning from ear to ear.

"Ah, here we are," he announced, clamping steely fingers into my shoulder. "Welcome, young man, welcome! Are you ready to show us what you've got?"

No, I thought, my mouth dry. *I don't want to do this. I'm not sure I can throw a set of knives at my girlfriend and not want to kill myself if I hit her.* But the ringmaster was giving me no option to back out. "Pete!" he called, and the skeletal thing sidled up, glaring at me with empty eye sockets. The ringmaster didn't seem to notice. "Give the young man your knives," he ordered cheerfully, "and let's start the show!"

Pete grabbed my wrist, yanked my arm up and smacked three copper, slightly curved throwing knives into my palm. They were about six inches long, edged along both sides, and razor sharp. A thin line of blood welled up from where one knife edge parted my skin, but I barely felt it.

In a daze, I let the ringmaster lead me across the circle and stop about thirty feet from where Kenzie was strapped to the giant target. A pair of clowns waited for us as well and silently flanked me as the ringmaster stepped away.

"Whenever you're ready, my boy," he said, gesturing at Kenzie. I looked numbly at the knives in my hand, then at Kenzie, facing me across the circle. *Okay, I can do this. I just have to hit the target and not her. No big.* My stomach twisted, and my hands shook as I picked up one knife with a hollow clink. *God, Kenzie, you have way too much faith in me.*

"One moment, my boy." The ringmaster raised his hand before I could pull my arm back. "I have an even better idea." Striding up to Kenzie, he beamed a smile at her, then turned to the "audience."

"Ladies and gentlemen!" he called, raising his arms. "We have a special treat for you!" Reaching into his coat, he pulled out a bright red candy apple, waved it around for effect, then placed it atop Kenzie's skull. Kenzie froze, eyes going wide, and the ringmaster beamed. "This brave young man will attempt to throw a knife and spear the apple right off this girl's head!"

My stomach dropped all the way to my toes. "No!" I protested. "That wasn't part of the deal."

"Oh, come now, it'll be fun." The ringmaster strode back to me, a warning in his bright grin. "You don't want to disappoint everyone, do you?" He waved back to Kenzie. "Hit the apple, and you and the girl can go. You get three tries. It shouldn't be that difficult, right?"

"And what if I refuse?"

"Then I will be disappointed, but I certainly cannot make you participate if you are unwilling or scared. But worry not." He nodded to the skeletal thing standing behind me and smiled. "Pete will do it. The show must go on."

Swallowing hard, I looked back at Kenzie and the tiny red target perched atop her head. *I can't hit that; there's no way I'll be able to pull this off. Not without killing or maiming her in the process. Dammit, Kenzie, this can't be what you were thinking.* The clown thugs stood silent and motionless at my sides, and the ringmaster looked on expectantly, gripping his cane. I could feel him getting impatient, though, and my mind whirled, trying to think. *If could just get to my swords. I'd stand a chance against these guys if I were armed...*

Oh.

Mentally, I kicked myself. Kenzie didn't volunteer me to throw knives at her; that hadn't been her plan at all.

Ethan, you're an idiot.

Spinning, I stabbed both clowns, sinking a knife deep into one's chest, then the other's. They gave a startled bellow, and as I yanked each blade out, seemed to deflate in on themselves, hissing like a balloon with a slow leak.

Grinning savagely, I turned on the ringmaster, but he gave a shout and sprang away, long legs carrying him half the length of the circle. "No!" he yelled, as I raised the knives and started after him. "Young man, please, sit down! You are ruining the show! Security!"

Three clowns rushed the circle. I turned to face them just as something bright whizzed by my face, cutting a stinging gash across my cheek. Glancing over, I saw Bull's Eye Pete silently draw another knife from the dozens on his belt and raise his arm to hurl it at me.

With a screech, something tiny and dark landed on his head, green eyes flashing. Razor snarled and dug his claws into the thing's bony eye sockets, making him howl and flail at his head, trying to dislodge the gremlin. I didn't think Razor would be able to stop him, but at least he was a great distraction.

The first clown reached me and lunged, trying to grab me in a bear hug. I ducked beneath the huge limbs and jabbed him in the gut with the knife. There was a squeaky hiss, and the clown staggered away, folding in on itself. As the other two barreled in, I flipped one knife in my hand, holding it by the tip, and raised my arm.

Sorry, Guro, I thought, and hurled the knife at the massive bulk of the clown. Even if I was the poorest shot in the world, it was like hitting the broadside of a house. The blade struck him right in the center, sinking deep, and the clown pitched forward, his body shrinking and losing form as it deflated in the dirt.

The last clown bellowed with rage and plowed into me like a bull. The breath left my lungs in a painful expulsion, and I fell backward with the clown filling my vision as it came down, as well. Hitting the ground, I stabbed up with the knife, bracing myself to be crushed. There was a pop, and the clown shuddered as it deflated on top of me like a giant air mattress.

Shuddering, I kicked myself clear and rose, one knife still

clutched in my hand. I saw Razor, clinging to the side of the tent, dodge the knife Pete hurled at him and scramble farther up the wall, buzzing insults at the furious knife thrower. At least the gremlin was keeping him busy. But where was the ringmaster—

Something hit me from behind, making sparks explode across my vision. I tumbled forward, managing to use the momentum to roll to my knees, though the world still spun dizzyingly around me. Dazed, I looked up to see the ringmaster, his huge mouth bared in a scary snarl, draw a sword from his skull-headed cane and raise it over my head.

"Not today, Ethan Chase," said a familiar voice out of nowhere, and the Thin Man turned into existence, appearing behind the ringmaster. His own blade flashed, almost too quick to be seen, and the ringmaster froze, his sword a few inches from my face. I scrambled back, lurching to my feet, as the ringmaster's head toppled forward and hit the ground with a thump. His body slowly collapsed, folding into weird angles like it was made of stilts, as his top hat rolled forward a few paces and hit my shoe.

I tensed, wondering if the ringmaster's death would cause this whole crazy reality to start fragmenting and falling apart, but nothing like that happened. Pete, however, let out a wail that set my teeth on edge and fled the ring, ripping through the tent and vanishing into the darkness.

I ran to Kenzie, cut through the leather straps and pulled her into my arms. She clung to me, heart pounding, and I hugged her tight, feeling my own heart race against hers. Razor landed on us, bouncing up and down and buzzing with excitement and fear, but I barely felt him.

"Quickly, Ethan Chase!" The Thin Man was suddenly beside us, with my swords and Kenzie's backpack, which he tossed to her. "There is no time. Take your horrid iron weapons before they ruin my gloves." He thrust my swords into my hands and yanked his arms back, shaking them like they stung. "Hurry, before the entire rest of the freak show arrives. We still have to find the anchor and destroy it."

"Humans." And Grimalkin appeared, perched atop a barrel, his golden eyes slitted impatiently. "This way, if you would. While you were wasting time, playing circus with the ringmaster and the clowns, I found the location of the anchor. Follow me."

A roar interrupted us. The Bearded Lady monster had flung aside the entrance flaps and stomped inside, her huge mouth gaping angrily as she saw us. More shadows appeared outside the cloth walls, deformed and twisted, starting to rip through the canvas with claws and teeth.

We ran, following the cat as he bounded to the cloth wall and slipped beneath. I slashed through the wall, and we fled back into the maze of tents.

As we ran, trailing the near invisible cat through shadows, mud and the mist that coiled around our feet, I started to hear the music again. Bright and cheerful, and definitely closer this time. The cloth walls suddenly fell away, and I stumbled into the open. A wide, muddy street stretched before us, lined with booths and carnival games.

At the end of the street, maybe a hundred yards away, a carousel spun in a slow, lazy circle. Unlike the game booths and the Ferris wheel, it glimmered with dozens of twinkling lights, though the creatures that made up the ride were definitely not child-friendly. Horses bared bloody teeth as they spun around on their poles, many twisted into unnatural positions of agony, their eyes mad and white. The other "mounts" were just as horrific. Slavering wolves, giant spiders and a bear with a small child in its jaws were a few of the nightmares frozen in plaster, all spinning around to the cheerful tune I'd heard before.

Kenzie, following my gaze, drew in a sharp breath. "That's the anchor," she said quietly. "The very center of the carnival."

"Yes," Grimalkin agreed. "Destroy the carousel, and this reality will disappear. Without the anchor, everything will fade back into the Between. You will have to do it quickly, though. The denizens that make up this world are none too pleased with you."

"Great. So, *how* do we destroy it?" I asked, looking down at the cat. Only to find that he was gone.

Something moved in the corner of my eye. I looked into the nearest game booth...as one of the teddy bears dislodged itself from the wall, crawled onto the counter and bared sharp little teeth at me. And then I noticed that *all* the toys, dolls and stuffed animals had turned their heads and were staring at us, eyes glowing like hot coals in the shadows of the booths.

I don't think I've ever run so fast in my life.

High-pitched voices shrieked and babbled at us as we fled down the fairway, and several things leaped off the walls, trying to grab us as we ran. A porcelain doll with a cracked face staggered into the road in front of Kenzie, holding up its arms; Kenzie kicked the thing away like it was soccer ball and didn't slow down. A red-eyed clown doll sprang at me from one of the counters, miniature butcher knife in one gloved hand. I smacked it away with my sword and kept running.

We reached the carousel, and as we got close, the animals came to life, snarling and thrashing against their poles, trying to bite us. I dodged a kick from a horse's hoof and slashed my sword at a giant, blood-drenched white rabbit as it came around. The blade hacked through an ear, causing it to clatter to the floor, but it didn't seem to affect the carousel itself.

"Get to the middle!" the Thin Man ordered, pointing

through the mob of shrieking, hissing animals. Our reflections stared back at us from the mirrored center, a dozen Ethans, Kenzies and Thin Men, gazing out of gilded panels. "Smash the mirrors," the Thin Man called, leaping onto the carousel. "The mirrors are the very center of this world. Destroy them and—" A dragon lashed out and clamped its jaws around his arm, and the Thin Man disappeared as he turned to deal with it.

I swore. "All right, guess I'm going in. Kenzie, maybe you can find something to throw at them? Maybe grab some baseballs from one of the booths?"

"Um, Ethan?" Kenzie said, her voice slightly strangled. "Not a great idea." I looked back and saw a flood of stuffed animals and dolls staggering down the road at us, their eerie red eyes like a swarm of ants. Beyond them, and closing from all directions, was an army of clowns and circus freaks, twisted, deformed and looking pissed as hell.

My blood went cold. "Okay, then," I gasped, turning back to the carousel, trying to find a break between snarling, writhing creatures. Spotting a hole between a leopard and the rabbit I'd smacked earlier, I grabbed Kenzie's hand and yelled, "Jump!"

We leaped onto the carousel. The rabbit screamed and clawed, gnashing long front incisors, but thankfully couldn't reach us. "Wait here," I told Kenzie, as the other animals eyed us balefully and bared their teeth. I winced. Getting through unscathed was going to be difficult, but I'd rather I be the one gored by that evil-looking unicorn than Kenzie.

Without waiting for a reply, I started toward the center. A wolf snapped at me; I dodged aside. A tiger raked its claws at my head; I twisted just enough to catch it on the shoulder rather than the face, though it still tore a chunk from my arm and made my eyes water with pain. The last few feet to the mirrors were blocked by the unicorn and the bear, and I paused, trying to find a good time to dart through.

Kenzie let out a yelp. I looked back to see a clown, its painted mouth gaping to show jagged fangs, grab for the carousel, miss and stagger away. But as we spun around, I could see more things leaping onto the edges, clinging to the poles as the carousel whirled ever faster and the animals roared with rage.

"Dammit." I spun, braced myself and dived through the opening, wincing as the unicorn's horn jabbed me in the back. Rolling upright, I charged a panel, raised my sword and brought the hilt smashing down on the surface as hard as I could.

The glass shattered. And so did everything else. My reflection exploded into a dozen fragments and collapsed, just as the carousel, the carnival and the sky overhead did the same. Shards of reality rained down on us, as I staggered back to Kenzie, yanked her to me and covered her body with mine as best I could. I didn't know what was happening with the clowns, the freaks and the killer toys; I just hoped we wouldn't be cut to ribbons in the blink of an eye. Shrieks and screams rang out, and the air filled with the roar of a million chandeliers crashing all at once. And then, dead silence.

Cautiously, I looked up.

The carnival was gone. The tents and clowns and eerie booths were gone. Kenzie and I stood at the center of an ancient, run-down carousel, plaster horses cracked and peeling and definitely not alive. Around us, the Between stretched out, dark and misty and endless.

I looked down at Kenzie. "You okay?"

She nodded, and I slumped in relief. "Well," she said, as Razor dropped onto a horse's head, buzzing, and the Thin Man wove his way through the mounts toward us, looking annoyed, "that was…horrifying. At least I can cross one more thing off the list of things I want to do before I die."

"Survive the clown apocalypse?" I guessed. She grinned at me.

"Nope. Join the circus."

I chuckled, shaking my head. Relief that we were out of that crazy place was making me kind of giddy. I was even thrilled to see the dark, empty creepiness of the Between. That's how glad I was. "You're a strange girl," I told her. "Brilliant, but strange."

She beamed. "That's why you love me."

"Yeah," I whispered. She sobered, gazing into my eyes, as I pulled her closer against me. "Though if you do ever join the circus," I murmured, holding her gaze, "promise me you won't volunteer for the knife thrower's assistant? I think I had at least three minor heart attacks tonight."

"Oh, I don't know," Kenzie said, a wicked look crossing her face. "It was kind of exciting. The two of us could perfect an act and take it on the road." At my mock horrified look, she smiled and brushed back my hair. "I trust you, tough guy," she murmured. "Even tonight in the ring, when I wasn't certain if you would throw the knife at my head or use it to stab the ringmaster, I trusted you. I know you would never hurt me."

"Humans."

Grimalkin's bored voice cut through the silence. I drew back, rolling my eyes, as the cat appeared on the saddle of a nearby horse. "I would say we are wasting time," he said, thumping his tail against the peeling paint, "but it never appears to sink in. Shall we go, before the Between starts manifesting hearts and balloons and other nauseating things?" The cat rose and leaped gracefully off the carousel horse, giving us a revolted look as he landed. "I shudder to think of the reality that might spring up around the pair of you. I believe it would be even more frightening than the carnival."

CHAPTER ELEVEN

VANISHED REALITIES

More wandering the Between. Okay, maybe *wandering* wasn't the right word, as the Thin Man seemed to know where he was going. But it sure felt like wandering, walking in endless circles through a creepy landscape that was always more of the same. I ached, from various wounds caused by throwing knives, tiger claws and unicorn horns. And now I was paranoid about stumbling into another pocket of reality, another whacked-out world that had sprung from the head of a batshit crazy fey. The carnival had been terrifying enough; I did not want to find myself suddenly trapped in an abandoned asylum, running from nightmares in long white coats wanting to "cure" me.

"Stop that," the Thin Man told me, as a stretcher rolled out of the fog, wheels creaking in the silence. It continued past us and disappeared into the mist, and I shuddered. "You're doing it again."

"Yeah, pardon me for being a little freaked-out by the whole evil carnival thing," I growled. "I guess I should be grateful it wasn't a mermaid or selkie that found the anchor and that the carnival wasn't underwater. You could've mentioned that we might run into something like that before we started."

"I did not think it likely we would find one," the Thin

Man replied. "Anchors are very few and far between. They are not simply lying around for anyone to attach a world to. You could wander the Between for a lifetime, a millennium, and not run across one." He gave me a look from the corner of one pale eye. "I was just as unpleasantly shocked as you when we stumbled upon that reality, but I am discovering that you have an uncanny ability to attract trouble, Ethan Chase. It is almost a talent."

"Yeah." I sighed. "Welcome to my world."

And of course, at that moment, we walked through some invisible barrier in the mist and fog...and the world changed.

"Dammit, not again," I groaned, wondering what kind of nightmare we'd gotten into now. It was not, at least, another carnival. Or creepy abandoned asylum. We stood at the edge of sleepy meadow, a huge yellow moon hanging overhead, so close you could almost see its cratered surface. Forest surrounded us, dark and tangled, and a narrow stream wound along the edges of the trees. Though it looked perfectly still and normal, there was something about the whole scene that bothered me. Not in the *this is straight out of a horror movie* way, just a faint feeling of disquiet.

In the center of the grove stood an enormous Victorian mansion. Towers and turrets soared into the air, spearing the night sky. Windows and balconies rose above us, archways and pillars were scattered around the stone walls, and a pair of huge stone lions guarded the end of the walkway.

"Wow," Kenzie remarked, craning her neck up to stare at the huge house. "Well, whoever owns this crazy reality, at least they have good taste."

Grimalkin sauntered up and leaped onto a nearby rock. "That," he stated imperiously, waving his tail, "is Leanansidhe's mansion."

I exhaled in relief. Never had I been so glad to see the lair of a dangerous, impossibly fickle faery queen in my life. Of course, I'd never seen the outside of her mansion, but I'd take Grimalkin's word that this was it. "Let's go," I said, and started toward the mansion. "The sooner we find Annwyl, the sooner we can get out of here."

"Hold a moment, Ethan Chase," the Thin Man said. I gave him a puzzled look, and he folded his hands before him. "I believe it best if you see the Exile Queen without me," he went on with a somewhat pained smile. "I do not think Leanansidhe would take kindly to having a Forgotten inside her home. And the Summer girl might react poorly if she saw me with you. I would not want to frighten her away." He nodded at the mansion. "You go on, meet with the Exile Queen. I shall wait until you return with the girl."

"Where will you be?" Kenzie asked.

The Thin Man waved an airy hand.

"I will be close," he said, gesturing back to the meadow. "Do not worry, I sense no danger in this pocket of reality. Leanansidhe, it appears, has a firm grasp on her territory. So, you go ahead, and when you are ready to leave, I will rejoin you."

He turned away, and as he did, vanished from sight.

Walking up the long gravel path to the steps, I figured out what was bothering me before. The meadow made no sound. There was a breeze; I could see grass stalks and branches waving in the wind, but there was no sound whatsoever. Not even the stream running along the edge of the forest made any noise. Staring at the grove was like looking at a very surreal, lifelike painting or a movie with the sound on mute. It was eerie, but then again, I'd take creepy quiet meadow over creepy killer carnival any day.

But that was still no reason to lower my guard.

With Grimalkin ambling behind us and Razor perched

on Kenzie's shoulder, we walked up the large marble steps to the huge double doors waiting for us at the top, and Kenzie rapped on the wood with the brass lion knockers in the center.

No answer.

"Try again," I told Kenzie, after a few minutes had passed in silence. She did, knocking a little harder this time, the raps echoing sharply in the complete stillness. Still, there was no answer.

"Well, that's not very encouraging," Kenzie said, staring at the mansion. "Do you think something's happened to her, or that she's just ignoring us?"

I frowned. No, something was definitely wrong. Leanansidhe might've been fickle, dramatic, unpredictable and prone to turning people into guitars when they annoyed her, but she'd always welcomed exiles and runaways into her home. Granted, she used them for cheap labor and to further her own ends, but she wasn't known for turning people away. Especially if she thought she could gain from them. "Let me try," I said, and walked up to the door as Kenzie stepped aside. But instead of using the knocker, I raised my sword and banged the hilt against the wood, making a hollow booming that vibrated up my arm.

This time, the door swung back with a whoosh, making me blink and step back. And Leanansidhe herself, the Dark Muse, Queen of the Exiles, towered over us. She wore a sparkly black gown and elbow-length gloves, and a bright mane of copper hair floated around her head. She stood in the door frame, regal, beautiful and looking dangerously pissed off.

"Well," she announced, her cold blue eyes fixed on me. "Ethan Chase. Haven't *you* made a mess of everything."

Uh-oh. *Now* what had happened?

"Well, don't just stand there, darlings," Leanansidhe snapped.

"If you're going to come in, come in. I have better things to do than watch you gape at me like frightened deer. Chop chop, doves. Move."

Kenzie and I shared a confused look, then stepped into the foyer and gazed around warily. At first glance, it looked the same—tile floors, marble columns, a huge fireplace against one wall and a baby grand piano in the corner. But there was something different about it, too. Something I couldn't quite put my finger on...

Leanansidhe shut the door with a bang that made me jump. She turned to face us, beaming a bright, brittle smile in my direction. "Ethan, darling," she said in a voice that made my insides shrink. "How good of you to stop by. I was just thinking about you."

Well, *that* was all kinds of ominous. I shared another glance with Kenzie and saw that she still looked just as baffled as me. I also noticed that Grimalkin had conveniently disappeared, and that Razor was hiding down Kenzie's shirt and making no noise whatsoever.

"Uh." I faced the Exile Queen again. "Something wrong, Leanansidhe?" I asked, trying to be diplomatic.

"Oh, why don't you tell me, darling?" Leanansidhe raised her arms, indicating the whole room. "You're a smart boy. Why don't you take a look around and see if anything comes to mind? Does anything seem *wrong* to you?"

I scanned the foyer again, trying to figure it out. Everything looked fine to me; nothing was broken, cracked, burned or damaged in any way. But Kenzie suddenly drew in a sharp breath and glanced at the Exile Queen.

"It's too quiet," she said. "Where is everyone?"

Of course. That was the thing that was bugging me. Leanansidhe's mansion was a haven for outcasts, and they were usually here in droves. Exiles, half-breeds and runaways alike, this was a last resort for those who had nowhere else to go, and the mansion was always teeming with fey. Not to mention a number of gifted humans Leanansidhe had "collected" over the years. All brilliant, musical or artistic in some fashion, and all completely nuts from living in the Between so long. The mansion seemed empty, devoid of life. Now that I thought about it, it was weird that Leanansidhe herself had opened the door; she usually had servants do that sort of thing for her.

"Where indeed?" Leanansidhe said, smiling down at us. "That is the million-dollar question, isn't it? You'll have to forgive me, doves, if I seem distracted. I've been rather busy of late. You see—" she fixed me with a piercing stare "—not long ago, I was out and about in the mortal world—on a business trip, mind—when there was this…oh, how should I put it…this *pulse* that went through the air like an electrical charge. It nearly knocked me down, it was so strong. Naturally, I was startled and started to ask this nice young lady if she had felt it, too.

"Do you know what she did, darling?" Leanansidhe asked, though she obviously had no intention of waiting for an answer. "She screamed. In my face. Right in the middle of a busy street. I had no idea what she was going on about at first, but you can imagine my surprise when I realized she could *see* me. Really see me. In fact—and here is the hilarious part, darling—*all* of them could see me, the entire squealing, bumbling human crowd. The barbarians surrounded me, talking all at once, screaming, taking pictures, attempting to *touch* me." Leanansidhe gave a dramatic sigh. "It was a rather trying afternoon."

I grimaced. "What did you do to them?"

"Oh, wouldn't you like to know, darling?" The Exile Queen gave me an evil smile. "But that is not the important bit of this story. Would you like to know the climax? After

I...*dealt with* the mortals, I returned home. Or, I tried to return home. And do you know what I found, Ethan Chase?"

Her eyes were almost glowing now, an icy, dangerous blue, making my insides shrink. "Nothing?" I guessed in a small voice.

"Bravo, Ethan Chase!" Leanansidhe applauded. I jumped, and the lights around us flickered. "*Nothing* is exactly what I found. The Between was gone. My home, gone." She snapped her fingers. "Vanished, like it never existed."

"But...it eventually came back," Kenzie ventured, and Leanansidhe turned her piercing gaze on her. "I mean, it's here now."

"Noticed that, did you, darling?" The faery's voice was cutting. "Yes, the Veil eventually re-formed, and I was able to return to the Between. But you know what didn't magically re-form?" She waved her hands around the room again. "This. My home. The center of my kingdom. That's why I've been so busy of late, my dove. I've had to rebuild from scratch. And all my humans, my artists and musicians and composers I've grown rather fond of all these years?" She fluttered a hand at the ceiling. "Gone. Lost. Ran off into the mortal realm when the Veil went down, and I haven't seen them since. I'm still rather perturbed about that."

Oh, crap. This wasn't going well. We'd escaped one dragon's nest only to land in an even bigger, nastier one. The Exile Queen stopped staring at Kenzie and smiled at me again, and I felt my insides shrink.

"And then, I start to hear things about *you*, Ethan darling. Rumors trickled in, from all corners of the Nevernever and the mortal realm. Such *interesting* stories, my dove. About you, and the Iron Prince, and how you both were responsible for the destruction of the Veil." She clasped her hands in front of her, giving me a mock inquisitive look. "Would you care to elaborate on that, darling? You see, I'm a little annoyed with you and the prince right now, and an explanation might make me less inclined to rip your intestines out through your nose and string my harps with them."

"Keirran stabbed me," I said, as Kenzie moved protectively to my side. I didn't know what she could do against the insanely powerful Exile Queen, but I did know she would try to do something if Leanansidhe made good on her threat. I had to get a handle on this situation—now. "We went to see the Forgotten Queen," I went on, "and she told him he could destroy the Veil and save all the exiles if he sacrificed someone whose blood tied him to all three courts. And then he ran me through and left me to die." Leanansidhe raised an eyebrow, and I made a hopeless gesture. "I didn't mean to destroy the Veil and make your kingdom vanish," I said seriously. "I would have tried to stop it, but I was kind of dead at the time."

She looked unappeased. "I'm afraid that is not much of an excuse, darling," she said, making my stomach drop to the floor. "It was your blood that destroyed the Veil, your life that caused this disaster. Intentional or not, the fault still lies with you."

"What about Keirran?" Kenzie demanded angrily. "He's the one who stabbed Ethan. He sacrificed him, knowing it would destroy the Veil. If you want to point fingers, Keirran is the one who made the choice, not Ethan."

"Oh, the Iron Prince has much to answer for," Leanansidhe agreed in a scary voice. "And he will feel my retribution before this is over, I assure you. But…" Her gaze sharpened, glaring at me. "*He* is not here. And he is only half of the equation. Everything that has happened, everything he has done up until this point, was made possible only with your help, Ethan Chase." She tilted her head, raising both brows. "Can you deny this, darling?"

Numbly, I shook my head. "No," I rasped, "but I'm trying to make it right."

"Make it right?" Leanansidhe let out a short bark of laughter. "Forgive me, darling, but it's far too late for that. Can you
return all my humans to me? Can you make the Forgotten
disappear? Can you undo the prophecy, now that it has been
set into motion?" The Exile Queen shook her head. "This is
a war, Ethan Chase. And you are not like your sister. You do
not command the power of Summer and Iron. You do not
have the son of Mab and the infamous Robin Goodfellow
at your side. You are a mere mortal with no power of your
own, a girl who is dying and a gremlin. How do you expect
to 'make things right,' Ethan Chase? How do you expect to
stand against the Forgotten and their queen?"

"I don't," I said, suddenly feeling very tired. "I'm not trying to stop a war. I don't plan to take on the Lady and the
Forgotten by myself. I'm just… I'm trying to save my family. What's left of it, anyway." I felt Kenzie press closer, and
her fingers briefly brushed mine, letting me know she was
there. I squeezed her hand in return. "If you want to kill me
for that," I went on, making Kenzie stiffen, "turn me into a
harp or a guitar or whatever, go ahead. But I'm the only one
who can stop Keirran now. The prophecy wasn't about the
Lady, it was about him. And me. One way or another, we're
going to have to face each other again."

"You can't take this out on Ethan," Kenzie broke in, now
squeezing my fingers in a death grip. "This wasn't his choice.
He did everything he could to help Keirran save Annwyl, and
Keirran repaid him by stabbing him in the back. And if you
think I'm going to let you turn him into a guitar—"

"Oh, darling, don't be ridiculous," Leanansidhe snapped,
rolling her eyes. "And I thought I was the dramatic one. Do
you honestly think I would turn the Iron Queen's precious

baby brother into a guitar? Permanently, anyway? No, dove."
She gave me a look of disgust. "If I wanted revenge, I would
not be so crass and obvious as that. Not when there are a
thousand other, more creative ways, to ruin someone's life.
So you can stop glaring at me, darling," she went on, looking
at Kenzie. "And Grimalkin can stop hiding. I am not turning
anyone into anything today."

"Please," sniffed a familiar voice. Grimalkin's, from the
piano bench. The cat looked up from washing his tail, like
he'd been sitting there all this time. "As if I have anything to
fear from the lot of you," he stated, and went back to groom-
ing himself. I felt Kenzie slump in relief.

"Though, I am curious, darlings," Leanansidhe went on,
after a brief glare at the cat, who seemed oblivious. "What
are you planning to do about the Iron Prince? Last I heard,
he had declared war on all the courts, even his own Iron
Realm, in front of every king and queen of Faery. Quite the
treasonous offense, you know. Punishable by death. It seems
our darling Iron Prince is entirely serious about destroying us
all." She shook her head. "Stupid, brazen boy. I didn't think
he had it in him."

"He doesn't," I said, making her blink. "He's...not entirely himself. There's this amulet that...uh...sort of sucked
out his soul."

The Exile Queen regarded me with those scary blue eyes,
and the air around us went very still. "This amulet," she said
in a quiet voice, "is it around the neck of a certain Summer
faery?"

I swallowed. "I take it you've seen Annwyl."

"Not in a long time, darling." Leanansidhe straightened
with a sniff. "Nor do I ever want to see the girl again. That
little harlot has caused me no end of trouble." Reaching over
her head, she pulled a cigarette flute out of thin air, stuck one

end in her mouth and puffed out clouds of violet smoke. "I never should have agreed to take the girl in the first place," she grumbled, "but you know our darling prince. Bats his eyes and gives you that wounded puppy-dog look, and it's nearly impossible to tell him no. And if *that* doesn't work, he'll just pester you constantly until you give in. Impossible child."

I almost smiled. Keirran *had* been like that, once. When I'd first met him. The prince of the Iron Realm had been chivalrous, soft-spoken and relentlessly polite even to his enemies. He was also stubborn, reckless and impossible, but at least he was civil about it, so it was hard to hold it against him. When I found out who he really was, I thought I would hate him. But my nephew had gone out of his way to treat me not only as family, but as a friend. And, shockingly, that's what he had become. Once upon a time, not very long ago, Keirran had been my friend.

Nothing like the cold, emotionless stranger who'd shown up in Tir Na Nog that day, his eyes completely flat as he'd told the courts, his own family, that they were his enemies now.

"I knew something was wrong when she came back with that…thing…around her neck," Leanansidhe continued, making my stomach twist. "Nasty bit of magic that was, darling. I don't know where she got it, but I did know that I didn't want it in my house. The wretched girl wouldn't tell me where she got it, either, only that it connected her and the Iron Prince, and that she couldn't take it off. I should have thrown her out then. But I let her stay, like the softhearted fool I am."

"Where is Annwyl now?" asked Kenzie.

"The last time I saw the Summer girl," Leanansidhe mused, "was a few nights after the Veil was torn away. She had been at the mansion when the Between disappeared. I don't know how she survived, or what happened to all the exiles and half-breeds in the house when the Veil went down. I just know I came back from the mortal realm that night, and the Between was no longer there. When the Veil re-formed and I was able to go Between again, nothing was left of my mansion but the anchor. Everything and everyone else was gone.

"A few nights later," Leanansidhe continued, "Annwyl came to me and announced that she was leaving. That something had happened with the prince, and she had to go before the amulet did anything else. Or something like that. I wasn't really listening at the time."

Kenzie blinked. "You didn't care that Annwyl was leaving?"

"You'll have to forgive me, darling. My home was gone, the Between no longer existed, and, to my mind, the girl had just told me she was partially responsible for its disappearance." Leanansidhe's eyes glittered as she twiddled her flute. "I wasn't in the most reasonable mood at the time. She was lucky I was exhausted from renovating. Otherwise I might've decorated my office with Essence of Summer Girl."

"What happened to her?"

The Exile Queen pursed her lips, blowing out a cloud of smoke that looked eerily like the Summer faery. The smoky image cringed back from some unseen terror, picked up her skirts and ran. "I told her to get out of my sight," Leanansidhe said, watching it scamper away, "and that if I saw her again, I would separate her lovely head from her shoulders."

She made a swift gesture with the cigarette flute, and the cloud faery's head tumbled from her body before both parts writhed away into nothing. Kenzie wrinkled her nose. "So, no, darlings," the Exile Queen finished. "I'm afraid I haven't seen the Summer girl lately. Like I said, I've been busy re-establishing my home from nothing."

"We have to find her," Kenzie insisted. "We have to get that amulet before it's too late. Did she say where she was going, what she was looking for?"

Leanansidhe sighed. "I have no idea what she's looking for, darling," she said. "But I do know where she went. Not that it will do you much good." She sucked on the cigarette flute and puffed out a long stream of smoke that curled through the air like a lazy river. "The Summer girl has gone to the border of the wyldwood," the Dark Muse intoned solemnly, "and past the River of Dreams. Beyond the territories of Summer and Winter, into the Deep Wyld."

I felt a chill in the large, cozy room.

"The Deep Wyld?" Kenzie echoed, sounding intrigued. "What is that? Another region of the Nevernever?"

"Yeah," I muttered, recalling the bits and pieces I'd picked up over the years about the Deep Wyld. Not much, but I did know that it was the deepest and darkest part of the Nevernever, a place into which the normal fey rarely ventured. No one knew much about the Deep Wyld, what it was like, what kinds of things lived out there. "Kind of like the wyldwood, but…bigger. It's supposedly the oldest part of Faery."

And probably the most dangerous.

"Exactly, darling," Leanansidhe agreed. "The Deep Wyld is the vast, untamed wilderness of the Nevernever, beyond the courts and the wyldwood and anything familiar. Only the bravest or most desperate venture across the River of Dreams and into the Deep Wyld. And many that do attempt that crossing never return."

"Really?" Of course, that news did nothing to deter Kenzie. Another region of Faery that was even more mysterious and dangerous than most? I could practically see her eyes sparkle at the thought. "But why would Annwyl go into the Deep Wyld?" she asked.

"Not a clue, my dove," the Exile Queen said flippantly. "It is said that many ancient secrets and forbidden knowledge lie in the darkest regions of the Deep Wyld. If Annwyl is searching for something in particular, whether it be knowledge or power, that is not a bad place to look. However, tracking a Summer sidhe through the wyldwood is difficult enough. If they do not want to be found, it is nearly impossible to find them. Tracking a Summer sidhe through the Deep Wyld, which is vaster, darker and infinitely more dangerous, is another matter altogether. You cannot simply rush after the girl with no hint as to where you are headed, darlings. You are going to need some sort of guide."

"We have Grimalkin," Kenzie pointed out, glancing at the cat on the piano bench. His eyes were closed. "He can show us the way, right?"

Leanansidhe sniffed. "Contrary to what Grimalkin would have you believe, darling, he does not know everything about everything in the Nevernever. Shocking, I know. But if you are going to attempt to find the Summer girl all the way in the Deep Wyld, there is only one who will be able to help you. And I believe our darling Grimalkin knows exactly who I'm talking about."

"You cannot be serious." Grimalkin's yellow eyes opened a crack and he glared disdainfully. "Summon *him*? To track a Summer faery through the Deep Wyld? I cannot say if he could even be bothered to respond to such a request."

"He would come if *you* asked, darling."

The cat flattened his ears. "I suppose if there is no other way," he said in a disgusted voice. "Though someone is going to owe me a very large favor when this is over. But worry not, humans." He gave me a slitted-eyed look of exasperation. "I will take care of everything, as usual."

"There is," Leanansidhe said, and the slightly evil smile was back on her face, "one more tiny little problem. You see, the Deep Wyld lies on the other side of the River of Dreams, which isn't a short walk from here, darlings. It will take you

many days of travel through the nastiest parts of the wyldwood
to reach it. How do you intend to get there?"

"Walk, I suppose," I muttered, though the thought of
tramping through the wyldwood for days on end wasn't pleas-
ant. And I was all too aware that we were running out of time.
"Unless someone can think of something better."

"Well, I have a suggestion, darling." The Exile Queen
waved her hand, and the cigarette flute writhed away into
tendrils of smoke. "I'm just starting to put my trods back together, and it just so happens that I have one working again.
It leads into the wyldwood, to a spot very close to the River
of Dreams. Still a day's walk from the river, but it will get you
to the border much faster than if you hiked there from here."

Instantly suspicious, I crossed my arms. "Uh-huh. And what
would the catch be? You're certainly not going to let us use
that trod out of the goodness of your heart."

"Why, darling, what an awful idea. We can't have rumors
like that circling around, can we? Think of the damage to my
reputation." Leanansidhe chuckled, as if the thought was lu-
dicrous, and shook her head. "Besides, Ethan Chase, you and
the prince have caused me no end of trouble. Some would
argue that you owe me."

"Fine." I sighed. "I guess I'll give you that." I raised both
arms in a shrug before letting them drop to my sides. "Let's
get it over with, then. What do you want?"

"Ethan, wait." Kenzie edged forward and turned us away
from the Exile Queen. Lowering her voice, she whispered,
"Let me bargain with her. Leanansidhe isn't mad at me, not
like you and Keirran—the price might be lower if I deal with
her."

"No, Kenzie," I murmured, and took her hand. "It's my
turn now. You've done so much already, made so many deals.

I know you would do this without a second thought, but…I think it's time for me to share some of that burden."

"But you hate bargaining with the fey."

"I know." Tugging her forward, I slipped one arm around her waist, keeping my voice soft. "It's not about me anymore. And I'm not going to be like Keirran and make deals that are too high, or promise something that will hurt others, especially you. But we do have to find Annwyl soon. And if bargaining with Leanansidhe will get us there faster, then I'm willing to do it. If the cost is something I can live with. Something we both can live with."

"Okay." She nodded slowly. "Just be careful, tough guy."

"I will. And if you think I'm going to end up as a harp or something, just kick me."

"I am not," Leanansidhe said in an annoyed voice as we turned around, "going to turn you into a harp, Ethan Chase. One, I already have a substantial collection. Two, you would make a terrible harp, far too whiny and brooding. No elegance at all. But that is beside the point." She straightened regally, staring down her nose at us. "Are you ready to hear my terms, darling?" she demanded. "Or should I not even bother wasting the breath, because we all know Ethan Chase does not bargain with faeries, and the price is going to be significant?"

I swallowed. Everything in me was telling me to refuse, but I forced myself to ask. "What's the price?"

Leanansidhe smiled.

"One year," the Dark Muse said in a low, eerie voice, "of your life, forfeited to me. All your ideas, all your dreams, fears, emotions, everything that you would have felt or experienced in those twelve months, will be mine."

My insides turned themselves into a knot.

"One *year*?" Kenzie demanded behind me. "Just for using

the trod? That's a bit much, don't you think? I gave you a month to get the Sight—why is it so high for Ethan?"

"Because, my darling," Leanansidhe said, "and don't take this the wrong way, but, you are not as important to the Nevernever as Ethan Chase. He is the Iron Queen's brother. He is part of a prophecy. His blood ties him to all three courts of Faery. He is intricately bound to our world, and a life like his only happens once in a blue moon." She shrugged. "Also, I'm still cranky about my Charles collection. Do you know how long it took me to gather all those humans? No, Ethan Chase." She held up a finger. "One year of your life, no more, no less. Of course, you can still travel to the Deep Wyld via the normal route. It will only take you, oh...three weeks, Faery time? If you don't run into trouble on the way."

"A year of my life, huh?" I murmured. "And there's nothing I can say or offer that would shorten that a bit?"

"Actually," Leanansidhe purred, "there is." Smiling, she regarded me over steepled fingers. "Your life is not the only one I am interested in. I'd be willing to split the cost with the other half who has caused me so much trouble. In fact, just for you, darling, I'll let you completely off the hook...if you promise me a year of the prince's life instead."

Kenzie gasped. "Can you do that?" she blurted, staring at us wide-eyed. "Promise away a year of someone else's life? Even if they don't agree to it themselves?"

"Normally, I can't, darling," Leanansidhe said. "But this is a special case. You see—" she gestured in my direction "—Ethan and the prince are tied together by more than blood. They are two halves of a prophecy, and that makes them, and this situation, unique. Keirran has already taken Ethan's life. Therefore, Ethan could tip the scales and take a portion of the prince's life in return. If he wanted to."

"But...Keirran is part fey," Kenzie said, furrowing her brow as she tried to understand. "Technically, he's immortal. How do you shorten the lifespan of something that can't die?"

"All faeries can die, my darling," Leanansidhe said. "They just don't wither and die of old age like you mortals. But you are a clever girl to remember that." She sounded begrudgingly impressed and annoyed at the same time. "I wouldn't be shortening the prince's life so much as taking a portion of it away. A year's worth of dreams, emotions, glamour, happiness, everything that he would hold dear."

"What would that do to him?" Kenzie asked.

"Who knows, dove?" Leanansidhe shrugged. "I've not made this type of bargain before, not with a faery recipient. All my dealings have been with mortals. Perhaps the prince will shrivel, become a shade of his former self for a while. Perhaps he will spend a year out of sorts, knowing *something* is missing, but unable to put his finger on what. It doesn't really matter, though, does it? The Iron Prince is your enemy now, the enemy of all true fey. Who cares what this will do to him?" She turned back to me expectantly. "So, what say you, Ethan Chase? You can take your revenge on Keirran right here. Take your vengeance for his betrayal, for killing you, his own family member, to save the Forgotten." At my hesitation, her voice became low and cajoling. "It's only fair, wouldn't you agree, darling?" she crooned. "'An eye for an eye,' isn't that one of your human sayings? Don't you think that Keirran should be punished for all the pain he's caused?"

"Yeah, but…" I scrubbed a hand over my head, thinking. Truthfully, and I might've been a rotten human being for admitting it, the offer sounded pretty tempting. Keirran had hurt so many people. Not just me, but Kenzie, Meghan, Ash, Annwyl, my parents, Razor, Guro, everyone in the Mag Tuiredh, the list went on. And in siding with the Forgotten Queen, he was endangering a hell of a lot more. I wanted him to pay.

I wanted him to know the consequences of his actions, and that I wasn't just going to roll over and accept that he'd tried to kill me. I wasn't okay with that, dammit. Just because he didn't have a soul anymore didn't mean I could excuse all the crap he'd put us through.

But…if I agreed, I wasn't just hurting Keirran. I'd be hurting Meghan, too. And that was something Keirran never got or understood; his stupidly reckless actions didn't affect only him as he'd once believed. He wasn't just hurting himself, he was hurting everyone who cared for him.

And, even if I was pissed at the prince, even if he deserved it, Keirran's life wasn't mine to trade away. That would make me just like him.

"No," I muttered, shaking my head. "No, Keirran is a bastard but…it's not my place. I won't do that to him, or Meghan."

"Very well, darling." Leanansidhe straightened, tossing her hair back. "It's your choice, after all. But the price for using the trod still stands. A year of his life, or a year of yours. What's it to be?"

I sighed, pushing down the fear, the savage twisting of my insides. "One year," I said cautiously. "Exactly one. And this will be at the *end* of my normal lifespan? I won't wake up as a vegetable when I'm thirty?"

"No, my dove." The Exile Queen shook her head with a smile. "If nothing happens to you, you will live a long, normal human life. It will simply be one year shorter than when you are supposed to die. I cannot tell you when that will be, darling. No one can tell you that."

"Kenzie." I looked at my girlfriend, who was watching all of this in somber silence. Her arms were crossed, but she didn't seem angry or like she wanted to protest. She just looked grim.

I stepped close, putting my hands on her arms, lowering

my voice. "If you don't want me to do this," I said, "I won't. I'm willing to make the deal, but you have to be all right with it, too." I wished I could've talked to my parents, but of course that wasn't going to happen. "I don't want to be like Keirran," I said to her bewildered look. "Making bargains and promises without thinking of anyone else. And you...are the most important person in my life now, so..." I trailed off, as Kenzie's eyes glimmered. "I want to be sure you're okay with this," I went on. "If you're not, it's all right. We'll find another way—"

"Ethan." Kenzie put a hand on my chest. Her eyes were still bright as she gazed up at me. "I'm not exactly okay with this, but...I'm certainly not one to tell you anything about making bargains with the fey. It would be super hypocritical of me to stop you now, even though I want to have you around as long as I can. But I know that's not possible." She held on to her smile even as a lump rose to my throat. "No one can live your life but you, and this is your choice, tough guy. Whatever you decide, you'll always have my support." She leaned up and kissed the corner of my mouth. "As long as you don't get yourself turned into a hamster or something," she whispered as she pulled back. "Then I might protest a little."

"Kissy," buzzed Razor from under her hair.

"Oh, please, turn him into a hamster already," Grimalkin remarked from the piano. I ignored them all and kissed her.

Leanansidhe was waiting patiently as I drew back, though Kenzie slipped her fingers through mine and held on, refusing to leave my side. There was a faint smile on the Exile Queen's face as she watched us. "Have you decided, then, darling?"

I nodded. "Yeah," I husked out, willing my heart to calm down. "I'm willing. I agree."

"One year of your life, forfeit to me, whenever that time may come." Leanansidhe raised a slender hand before I could answer. "Last chance to back out, darling. Once you commit, it is permanent. Your next words will decide this bargain, so be very sure. In exchange for use of the trod that will take you close to the Deep Wyld, you will agree to give up one year of your life to me. Yes or no?"

Kenzie squeezed my hand. I swallowed hard, took a deep breath and answered, "Yes."

I braced myself, but I wasn't prepared for what felt like a fist of ice plunging into my chest, grabbing something vital and ripping it out again. I gave a breathless cry and would have fallen, but Kenzie grabbed my arm, planting her feet as she took all my weight, keeping me upright.

Panting, I caught myself and gave her a grateful look as I straightened. Leanansidhe hadn't moved, though her eyes were closed and her hair fluttered and writhed as if caught in a strong wind.

"You okay, tough guy?" Kenzie whispered.

"Yeah," I gritted out, as the pain faded and my muscles finally loosened. For a second, I felt the gaping hole somewhere deep inside, before I sucked in a breath, and it filled once more. "I'm all right. Thanks."

Leanansidhe opened her eyes and beamed. "Splendid, darling!" she announced, and it could've been my imagination, but she seemed brighter, more vibrant and alive. I wondered if I looked any different to the fey around me, if they could sense something wasn't quite right. That I wasn't completely whole.

It didn't matter, I told myself. It was one year, and nobody knew when they were going to die. I could give up a year if it meant saving my family, my friends and the rest of this crazy world. Whatever happened, whatever the future brought, I would just make the most of the time that I had. Kenzie had taught me that.

Though a few short months ago, I would never have made

this kind of bargain. Before Kenzie and Keirran crashed into my life, before the Forgoten and the Lady, before the Never-never chose me as its human champion, I hadn't wanted anything to do with the fey. I'd barely wanted anything to do with my immortal family. Everything was different now. I was willing to give up a lot more, even my own life, to save everything I'd once despised.

I...sure have changed.

"Well." Leanansidhe clasped her hands. "I believe that concludes our business transaction, Grimalkin, darling..." She looked at the cat, who had curled back up on the piano bench with his tail over his nose. "Be a dear and show them the way to the trod. You know where it is, right? Oh, and if you're going to bring that horrid thin Forgotten through my house, do not let him anywhere near...well, anything really. I don't want him sucking the glamour off the walls. Ethan, darling?" She smiled at me. "I wish you luck. And if you do end up facing Keirran in the near future, be a love and kick his royal little ass for me, would you? I would appreciate it. *Ciao*, darlings."

A wind whipped through the foyer, tossing Kenzie's hair and making the fire in the hearth flare up with a roar. When it died down again, the Exile Queen was gone.

"Well," said a high, familiar voice, as the Thin Man turned into existence from a corner. "I do believe I am offended."

CHAPTER TWELVE

THE GNOME BRIDGE

Back into the Nevernever yet again. I was beginning to feel a little run-down, as we'd been hopping from real world to wyldwood to Between and back again, with hardly a chance to rest or eat or catch our breath. At least Kenzie had gotten a few hours' sleep that night in the tree, though she was beginning to show signs of exhaustion, too, despite trying to hide it. I was concerned about her health and trying hard not to be overbearingly protective as we trailed Grimalkin through several long, narrow corridors that led deeper into the mansion.

Which didn't seem entirely solid the farther we ventured into its halls. Corridors would waver in the distance, shimmering like heat waves. Or they would flicker like they were in danger of disappearing. We passed several large rooms that were completely empty and others where ghostly furniture faded in and out of existence, as if there wasn't enough glamour to make them completely real. Once, Kenzie paused outside a door, and I peered over her shoulder to see everything beyond the frame floating in midair. Sofas, chairs, a coffee table, lamps, a bookshelf, all drifting lazily around the room like astronauts on a space station. Quickly, I pulled her away, hoping Grimalkin could get us to the trod without the floors vanishing or us falling through the stairs or something.

Finally, the cat led us down a long flight of stone steps into Leanansidhe's dungeon-like basement. Torches flickered in brackets on stone pillars, and the floors were cold and damp. It looked much smaller than when I'd been down here last, or maybe it just seemed that way because I couldn't see past the sputtering torchlight. Beyond the circles of orange light, there was nothing but black.

"Here," Grimalkin said, sitting in front of a stone archway. A pair of gargoyle heads each held a flickering lantern on either side of the arch, but much like the rest of the room, I couldn't see anything but darkness through the frame. "This is the trod that will take you to the border of the Deep Wyld," the cat went on, angling an ear back at it. "From here, the River of Dreams is not far. I will issue this one caution, however. The Deep Wyld is not like the wyldwood. It is far more danger-ous, far easier to become lost and far more likely for mortals to stumble upon things they should not touch. Do be care-ful, humans." Grimalkin sighed, waving his tail as he turned toward the arch. "I would hate to have to explain to the Iron Queen how her brother was eaten by carnivorous mushrooms because he did not watch where he put his feet."

"Carnivorous mushrooms?" Kenzie looked back at me and grinned. "Kind of like the Goombas from Super Mario Broth-ers? Don't worry, if you see any evil mushrooms, just hop on their heads—that'll kill them."

I gave her a bewildered stare. "What?"

"Super Mario Brothers!" Kenzie exclaimed, frowning. "Mario, Luigi, Bowser? It's a classic." When I still looked baffled, she rolled her eyes. "You're a boy. How do you not know your video games?"

I smirked. "Possibly because I was more concerned about *real* monsters that could eat me."

"Oh, whatever. When we go home, I'm going to borrow Alex's Nintendo and introduce you to Super Smash Brothers." "Mushrooms." Razor, perched on Kenzie's shoulder again, wrinkled his nose. "Bleh. Nasty, evil mushrooms. Like kitty." The Thin Man shook his head. "Oh, this is going to be *quite* the experience," he sighed, and followed us through the arch.

It took us a few hours to reach the river. The wyldwood was still as dark, tangled and uninviting as before, and I wondered how this mysterious Deep Wyld could be any worse. I had no doubt it *was*, of course. Because that's how things in the Never-never always worked. Things were never so twisted, awful and completely horrifying that they couldn't get even worse.

Well, that's a cheerful thought, Ethan. You're just a ball of sunshine today, aren't you?

My bad mood continued to worsen the farther we hiked, punctuated by occasional spikes of temper whenever I stumbled over a log, or a vine snaked around my foot and deliberately tripped me. Adding to my grievances, my many small cuts and gashes throbbed, making me even more irritable. I was, I realized, getting tired of Faery. I was tired of its wars and power struggles. I was tired of its stupidly dangerous landscapes that defied logic and sanity and would drive you nuts if you thought too hard about it. I was tired of faeries and faery bargains and quests and impossible choices. I was tired of it all.

"Hey," Kenzie said when we stopped for a short break. Grimalkin was sitting on a log in a rare patch of sunshine, washing his tail, and the Thin Man had disappeared to somewhere or other. I was leaning against the trunk of a massive tree, feeling cranky and antisocial and wishing this journey was just done already, when Kenzie walked around with a granola bar in hand. Her eyes were worried as she gazed up at me. "You okay?"

I took the offered bar with a short nod. "Yeah. I'm fine."

"You sure? You haven't said much since we left Leanan-sidhe's, and you've got that broody *I hate everything* frown going on. Are you—"

"I said I'm fine," I snapped, making her jump. Razor hissed at me and vanished down her shirt, and Kenzie's eyes flashed.

"All right, tough guy, point taken." She stepped away, not quite able to mask the hurt and anger on her face. "I'll leave you alone."

I sighed. "Kenzie, wait." She turned back warily, and I raked a hand through my hair. "I'm sorry," I offered, dropping my arm. "I didn't mean to snap at you. I'm just...tired, I guess."

She blinked, watching me in concern. "You gonna be okay?"

"Honestly? I don't know." I looked down at my hands, fiddling with the wrapper of the bar, feeling her gaze on me. "It's just...everyone is counting on us, you know? And there's a lot that could go wrong. We have to find Annwyl, who could be anywhere right now, convince her to come back with us, and somehow make it to Keirran, who is probably on the other side of a freaking army. And if we do manage all that, if we somehow make it to Keirran without dying, we have to convince him to destroy the one thing that's been keeping Annwyl alive. So that she can die. So that he can get his damn soul back." I scrubbed a hand across my eyes, shaking my head. Kenzie continued to watch me, saying nothing, though her eyes were sympathetic now.

"I haven't seen my parents in months," I muttered. "I don't know what they're doing, what's going on in the mortal world or how much time will pass before we're finally done here. Everything is so screwed up. My sister is going to war with my nephew, my best friend killed me so the Lady could rise to power and the only way to stop all of this is to let another of our friends die. And I..." *Have somehow become the champion of Faery itself. No pressure there, right?*

Leaning my head back, I stared up at the canopy of the wyldwood, feeling the ugly truth steal over me. I was exhausted, I was sore and my head ached, but truthfully, I was just scared. So much rested on us finding that amulet and destroying it, but what if we couldn't? What would happen to my family if I couldn't bring Keirran back? If the First Queen actually won?

I heard Kenzie take off her backpack, set it on the ground and pick her way over the roots to stand beside me. Putting her hands behind her, she leaned back against the wood, gazing into the forest. Razor climbed out of her shirt, muttered, "Grumpy boy" in my direction and scampered up the trunk, disappearing into the branches.

"I'm scared, too," Kenzie said after a moment. Surprised, I glanced down at her, but she was staring into the trees, her gaze distant. "I know I'm not as close to this world as you are, but I do know what's at stake. I'm worried for you, my parents, Alex, Razor and...and I can't even think about Annwyl right now. I keep hoping there's another way, that we'll find another solution, so Annwyl doesn't have to..." Her voice shook a bit on that last part, before she took a quick breath and turned back to me.

"It sucks," she admitted, her eyes going dark. "Sometimes the world is like that. Sometimes we just have to play with the hand we're dealt. But let me ask you this—would you trust this to anyone else? You said the Nevernever itself chose you, a human with no special powers, no magic or glamour or anything. There has to be a reason for that, and I think it's because no one else can do it. It has to be you, tough guy."

"I thought you didn't believe in fate or destiny."

"I don't." Kenzie shrugged. "There's always a choice, Ethan, even if between running away and facing the thing that scares us head-on. Even if all paths lead to the same place." She paused a moment, staring up into the canopy, her voice going soft. "How we get there, and what we do on the way, that's always up to us."

"Humans." Grimalkin appeared on a moss-covered stump. He didn't saunter around the tree; I hadn't seen him hop onto the log. He was just there. "I am going on ahead," he stated, blinking at us languidly. "Our thin friend should be able to take you the rest of the way."

"What?" I scowled at him. "You're leaving? Now? Why?"

"I must meet with our contact and make the necessary arrangements for your crossing into the Deep Wyld, since it appears I must do everything around here," the cat said in a weary tone of voice. "Worry not, human. We will meet again soon."

Leaping to the ground, he stuck his tail in the air and trotted toward the brush. "I trust you will be able to go on without getting into too much trouble," he said as he slipped beneath a clump of ferns and disappeared. "The River of Dreams is not far. If you could refrain from tedious human chatter and the tendency to fall all over each other, you might reach it before nightfall."

Night did fall before we reached the River of Dreams, and it fell quite suddenly. As in, one second we were walking through the hazy gray twilight of the wyldwood, the next, it was dark. Like someone had flipped a switch. Kenzie startled, and I immediately went for my swords, certain that whatever had killed the lights was waiting in ambush, and we were seconds away from an attack.

"Don't panic, Ethan Chase," the Thin Man said as I turned

in a wary circle, scanning the darkness and shadows. "This is perfectly normal. Do you hear that?" He tilted his head, and at that moment, I heard it, too. A dull murmur filtering through the trees, the sound of moving water in the distance. The Thin Man smiled. "We are very nearly there."

I didn't know what to expect from something called the River of Dreams, but whatever I had imagined—stars and dreamers and pirate ships floating down a lazy current—it was nothing compared to the real thing.

"Wow," Kenzie breathed a few minutes later, her gaze awed as she stared over the water. "That's just... I think *wow* covers everything."

I didn't answer, feeling like my eyes weren't big enough to take everything in. We stood on the bank of an enormous black river, the inky surface reflecting the night sky, until they seemed to merge together. The water was full of stars, moons, constellations, and the longer I stared at it, the more I felt like I was in danger of tumbling into the void. I couldn't even see my own reflection in the glassy surface. Though I could see other things beneath the water or floating along the top. A violin, a stuffed bear, a huge fat goldfish the size of a basketball. A log drifted past, spinning lazily in the current, and a red fox peered out at me with bright orange eyes. Spheres of light, either balls of faery fire or gigantic lightning bugs, hovered over the surface as well, only adding to the dazzling confusion.

"The River of Dreams," the Thin Man said, standing at the edge of the water with his hands clasped behind him. He sounded...not sad, but contemplative. Wistful. Eyeing me and Kenzie, his mouth twitched into a smile. "Do you know how many mortals have stood on these banks, Ethan Chase? How many have seen the River while awake? None in my lifetime, and I have lived a very, very long time."

"It's amazing," Kenzie whispered, unable to tear her eyes away. Razor, perched on her shoulder, seemed entranced, as well. The Thin Man blinked as she took a step forward.

"I would not stand too close to the edge, my girl," he warned. "This is not the nightmare stretch, but that does not mean you want to lean too far over the water. If you fall in, the river might be unwilling to let you go."

A loud gurgle interrupted him. I looked up, just as a portion of river boiled, and a freaking *house* rose out of the water, pointed yellow roof stabbing into the air. The house was perched on the back of an enormous turtle, which turned its head to stare at us with glassy black eyes. I was frozen, but the massive reptile blinked lazily, as if we were beneath its notice, turned and swam off, carrying itself and the house down the river, until it sank into the depths once more and was lost from view.

I swallowed the dryness in my throat. *Okay, that was terrifying. Stepping back from the edge now.*

Kenzie, too, had moved a few swift paces away from the water. "The Deep Wyld is on the other side, isn't it?" she asked, as the ripples from the monstrous turtle began to die away. "How are we getting across? Is there a dock close by? Somewhere we can catch a boat?"

"No." The Thin Man turned to stare at us, frowning. "There is only one ferry that travels the River of Dreams," he said, somewhat mysteriously, I thought, "but it is not for *crossing* the river. I doubt we will see it here, and even if we do, it will not stop for us, I'm afraid."

"Okay." Kenzie gave the water's edge a leery glance. "I hope you don't expect us to swim."

"Patience, my dear." The Thin Man held up an impossibly slender finger. "The River of Dreams is very long, and we are not the only ones who wish to cross it tonight. Worry not. Hopefully, it will be here soon… Ah, there it is. Perfect timing."

I turned, hearing Kenzie gasp in surprise.

Spanning the length of the River of Dreams, where nothing had been before, was a bridge. A very old bridge, made of wood, stone and rope, creaking softly in the wind like it would snap at any moment.

I stared back at the Thin Man. "You've got to be kidding me."

"No, Ethan Chase. That is the bridge to cross the River of Dreams," the Thin Man said, seemingly baffled by my reaction. "You should consider yourself lucky. Sometimes the bridge does not appear for several hours. Sometimes it does not appear at all. Like I said before, the River of Dreams is very long. You can't expect the bridge to just appear with a snap of your fingers."

"That's not what worries me."

"Then what is the problem here, Ethan Chase?"

"The problem is I don't want to wind up in the middle of the River of Dreams if that rotten thing decides to snap. Or vanish into thin air."

The Thin Man shook his head. "You are being ridiculous, my boy. The bridge has existed for a very, very long time. It has never failed. Also, may I remind you that there is no other way to cross the River of Dreams, unless you are planning to swim. Which I *do not* recommend. There are far more dangerous things in the water than what you have seen tonight." With a sniff, he straightened, tugging on his coat sleeves. "I am going now," he announced with great dignity. "Feel free to join me when you are done being paranoid."

He turned, briefly disappearing from sight, and walked down the bank to where the bridge loomed ominously. I sighed, shared a look with Kenzie and Razor, and hurried after him.

Two ancient moss-covered stones marked the entrance to the rickety walk of wooden boards stretching precariously over the water. The handrails were a couple of old ropes on either side, and I could see the river through the gaps between the planks. The Thin Man strode onto the bridge without hesitation, but Kenzie paused, crouching to peer at one of the stones, Razor lighting up the surface with his neon grin.

"There's...something here," she muttered, brushing at the mossy coating. "Words, or a message, or something. I can't read it. It's too worn away."

Up ahead, the Thin Man had turned back and was giving us an impatient stare, tapping long fingers against his arm. "Come on," I said, pulling Kenzie to her feet. "We can't worry about it now. Hopefully it's not important."

Carefully, we started across the bridge, Kenzie in front with Razor clinging to her neck, while I followed close behind. The planks creaked horribly under my feet, the ropes felt rotten as hell and I held my breath every time a breath of wind made the whole bridge sway. Below us, the River of Dreams glittered and churned sluggishly through the many holes in the wood. Once, I made the mistake of looking down, just as a huge pale eye rose out of the water, staring up at me. Before I could say anything, it blinked a filmy blue lid and sank back into the depths. I bit down a hysterical gulp and concentrated on moving forward, keeping my steps as light as I possibly could.

In front of me, Kenzie gave a shudder. "Did you see that?"

"No," I muttered stubbornly. "I didn't, and I'm not thinking about it. Don't look down. Just keep walking."

"I would," Kenzie whispered in return. "But there's a gnome blocking my path."

"What?" I peered over her shoulder. Yep, there certainly was. A short bearded faery with a nose like a shriveled apple, staring up at us with his arms crossed to his chest. A few paces beyond, the Thin Man glanced back with a frown, but the gnome didn't seem to notice him.

"Hello, humans," he said, his voice like a squeaky wheel. "Lovely night, isn't it?"

"Um." Kenzie glanced at me, confused. I shrugged and put a hand on my sword hilt. "Yes? I guess so?"

"Excellent, excellent." The gnome rubbed his palms. "Don't meet many humans on my bridge, wanting to cross into the Deep Wyld. Very brave, you are. I do hope you don't get yourselves eaten."

"But you're a gnome," Kenzie pointed out, making him cock his head. "Aren't bridges guarded by trolls?"

"Not all bridges are troll bridges," the gnome exclaimed, sounding faintly offended. "Just because trolls like to lurk under them does not give them exclusive rights to every bridge in the Nevernever. I am a bridge gnome. This is my bridge."

"Okay," I muttered, closing my fingers around my sword. "Sure. So, how 'bout you step aside now and let us pass?" Kenzie kicked me lightly in the shin, and I winced. "Please."

"Yes, yes, yes." The gnome bobbed his withered head. "I'm sure you have much to accomplish. So, if you would kindly pay the toll, we can settle our debts, and I will get out of your way."

"Toll?" Kenzie asked. "What toll?"

"Well…the toll for using my bridge, of course." The gnome frowned, lacing his arms behind his back. "Those are the rules. *All tolls must be paid upon request.* Didn't you see the sign? It's right at the entrance, clear as day."

Kenzie turned to give me a brief, unreadable look. I grimaced. "What about him?" I asked, nodding to the Thin

Man, who was still watching us several yards down. "I notice he didn't have to pay any toll."

"Well, no." The gnome glanced over his shoulder. "The mayor is exempt from paying the toll. As are all residents of the Deep Wyld, if they decide to use the bridge at all. Most do not. You are outsiders. Therefore, you must pay the toll."

"Just out of curiosity," Kenzie asked, "what if we can't?"

"Then I will take my bridge and leave. And you can swim the rest of the way to shore."

"Okay, fine." I sighed. I didn't like the idea of paying yet another price, but I liked the notion of getting dumped into the River of Dreams even less. "What's the stupid toll?"

"Oh, something very simple," the gnome said, looking us both up and down. "I think…your firstborn child. Yes, that should be sufficient."

I took a breath to say *Screw that!* or something to that effect, when Kenzie elbowed me in the ribs, making me grunt. Startled, I frowned at her, but her attention was on the faery in front of us.

"I'll give you a ring," she said calmly, and the gnome arched a brow at her. "It's silver," she continued. "With a pink gem in the middle. It belonged to a princess, once."

The gnome cocked his head, intrigued. "A princess?"

"Yes. Princess Alexandria St. James." Kenzie's voice was completely serious. "She was the previous owner. I'd give you the tiara that goes with it, but the princess lost it when she was trick-or-treating."

The bridge gnome pondered this a moment. "Let's see this ring," he said at last.

Kenzie unzipped a side pocket of her backpack and drew out a gaudy plastic ring. It was a kid's toy, the kind you'd find in bargain bins at dollar stores. The fake pink gem sparkled in the dim light, and the gnome's eyes gleamed as he followed it.

"Well…" The gnome tapped his foot, trying and failing to sound reluctant. "I don't know, human. It is just a ring, after all. Even though it belonged to a princess…"

Kenzie shrugged and withdrew her arm, closing her fingers around the ring to hide it from view. "If you don't want it…"

"No, no, no. That's not what I meant." The gnome let out a huff. "Very well. I accept your toll. But only for you," he added quickly. "The boy will have to give me something else."

"Uh," I hedged, as the bridge keeper shot me an expectant look. I didn't have anything to offer except my swords and the clothes on my back. And tromping through the Deep Wyld naked or unarmed wasn't an option. But Kenzie put a hand on my wrist and leaned in with a smile.

"It's okay, tough guy. I gotcha covered." Reaching into the bag again, she pulled out a plastic bracelet, the stretchy kind with shimmery, multicolored beads, dangled it in front of the gnome, and the faery's eyes lit up the same way as before. "Do we have a deal?"

Kenzie smirked, shaking her head, as the gnome nodded once and vanished, taking the pieces of costume jewelry with him. "Firstborn child. *Please*," she muttered as we continued down the last part of the bridge, where the Thin Man waited on the other side. "Why do they always open with that?"

I gave her an alarmed look that was only half-teasing. "You're getting almost scary good at this," I said, making her chuckle. "Did you take classes or something on how to bargain with the fey before you came back?"

"No, but it's not that hard…once you realize a few things." Kenzie held up a finger. "One, never accept their first offer. Two, everything is negotiable. Three, when presented with a choice, faeries will almost always choose to have something *right now*, rather than have to wait for something better." She snorted, rolling her eyes. "Cheap costume jewelry now or firstborn child in a few years? Yeah, they always go for the shiny."

I shook my head in disbelief. "You're brilliant," I told her. "You know that, right?"

"Just observant. And a fast learner. I can't swing a sword around, so I go with my strengths. And *you...*" she went on as we finally reached the opposite bank, where the Thin Man was slouched against a rock, waiting for us. "Why didn't you mention this was a toll bridge? You didn't think that was an important bit of information to share, before we were stuck in the middle of the river?"

"Apologies, my dear." The Thin Man pushed himself off the stone. "It has been a very long time since I've used that bridge. I forgot about the toll. Especially since I have never had to pay one. But everything worked out in the end, didn't it? And here you are, on the other side of the river." He waved an arm at the tangle of black forest behind him. "Welcome to the Deep Wyld, humans. It is only going to get more interesting from here."

CHAPTER THIRTEEN

GRIMALKIN'S GUIDE

"Why are we waiting around, again?" I asked, pacing up the bank to where a small fire crackled in a shallow pit. Kenzie's magic survival pack also contained a lighter and a tiny bottle of lighter fluid, and after a couple false starts I'd managed to coax a tiny flame to life, then fed it twigs until it could sustain itself. I had no idea why we were camping on the banks of the River of Dreams, but the Thin Man had told us we had to wait awhile before heading into the forest after Annwyl. Kenzie was sitting on a log close to the fire, and Razor was perched at its edge, tossing leaves into the flames and poking it with a stick, but I was getting impatient.

"Come on," I told the Thin Man, who was sitting in the sand near the fire, the flat edge of his profile turned toward the flames. "Why are we sitting here? You know the Deep Wyld. You can get us through. We should be looking for Annwyl, not roasting hot dogs and making s'mores."

"Mmm, s'mores," Kenzie remarked in a wistful voice. "Hot dogs. Man, I could really go for some real food right now."

The Thin Man smiled at Kenzie, then gave me an aggravated look. "And where do you suggest we start looking, Ethan Chase?" he asked in a sharp voice. "Do you see that forest behind us?" He didn't point to the tangle of trees and undergrowth, but I glanced at it anyway. "That is the Deep Wyld. It is not like the wyldwood. You cannot simply march merrily through without knowing where you are going. If you thought it was easy to get lost in the wyldwood, you haven't seen anything yet. If you stumble or lose sight of the path for even a moment, the Deep Wyld will swallow you whole.

"I do not know where the Summer girl is," the Thin Man continued, as I gave the forest another wary look. It might've been my imagination, but the shadows that marked the edge of the Deep Wyld looked closer. "I do not know what the Summer girl is searching for. The Deep Wyld is far too vast to wander about blindly, hoping we will stumble into her by chance. If we are to have the barest sliver of hope in finding her, we must wait for the cait sith's contact." The Thin Man took off his bowler hat and twirled it between his fingers. "We must be patient awhile longer. The cat said he would be here, if he decides to come at all."

"Yeah, it's the 'if he decides to come at all' part that bugs me," I muttered, but turned and wandered back to the fire pit. Kenzie scooted aside on the log, making room for me.

"Feeling better?" she asked, as I plunked down and stared moodily into the flames. I shook myself, realizing I was "brooding" again, and leaned against her, resting my head on her shoulder.

"No." I sighed, as her slim hand came to perch on my knee. "But I'll try not to whine about it anymore. You're right. I'm always going to be a part of this world. I may not like it, but... this is my family." I shrugged and felt Kenzie look down at me. "Time to stop running, I guess, and accept the fact that I'm never going to be normal."

"Normal is highly overrated," Kenzie said cheerfully. "I used to think all I wanted was normal, but then I met you. Normal isn't Thin Men and shadow monsters and talking cats, and crazy adventures through a real-life faeryland. Normal isn't camping on the River of Dreams with your boyfriend who, oh, by the way, is the brother of a faery queen."

"Normal isn't being chased through a nightmare carnival by ugly clowns and creepy dolls that come to life."

"Yes, well, we're just not going to talk about that," Kenzie said with a shiver. "*That* is right out of a horror flick, which doesn't count, because no one wants to be part of that. Ugh." She shivered again, and I chuckled, though her next words froze me in my seat. "Normal…isn't wishing you could just stay here, in Faeryland, because back home are doctors and tests and all those things you wish you didn't have to face." Worry and dread rose up, making my insides turn, but Kenzie shook herself with a forced smile. "So, I guess I'm just as un-normal as you, tough guy. We make a good pair, huh?"

"Hey." I sat up, drawing her close. "It's all right," I murmured, smiling ruefully. "Normal isn't the girl I fell for."

She kissed me. I closed my eyes, letting myself relax into her. My hand rose, cupping her cheek, and her fingers trailed down my chest, making my breath catch. For a moment, I forgot about Keirran, Annwyl, the amulet, the war, and just lost myself in Kenzie.

I felt her smile as we drew back, my senses still reeling from the feel of her lips on mine. "That's strange," Kenzie murmured. "That's the longest we've ever gone without Razor shouting 'kissy kissy' and interrupting us."

"Maybe he's getting used to it," I muttered, leaning forward to kiss her again. But Kenzie turned her head and gazed around, looking for the gremlin. I glanced at the edge of the fire pit where I'd seen Razor last, poking at the flames.

He wasn't there.

"Razor?" Kenzie stood, scanning the area for the missing gremlin. I rose, too, silently cursing him as I looked around.

At first, I didn't see anything. But then I noticed his tiny black body moving down the river bank. The gremlin seemed entranced by a small green light that bobbed and hovered in the air just out of his reach, drifting slowly toward the edge of the water.

I nudged Kenzie, nodding down the bank, and she frowned. "Razor!" she called, stepping away from the campfire. "Hey, get back here. Don't get too close to the water."

The gremlin ignored her. The light hovered in place for a second, and he lunged, swatting at it with long arms, but it zipped away. He buzzed and snatched at it again; it darted even closer to the water.

Kenzie sighed. "Dammit, Razor," she muttered, picking her way down the bank toward him. He hopped onto a rock, hissing and making garbled noises at the light, now floating just out of reach over the water. Kenzie plucked him off the rock, and he gave a disappointed buzz. "Come on, little man, let's get away from the edge before something drags you—"

A slimy black tentacle erupted from the surface, coiled around Kenzie's leg and yanked her into the river. She screamed once, before the water closed over her head and she disappeared.

I flew down the bank, drawing my sword, as Razor screeched and scuttled back and forth, buzzing wildly. Wading into the River of Dreams, which was shockingly cold and clung to my jeans like frozen hands, I splashed to where I'd seen Kenzie go under, searching desperately for any sign of her.

"Kenzie!" My voice echoed over the surface, high-pitched and frantic.

And then, her face broke the surface with a gasp and an explosion of river water. A dark tentacle was coiled around her neck like a huge snake, dragging her back even as she struggled to stay afloat.

I lunged forward and reached Kenzie just as she went under again, leaving behind a swirl of dark water. But I caught a gleam of black through the murk, something long and shiny, vanishing into the depths. Praying I wouldn't hit Kenzie, I surged toward it and brought my sword down as hard as I could.

The blade struck something hard and rubbery. There was a muffled screech somewhere below the water, and the tentacle recoiled. Kenzie thrashed to the surface again, gasping and choking, and I pulled her against me.

The water around us churned angrily, and several black tentacles erupted from the depths and circled into the air. I kept one arm around Kenzie, the other gripping my sword, as the first of the tentacles shot toward us. I lashed out with my blade, cutting it in two, and dark ichor sprayed everywhere as the thing writhed back before vanishing into the water.

The rest of the tentacles snaked in. I sliced at one, cutting deep, slashed at another and felt a slimy rope curl around my arm. Before I could register that I was in trouble, there was a flash of silver, and the tentacle thrashed away, leaving the end still coiled around my arm.

"Don't just stand there, Ethan Chase," the Thin Man snapped, turning briefly into view as he jabbed at another tentacle. "Fall back. Get out of the river already!"

Oh, right. Good idea. Protecting Kenzie, I edged back toward shore, swatting and hacking at the tentacles that grabbed at us. There were a lot of them, but between me and the Thin Man, we managed to fend them off. The closer we got to shore, the more frantic they grew, and I pulled my second blade to deal with the increased attacks.

My feet hit dry land, and I whacked a coil away before shooting a split-second glance at Kenzie. "Go!" I told her. "Up the bank. Get away from the water—"

Something warm snaked around my ankle and yanked me off my feet. I hit the ground on my back, driving the wind from my lungs, and felt myself being dragged back into the river. I managed to suck in a breath before my head went under and I was pulled down into the murky darkness.

Trying not to panic, I whacked at the thing around my leg, grazing it, but another tentacle reached up and looped around my chest, pinning my arms. I managed to keep hold of my swords, but couldn't do much else as I was dragged farther into the depths.

Something rose from the bottom of the river, coming toward me. In the darkness and murk, I could just make out an enormous black blob, two pale fishy eyes fixed on me. A mouth gaped open, filled with lamprey-like teeth, and my heart seized up as the tentacles drew me toward it. I kicked wildly, thrashing in the thing's grasp, but with my arms pinned I could only watch as the teeth loomed closer.

There was a flash of silver beside me, a slender blade stabbing from the darkness, piercing the band around my chest. The tentacle spasmed and recoiled, loosening enough for me to free my arms. With the gaping mouth only a foot away, I stabbed up with everything I had and sank the steel blade between two curved fangs.

A muffled roar went through the water, vibrating against my skin, and I was free. Kicking out, I swam for my life, breaking the surface with a gasp and immediately heading for shore. Kenzie and Razor were at the water's edge again, eyes wide as I staggered out of the river. My lungs burned, and the ground didn't feel as solid as it should, swaying under my feet as I stumbled onto dry land.

"Ethan!" Kenzie rushed toward me, taking my arm as I nearly fell to my knees in the mud, feeling my heart hammer in my ears. Close behind me, the Thin Man emerged from

the river, shaking water from his blade and giving me an exasperated look as he grabbed my sleeve in long fingers. Together, we scrambled up the bank, Kenzie and the Thin Man
half dragging me, until we were about a hundred feet from
the water's edge. Only then did I collapse, panting, never so
happy to feel solid earth under my palms.

Razor let out a screech and scrambled to Kenzie's shoulder, frantically pointing back to the river. I looked up, and
my blood chilled as a long black tentacle rose into the air,
followed by another, and another, as the huge, amorphous
blob pulled itself onto the bank. Eyes gleaming, it opened its
mouth to bare the circle of jagged lamprey teeth and slithered
forward with a hiss.

Grabbing my swords, I staggered to my feet. But as I raised
my weapons, the tentacles reaching for us suddenly retracted as
if stung. The octopus-blob thing lurched to a halt, peering at
us with blank silver eyes. Then, with a hiss, it turned and fled,
tentacles carrying it over the ground and back down the bank.
There was a splash as it reached the river, and then silence as
it sank back into the depths and disappeared from sight.

Frowning, I glanced back at my companions. "What the
hell just happened?"

Kenzie, looking just as baffled as I felt, shrugged. "Maybe
you scared it off?"

A low chuckle echoed behind us from the edge of the trees.
"The fox does not run away from the mouse, little human,"
rumbled a deep, gravelly voice that made the hairs on the
back of my neck stand up. "Unless, of course, it knows the
bear is coming."

Heart in my throat, I turned.

Something watched us from edge of the forest, nearly invisible in the shadows, except for a pair of gold-green eyes
shining with subtle amusement. Something huge and black,

THE IRON WARRIOR 189

with shaggy fur spiked out in every direction. It gave another chuckle and padded into the moonlight.

A wolf, I realized as it slid out of the dark. A black wolf... the size of a freaking Budweiser horse. The top of my head barely reached its huge shoulders, and its jaws were about the length of my arm. It was smiling as it padded into view, its tongue lolling out between rows of slick white fangs. I quickly stepped in front of Kenzie, raising my swords as it loomed closer, and the massive wolf snorted in clear disgust.

"Ugh, why must we go through this silly dance every single time I meet one of you?" it rumbled, making no sense whatsoever. I'd never seen this thing before and would certainly remember meeting a giant-ass wolf that could talk. The huge canine shook his head. "Do you think those little toys will hurt me, boy?" it asked in an overly patient tone, its teeth flashing in the dim light as it spoke. "Do you even know who I am?"

"I do," the Thin Man said, startling me. The tall faery stepped up beside me, narrowing his pale eyes, and the wolf stared back, unblinking. "I remember you," the Thin Man said softly. "When you came through my town. I remember you and the Winter prince, the Summer jester and the seer. That seer—the one whose time was already up—she should have never left Phaed. I knew it was folly to let her go, but you and the prince refused to leave her behind." The Thin Man's voice grew hard, bitterness seeping into his words. "I could have stopped them there, even the Winter prince. But you were the one that helped them escape, escape with *her*, and because of that one oversight, this entire mess came to pass." He pointed at the wolf with a long, stabby finger. "If not for the seer, the Winter prince would have failed, but because she lived, the prophecy was set into motion. If the First Queen and the Iron Prince emerge victorious, let it be on your head."

The wolf growled, showing his enormous fangs and making the ground vibrate. "You did not know what would happen any more than I did," it rumbled, the spikes on the back of its shoulders bristling angrily. "Nor could you know what might've happened, had the Winter prince *not* fulfilled his quest. Perhaps a future worse than this one. Perhaps he would have become a monster even more terrible than the First Queen."

"Or perhaps he would have died, and the child of prophecy, the one who is responsible for bringing the First Queen to power once again, would never have been born!"

"Hey!" Kenzie stepped between the Thin Man and the wolf, glaring at them both. "Stop it, both of you," she ordered, as the Thin Man blinked and the wolf pricked his ears in amused surprise. "This isn't helping anything. Who cares who did what, and who's responsible for which prophecy? We can't go back and change it. So, instead of pointing fingers at each other, why don't we try stopping it now?" She turned to face the huge wolf, back straight, completely unafraid. "I take it you're the guide Grimalkin told us about?" she asked, while I held my breath and tried not to imagine those massive jaws biting her head off. "The one who can help us find Annwyl?"

The wolf stared at her, then barked a guttural laugh, making me jump. "The little human has teeth," he remarked, and lowered himself to his haunches, giving Kenzie an almost approving look. Sheathing my blades, I edged up so that I was standing beside her, just in case. Even sitting down, the wolf towered over her. "But you are correct, little mortal. I am the best tracker in the Deep Wyld, the wyldwood and all the Nevernever. The wretched cat informed me that you were searching for a Summer gentry that had crossed the river into the Deep Wyld. He suggested I might lead you to her." He snorted, curling a lip in disdain. "Normally, such effortless hunts are a waste of my time, but the cat would not call on me if it was not important." He panted, baring shiny teeth in an evil grin. "And I would never turn down the opportunity to hold a favor over his arrogant, insufferable head.

"Well, then." Stretching with easy grace, the wolf glanced at me and the Thin Man. "Shall we get on with it, then? I smelled a Summer gentry passing through not long ago, so the trail will not be difficult to find."

"What about Grimalkin?" Kenzie wondered.

The wolf shrugged.

"The cat is not coming. He said he wouldn't be joining you this time, something about returning to the realm that needed him. Good riddance, if you ask me. Listening to him talk makes me want to snap his head off." The wolf rolled his glowing eyes. "Let's go. The sooner we get this done, the better. But, I do suggest you stay close, little humans. The Deep Wyld is not a place that takes kindly to trespassers. Don't leave the trail, and don't wander off by yourselves. If you stare into the trees and something stares back, ignore it and keep walking. If something calls your name, ignore it and keep walking. With any luck, you'll leave the Deep Wyld with the same number that you started with."

"We're here for Annwyl," I reminded the wolf, as he turned and padded soundlessly toward the tree line. "We should leave with one more than we started with." He snorted without looking back.

"I know."

CHAPTER FOURTEEN

CHICKEN BARGAINS

Surprisingly, the journey through the Deep Wyld was not as treacherous as I feared. Though it could have been, I suspected, far more dangerous than the river, or the wyldwood, or any realm we'd encountered so far. Unlike the hazy gray twilight of the wyldwood, this forest was almost pitch-black. The canopy shut out the sky, and Kenzie's mini-flashlight beam seemed weak in the absolute darkness of the Deep Wyld. I could feel eyes on me from every angle, watching from the trees and shadow.

Back in the wyldwood, things moved through the brush and in the corners of your eyes, just enough to make you paranoid. In the Deep Wyld, the feeling of being watched was constant to the point of driving you crazy. As if the entire forest—trees, rocks, even the darkness itself—was watching you, judging you, and if you stared back too hard, you might see something horrible.

Apparently, I wasn't the only one on edge.

"Do you feel like we're being watched?" Kenzie asked after several minutes of hiking. Razor, perched on her shoulder, gazed around with huge green eyes and occasionally mumbled something under his breath, showing a glimmer of neon light.

"Yeah." I nodded. "I do." I checked my swords, making

sure they were still there, at my waist. "Wonder how long it'll be before something comes leaping out at us?"

A few paces ahead, the wolf snorted.

"Don't worry so much, little humans," he growled, glancing back at us. "Nothing will attack you here."

"How can you be sure?" Kenzie asked.

"Because you are with me," the wolf replied.

"Right," I muttered, unconvinced. Yeah, the wolf was huge, and strong, and scary, but I'd seen things like giants and dragons that were way bigger. "And who are you, again?"

"Not very bright, are you?" was the rumbled answer. "I am Wolf, Ethan Chase. Every story, every tale that you've heard that had a wolf in it, that was me. The Grimm brothers, Aesop the storyteller, even your modern fable of a man who becomes a beast the night of the full moon. Those stories are all mine. You should know who I am."

"Oh," I said, as it finally clicked. Not a wolf. *The* Wolf. The one who ate Red Riding Hood's grandma, terrorized the Boy who cried Wolf and threatened the three little pigs. The Big Bad Wolf himself.

I shut up after that.

A while later, we stopped at a small stream. How long we'd been trekking through the Deep Wyld, I couldn't say. Hours or days, for all I knew. The Wolf never slowed except to sniff the ground or the air, testing the wind, and then he was off again. A rickety wooden bridge spanned the banks of the stream, even though it was barely three feet across, and the Wolf sniffed that, too.

"She's been here," he said, curling a lip. His fangs flashed briefly in the darkness as he pulled back, wrinkling his nose, and I frowned.

"Something wrong?"

"Not for me. But you might want to see this."

Warily, I walked around to the bridge entrance. Someone had nailed a chicken's head and feet to each of the wooden posts. A few blood-caked feathers fluttered in the breeze, and I joined the Wolf in wrinkling my nose.

"Ew," Kenzie said, echoing my sentiment. "What the heck is that?"

"It's a warning," the Wolf said. "Whoever put this up is telling people to stay away. Not a problem in itself, but if it's the person I think it is, your girl could be in a lot of trouble if she passed through here." He shook himself, then sprang lightly over the stream, looking back with glowing eyes. "Let's go. And don't touch the water. You'll turn into a frog if you drink it."

We crossed the bridge, being careful not to touch the grisly remains, and continued into the Deep Wyld.

"At least we're on the right track," Kenzie commented, as Razor perched on her shoulder and muttered, "Bleh, chicken heads. Bleh!" over and over again. "Maybe we'll catch up to her soon."

"I hope so," I muttered. "This place is starting to…"

Somewhere in the woods, a branch snapped. Stopping in the middle of the trail, I pulled Kenzie to a halt, frowning.

"I heard something," I growled. Kenzie immediately shushed Razor and fell silent, head cocked as she listened. Up ahead, the Wolf had also paused, ears pricked and head raised to the breeze.

Something was coming toward us through the trees. Something massive. Something that caused the ground to shake and the branches of the trees to sway wildly back and forth.

The Wolf whirled around, bristling.

"Move!" he snarled at me. "Get out of sight, humans. Now."

We scrambled around a tree as the crashing and snapping got louder. The Thin Man vanished, and the Wolf melted into shadow, as something huge and heavy continued to stomp its way toward us.

When I peeked around the trunk, my mouth nearly fell open in astonishment.

It was…a house. A flipping *house* was walking through the forest, on a pair of gigantic chicken legs. Incredulous, I blinked hard and looked again, making sure I was seeing this right. Yep, it was definitely chicken legs. The gnarled yellow talons squelched mud and snapped branches in their wake, carrying the ramshackle wooden hut through the trees with every stride. I could only stare after it, gaping, as the house with chicken feet walked past, trailing a curl of smoke from the chimney, and continued into the forest.

"O-kaaay," Kenzie remarked after the crashing had died down and the woods were silent again. "I'm not crazy, am I? Everyone else just saw a house walk by us, right?"

Razor buzzed and nodded vigorously, ears flapping. "Funny house!" he exclaimed. "Funny house, funny feet, ha!"

"Blast it all," said the Thin Man, emerging from behind a tiny sapling that was more twig than tree. "Unfortunate that she is lurking about this area of the Deep Wyld. I was hoping we could avoid her. Can you still pick up the girl's trail?" he asked the Wolf. "Is it still around? Where does it lead?"

The Wolf stared at us and didn't answer. I sighed. "It's going in the same direction, isn't it?" I guessed.

He grinned. "The hunt just got interesting."

We followed the house, which was pretty easy since it left a giant, house-sized trail of destruction behind it. Crushed vegetation, snapped limbs, broken branches and huge, chicken-shaped footprints in the dirt. Eventually, we came to a small clearing, where you could almost see the sky through the massive trunks surrounding the glen. The house sat, or crouched, or perched, in the very center, the legs now folded underneath it. A fence surrounded it, but the closer I looked, the more it seemed that the posts and railings were made of bone, topped with various skulls. Several chickens milled around the yard, scratching and pecking, seemingly unconcerned that a freaking house had just marched up and plopped itself down inside the fence.

Kenzie nudged my arm. "Look at that," she said, pointing to a crude wooden X near the perimeter of the trees. More skulls and chicken feet dangled from it, spinning lazily in the wind. The Wolf snorted.

"More keep-out signs," he sniffed, and gave an exaggerated yawn. "As if that would stop me. Well, humans? Are you going down there or not? I'll wait for you here. Probably better that way, trust me. No one wants to look up and see a wolf on their doorstep."

"And you're certain Annwyl went down there?" I asked.

"I can smell the girl's trail from here," was the growled answer. "It leads straight to the front gate and does not return. If she is still alive, she never left that house."

"Foolish girl." The Thin Man shook his head, staring at the house with grave eyes. "Foolish, or desperate. Some old powers you do not seek out, for any reason."

"Why?" Kenzie asked, watching as the house shifted, creaking and groaning, before it was still again. "Who lives here, exactly?"

"A witch," the Wolf said, curling a lip. "Old, though not as old as me. She travels the Nevernever in that ridiculous house of hers, sometimes in the wyldwood, sometimes in the Deep Wyld, never in one place for long. She doesn't bother me, and as long as she stays out of my hunting grounds, I return the favor. Still, she has many names and many legends of her own in the mortal realm. It's best for you humans to be cautious when dealing with her."

"It's best not to deal with her at all," the Thin Man added, crossing his arms. "But, if we must, we must. Again, it cannot be overstated how careful you must be, humans. The witch of this house is indeed old and powerful, and also quite unpredictable. She might help, or she might attempt to trap you into making a deal you will regret. So do watch what you say around her."

Kenzie sighed and shared a glance with me. "Normal day in Faeryland."

I gave a weary nod. "You know what to do if I'm about to sell my soul."

Together, we stepped away from the trees and walked steadily toward the house. As we drew close to the fence, which *was* made completely of bones, the front door creaked open and a bent old woman hobbled down the steps into the yard. Tangled white hair hung around her face; her skin was lined and shriveled like a walnut, and a ragged shawl was wrapped over bony shoulders. She looked like somebody's grandmother but also like every witch in every fairy tale I'd read. The only things missing were the black robes and pointy hat.

She noticed us immediately but didn't seem surprised. Instead, she continued down the steps, clutching a wooden bucket in one gnarled claw. The chickens, instead of swarming for the food, scattered before her, running to different corners of the yard. The witch dumped the bucket of scraps on the ground and turned, fixing us with beady black eyes.

"Well?" Her voice squeaked like a rusty hinge, as she raised thin white brows at us. "Are you going to come in, boy, or are you going to stand there and gape until something flies in to roost?"

I swallowed. "Um." I glanced at the Thin Man. He gave his head a tiny shake, echoing my feelings. Stepping into the witch's yard didn't seem like the brightest of ideas right now. "Actually, we're just looking for someone," I said, turning back to the witch. "A Summer sidhe. We thought she might've come through here."

The witch sniffed and set the bucket atop a large wooden cask. "Is that a statement, human, or a question? Don't waste my time with stories I care nothing about. If you want to ask me something, ask."

"Fine. Have you seen a Summer sidhe called Annwyl?"

"Better." A sly smile curled the witch's bloodless mouth. "Yes, Ethan Chase," she crooned, making my skin crawl. "I have indeed. But that is not the question you should have opened with. I have *seen* her in the Summer Court and the wyldwood, in the mortal realm and Tir Na Nog. I have seen the Summer girl many a time, in many different places, and you had best start asking smarter questions, or this is going to be entirely too easy for me."

I groaned, raking my hands down my face. "Kenzie," I muttered, feeling a headache start to throb behind my eyes. "Help."

Kenzie stepped forward, brushing my arm as she faced the witch over the fence posts. "Will you please tell us," she began in a quiet, firm voice, "to the best of you knowledge, where Annwyl of the Summer Court is right now?"

"Ah," said the witch. "A far smarter question. Your friend is much better at this than you, Ethan Chase. I do indeed know where you can find Annwyl of the Summer Court. The girl came to me not long ago, seeking answers, as most do. She seemed quite desperate, as most are, by the time they come to me. She had already been to the wyldwood and the mortal realm, and both were unable to help."

"Why?" Kenzie asked, then quickly added, "What was the question she needed an answer to?"

The witch's smile faded. "She wanted to know," she said in a grave voice, "how to destroy the amulet she was bound to."

Kenzie's eyes widened. "But that would kill her," she exclaimed. "Without the amulet, she would Fade away to nothing. She had to have known that."

"She did," the witch said calmly. "It would not deter her. She was determined to see it destroyed, and she wanted to know if I knew how."

"And do you?" Kenzie asked.

The witch gave her a level stare. "I do," she replied. "I do indeed. But you don't need that information, do you?" She eyed me and the Thin Man. "You already know how to destroy the amulet," she said. "That is not the reason you are here. No, you have come for *her*."

"Yes," the Thin Man said, stepping forward. "You know the danger, old mother. You must have heard the rumors, even out here in the Deep Wyld. The First Queen has returned, and the child of prophecy leads her army of Forgotten against the courts. If she succeeds, the days of blood and darkness will swallow the Nevernever whole, and nothing will be safe. You cannot hide from her forever, even in the Deep Wyld. That girl holds the key to victory against the First Queen, even if it is the smallest chance."

The witch glared at him. "I am well aware of this, forgotten one," she snapped, showing a flash of jagged yellow teeth. "Which is why the girl is not rushing off to confront the Iron Prince and doom us all. The First Queen knows about the amulet, and the Forgotten would kill the Summer girl before she could ever reach the prince. They are likely still searching for her, for all of you." She looked down her crooked nose at us. "I knew you would come here, Ethan Chase," she stated smugly. "If not you, then someone else. Your sister, perhaps. Or that insufferable Goodfellow. Eventually, I knew someone would arrive looking for the girl and the amulet. So, I kept her safe. Hidden." Her lips twisted in a faint smirk. "Though *she* might not see it that way."

"Where is she?" I asked. "We know she's here. Where are you keeping her?"

The witch's grin widened, and she gestured to the yard behind her, at the dozen or so chickens milling about the grass. For a second, I didn't know what she meant; I didn't see Annwyl anywhere in the yard, or among the flock. Then my stomach twisted with horror at the realization, and Kenzie gasped.

"Yes," the witch said in a pleased voice. "She is here. Isn't this better, Ethan Chase? No Forgotten will come for her on my land. No traitor princes will think to look for her here. Your Summer girl is perfectly safe, hidden from the First Queen, and has everything she needs."

"Change her back," I said firmly, narrowing my eyes. "Right now."

"Are you certain, boy?" The witch glanced at the flock, still smiling. "She is much happier like this, no burdens, no responsibilities. She doesn't remember her past life and is perfectly content scratching about with her fellows. Are you sure you want me to restore her to how she was, knowing she will most certainly die?"

I swallowed hard. "I'm not leaving her like that," I growled. "We need her, and the amulet, to stop Keirran. So, please, change her back."

The witch chuckled. "I suppose I could do that," she began, making me slump in relief. "Though I don't see what *I* would get out of it." She pondered a moment, then snapped her fingers. "Here is a fun game, Ethan Chase," she cackled. "I'll let you take the Summer girl and the amulet, free of charge, and I'll even agree to change her back—" she gestured to the flock behind her "—*if* you can pick her out from the rest. Bring me the right bird, and I'll let you all go."

My stomach dropped. "And if I choose wrong?"

"Then one of your friends will become a happy member of the flock," the witch said. "And you can try to guess again. But, be warned. I am only agreeing to let *one* bird go tonight. Whether it is the Summer girl or your little human friend will be up to you." She grinned, showing a mouthful of jagged teeth. "So I would try to get it right the first time, Ethan Chase."

"Dammit." I raked a hand through my hair, looking helplessly at the others. If I guessed wrong, and Kenzie paid the price… "No," I told the witch. "I won't do this. There must be something else you want."

"There is nothing else that I want," the witch said calmly. "I have all that I need. You have trespassed onto my land, and there is a price to pay regardless of the circumstances. I've given you your task, and if you want the Summer girl to leave this place, you know what must happen. That is the deal, and neither you nor your clever human friend will change my mind. Take it or leave it, Ethan Chase."

Kenzie moved close and put a hand on my arm. "You can do this, Ethan," she murmured, and I shook my head in protest. "You have to," she went on. "It's the only way to find Annwyl. We can't turn back now."

"I can't," I said through gritted teeth. "What if I guess wrong? I'm not going to put you in danger like that. I'm sorry, but I refuse to have a chicken for a girlfriend. That's not going to happen."

"Ethan." Kenzie squeezed my wrist. "We've come all this way," she whispered. "We have to get Annwyl and the amulet back to the wyldwood before the war starts. It's the one chance we have at stopping Keirran and the Lady." I took a breath to argue, but she overrode me. "Your family is depending on you. We have to bring him back."

I slumped. "Dammit, Kenzie. You had to bring up Meghan, didn't you?" But she was right, and we both knew it. Shooting a glance at the yard, at the dozen or so chickens I had to choose from, my insides churned. So many, and they all looked exactly the same. "Any tips for chicken wrangling in that animal trainer head of yours?" I asked desperately.

"Not really my area of expertise," Kenzie replied, glancing into the yard. "But…all animals respond better to patience and slow movements. Try not to chase them around. If Annwyl is in there, if there's any part of her left at all, maybe she'll recognize you."

"Boy," the witch said, sounding impatient. "Time is wasting, and I have a kettle on the stove. If you are going to do this, get on with it."

I squeezed Kenzie's hand. "All right," I muttered. "Wish me luck." *For both our sakes.* Swallowing the dryness in my throat, I opened the gate and stepped into the yard.

Okay, this was probably the *stupidest* thing I'd ever agreed to do, and that included all of Keirran's high jinks as we'd trailed him to one end of the Nevernever and back. Yeah, following Keirran had led to my death, but at least no one had ended up as a chicken.

The flock eyed my approach from different corners of the yard, beady eyes glassy and blank as they milled around with nervous clucks. None of them looked like they recognized me.

I took a few steps toward them. They skittered away. I took another few, to the same result—fearful squawking as they ran behind logs and bales of straw. They wouldn't let me near them.

We were so screwed.

Behind me, the witch let out a cackle. "Having trouble,

boy?" she called, and I resisted the urge to flip her off. "Try cornering them between the haystacks and the water barrel. I'm usually able to trap a couple of them there."

"Right," I muttered, and took a step toward the water barrel, where a trio of hens huddled. They tensed, ready to run, and I stopped.

Wait a second. This is exactly what she wants me to do—chase them around like an idiot until they're scared and exhausted and too terrified to come near me. What had Kenzie told me a few minutes ago? *Animals respond better to patience and slow movements.* I couldn't stomp after chickens like a giant, hoping to gain their trust. Even if Annwyl's scrambled chicken brain sort of recognized me, chasing them around would just freak her out.

I stared at the three birds in the corner. Two of them tensed, ready to run, but one hen peeked out at me with wary eyes, as if it was unsure whether to flee or not. If I made any motion toward her at all, she would.

Okay, then. Annwyl, wherever you are, I hope there's enough of you still in there to remember me.

Very slowly, I sat down, crossing my legs in the damp, cold grass. The chickens watched from the edges of the yard, a few curious, but most of them still wary. I shot a quick glance at the spot the one hen had been, but she was no longer there.

God, I hope this works, I thought, and closed my eyes.

For a few minutes, I remained absolutely motionless, counting my breaths, listening to the shuffle of chicken feet and the warbled clucks around me. I heard Razor buzz something to Kenzie, who shushed him immediately. Thankfully, the witch didn't move, either. It would've sucked a lot if she did something to freak the chickens out, though now that I thought about it, there was nothing in the agreement that said she *couldn't* interfere. I was relieved that she was letting me do this in peace, but I could still feel her gaze burning the back of my neck.

Hope she doesn't turn Kenzie into a chicken for the hell of it, I thought, just as there was a tap on my shoe.

Cautiously, I opened my eyes. A small red hen stood at the toe of my boot, cocking its head at me. I couldn't tell if it was the same chicken from before or not, but it was the only one that had ventured close. For a second, I stared at it as my heart started to pound. What if this wasn't the right bird? What if I guessed wrong?

Come on, Ethan. You're going to have to choose sometime.

The hen blinked, peering up at my face, as I gave it a hopeful smile.

"Hey, Annwyl," I whispered.

The second the words left my mouth, the chicken started to glow. It grew brighter and brighter, its features melting into the light, until I had to look away. When the glow faded and I was able to turn back, there was no longer a chicken standing there.

Instead, a slight, beautiful fey girl sat next to me in the grass, looking bewildered. Wavy chestnut hair tumbled down her back and shoulders. Her ears were long and pointed, and her huge green eyes stared at me in a daze.

"Ethan...Chase?" Annwyl whispered, as the breath left my lungs in a rush and I nearly collapsed in relief. "Why are you here? I thought...I heard you had died."

I managed a tiny smirk. "Yeah, well, rumors of my death were highly exaggerated."

She looked confused, but suddenly her hand went to her neck. "The amulet," she gasped. "It's gone!" I started to answer, but her eyes shifted, anger crossing her normally passive face. "Where is it?" she demanded. "Ethan Chase, what have you done?"

CHAPTER FIFTEEN

ANNWYL'S QUEST

Aw, crap. Now what?

Annwyl leaped to her feet, looking frantic, and I scrambled upright, as well. "Where is the amulet?" she demanded again, staring at me. "Is it destroyed? Is it lost? Where is it, Ethan Chase?"

"Easy." I held up my hands, taking a step back. Annwyl's eyes glowed a scary green, and the grass around her feet started to writhe and coil. Chickens scattered to all corners of the yard, squawking in terror, as the previously docile Summer fey snapped and pulsed with the energy of a storm.

"Annwyl, calm down," I said, raising my voice to be heard over the chickens and the hissing of plants. What the hell was happening? I'd never seen Annwyl like this. "I don't have it, okay? We thought it was with you."

"It is not." Annwyl did not look like she would calm down anytime soon. "But I did have it. It was in my possession when I came here." She glared around the yard, her gaze lingering on the house, before turning on me again. "Where is it?" she almost whispered. "I need to find it now!"

"Enough!" The witch swept up, scowling, and Annwyl turned a furious gaze on her. But Kenzie and the Thin Man hurried across the yard toward us, and at the sight of the tall

Forgotten, the Summer faery shrank back, more frightened of him than the old woman beside me.

"The Thin Man!" she seethed, and thorny vines erupted from the ground, coiling back like snakes. "Get back! I will not go with you! I must find the amulet and Keirran."

"Annwyl, stop," Kenzie implored, holding out a hand. "It's all right, he's with us now—"

"Why are you here?" Annwyl interrupted, ignoring Kenzie as she glared at the Thin Man. The tall Forgotten started to answer, but the Summer faery overrode him. "I know you've come for me," she said. "I cannot go to your Forgotten town. I must get to Keirran before it's too late, and you will not stop me!"

"I have no intention of taking you anywhere, my dear!" the Thin Man shot back. "If you would only listen to your friends, you would realize that. Calm down before you hurt someone."

"Annwyl!" I shouted, grabbing her arm. "He's telling the truth. We came here to get you and the amulet. Take it easy."

She did not take it easy but turned on me again, eyes flashing. "Where is the amulet, mortal?" she demanded, sounding more like Titania than the Annwyl I had known. "Tell me now!"

"I said enough!" The witch waved her hand, and the vines and roots snaking around the Summer faery froze, then slithered back underground. Annwyl blinked, startled, as the wind died down, the grass stopped roiling, and the land returned to normal once more. Only the chickens fluttering about the yard still squawked and gibbered at the top of their lungs.

"Stop this foolishness," the witch continued, glaring at the faery. "This is not helping anything. You are so blinded by your feelings for the Iron Prince, you cannot see what is at stake. Look at what you are doing to your friends who have traveled so far to find you."

Annwyl went pale, and the scary light faded from her eyes. "Ethan," she whispered, glancing at me. "Kenzie." She shook her head, like she was just now recognizing us. "I'm sorry. Forgive me. I guess...I panicked."

"Yes," the witch agreed before we could say anything. "You did. And this is precisely why I changed you, girl. So ready to rush off to your destruction, to throw your life away. Even if you managed to reach the Iron Prince through the army of Forgotten, do you really think he would hear you now?"

I jerked in surprise, but Annwyl turned calmly, facing the witch down. "He would," she said. "I told you before. He would listen to me. I would have made him see."

"No. You would have died. And the prince would have lost his soul forever." The witch narrowed her beady eyes at the Summer fey. "You could not have done this alone, but you would not listen to those older and wiser than yourself. So, I made the decision to keep you and that cursed bit of magic safe, for your own good, until someone appeared who could help."

"What?" Kenzie turned from me to stare at the witch, frowning. "If that was the case, then why make us go through all this crap? Why not just turn Annwyl back and be done with it?"

Her thin mouth twitched. "Because I have a reputation to uphold, my dear. And if the boy could not figure it out, I did not have any hope that he could reach the Iron Prince. Besides, it was amusing. Living out here with almost no visitors, I take my entertainment when I can."

She cackled, then reached into her shawl and drew forth a familiar copper disk on a leather cord. My skin crawled at the sight of it, and the Thin Man recoiled as the witch held it up. The amulet, the thing that had trapped Keirran's soul, dangled from the cord, twirling in the breeze.

"I believe this is what you are looking for."

For a moment, Annwyl looked like she might lunge forward and snatch the amulet from the witch's crooked fingers. But she took a deep, calming breath, and when she spoke again, her words were steady.

"Are you going to return it to me, or is this something I must bargain for?"

"Pah, I would not bargain for this cursed thing," the witch said, curling a lip in disgust. "It is your burden to bear, not mine. I will, however, issue this one warning. The Iron Prince, as you knew him before, no longer exists. His soul has been missing from his body for far too long. The longer you use that amulet to sustain your own life, the more it is in danger of vanishing completely."

Annwyl shivered but nodded. "I understand," she whispered, and the witch held out the cord. The Summer faery took it and carefully draped it around her neck, where the amulet pulsed like a sullen heartbeat.

"Well," the Thin Man sighed, as Razor crawled out of Kenzie's shirt and waved to Annwyl, buzzing happily. "Here we all are."

"Yeah," I muttered. "I get the feeling that was the easy part."

"So, let me get this straight," I said, as we left the witch's house, heading back into the forest. "You came here hoping to destroy the amulet. Knowing that it would kill you if you did."

"Yes," Annwyl said calmly. "After I heard…what Keirran had done to you in Ireland, what he brought about, I knew that something terrible had happened to him. He couldn't be the same. The Keirran I knew would never do something like that. I knew the amulet had to be responsible. I could *feel* it, constantly eating away at him. I couldn't stand the thought that by saving my life, Keirran had become *that*. What they're calling him now—the Soulless One. The Destroyer of the Courts.

"So, yes," Annwyl went on. "I began searching for a way to undo the amulet. I first tried seeking out its creator, the mortal in the human world. But…it appears I cannot make myself visible to humans anymore. Maybe because I'm so close to the Fade, only the amulet is keeping me alive. But mortals in the human world can neither see nor hear me, so I could not ask your Guro how to break this curse."

"So, that was the presence Guro was talking about when we went to see him," Kenzie said. "It was you."

Annwyl nodded. "I thought the human could sense me. But I still could not make myself known. And by that time, word of what Keirran had done had spread. My own kind would not help me. Leanansidhe might have killed me had she not been so preoccupied with her mansion's disappearance. So, I went into the Nevernever, looking for anyone who might give me the answer I sought. Eventually, I heard that the Bone Witch had journeyed across the River of Dreams, back into the Deep Wyld again, so I made my way here."

"But…" Kenzie's forehead scrunched up. "Weren't you exiled from the Nevernever?" she asked. "Wasn't that how this whole mess started? How did you get back?"

"When the Veil disappeared," Annwyl replied, "all of the old seals and barriers the rulers had placed on the trods vanished, as well. The exiled fey found they could suddenly return to the Nevernever, and many have. But it's too late for me." She lightly touched her chest, where the amulet was hidden beneath her dress. "I was too close to the Fade. I don't know if I'm even really alive anymore, or if I'm just a memory that can't die. Right now, the amulet is the only thing keeping me here. Even now, back in the Nevernever, without it I would Fade away completely."

"Annwyl." Kenzie's face was sympathetic and angry at the same time. "I'm so sorry," she whispered, and her eyes glimmered. "This isn't... It's just not fair! You didn't ask for any of this. It's not your fault that Keirran went completely stupid."

"It's all right." Annwyl gave a small smile. "I'm...tired, Mackenzie. I've lived a long life, longer than most. I have fewer regrets than joys, fewer sorrows than happy memories." She looked away, into the trees, her voice the barest murmur. "I'm not afraid. It's time to stop lingering and move on. Keirran is the last piece I must take care of."

There was a ripple of movement in the darkness ahead, and the Wolf melted soundlessly out of the trees. Annwyl stiffened, eyes going wide with fear and awe as the huge creature padded toward us, but she didn't panic, even when the Wolf swung his massive head toward her, sniffing the air.

"I take it this is the one you came for?" he growled, his voice making the leaves vibrate overhead. "You didn't tell me she was one of them."

"One of who?" Kenzie asked.

"Them. The Fading Ones. The Forgotten, as you call them." The Wolf snorted in disgust. "She reeks of stolen magic, of forbidden glamour, yet she herself is not entirely here. And there is something else. Something...dark. Angry." His muzzle curled, revealing fangs, and he pressed forward threateningly. "It sort of makes me want to bite her head off."

"Well, restrain yourself," Kenzie snapped, stepping in front of the Summer fey. "No one is biting anyone's head off. You, stay." She glared at the Wolf who, while he didn't look exactly intimidated, snorted and backed off a step. "We have to get back to the wyldwood and look for Keirran," Kenzie went on, glancing at the rest of us. "Any ideas on how we're going to do that?"

"Quickly, would be my advice," came a voice overhead. A pair of glowing eyes floated in the branches above, a moment before Grimalkin materialized on a tree limb. "I see you managed to locate the Summer girl and the amulet," the cat said, sounding as if he had doubted our ability to accomplish that. "And the dog remembered his end of the bargain and did not bite anyone's head off out of habit. I suppose wonders never cease."

I expected the Wolf to snarl and bare his teeth, but to my surprise, he only chuckled. "Don't be a sore loser, cat," he rumbled. "Remember, you had to ask for my help. I look forward to reminding you of that at every opportunity."

"Hmph." Grimalkin sniffed, looking bored. "I suppose the less intelligent have to reassure themselves however they can," he mused. "I, on the other hand, have been busy with important matters. Ethan Chase…" That gold gaze shifted to me. "The First Queen has invaded the wyldwood," he said, making me jerk up. "The courts are now at war. A multitude of Forgotten stands between you and the Iron Prince, not to mention the Lady herself. Going after him now would be most unwise."

"Great. So what are we supposed to do?"

"That I cannot tell you. However, the courts have set up camp at the edge of the wyldwood and Arcadia," Grimalkin went on, curling his tail around himself. "The Iron Queen is among them, as are the rulers of Summer and Winter. Perhaps they will have a solution. One more feasible than charging headlong at the Iron Prince through a horde of Forgotten and getting yourselves torn to shreds."

Back to the wyldwood. Back to Meghan and the rest of the courts. I wondered if she would be angry with me; I had promised her I'd stay away from the battlefield if it came down to war with the Forgotten. *But...* I glanced at Annwyl, watching in somber silence. *This is my family. I can't stay away. I have to try to save him.* The Summer girl gave a tiny nod, as if she knew what I was thinking, and my stomach turned. *Dammit, I just wish I could save Annwyl, too.*

"All right," I said, and looked to the Thin Man, who hadn't said much since we'd left the witch's house. "Back to the wyldwood, then. Can you take us there? Through the Between?"

He raised a razor-thin eyebrow. "Not here," he said slowly. "One can only part the Veil where it is weak, and I know of only one place in the Deep Wyld where the barrier between worlds is that thin. We would have to cross the River of Dreams to find a spot where I could take you into the Between."

I sighed. "I guess if that's the only way," I muttered. "But we're running out of time. And call me cynical, but I can't see us not running into some kind of trouble on the way back, either."

The Wolf shook his massive head.

"There will be no trouble," he stated in a deep, firm voice. "Nothing will dare come close. I'll take you back myself."

Kenzie blinked. "You will? Why?"

"I'm old, little girl." The Wolf regarded her with solemn green eyes. "Older than the witch. Older than even your thin friend over there. I remember the days when the First Queen ruled. The courts have forgotten—purposely, I suspect—but those were chaotic, bloody times. The world lived in fear of us, terrified of the Good Neighbors and the creatures that lurked in the dark. She would bring those days back, if she could."

"I don't understand," Kenzie said. "All that fear and glamour and belief? Isn't that what you want?"

"Chaos and panic and mortals running around like headless chickens?" The Wolf barked a laugh. "It would be highly amusing. But the world has changed. Those days are gone. And I know what humans are capable of now. They no longer worship the things they fear. They try to eradicate them." His eyes narrowed. "The First Queen would bring destruction to the Nevernever even as she tried to save it. The Veil cannot be allowed to disappear again. So if you need someone to carve a bloody swath through ranks of Forgotten to get to the First Queen and her little Iron pet, I'm the best one for the job."

"Oh, goodie," said Grimalkin, rising from the branch. "And now we have picked up the dog. I will inform the Iron Queen of your imminent arrival, and to prepare for the smell."

He waved his tail once and was gone. Razor bared his teeth in the direction the cat had been and hissed. "Evil, bad kitty," the gremlin muttered. "Tie rock to tail and throw in lake, ha!"

The Wolf chuckled in approval. "At least one of you has good taste."

As the Wolf predicted, we did not run into any trouble on our way back through the Deep Wyld. Though there was one tense instance where a boulder uncurled and stood up, revealing it was actually a wrinkled gray giant with mossy hair, yellow tusks and arms down to its knees. Wolf and giant stared at each other for a few terrifying heartbeats, before the two-legged monster took a step back and shambled off into the trees

The bridge was waiting for us as we left the tangled forest, which was somewhat of a shock. And a very grumpy bridge gnome informed us that a bossy gray cat had already taken care of the toll, and that we were free to cross as we pleased. Why he couldn't have done that the first time we crossed, I had no idea, but it was, after all, Grimalkin. Once we were back in the wyldwood, the Thin Man quickly found a spot where the Veil was thin, and we slipped into the blank grayness of the Between once more.

"Hmm," the Wolf remarked as the curtain of reality closed behind us. Like Razor, his eyes glowed a hazy green as he gazed around the lightless landscape. "So, this is the Between," he mused, his deep voice echoing through the fog. "I was in a town very much like this, I think. It smelled of nothing, and its residents tried to suck the glamour right out of us."

"That was my town," the Thin Man said flatly. "And you shouldn't even have been able to find it. I still have no idea how the lot of you managed to stumble into Phaed, but it has caused quite the headache, hasn't it? And now we must fix this mess a certain Winter prince has caused, or the Nevernever and the Between could be lost forever."

The Wolf growled. "Don't blame me. *He* was the one who wanted a soul. I tried warning him." His gaze slid to Annwyl. "You people and your souls. First, we had to find one, now we have to return one." He wrinkled his muzzle in disgust. "What good are they, except to cause grief?"

"I don't know," Annwyl said softly, touching the cord at her neck. "But Keirran's always felt so bright. Perhaps if I had one of my own, I wouldn't be Fading away. I guess I'll never know now." She sighed and gazed into the distance, her voice almost wistful. "It won't be long before my time is done."

"Noooo," Razor moaned from Kenzie's shoulder. "No leave. Stay, pretty elf girl. Stay."

Well, I had picked up quite the party, hadn't I? I wondered what Meghan would say when I walked into the faery camp with Kenzie, Annwyl, a gremlin, the Thin Man and the Big Bad Wolf trailing behind me. I wondered what the *other* rulers would think.

Guess I'd find out soon enough.

"How far to the border of Arcadia?" I asked the Thin Man.

"Not far," the tall faery replied. Gazing around the empty landscape, he sighed and turned away, raising a hand. "Follow me, and let's try not to stumble upon any other realities this time."

"No arguments there."

We didn't stumble into any pockets of reality, and when the Thin Man parted the Veil once more, we stepped into the familiar murk and tangle of the wyldwood.

"Arcadia is that way, I believe," the Thin Man said, pointing in a random direction. "Though I am not certain where the courts would set up camp. The cait sith only mentioned they were at the border of the Summer Court and the wyldwood."

The Wolf cocked his shaggy head. "I hear rushing water," he stated, and lifted his muzzle to the wind. "And I smell… many fey. Summer, Winter " his lip curled back from his fangs " and Iron."

"That must be the army," I said, ignoring the twist in my stomach. Meghan was close. As was the war and probably the First Queen. Soon, I would have to face both my sister and the Iron Prince, and I had no idea which one scared me the most.

Nothing for it now.

Taking a deep breath, I started forward, toward the camp, my sister and maybe the final fight with my nephew.

CHAPTER SIXTEEN

UNDER IRON'S BANNER

There were probably a few thousand tents camped along the river's edge.

"Wow," Kenzie murmured, gazing into the valley, which looked like some sort of crazy circus or refugee camp. Nearly all available space had been taken up by tents, and fey of every description wandered the narrow paths between. However, I noticed a distinct separation in the tents belonging to Summer, Winter and Iron. The three courts kept solely to their sides of the field, not mingling or interacting with the other territories. At least, that's what I assumed, based on the different colors of tents clumped together: shades of green and brown for Summer; black, red and blue for Winter. The Iron court was easy to spot. Not only did it sit far away from the other courts; the area around it looked slightly sick. Trees were withered and bent over, plants were in the process of dying, and even the grass looked dead. I figured such a large amount of Iron fey sitting in the middle of the wyldwood was slowly poisoning the land around them, but nothing could be done about it. Meghan's court was too powerful an ally not to participate in the war with the Forgotten. Of course, once the fighting was done, Summer and Winter would probably waste no time kicking the Iron fey out of the wyldwood and back to Mag Tuiredh. I wondered how Meghan had been able to put up with them for so long.

"Ugh," the Wolf growled as he stared into the valley. He backed away from the edge. "Too crowded for my taste," he said. "You four go ahead. Meet with your rulers, do whatever you have to do. I'll stay back, keep an eye on the perimeter. Make sure there are no Forgotten sneaking around the edges."

"You sure, Wolf?" Kenzie asked. The Wolf panted a grin.

"Oh, trust me, it's better this way. There'd probably be a panic if I went strolling down there now." He shook himself, then turned back into the forest. "I'll be close. If there's trouble, just scream."

Loping into the trees, he disappeared.

Stepping out of the forest, we headed toward the river and a wooden bridge that spanned the bank. Two sidhe knights guarded the entrance of the bridge, tall and slender, in blue-and-white armor with icicles growing out of the shoulders and helmets. The Winter knights glared at us as we approached, gauntleted hands dropping to their icy swords.

"Hold," one growled as we stopped a few feet from the posts. "Identify yourselves, humans. This camp is off-limits to your kind."

"My name is Ethan Chase, brother to Her Highness the Iron Queen," I said, cringing at how douchy I sounded. But, as I discovered, the fey responded better to rank and pomp, and usually bowed to protocol. "Let us pass. I have an important message for my sister."

The Winter knights eyed each other. It was obvious they didn't care to be bossed around by a human and were stalling for a way to refuse. I crossed my arms and tried to look impatient and important. The knights finally dropped their hands from their sword hilts.

"Very well," one of them said reluctantly, and stepped aside.

"You may pass, Ethan Chase. The Iron Queen's tent is on the east side of the camp."

"Wait," the other said, just as I relaxed. His gaze slid past Annwyl and Kenzie—thankfully, Razor had hidden down her shirt—and fixed on the Thin Man, waiting quietly behind us. The knight's cold blue eyes narrowed, and he suddenly drew his sword.

"Forgotten!" he snarled. "That is a Forgotten! Traitor!"

He started forward, a murderous look in his eyes. I drew my swords and stepped between them, blocking his path.

"Not another step," I warned.

Smirking, he tried shoving me aside using brute force; I dodged his arm, stepped in and put the tip of my sword against his breastplate. The icy armor frayed apart where it touched the steel, dissolving in the air like colored mist, leaving a small hole behind. The knight froze, staring at his ruined breastplate, and I smiled coldly.

"Last time I'll ask nice."

"How dare you bring that abomination here!" the knight spat, switching to indignant rage now that raw violence had failed. "How dare you bring a Forgotten into our very midst? The rulers will never stand for it."

"Will you relax? He's not with the First Queen." I spared a split-second glance back at the Thin Man to make sure he was still there. He was, watching the knights calmly, an almost amused expression on his narrow face. I supposed if he was in any real danger, he could essentially make himself invisible. As long as he faced his opponents head-on, he couldn't be seen. *Must be nice.*

"He's on our side," I insisted, as the knight gave me a blatant look of contempt. "He's working with us to stop the First Queen and the rest of the Forgotten, so everyone can just calm down. And we have important information on the war, information that all the rulers will want to hear. But, hey, if you don't want to let us pass, let it be on your head when the Iron Queen finds out."

The knights glared at me. "Wait here," one finally ordered, taking a stiff step back. "I will inform the rulers of your arrival. They can decide what to do with you and your...friends."

Spinning on a heel, he marched rigidly into camp, while the second knight returned to his post, still watching me with hooded eyes.

"Charming," Kenzie said, as Razor peeked out of her hair and made faces at the retreating knight. The Thin Man sighed.

"I was afraid this might happen," he said, and cast a tired glance back at the trees. "Perhaps I should go," he mused. "Join the Wolf in waiting for you at the edge of the forest. I would not want our mission jeopardized because of the suspicion of the courts."

"No," I said. "We wouldn't have gotten this far if not for your help. You're staying with us. The courts are just going to have to suck it up and act like reasonable adults for once."

The Winter knight did not return, but after several tense minutes, the clanking of armor could be heard coming toward us, and a squad of Iron knights marched up to the bridge. "Prince Ethan," the one in front called. "Please, forgive the wait. If you and your friends would accompany us, we will take you to the Iron Queen."

I breathed out in relief. Meghan herself had called for me. No having to argue our way past an irate Mab or Titania. We were going directly to see my sister.

I hoped she wasn't too angry that I had snuck off without her permission. Again.

Glowering, the Winter knight stepped aside to let us pass. I was sorely tempted to smirk at him as we crossed the bridge, but I had just made that "reasonable adult" comment a moment ago, so I refrained. The Iron knights surrounded us, keeping a wary eye on the Thin Man as they did, and we started through the camp.

Faeries stared at us, curious and suspicious, as we followed the knights down the muddy streets. Of course, we had to go through the Unseelie side of camp to get to Iron's territory, so most of the fey—goblins, redcaps, ogres and the like—looked like they might have attacked us if we hadn't been surrounded by a wall of iron and steel. Several redcaps trailed alongside the knights, staying just out of reach, and snarled or hurled insults at us, the Thin Man especially. A chill hung over everything, and the air was thick with tension and the threat of violence. Everyone here was twitchy, I realized, eager for battle and bloodshed. I kept one sword out, just in case, and wondered how close the First Queen's army was and how soon before all hell broke loose.

We finally stepped free of the Winter camp, much to my relief, and the mob of Unseelie fey soon disappeared as we crossed into Iron's territory. The city of tents looked much different under Meghan's banner. Unlike the wild chaos of the Unseelie camp, where the dwellings were thrown together in haphazard rows wherever there was room, the tents here were organized in perfectly straight lines, almost like a grid. Instead of torches, lampposts flickered on the corners, iron poles growing right out of the earth. Faeries still stared at us curiously: hacker elves, wire nymphs, Iron knights and swarms of the ever-present gremlins all watched us as we made our way through the camp. But, notwithstanding the gremlins, many of them bowed or nodded as I passed, still treating me like a prince. It made me uncomfortable, but it was better than being called a "tidbit" by a shark-toothed redcap itching to take a chunk out of me.

As we passed beneath a watchtower, a gaggle of buzzing,

high-pitched voices rang out, and a swarm of gremlins appeared, clinging to the tower walls. They chattered and waved, garbling at us in their nonsensical language and sounding like a staticky radio station.

Razor popped out of Kenzie's hair, a huge grin crossing his face as he bounced and waved back, buzzing nonstop. Kenzie winced, tilting her head as she waited patiently for the gremlin's excited flailing to stop. Razor turned to her, ears pricked, expression hopeful, and she smiled.

"Go on," she said, and the gremlin took off, shooting up the tower to join the rest of the swarm. They laughed and shrieked in maniacal joy, jumping all over each other, until the entire throng skittered away and was lost from sight. Kenzie shook her head.

"He'll be back," she sighed, as their buzzing voices faded away on the wind. "Can't keep him away, I'm afraid. Did you know I spent about a month teaching my dog to ignore gremlins? My dad and stepmom thought he'd gone nuts, barking at things that weren't there." Her face fell then, her eyes going dark. "I wonder what they're doing now?" she murmured, almost to herself.

My stomach turned. What were *my* parents doing now? What was going on at home? I knew months had passed in the real world since I saw my parents last, the morning I snuck off to New Orleans with Annwyl and never returned.

"Prince Ethan?" A knight's voice broke me out of my musings. We had stopped at the entrance of a gray tent, much larger than those around it and guarded by another squadron of knights. I realized we stood in the very center of the Iron camp, and the banner of a huge white oak fluttered in the wind atop the tallest pole. "We're here, sire," the knight said with a short bow, and gestured to the tent flaps. "Her Majesty is waiting for you inside."

I licked my lips, took a furtive breath and stepped through the flaps.

Inside the tent it was dim and cool. A large table stood in the center of the room, a map of the Nevernever spread across it. Colored pins had been pressed into the surface, marking skirmishes or battles or sightings of Forgotten, I didn't know. I glanced quickly around for Ash and saw that neither he nor Puck were present.

But Meghan stood at the far end of the table, surrounded by Iron fey and looking imposing in a suit of silvery battle mail, a sword dangling at her side. Her hair had been pulled back, fully exposing her pointed ears, and she wore a glittering circlet of wire and steel on her brow. My skin prickled. This was the first time I'd seen her like this, a true Faery Queen, powerful and terrifying, ready to defend her lands.

"Rylan's scouts are monitoring the situation, Your Majesty," one of the faeries was saying. "They will inform us if there are any developments, but so far there have been no new sightings of Forgotten anywhere in the wyldwood."

"Any sign of the First Queen, yet?" Meghan asked.

"No, Majesty." The faery shook his head. "There have been no sightings of her or Prince—" he stumbled over the word, looking pained "—or Keirran, in the wyldwood or anywhere in the Nevernever."

The Iron Queen nodded. "Very well," she said. "Keep monitoring the situation and let me know if anything changes. If Keirran or the First Queen appears, inform me at once."

"Yes, Your Majesty."

"That will be all. Dismissed."

The fey in the room put a fist to their hearts, bowed and shuffled out, weaving around us with polite nods. The Iron Queen remained at the table, gazing down at the surface, until they were gone, and silence descended on the room.

"Ethan." Meghan looked up from the war table. Her blue eyes were weary, sad, as they met mine across the room. "This is not where I wanted you to be, little brother," she said, and her voice was more resigned than angry. "You should be home, not on the front lines of this madness. You promised me that you would stay away from the war."

I swallowed. "I'm sorry, Meghan. But I can't. This is my fight, too."

"Stubborn." Shaking her head, Meghan came around the table, her gaze flicking to the Thin Man standing behind me. For a moment, a steely look crossed her face as she recognized the tall faery for what he really was. "And you are...?" she asked, a note of warning in her voice.

The Thin Man bowed. "An acquaintance of the family," he said in polite tones. "You might not realize it, Iron Queen, but I have been watching you and your kin for quite some time. We are more connected than you know."

"He's a friend, Meghan," I broke in, as the queen continued to regard him with suspicion. "He wants to stop the Lady and the Forgotten. He's been helping us find a way to bring Keirran back."

At Keirran's name, Meghan blinked, and her gaze shifted to me, the sudden hope within making my insides tighten. "Then...you have found a way?"

"Yeah," I said, and hesitated. "Well, sort of. It's complicated."

"Complicated." Meghan briefly closed her eyes. "I saw Keirran at the Tir Na Nog council," she went on. "I heard what he said. I know how strong he is, the great danger he poses to the Nevernever. I cannot allow my son to destroy those I care about." Her gaze lingered on me. "I made a promise to my people that I would protect them, from *all* threats. Even if the greatest threat comes from my own blood." She blinked rapidly, banishing the tears that were beginning to shine through, and stood firm. "I am queen. It is killing me but... I cannot let Keirran destroy this world, or the people whom I love. I will do anything to bring him home, but if he cannot be saved..."

"No." This time, it was Annwyl who spoke up, surprising me. The Summer girl stepped forward, her gaze beseeching, to face the Iron Queen.

"Your Majesty," she whispered, dropping her gaze as Meghan turned to her. "My name is Annwyl, former hand-maiden to Titania of the Summer Court. And I..." She trembled, took a deep breath to steady herself. "I am the one responsible for Keirran's betrayal."

"Annwyl," Kenzie broke in, as Meghan stared at the Summer faery, her expression unreadable. "That's not true. You didn't make Keirran do anything. Everything he did, he had a choice. We all did. Don't blame yourself for his actions."

Annwyl shook her head. "I was weak," she said, still not looking at any of us, especially not Meghan. "I knew I shouldn't have met with him. If I had only heeded the laws back then, none of this would have happened."

Meghan gave a slight frown. "Annwyl," she said slowly, as if just coming to the realization. "The Summer girl from Titania's court," she mused. "You...are the one Keirran fell in love with?"

"I am so sorry, Your Majesty," Annwyl said, and dropped to her knees, staring at the ground. "This whole mess can be traced back to me. Titania wanted me to meet with Keirran, to seduce him and earn his affections, and I couldn't refuse the queen. I met with the prince several times, knowing I would have to betray him in the end, that Titania would demand it. But..." Her voice trembled, and she clutched her hands to her chest to stop them from shaking. "When she ordered me to ask Keirran to kill one of her rivals, a Winter Court gentry, I couldn't do it. I had never disobeyed her before, and I knew she would exile me for treason, but I refused my queen's direct command for the first time in my life and was banished to the mortal realm. Because I had fallen for Keirran, as well.

"I knew our relationship was forbidden," Annwyl continued. "I knew we shouldn't be together, even if Keirran scoffed at the old laws. I should have broken his heart that first time, convinced him that I despised him, that I blamed him for my exile. It would have been kinder in the long run, to let him go. I should have let him go." Her eyes glimmered, and she finally looked up, meeting Meghan's gaze. "It's because of me that Keirran made all those bargains, and it's because of me that he went to see the Lady that night. Your brother died, and Keirran lost his soul…because of me."

Meghan closed her eyes. "Annwyl," she said quietly, and the Summer girl winced, as if bracing herself for punishment. But the Iron Queen's voice was calm as she opened her eyes and gazed down at her. "Stand up. Look at me. Falling in love is not a crime. Even if a relationship has been forbidden by the courts. I know my son. It is extraordinarily difficult to change his mind, about anything, once he makes a decision. I'm sure you have discovered how stubborn he can be." Annwyl gave a tiny laugh that was part sob as she rose, and Meghan smiled sadly. "I knew Keirran had fallen for someone," the Iron Queen went on. "He tried to hide it, but a mother always knows. I just hoped that whoever had captured his heart would treat it carefully, because he is very much like his father in that once he loves someone, he does it completely." A pained look crossed her face, before it was composed again. "I don't blame you for Keirran's decisions. I cannot be angry at you and Keirran for falling in love. You protected him from Titania at the cost of your own freedom. That is not the decision of a faery who is merely playing the game."

"Your Majesty is too kind," Annwyl said, and her voice was somewhat choked. "But I don't deserve your sympathy. Not when I have this."

Slowly, Annwyl reached for the cord beneath her dress and pulled the amulet into the light. The copper disk glimmered in her hand as she held it up, staring at it like a live scorpion rested in her palm.

"This...is what is keeping me alive," Annwyl whispered, as Meghan looked down at the amulet and went pale. I wondered if my sister could feel the dark magic pulsing within the copper disk. Or—and my stomach turned at the thought—could she somehow sense what the amulet truly contained? "This is what my existence is worth," the Summer faery went on, her own expression wrinkling with disgust. "Keirran's soul, and the destruction of the courts. I didn't want this," she whispered, as the metal disk reflected in her eyes. "I would have happily Faded away if I had known this would turn him into a monster."

"This is the amulet Ash was talking about?" Meghan asked. "This is what contains Keirran's soul?" And though her voice was still calm, I could hear the bridled fury, horror and despair beneath. Annwyl must've sensed it as well, for she went white to the point I thought she might pass out. But she nodded firmly.

"Yes, Your Majesty."

"Can it be destroyed?" Meghan asked in that same calm voice. Her eyes gleamed as she stared at the amulet, and I felt the immense power gathering around her, like the energy before a storm. As if she would shatter it herself in a moment. "Would that free Keirran's soul and return him to us?"

"It can be destroyed," Annwyl said slowly, her voice trembling. "But..."

"Keirran has to do it," I finished, and Meghan's gaze flicked to me. "Of his own free will. He has to make that choice himself."

"I see," Meghan murmured, and the energy around her flickered and died. I watched the realization creep over her, the same huge problem that had been plaguing me ever since I left Guro's house. How the hell were we going to convince Keirran, the self-proclaimed Destroyer of the Courts, to shatter the amulet himself? "And do you have a plan for how you're going to do that?" Meghan asked, as if reading my thoughts.

Not really, I thought, but thankfully Annwyl beat me to it. "I will talk to him," the Summer faery said. "He'll listen to me. At least, I hope he will." She closed her eyes, her voice dropping to a whisper. "I hope he is not so far gone that he has forgotten about us."

I nodded. "If Keirran will listen to anyone, it'll be Annwyl," I told Meghan. "The only problem will be *getting* to him. We don't really know where he is, except that he's never far from the First Queen, and that there's probably going to be a huge army of Forgotten between us."

Meghan's brow furrowed. "Ash and Puck are scouting the area where the Forgotten were last seen," she said. "There have been skirmishes along the borders, places where the Forgotten pop up out of nowhere, but we've never glimpsed the real army. No one has seen Keirran or the First Queen, either, though we suspect the Forgotten are getting ready to launch a full attack. If we can somehow reach Keirran before that happens, we can save him at the very least. But if he attacks with the Forgotten…" Meghan trailed off, shaking her head. "Even if I cannot strike the final blow, the other rulers will show him no mercy. If Keirran leads the Forgotten to war, we cannot hold back. The First Queen cannot be allowed to win."

"Iron Queen," the Thin Man said, and stepped forward. "If

I may… I have information about the First Queen that your people might not. I am willing to share it with you, and everyone, in the hopes that we *can* defeat the Lady. But we must work together. The First Queen of Faery ruled for a very long time before she was finally overthrown and forgotten. Do not underestimate her. She is not an opponent to take lightly."

Meghan nodded and straightened, looking at all of us. "I will call for a war council," she announced. "Mab and Oberon will want to hear this, and I want to explain the amulet to them. Maybe convince them not to slaughter Keirran on sight." Her eyes flashed, that dangerous energy swirling around her again, before she moved away. "I'll need to call a few of my forces back, so it could be a few hours until they show up. Until then, I'll have someone clear out a few tents. You all look like you could use the rest. Annwyl—" she glanced at the Summer faery "—I know that staying in the Iron camp is probably unpleasant for you. Will you be all right? I can speak to Oberon if you want to stay within Summer."

"I'm grateful, Your Majesty," Annwyl replied. "But there's no need. I…I don't feel the iron sickness like I should. Maybe the amulet sucks it away, but…" She looked down at her hands. "I don't think I'm entirely here, anymore. And, after what happened with Keirran and the Summer Queen, none of my kin really want me around. Titania made it very clear, within Arcadia at least, that I was the cause of Keirran's betrayal. There were even rumors that I was the one who ordered Keirran to attack the queen, to force her to lift my exile. So, I am not welcome in the Summer Court any longer, and there are likely those within Summer that wish me harm. If it's all the same to you, I would rather stay on this side of the border."

Meghan's gaze was sympathetic as she nodded. "Of course," she replied. "And don't worry about Titania. None of her servants will dare cross the border into Iron. You'll be safe here."

The Thin Man cleared his throat. "I, on the other hand, believe I will excuse myself," he said, tipping his hat to the queen. "Not to be rude, but I am finding the effects of your Iron kingdom unpleasant. I believe I will be elsewhere until you have need of me. Ethan Chase—" he glanced in my direction "—I will be close. Do not go after the prince without me."

He turned...and disappeared.

Meghan sighed. "Councilor Fix," she called quietly, and the packrat who had been busily scribbling notes shuffled forward, blinking. "Will you please arrange tents for Kenzie and Annwyl? We should have the space for it. See if you can get them something to eat, as well. Ethan—" she looked at me "—I want to speak with you a moment alone."

The packrat nodded and waddled from the tent, beckoning Kenzie and Annwyl to follow. Kenzie paused, looking at me, and I nodded. "Go on," I told her. "Go get food. I'll be all right." She hesitated, then followed Annwyl and Fix outside. There was a brief flash of sunlight as she pushed through the tent flaps, and then they were gone.

Alone with the Iron Queen, I held my breath, wondering if she would lecture me on wading right back into this mess, when I'd promised her I'd stay away. Meghan paused as if waiting for everyone to be out of earshot before turning to me.

"I spoke to Ash the night we came back from Tir Na Nog," she said, making my stomach drop. "He told me he let you and Kenzie out of the palace. He said you might be able to help Keirran, that a mortal who isn't bound by Faery law might succeed where we could not. Is that true?"

I nodded. I hadn't wanted to rat Ash out, but if he'd already confessed, there was no reason to deny it. "I know you wanted me to stay out of this," I told her, "but I can't just sit at home, knowing you and Keirran are out there, probably fighting each other. That would drive me completely nuts. Even if I don't have faery blood, I'm part of this family, which means I'm part of this war, whether you like it or not. Also…" I scrubbed the back of my head. "Don't blame Ash entirely. If he hadn't let us go that night, Kenzie would've insisted we do something anyway. And we'd probably be right back here."

Surprisingly, Meghan smiled. "I was furious with him," she said, "but he told me to have more faith in the human part of my family. I guess he was right. I have to remember that you've grown up, just like I had to." She gave me a wistful, slightly sad look. "Your birthday was three weeks ago in the mortal realm, did you know that?" she went on, making my brows shoot up. "You're eighteen now, Ethan. You're not a kid anymore."

I'm eighteen? The notion shocked me. I was legally an adult. It was a bittersweet realization. Eighteen had been the magic number that represented freedom, on many levels. On the one hand, I wasn't required to go to school or live with my parents. On the other, I hadn't really gotten much of a childhood, not a normal one, anyway. Meghan had been absent for much of it, and those years were truly gone now. I could never go back and relive them, hoping that my sister would come home and our family would finally be complete.

Meghan nodded, smiling faintly. "You've grown up so fast," she murmured, walking forward. Nostalgia colored her voice. "I still remember when you were four, wanting me to tell you and Floppy a story, so the monsters in your closet would go away."

I chuckled, shaking my head. "I haven't been that for a long time, sis."

"I know." Meghan stopped about a foot away, blue eyes solemn now as she gazed up at me. "And I know I've missed so much of your life, Ethan. I wish I could've been there, to watch you grow up. But, you have. And you've grown up into someone…that I'm so proud of." Her palm pressed against my cheek, brushing hair from my face. "I love you, little brother," she said, looking me right in the eye. "You've become more than anyone could have guessed, and no matter what happens, you will always be my family. I want you to know that, before you have to face Keirran again. Even if I couldn't be a part of your life, I was always thinking of you."

I swallowed hard. "We'll save him," I told her. "I swear it, Meghan. Even if I have to knock some sense into him myself. We'll bring Keirran back, and then we'll take down the First Queen and the Forgotten together."

She nodded, but her eyes were distant. "I hope you're right," she whispered. "I hope you can change the prophecy where I failed."

"I will," I promised. "And, Meghan?"

She was already pulling away, but paused, gazing back at me. I took a quick breath. "I don't blame you," I said softly, "or Ash. Or Keirran. I know…I realize now, it had to be this way. Took me a while, but I think I finally got it." Meghan's eyes glimmered, and I forced a wry grin. "So, no more whining from me about not visiting on my birthday or spring break or whatever. I'll just be happy to know that everyone in my family is alive."

Meghan smiled, even as a single tear slipped down her cheek. "That's always been my hope, as well."

Exhausted as I was, I couldn't sleep. Maybe because I was antsy for the upcoming council, though I knew that was likely several hours away. Or maybe because my brain wouldn't shut up and leave me alone. After devouring a bowl of stew and bread in my tent—finally, real food—I lay on my cot in the darkness, staring at the ceiling while my mind looped in endless circles.

We were close. Close to the end, however that might turn out. The Lady and the Forgotten were out there, as was Keirran. We had fought our way through the wyldwood, the Between and the Deep Wyld to find Annwyl. We'd rescued her and the amulet. We knew how to free the soul trapped inside. The pieces were all in place.

And it would all be for nothing, if we couldn't convince Keirran to destroy the *anting-anting* himself.

And even if we do convince him, I thought, *what then? The war isn't going to stop. The Forgotten aren't going to give up just because Keirran gets his soul back. Meghan and Ash have been worried about him, sure, but the real threat is the First Queen. Maybe that was her game all along; have the courts so focused on Keirran, they completely forget about her until it's too late.*

Whatever her reasons, the First Queen's ploy to use Keirran against the courts was a brilliant one. Whatever they might say, even if they knew better, Meghan and Ash would not strike down their own son, and the fey of Mag Tuiredh would probably hesitate to kill their former prince, as well. And Keirran was dangerous enough and powerful enough to pose a real threat to everyone but the rulers of the courts. So, what did you do? Slaughter him and face the terrible grief and wrath of the Iron Court and its queen, or let him live to wreak havoc as he willed it? A pretty crappy situation all around.

So that left us. Me, Kenzie, Annwyl, Razor and the Thin Man. To break through a Forgotten horde, find Keirran and talk some sense into him. Provided we could even find Keirran. And that he would listen to us if we did.

Groaning, I pressed the heels of my palms into my eyes. Same old fears, same old arguments, with no answers in sight. My thoughts felt like a hamster running on a wheel, spinning and spinning and getting nowhere. I wondered where Kenzie was, if her thoughts were driving her crazy, too.

"Ethan?"

A soft tap on the outer wall drew my attention to the door, and my heart leaped. "You in there, tough guy?" came Kenzie's soft, hesitant voice. "Are you asleep? Or are you lying on your bed obsessing about everything your sister told you this afternoon?"

I snorted. "I'm *planning*," I told the silhouette on the other side of the flap, "not obsessing. There's a difference."

"Uh-huh." The voice sounded severely unconvinced. "Well, whatever it is, are you decent, or should I come back later?"

"No," I answered, not moving from the cot. "I'm decent. Come on in."

The flap rustled as it opened, and a moment later, Kenzie's face appeared above me. She held a small lantern, and the light cast flickering shadows over her face and the cloth walls of the tent. "This," she announced with a smile, "does not look like planning to me. This definitely looks like obsessing."

I sighed in defeat. "Fine, I'm obsessing. Did you track me down just to point that out, or was there another reason?"

She grinned, put the lantern on the floor and plopped down to sit beside me, making me grunt. "Just keeping you honest, tough guy. If I didn't point it out, how would you know you were doing it? You might overobsess and miss out on the obvious thing right in front of you. Besides—" her voice softened a bit "—with everything going on, I couldn't sleep, either. And I didn't want to be alone." She turned to me with a bright grin. "So, I thought I would come pester you, so we could not sleep together. And...um... Yikes." Her face turned beet red as she realized what had just come out of her mouth. "Open mouth, insert foot, Kenzie, geez." Hunching her shoulders, she started sliding off the cot. "Right. I think I'm gonna find a nice hole to crawl in now."

Laughing, I snaked my arms around her waist and dragged her back. "Oh, no. Not a chance," I said as she yelped. "Considering *I'm* usually the one who says all the stupid crap, this is too good to pass up. You're not getting off that easy."

She struggled. Halfheartedly. "I do not say stupid things," Kenzie protested, trying to wriggle, unconvincingly, out of my grip. "That's *your* department, remember? I'm the smart one, you're the angry, stabby one. That's how this partnership works."

"Uh-huh." I grinned and did not relent. "What was that a few seconds ago, then?"

"I have no idea. I've blocked it from my memory."

"Right." I pinned her to the mattress, holding her wrists above her head with one hand. She smirked up at me, defiant, her lips just inches from mine…and I suddenly forgot what I was going to say.

So I kissed her instead.

Kenzie let out a tiny sigh and relaxed into me, her lips warm on mine, soft and caressing. I felt her tongue flick my bottom lip and parted my mouth to let her in, a groan escaping my throat. Her body shifted on the mattress, subtly arching into me, and all my nerve endings shot to attention.

I kissed her deeper, and she moaned, tilting her head to give me access to her neck. I trailed kisses down her jaw and throat, hearing her gasp, feeling her hands running the length of my back, sliding beneath my shirt. The touch of her soft fingers against my bare skin made me jerk up, shivering, to look into her eyes.

"Kenzie…" My voice came out a ragged whisper. My heart was pounding, and the feeling in my chest was caught somewhere between elated and terrified. Kenzie gazed up at me, beautiful and perfect, and I wanted nothing more than to lean down and kiss her, feel her, draw her into me until nothing separated us. My fingers tangled in her hair, aching to touch her, to trace her warm skin. But I forced myself to be still and gaze at the girl in my arms. I had made her a promise, and this decision wasn't mine. I wouldn't move another inch unless I knew she was certain.

"I can stop," I told her. "It doesn't have to be tonight. But, if we keep going..."

Her fingers stroked my cheek. "I want this, Ethan," she whispered, making my heart turn over. "I think...I think I'm ready." She trembled, but her voice remained calm, resolute. "I've never felt this way, about anyone. While I still have the chance, I want it to be tonight, and I want it to be with you."

"Are you sure?" My own voice was not nearly as calm as hers, emerging as a somewhat choked rasp. She nodded, her eyes dark with emotion as she gazed up at me, and I swallowed the nerves crawling up my throat. "Kenzie, you know that I haven't... With the fey around, I never got close enough to anyone to..."

I could feel my face heating like an inferno at the confession. For so long I'd pushed people away, kept my distance, for fear of what the fey would do if I got close. I thought I was destined to live my life alone, caring for no one, so the fey wouldn't care about them, as well. Falling in love had not been part of the plan.

But Kenzie smiled and gently pulled me down, kissing me so that the words, and my last remaining fears, died in my throat. "No one's judging, tough guy," she whispered. "And—finally—no one is here but us. We'll figure it out together."

And, as the night went on and a predawn stillness settled over the Nevernever, we did.

CHAPTER SEVENTEEN

THE SECOND COUNCIL

"Ethan Chase?"

An insistent tapping wrenched me out of a comfortable sleep. Blearily, I cracked open my eyes, glaring at the far wall and the packrat-shaped silhouette beyond the tent flaps. I was warm, a heavy quilt covered my body, and most important, my arm was still curled around a sleeping Kenzie. For maybe the first time since I'd come to the Nevernever, I was reluctant to move.

Tap tap tap. "Ethan Chase?" *Tap tap tap.* "Are you in there? Are you awake?"

"No," I growled over Kenzie's shoulder. "Go away."

The packrat hesitated, maybe confused by the obvious lie out of my mouth, or that I'd given him an order he couldn't obey. "Forgive me, Prince Ethan," it continued timidly, "but Her Highness the queen has requested your presence. The prince consort and Robin Goodfellow have arrived. The war council is about to start."

I sighed. "All right," I called softly, hoping I wouldn't wake Kenzie just yet. "I'm coming. Tell them I'm on my way."

The silhouette bobbed and shuffled off, taking its annoying *tap-taps* with it. I levered myself to an elbow and gently pulled back the quilt, just enough to reveal the girl beside me.

As usual, Kenzie was dead to the world, sleeping soundly, her beautiful face free of worry and stress. Damn, I loved her. I wished we could've had a little more time. Without faery wars, politics and ancient Forgotten queens screwing everything up.

But wishing never worked in the Nevernever. Not like you wanted it to.

I kissed Kenzie's shoulder, then nuzzled below her ear, slipping an arm around her waist. She stirred with a sigh, then dark brown eyes cracked open to peer back at my face.

"Hey," I greeted, and she gave me a sleepy smile that made me want to kiss her all over again. I restrained myself, remembering what was at stake. "This is going to suck, but the war council is here. They're waiting for us."

Her nose wrinkled, and she groaned, trying to pull the covers over her head. "Five more minutes," she mumbled.

I chuckled. "Yeah, sadly, faeries aren't known for their patience. I don't think that will go over well." She groaned again, and I kissed the back of her neck. "You don't have to come," I told her, sliding back off the cot. "Stay here and sleep if you want. But I have to go."

She *harrumphed* and sat up, pulling the quilt around herself. "No, I'm coming, too," she sighed as I yanked on my jeans, then grabbed my T-shirt at the foot of the bed. "No rest for the weary, I suppose."

I pulled my shirt over my head, then searched around for my sword belt. "Look on the bright side," I said, dragging it out from beneath the cot. "At least Razor didn't pop in last night screaming *kissy-kissy* and making me want to kill him."

"I wonder where he is?" Kenzie mused, gazing around the tent, as if the bat-eared monster could be hiding in the shadows. "I hope he's okay with the other gremlins, wherever they are."

"I'm sure he'll show up eventually," I said, buckling my

swords to my waist. "Probably at the most inopportune time possible." Grabbing my shoes, I strode to the bed, bent down and kissed her on the mouth. "I'll wait outside," I told her, pulling back. "Take your time, but if I start to hear snoring, I'm going on without you."

Kenzie frowned. "I don't snore! Do I snore?"

"Um. I should go," I answered, and fled the tent.

Outside, the sky was still dark, but the Iron camp itself pulsed with gentle light, from the lampposts on the corners, to fey carrying lanterns, to the metallic fireflies that blipped through the air in shades of orange, blue and green. It was peaceful, quiet. The calm before the storm.

Kenzie emerged from the tent and yawned, stretching her arms over her head. I slipped up behind her, winding my arms around her waist, and kissed the side of her neck. "Ready?"

"Not really," she sighed, leaning into me. "But I guess we can't keep them waiting any longer."

I laced her hand through mine, and we walked through the quiet streets of the Iron camp, passing knights and the occasional wire nymph, until we reached the large commander's tent in the middle. A trio of Winter knights waited on one outside corner, glaring at the squad of Summer knights on the opposite side, so it looked like Mab and Oberon were already here. Ignoring the dark looks from Summer and Winter, we walked up to the entrance, nodded to the lone Iron knight who guarded the door, and slipped inside.

Meghan stood at the head of the table again, which was surrounded by fey once more. Only this time, instead of scouts and random Iron fey, all the heavy hitters of Faery stood shoulder to shoulder with each other. Oberon was there, and Titania the Summer Queen, looking like she would rather be anywhere else. Mab stood across from them, radiating power and causing one side of the table to be edged with frost. Ash stood to one side of Meghan, appearing grim and protective, and Robin Goodfellow leaned casually against a wall with his arms crossed and faint smirk plastered to his face, as if he found all of this secretly amusing. There were other faeries in the room: scouts and lieutenants, Glitch and one very large troll captain, but those six were the only fey that mattered.

Well, seven, really.

Annwyl stood a little behind Meghan, head bowed, eyes downcast, almost invisible. If it wasn't for the dull glint from the amulet, I wouldn't even have noticed her standing there. She seemed...less real than the faeries surrounding her, more shadow than anything, and the rest of the fey didn't appear to notice her, either.

They *did* notice me and Kenzie when we walked into the room. "Ah, there he is," Puck announced, grinning as we approached the table. His green eyes flashed mischievously as he gave us a mocking salute. "All hail the conquering hero. Winning battles before the war even starts, hey, Ethan Chase?"

I willed my face not to turn red. Off to one side, Glitch coughed loudly, covering his mouth with a fist, and Meghan and Ash shared a brief, secret smile. I forced my thoughts away from what that could mean and reminded myself to punch Goodfellow in the jaw before this was all over.

"If we can get back to business." Oberon's voice was not amused, and the murmurs from the rest of the fey swiftly died down. "Now that the mortals have finally arrived, perhaps you can tell us why you have summoned this council, Iron Queen?"

"Yes." Meghan took a step forward, standing tall as she faced the rest of the table. "There has been a new development regarding Keirran," she announced, commanding everyone's attention instantly. "I realize no one has seen Keirran or the First Queen, but I believe this is important enough to call a council. There might be a way to stop Keirran without killing him, to break whatever hold the First Queen has on him."

"And why would we do that, Iron Queen?" Titania asked, her smooth, high voice making me bristle with dislike. "Your son is a traitor to Faery. He betrayed us all and sided with a usurper, an offense punishable by death. Prince Keirran will show us no mercy. By his own admission, he seeks to annul the courts. Why should we stay our hand?"

"Because he is still my son," Ash said in a cool, low voice, staring the Summer Queen in the eye. "And no matter what Keirran does, whatever madness drives him to betray his own, that will not change." A thread of steel entered Ash's voice, a promise and a subtle threat to everyone there. "I will not allow my son to be destroyed in front of me. Not when there is a chance to save him."

"I have to agree with ice-boy," Puck added, pushing himself off the wall. "This—this whole war and destruction and gloom and doom thing—isn't like the princeling. I mean, I've known the kid most of his life. I practically helped raise him, despite frequent threats on *my* life. It's like certain unnamed parties didn't want me teaching him the good stuff." He grinned at Ash across the table, before sobering. "Keirran would never want this," Puck went on, shaking his head. "And I'm kinda uncomfortable with the thought of taking him out if the real problem is that he's lost his soul."

"And what of the prophecy?" Oberon asked. "We all knew this was coming, and despite what Keirran was, the warning remains. *The Iron Prince will unite the courts or destroy them.* He has already chosen his path, and it is Destroyer. No one can argue that."

"Um." Kenzie's voice surprised us all. Stepping around me, she walked up to the table as a couple dozen faeries all turned to her. "Not to be rude," she said, as Oberon and Mab regarded her with varying degrees of curiosity and amusement, "but, based on the wording of that prophecy, Keirran has already united the courts."

Mab frowned. "Explain, human," she said flatly. Kenzie rubbed her arm.

"Well, the prophecy didn't exactly say he had to bring the courts together himself. But...he *is* the reason you're all here tonight. Together. Under one banner—Summer, Winter and Iron." Kenzie gazed around the table, at all the rulers, and shrugged. "So, if you look at it that way, then Keirran *has* united the courts. *Against* him, sure, but the prophecy didn't say how or why. So, if he's already united the courts, then that means he doesn't necessarily have to destroy them."

For a moment, there was silence, as all the fey, the kings and queens of Faery itself, appeared to be struck speechless. Or at least pondering Kenzie's statement. Puck opened his mouth once, closed it, then leaned toward me.

"So, how did such a smart girl end up with you?" he muttered.

I snorted. "You got me."

Meghan shook herself. "Regardless," she said, taking control of the meeting again, "we think we have the answer to returning Keirran to himself." She raised a hand, and Annwyl stepped up meekly, eyes still downcast. I heard Titania's sniff of disdain and clenched my fists, remembering what the queen had done to her. The amulet pulsed around the girl's neck like a sullen heartbeat, and some of the other fey drew back from the table edge.

"How interesting, Iron Queen," Titania said, contempt oozing off her honeyed voice. "You have brought the prince's disgraced, forbidden lover back into the Nevernever. Flaunting your disrespect for our laws, just as you and the Winter prince flaunted them years ago. Like mother, like son, I suppose."

"Annwyl chose to come here," Meghan said calmly, as I seethed with loathing toward the Summer Queen, wishing Meghan would just lose it and shove an iron pole up Titania's ass. "She is under the protection of the Iron Realm, and you will not force her to leave again, Queen Titania. Her exile is over."

"What is that thing she is wearing?" Mab inquired, staring at the amulet glimmering in the dim light. "I can feel its anger from here. A cursed object to be certain."

"Yes," Meghan agreed. "This is the item responsible for Keirran's change of heart. Why he sided with the First Queen and the Forgotten. Why he has turned on us. If it's destroyed, we hope Keirran will return to the way he was."

"Then why not destroy it now?" Oberon wondered, and the air around him crackled, like the energy before a lightning storm. "Place the cursed thing on the table, and we will take care of it here."

"No," I said quickly. "It doesn't work like that."

All eyes shifted to me. "No one else can destroy the amulet," I said. "If you do, you're pretty much assuring he'll lose his soul forever. Keirran has to do it himself."

Another moment of silence as the circle of fey realized what that meant. "Then," Oberon said slowly, "someone must take the amulet to Keirran, and either convince or trick him into destroying it. How do you expect to accomplish this, Iron Queen?"

"I will do it," Annwyl said, quiet but firm, lifting her eyes from the table. "If I can get to Keirran, I can talk to him. He'll listen to me. I can convince him to destroy the amulet."

"And how do you expect to reach the Iron Prince, much less convince him?" Mab wanted to know. "No one has seen Keirran, or the Forgotten army, anywhere in the Nevernever. You cannot speak to someone who is not here."

"Ah...I believe I can help with that," said a voice, and the Thin Man appeared in the corner. Fey jumped, put their hands on their swords, uncertain whether or not to attack. Meghan raised an arm.

"Hold," she said sharply. "I called him to this gathering. He is not an enemy. If you all would listen to him, he's here to help."

"A Forgotten?" Oberon gave the Thin Man a suspicious look, his face cold. "Why would you help us?" he demanded. "Your queen intends to destroy the courts, remake the Never-never and give it to her followers. What do you seek to gain from opposing her?"

"She is not," the Thin Man said firmly, "my queen. You all have forgotten the days before, when the Lady ruled. You chose to purge it from your memories, erase all knowledge of the First Queen, so that not even the Nevernever remembers what it was like before the courts existed. But a few of us remember. Oh, yes, a few of us know what will happen if the First Queen wins this war."

"Which is why the amulet must be destroyed," purred a familiar voice, and Grimalkin looked up from the middle of the table, his tail curled around his legs. Nobody seemed shocked to see him. "The Lady's secret weapon is the Iron Prince," the cat went on, slitting his eyes at us. "On her own, she is powerful, yes, but he is the instrument that will bring destruction to the courts and the Nevernever. The prophecy is not about the First Queen. The Iron Prince has always been the key."

"As I believe you know, the Iron Prince has learned how to open the Between," the Thin Man said, picking up where Grimalkin left off. "That is how he has been able to avoid detection, and that is how the First Queen has been hiding her army of Forgotten. The prince will be with the Lady in the Between, so naturally, you will need someone to part the

Veil, enter the Between and find him. And, as I am the only one here with that skill, I guess it falls to me." He pointed to me. "I can take Ethan Chase and the Summer girl into the Between to find the prince. Beyond that, any convincing will be up to them."

"If this creature can open the Veil," Mab said, "let us march our armies into the First Queen's territory and force them to engage us now."

"Ah, no," the Thin Man said with a grimace. "I cannot do that. Sending a whole army through the Veil takes tremendous power—power I myself do not have. Not only that, the Veil is still quite unstable. Packing that much glamour, power and emotion within the Between could have disastrous consequences. The Forgotten have no glamour and little to no memories, so they can slip between worlds without leaving any scars of their passing. That is not the case with your armies or yourselves. A war in the Between itself might very well tear it apart again. Perhaps permanently this time." The Thin Man narrowed his pale eyes. "And I do believe that is exactly what the First Queen wants."

None of the faery rulers argued with him, not even Titania. "So, fighting in the Between is a no-no, got it," Puck remarked, and shrugged. "Okay, then. Let's say Ethan and Annwyl convince the princeling to stop being a jerk and come home. Yay for that. Anyone have any ideas on how to lure the First Queen out of her safe little hidey-hole? Maybe she likes cake?"

"Master!"

A shrill cry rent the air before anyone could reply, and Kenzie jerked up. A second later, a tiny streak of darkness flew through the opening and launched itself at Kenzie with a cry.

Mab rolled her eyes. "Apparently we cannot get through even one meeting without cats and Forgotten and Iron fey popping in whenever they please," she remarked, as Razor scrambled all over Kenzie, buzzing in a shrill, frantic voice. "What does the creature want, mortal? Silence it or get it out."

"Razor!" Kenzie snatched the gremlin off her shoulder and held him at arm's length. He hissed and crackled like a bad radio station, and she frowned. "I don't understand gremlin, Razor. English! What's going on?"

"Master!" Razor squawked. "Master coming! Master coming now!"

My blood chilled as, almost at the same time, the tent flaps opened and a Summer knight dropped to a knee in the frame.

"Forgive me, Your Majesties," it gasped. "But there is a large horde of Forgotten approaching the Summer side of the camp. We think they mean to attack!"

"Ready the troops!" Oberon boomed, striding from the tent. "Gather our knights and protect the front lines! Go!"

Chaos erupted. Mab's voice rose alongside Oberon's, calling for her warriors, gathering them for battle. Meghan nodded to Ash and Glitch, and the two fey strode off, probably to take control of the Iron Realm's forces and prepare them for war. I drew my swords, staying close to Kenzie and Annwyl, as faeries swarmed around us, heading for the Summer side of the camp. Gripping my blades, I started to follow.

"Ethan!" Meghan turned, the mantle of the Iron Queen surrounding her, snapping with power. "Keep back from the front lines," she ordered, her tone brooking no argument. "Stay here where it's safer. I don't want you in the thick of things."

"Dammit, Meghan, I can fight—"

"I know you can," the Iron Queen interrupted. "But you have something else to do, Ethan, you and Annwyl." She glanced at the Summer faery, a flicker of anguish crossing her face, before turning to me again. "Your fight isn't with the Forgotten. It's with Keirran. If no one else can save him, I must depend on you. So, please." She grabbed my shoulder. "Stay here. Protect Annwyl and Kenzie. Will you do that, for my peace of mind?"

I slumped, nodding. "Yeah," I muttered. She was right; much as I wanted to stand with her and the rest of my family, I couldn't go throwing myself into battle with the Forgotten. I still had to deal with Keirran.

Meghan squeezed my shoulder, her eyes intense. "Stay safe, little brother," she whispered, a sister once more, and whirled away. I watched her stride after the other rulers, knights and other Iron fey falling in behind her, and made my own promise to see her again when this was all over.

I walked back to Kenzie and Annwyl, who were hovering close to Meghan's tent as the rest of the army rushed past them. Razor perched on Kenzie's shoulder, eyes wide as he pressed close, muttering nonsense.

"You okay, tough guy?" Kenzie asked, watching me with concern. She seemed nervous about the impending attack but not frightened. Behind her, Annwyl watched the fey prepare for battle with the same calm resignation she did everything now. I sheathed my swords, then reached for Kenzie and pulled her close, wrapping my arms around her. Razor was either so anxious or shell-shocked that he didn't even grin at me.

"We should probably find somewhere safe to hole up," I muttered, watching the last of the Iron fey scurry off after their queen. "From the looks of it, things are going to get pretty crazy."

"Do you think Keirran will be with the Forgotten army?" Annwyl asked, her voice distant as she stared after the rulers. I frowned at her.

"Even if he is, you can't go charging after him yourself, Annwyl," I warned. "He'll be surrounded by Forgotten, and there will be faeries fighting and tearing each other apart. It's too dangerous to look for Keirran now."

"I know," she answered, much to my relief. "I understand what's at stake, Ethan Chase. I won't endanger that."

"Smart girl," said the Thin Man, turning into existence beside us. "Glad to see that we are all keeping our heads." His gaze rose past us, following the direction where Meghan and the kings and queens of Faery had vanished into the dark. "Strange that the Forgotten would choose to attack now," he mused, narrowing his eyes. "This seems most unlike them. Why march at us head-on when they can all slip through the…"

His eyes widened. "Oh, you clever boy!" he hissed, and strode forward. "Call them back!" We all stared at him, and he whirled around, vanishing from sight for a split second. "The army must fall back! The rulers must return at once! The Forgotten are about to ambush us from behind!"

"Ethan!" Kenzie gasped. "Look!"

I spun. Behind us, a crack appeared in the air, a tear in the fabric of reality. As I watched, horrified, it swiftly widened, showing the misty darkness of the Between beyond. And then a flood of shadows and glowing yellow eyes poured out of the breach like ants and swarmed to attack us.

CHAPTER EIGHTEEN

THE DESTROYER

"Run!"

I pushed Kenzie forward as Razor gave a screech of terror and bounced away. "Go!" I yelled. "We have to get to Meghan and the rest of the army. Go!"

They went, sprinting through the tent aisles, the Thin Man and myself close behind. I spared a glance over my shoulder and saw the massive horde of Forgotten still pouring from the gap, a flood of dark shadows. Some were normal-sized; some were larger and malformed, with huge heads and arms that dragged the ground when they walked. A few were enormous, towering over their smaller kin as they lumbered forward. I saw a dozen different types of Forgotten in one glance, but they were all blurred, indistinct shadows with wisps of darkness trailing behind. Featureless silhouettes except for their glowing yellow eyes.

And they were catching up. A pack of lean, doglike things raced toward us, making no noise as they leaped over tents and between aisles. One raced beside me, snapping pointed jaws at my ankles, and I cursed as I drew my sword. It leaped aside as I slashed at it, and the rest of the pack closed in. I felt one's teeth snag my jeans and stumbled with a stab of fear, barely catching myself. If I fell, that would be it. The dogs would maul me to death, and I'd be swallowed whole by a black flood of Forgotten.

Snarling, I hacked at one dog and saw it erupt in a billow of shadow before it disappeared. At the same time, another pair of sharp fangs closed around my ankle, and I felt myself falling.

Just as I hit the ground, there was a blur of darkness, much bigger than the Forgotten hounds, as something huge bowled into the pack with a roar, knocking them aside like stick figures. The pack yelped and scattered, and I shoved myself upright as a massive furry creature bounded to my side, long fangs flashing in the darkness.

"Wolf?"

"Go!" the massive faery snarled, facing the oncoming horde. "I'll slow them down. Move!" Baring his teeth, he roared a challenge, making the ground tremble, and sprang forward, straight for the army of Forgotten. Who, though I couldn't be sure, seemed to hesitate as the enormous Wolf barreled toward them like a freight train. Then Kenzie dragged me to my feet, and we continued to run.

I caught a glimpse of silvery battle mail between tents and angled toward it, feeling the silent flood of the Forgotten at my back. "Meghan!" I howled, and the figure turned, eyes going wide as she spotted me. "Meghan, turn the army around! The Forgotten are here—"

There was a blast of wind overhead, and a huge, winged Forgotten landed in front of us with a shriek. Flaring dark, spiny wings, it reared back to strike.

A streak of lightning descended from the sky, slamming into the Forgotten, which exploded into a cloud of smoke and writhed away. Meghan stood in the center of a cyclone, one arm outstretched, her hair whipping about in the gale. Her eyes glowed a piercing blue-white in the darkness, and as the Forgotten surged forward, she raised both arms toward the oncoming horde.

The ground trembled, then erupted in a tangle of metal roots and vines that glittered and scraped as they coiled into the air. They surged into the Forgotten, smashing and crushing, flinging shadowy bodies away, and a thick black mist began boiling out from the edge of the army.

Gasping, we backed away from the carnage, as the sheer numbers of the horde began pushing through. But with a shout, the troops of Summer, Winter and Iron raced past the Iron Queen, slamming into the waves of Forgotten, and all hell broke loose around us.

I retreated with Kenzie and Annwyl, trying to keep myself between the girls and the battle raging on all sides. I caught glimpses of the Thin Man here and there, slashing at things around us, but concentrated on keeping Kenzie and Annwyl safe. A Forgotten knight rushed us, swinging a huge black sword at my head. I dodged, rolling under the blow, and slashed at his legs as I came up again. He staggered, and I plunged my other sword through his back, making him dissipate in a coil of mist. A swarm of small, pointy-eared things bounced around me, jabbing with sharp little daggers, making me dodge and dance around to avoid being stabbed. One of them darted past me and up Kenzie's leg to her shoulder, but was shoved off by a furious shrieking Razor and booted away by Kenzie when it hit the ground. I cursed, slashed the last of the tiny creatures into nothing and rushed toward her.

"Ow," she muttered, cradling her arm as I hurried up. Blood was oozing down her skin, making my breath catch in horror. "Little bastard had sharp claws."

"Dammit, we're too exposed out here," I growled. We had to find a safer spot or risk getting torn to shreds. Meghan was gone, having disappeared into the fray, though the swirling storm overhead and the flashes of lightning told me she was still kicking Forgotten ass. I couldn't see the other rulers, but I figured they were out there somewhere, wreaking havoc. A six-legged Forgotten sprang at me, teeth bared, but a tree root uncurled from the ground and smashed it to the earth. Annwyl winced, swaying on her feet, and Kenzie caught her as she staggered. I made my decision.

"Come on," I told them both, raising my swords. "Fall back. Let's get to the river. At least we'll be protected on one side there."

They nodded, but a Summer knight suddenly went hurtling by, hitting the ground a few feet away and rolling to a crumpled stop. The ground trembled, and a huge, four-armed Forgotten lumbered forward, smashing knights aside with a pair of clubs. A single eye in the center of its blocky face peered down at me as it roared and raised the weapons high overhead.

A flurry of gleaming ice daggers spun through the air, striking the Forgotten in the face, and it staggered back with a bellow. Ash strode toward us, blue ice-sword unsheathed, and the giant howled a challenge, whirling to face him.

It didn't see the lean, red-haired faery sprint up behind it, launch off its meaty thigh and plant a dagger in its back as it came down again. Howling, the Forgotten flailed, completely forgetting about us in its quest to smash Puck into the ground. Puck laughed and danced around the giant's legs, avoiding the two clubs that swung at him, sometimes missing by centimeters. The Forgotten bellowed in fury as the Great Prankster led it farther away, and I slumped in relief.

"Are you three all right?" Ash asked, giving us a concerned look as he strode up. His silver gaze went to Kenzie's arm and narrowed. "Mackenzie, you're bleeding. Ethan, you need to get them away from here. Now."

I nodded. "Where?" I asked, and Ash pointed behind him.

"Head toward the Summer side of the camp. The fighting hasn't quite reached there yet. Look for the watchtower by the river. You'll be safe if you make it inside." He raised his sword. "Get going. We'll hold them off."

A whoop caught our attention. Puck stood on the end of the Forgotten's huge club, grinning devilishly as the giant scanned the ground, not seeing him perched there. Reaching over, the red-haired prankster tapped its shoulder, and the Forgotten jerked up, bellowing in anger as Puck waved cheekily.

"Right here, ugly."

Ash sighed. "Go," he told us, as the Forgotten smashed at Puck with the other club, and ended up hitting itself in the arm as Puck leaped away. "Protect yourselves. We're starting to push them back, so hopefully this will be over soon. Go!"

I grabbed Kenzie's hand and went, hearing Puck's mocking laughter behind me as I did. We dodged and wove our way through faeries and Forgotten, avoiding the fighting as best we could. A Summer and Winter knight fought side by side, icy sword and fiery spear whirling in tandem. A pack of goblins swarmed another large Forgotten, stabbing with their bony knives until the giant, leaking smoke from a dozen wounds, finally dissolved into mist.

"Behind you, Ethan Chase!" came the Thin Man's voice, and I spun, slashing with my blade. A Forgotten, swooping from the air, met a sudden end on my sword edge, and the Thin Man appeared beside me, gesturing toward a line of tents ahead.

"We're almost there! The watchtower is on the other side of the—"

I felt a pulse go through the air, a sudden surge of immense power, before a shrieking gale ripped the row of tents from the ground and scattered them and several fey in every direction. I staggered back, shielding my face as wind buffeted me, crackles of electricity raising the hair on my arms.

Wincing, I looked up, and the blood froze in my veins. Keirran was walking toward us, hair and cloak snapping in the wind, strands of lightning flickering all around him. His sword was at his side, and his eyes glowed blue-white with power. The look on his face was terrifying—murderous and completely without emotion.

A line of Winter knights rushed him; Keirran waved his hand and lightning streaked from his palm, slamming into the warriors and flinging them back. Roaring, a huge green troll bore down on the prince, tusks and claws gleaming as it barreled toward him. Keirran casually flicked a glance at it, and the troll froze midstride as ice coated its body, turning it into a statue. With a gesture from the prince, the enormous faery shattered, raining to the ground in a thousand glittering shards. I cringed, and Keirran's cold, emotionless gaze flickered to me, a faint smile crossing his face.

"Hello, Uncle."

"Kenzie, get back!" I shouted, drawing my swords as Keirran raised a hand, and a blinding streak of lightning shot toward me. I felt the deadly charge of electricity sizzle through the air and didn't even have time to blink as the lightning bolt slammed into a tree two feet away, splintering the trunk and setting it on fire. I dived aside, rolling to my feet to face my nephew, who looked mildly annoyed that I was still alive.

"Keirran, don't do this."

He shook his head. "You're too late, Ethan," he said calmly. "Summer and Winter will fall, as will the Veil, and once that happens, once the mortal world can see us permanently, no faery will have to fear Fading away again."

"That's not a solution, Keirran!" I shouted, circling around him, away from Kenzie and Annwyl. "What do you think humans will do once they can see the fey? You think we're all just going to get along? People are going to get hurt! Fey are going to be killed! You can't go through with this!"

"I am going through with it," Keirran replied. His voice sent shivers up my spine; it was flat and emotionless, his eyes blank as he watched me. "Because that's what the Lady desires, and I will be the instrument to carry it through. This is my destiny, Ethan. You and I, we were always meant to become enemies." He raised a hand, cold Winter glamour swirling around him, coating the ground with frost. Spears of ice formed above his fingers, crinkling sharply as they grew into existence, making my gut knot. "I'm sorry it had to be this way."

"Keirran, no!"

Annwyl's voice rang out, and the Summer girl stepped in front of me, facing the prince down. Keirran hesitated, the ice spears trembling overhead as he stared at her.

"This isn't what you want, Keirran," Annwyl said, her voice somehow rising over the howl of the wind and the shrieks of battle around us. "I know this isn't you. The Keirran I know, the Keirran I love, he would never turn on his family. On all of us. Please—" she held out her hand "—you can still stop this. Come back to us. Come back to me."

"Annwyl." For just a moment, Keirran's voice shook, and he closed his eyes. When he opened them, they were the same: cold, blank, resigned. "I loved you, once," he murmured, and my heart sank. "I think, deep down, a part of me still does." He shook his head, and his voice grew hard again. "But it's far too late for me now. I can't ever be that prince you knew before. And if you stand in my way, I won't show any mercy." Annwyl's face went white, and Keirran gave a sad smile. "Hate me now, but everything I've done was for you."

"Keirran!" Annwyl started forward, but Keirran gestured

sharply with his other hand, and a blast of wind slammed the Summer faery aside, causing her to tumble to the ground. At the same time, he flung out his arm, and the cluster of lethal ice spears flew toward me.

I winced and turned away, bracing for a dozen icicles to slam into my body. I felt the wind from their passing, heard the thumps as they struck the ground and trees around me, felt the burn of cold as they left trails of frost on my skin... but no pain.

I glanced up, and saw Keirran looking as surprised as I felt. A field of ice spears surrounded me, glittering in the moonlight, but the space around my feet was clear. Every single one had missed me.

"Oh, yeah." I grinned and looked back at Keirran, raising my swords. "Forgot about that. Apparently, the Nevernever chose me as its champion. I'm immune to magic and glamour now. Isn't that a fun little fact? Kinda levels the playing field."

Keirran scowled. Raising his hand, he sent another flurry of ice spears at me. This time, I didn't move, watching as they veered to the side, never touching my skin. He gestured, and a lightning bolt flashed from the air, curling around me to slam into the ground, leaving a smoking hole in the dirt. A pulse of glamour went through the ground a second before a tangle of roots and vines erupted, writhing and coiling madly, thorns and woody talons raking the air, but nothing touched me.

I smirked, walking forward through the storm of Winter and Summer glamour, feeling it slide and pass over my skin. "Looks like you're not the only one who's destined," I said, as Keirran's face darkened with every step I took. A surge of cold swirled toward me, veered away and turned a nearby tree into an icicle, shattering it a moment later. "If you want to kill me, Prince, you're going to have to do it the old-fashioned way."

Keirran's eyes narrowed to icy slits. "So it seems," he murmured, and raised his own weapon as I approached. "Very well. If that's the case, then I guess a sword through the heart is the only alternative—aagh!"

He jerked, arching back, as a slender blade punched through his shoulder, spraying blood as it tore through his armor. The Thin Man, his mouth set into a grim line, appeared for a split second behind the prince, clutching the blade sunk into Keirran's shoulder. The prince whirled, tearing free of the sword, and slashed at his assailant with his own weapon, but the Thin Man was already gone.

"Keirran!" Annwyl cried, as the prince staggered, clutching his shoulder. Blood dripped from his fingers and spread over his shirt as he glared around, searching for his attacker. The Thin Man appeared beside me, the prince's blood smeared across his sword, his face solemn. I grabbed his arm.

"Hey! What the hell are you doing?"

"What I must, Ethan Chase." The Thin Man wrenched his arm from my grasp. "You heard the Iron Prince. You heard the confession from his own lips. He is not going to stop, and if we let him live, he will destroy the Veil with the First Queen. I waited this long in the hopes that the Summer girl would be able to reach him, but now that she cannot, our course is clear. The Iron Prince must die." His pale gaze shifted to me. "And you must kill him."

My stomach dropped. "No," I rasped, glaring at the Thin Man. "I can't. Not yet."

"But I can, Ethan Chase," said a smooth, feminine voice behind us.

A streak of lightning shot from the air, slamming into Keirran as he straightened, flinging him back. Annwyl cried out as he struck the ground several yards away, and I whirled to see Titania the Summer Queen striding forward, her lips curled in a savage grin.

"Prince Keirran," Titania called, eager and unmerciful, as Keirran staggered to his feet, wind and dust whipping around him. His eyes glowed as he glared at the Summer Queen. "I have been waiting for you. We have unfinished business, you and I." She raised her hand, and a swirl of black clouds appeared overhead, flickering and deadly. "You will not escape me a second time. If the Chase boy will not end your life, then I will!"

"No, you will not!" A blast of snow and frigid air, and Queen Mab appeared, grabbing Titania's arm before she could bring it down. "You will not slay any of my kin!" Mab hissed at the other queen through bared teeth. A squad of Winter knights appeared, marching toward Keirran with ice spears raised, as Titania spun on Mab. "I will not allow it!" the Winter Queen snarled "The Iron Prince is not yours to destroy!"

"How *dare* you!" The Summer monarch wrenched her arm back, eyes flashing, and the two faeries faced off in the center of the field, glamour swirling around them.

Okay, this was getting nuts. I winced, afraid the two queens would lay into each other right then and possibly blow the entire camp to smithereens in the process, but Keirran threw up an arm, and a flash of light shot from his fingertips, spearing into the air and turning everything white for a split second. The ground started to shake, and a hedge of thorns and bramble clawed its way up from the ground, forming a spiny, bristling wall between us and Keirran. In the time it took for me to blink, the barrier shuddered and turned to iron, blackened and poisonous, and still crawling toward us over the ground. The knights halted, falling back from the creeping metal barrier with alarmed cries, and thankfully caused enough of a distraction to stop the queens from attacking each other right then.

The sounds of battle faded. Panting, I looked around.

From what I could see, the fighting had nearly stopped, and most of the Forgotten army was in the process of fleeing. I wondered if the beam of light Keirran had thrown up was some sort of retreat signal. I looked around at the carnage left behind—churned ground, blasted trees, ice daggers sticking out of everything—and felt my heart pound. Where was Kenzie? She had, very wisely, gotten out of the way when Keirran attacked, but then everything had gone insane, and I'd lost sight of her. Had she gotten caught in the cross fire? I'd never forgive myself if she'd been hurt, again.

"Kenzie!" I called, looking around wildly. A few yards away, Annwyl stared at the wall of thorns, her gaze unreadable. Mab was ordering her knights to tear it down while Titania glared sullenly. I didn't see the Thin Man anywhere, but he was the least of my worries. "Kenzie!" I yelled again. "Can you hear me? Where are you?"

"Here." She emerged from behind a stack of crates, looking pale and shaken, her hair tossed by the wind, but otherwise fine. Relief flared, and I caught her as she rushed up, crushing her to me.

"You okay?" I whispered into her hair, and she nodded, though her heart was pounding wildly beneath her shirt. I relaxed with a sigh. "You didn't jump in," I murmured, surprised. "I thought for sure you would tackle Keirran or try to talk him down." Kenzie grimaced.

"Well, last time I tried, I got slammed in the back with a lightning bolt and spent four months in the hospital," she answered in a shaky voice. "And with all the lightning and wind and ice flying around, I figured it would be better to let the guy who's immune to it all handle it this time." She squeezed my waist. "Though you did nearly give me a heart attack once or twice, with all those near misses. He really was trying to kill you." Her voice broke, and she pulled away, shaking with anger…or grief. "Keirran has gone completely dark side on us, hasn't he?" she whispered, gazing at the bramble wall, where the knights had almost hacked it down. I knew they wouldn't find him on the other side, that he was already gone. Kenzie's eyes glimmered, and she shook her head. "What are we going to do?"

"I don't know," I whispered back. Anger, guilt and despair burned my insides, making me feel sick. Keirran wouldn't listen to us; we hadn't been able to reach him. Not even Annwyl had been able to get through, and she had been our final hope. What chance did we have of convincing the prince to destroy the amulet? We couldn't even keep him from trying to kill us all.

"Master," Razor whimpered on Kenzie's shoulder. "Master bad. Master bad."

"Ethan Chase," the Thin Man said, appearing beside us and making Razor hiss. His pale eyes were sympathetic but stern. "I think you know what you have to do now. The next time you see the Iron Prince, you must kill him.

"We tried, my boy," he continued gently, as I stiffened in protest. "The Summer girl tried…and failed. The Iron Prince will not hear us. He will not destroy the amulet of his own free will. And the stakes are too high to allow this to continue. You heard what the prince said. About the Lady. About the Veil." He looked at what was left of the bramble wall, his face grim. "She intends to destroy it for good. And she will use the Iron Prince to accomplish her goal. As long as he lives, the courts will not be able to stop her. Not when they are so busy fighting among themselves. This attack will not be the last. The Forgotten can strike anywhere, at any time. And each time they do, each time the First Queen sends them through the Veil, she destabilizes it a little more. That has been her plan all along, I believe. Using the Iron Prince and the war to weaken the barrier, until she shatters it completely." The Thin Man turned back to me, his voice hard. "Once the queen rallies her forces, the prince will lead them through again. We must stop him before that happens. We must go into the Between and kill him ourselves."

"No," Annwyl whispered. She had drifted close and was staring at us with glazed green eyes, her face slack with horror. "Ethan Chase, please," she said, looking at me. "I can reach him. Let me try again."

"There is no time to try again!" the Thin Man snapped. "The Iron Prince must be stopped. Look at the damage he has caused, the lives he took, in a single night! He is using the full extent of his power, and we cannot hold back any longer. Your feelings for him will doom us all."

"Annwyl," Kenzie said, still pressed close to me. "I don't want to accept it, either, but…maybe he's right. Keirran might be gone. I mean, if Ethan wasn't immune to glamour now, he would've killed him. Again. How many chances can we afford to give him?"

"Please," Annwyl whispered, her eyes filling with tears as she stared at me. "I'm begging you. One more time, Ethan Chase. He is your family, your blood. One last chance."

I gazed across the field without answering. The knights, now joined by several fey of both Summer and Winter, had finally hacked their way through the bramble wall. As expected, Keirran was nowhere to be found. He'd probably slipped back into the Between as soon as he'd thrown up the distraction and was on his way to the Lady right now. Because we couldn't stop him.

"You!"

I jumped as Titania's furious voice rang over the field, but for once, it wasn't directed at me. The Summer Queen strode across the field, her blazing glare fixed on Mab, who awaited her with ice spreading out from her feet.

"Curse you!" Titania spat, as the air around the two queens swirled into a dangerous cyclone. "Curse your interference, Mab! I had the Iron Prince where I wanted him. I could have stopped him tonight, had you not interfered!"

"That is my grandson," Mab hissed in return. "The only kin of my last remaining child. I will not have him killed by the likes of you."

"I warn you, Mab." Titania drew herself up, eyes flashing. "You are moments from being at war with the Summer Court, as well."

Mab sneered. "Is that a threat, Summer Queen? Do you think I am afraid of you and your pathetic court?" Her lips curled in a savage, dangerous smile. "Any time you wish to experience the wrath of Winter, we are happy to oblige."

"Someone needs to stop this," Kenzie whispered in a warning voice. I couldn't agree more, but I didn't want to be the one to step between two pissed-off Faery queens. Titania swelled with fury, wind and lightning screaming around her, and Mab straightened, too, icicles spearing out of the ground to claw the air. They each raised their arms, and the ground started to shake. I whispered a curse, then shoved away from Kenzie.

"Stop it!"

Both queens turned, pinning me with blazing, scary eyes. I strode forward, trying to put distance between myself and Kenzie in case a lightning bolt or ice storm suddenly came my way. "This isn't the time to fight each other," I said, glaring at the queens with more bravado than I felt. "If you declare war on the other court, you'll just be helping the First Queen. You'll be playing right into her hand, and she'll be laughing at you all as she takes over the Nevernever and destroys the Veil. Is that what you want?"

"You dare, mortal?" Mab asked softly, and several sharp icicle points turned in my direction. "You dare speak to a queen of Faery like that?"

"Someone has to," I heard myself saying, and gestured to the torn landscape, suddenly furious myself. "Look around us. If you haven't noticed by now, Faery is being torn apart, the Veil is being shredded, and the First Queen is still out there while you two are having a pissing contest. I might just be mortal, but *my* world is being threatened, too. If the Veil goes down, it'll be hell on earth for everyone, not just the Nevernever. So I'd kinda like to stop that before Keirran and the First Queen unleash the faery apocalypse. And the two of you aren't helping by being at each other's throats all the time!"

Several ice spears flew at me, insanely fast. My insides cringed, but I forced myself to stand tall, facing them as they veered off at the last second, sticking into the trees and mud behind me. Mab stared in surprise, and I used that pause to tell my heart it could start beating again.

"What is going on here?"

A surge of energy announced the arrival of the Iron Queen. Meghan strode through the crowd, Oberon beside her, and the throngs of fey quickly fell back. Ignoring Mab and Titania, Meghan walked straight to me, her gaze concerned as she gripped my arms, blue eyes searching.

"Ethan? Are you hurt? What happened?"

"Keirran," I muttered, and Meghan went rock still. "He was here. I'm sorry, Meghan. I couldn't stop him."

"The Iron Prince has fled back to his Lady," Titania announced, as Meghan squeezed my arms and straightened, turning to face the other rulers. "He has gone into the Between, and we must follow him. Open the Veil," she ordered, looking at the Thin Man. "This has gone far enough. The Iron Prince and the First Queen will not hide from us any longer. We will go into the Between and find them ourselves. Open the Veil, Forgotten."

"No," the Thin Man answered. "I will not."

Titania stiffened with fury and outrage, but Oberon raised his hand, silencing her outburst. "I will not hasten the destruction of the Veil any more than I already have," the Thin Man continued. "Bringing any of you—" he gazed around at the four rulers "—into the Between will put too much strain on the Veil. It is already dangerously weak. A surge of power that strong could dissolve it completely."

"Then what do you expect us to do?" Titania spat. "Sit here and wait for the Forgotten and the Iron Prince to attack again?"

"No," I said, and stepped forward. "I'm going in after Keirran, right now."

They all stared at me. "The Forgotten might still be retreating," I went on. "If we hurry, we might be able to get to him before he reaches the First Queen."

"We, Ethan Chase?" Mab wondered.

"Yeah." I nodded at the small group around me. "Me, Annwyl, Kenzie and the Thin Man. We won't pose a threat to the Veil, and hopefully we'll be able to slip through the Between without the Forgotten noticing we're there."

Meghan frowned. "It'll be the four of you against the Forgotten, Keirran and the First Queen," she said. "If you're discovered, you won't have a chance. I don't know if I can let you do this, Ethan."

"I have to, Meghan." I faced my sister tiredly. "It was always meant to be me and Keirran in the end. I can't do anything about the First Queen, or the Forgotten, but I can try to save Keirran." *One way or another.*

Meghan sighed. "Are you sure you can do this? Alone?"

"He won't be alone," came a deep voice, as Ash, Puck and the Wolf padded up together. I froze as Ash turned his cool gaze on us. "We're going with him," the dark faery said, his firm voice leaving no room for argument. "If we can find the First Queen, we might be able to stop her."

"Yep," Puck agreed, lacing his hands behind his skull. "And hopefully, our illustrious presence won't make the Between go wonky and poof out of existence." He glanced at the Thin Man. "That won't be a problem, right, Slim Shady?"

The Thin Man frowned. "It might," he said uncertainly. "Two legends and a former Winter prince? I don't know if the Between will be able to take it."

"Risk it," Ash said, narrowing his eyes. "This is our best and only chance to reach Keirran and the First Queen. If she won't come to us, we'll have to go to her."

"And if it destroys the Veil in the process?"

Someone yawned, loudly and mockingly, a few feet away.

"I do not think you have to worry about that," purred Grimalkin, appearing on a nearby shattered stump. Curling his tail around his feet, he regarded us lazily. "The Veil will survive," he stated in a bored voice. "Regardless of what he might believe, Robin Goodfellow is not going to be throwing around the power of a king or queen of Faery. The dog's strength comes from story and legend. He has no magic of his own except the annoying ability to not die when he should. And the former Winter prince is no longer fey, not completely. Taking them into the Between will be a risk, but it might be your best option for any hope of victory tonight."

The Wolf rumbled an agreement. "The cat has a point," he said, curling his lip as if those words were somehow distasteful. "Two humans, a Fading Summer girl and a Forgotten won't be able to stand against an entire army. We can at least get you there."

"Oh, very well," the Thin Man snapped. "But no one else. We're already pushing the boundaries of what the Between can take." He scowled at us all—me, Annwyl, Kenzie, Ash, Puck, Wolf—and sighed. "Shall we go, then? I believe you want to find the Iron Prince and the Lady soon, before the Forgotten have a chance to regroup."

I nodded before I had a chance to think about it. "Yeah," I said. "Let's go. Right now. The sooner the better."

"As you wish," the Thin Man murmured. "Wait here. It will take me but a moment to find where the prince went through."

He strode off toward the hole in the bramble wall the knights had torn through. Guiltily, I looked at Kenzie, wondering what she was thinking about all this. She gazed calmly back, and I swallowed. "Are you okay to do this?" I asked softly. "Go into the Between again?"

Kenzie smirked. "Trying to leave me behind again, tough guy?"

"No." I shook my head. "I'll always want you with me, no matter what we're facing. But I want you to be sure. You don't have to do this, Kenzie. This is family stuff. If Keirran... kills me, he'll go after you, too. I won't be able to protect you from him."

The smirk widened. "If that happens, *he's* the one who's going to need protection," Kenzie replied, only half joking, and stepped close to me. Her arms slid around my waist, pulling me against her. "We started this together, Ethan," she said, smiling up at me. "We end it together. No matter what."

"Kissy kissy!" Razor buzzed, as I lowered my head and did just that.

"Ethan Chase," called the Thin Man as we drew apart. "It

is time." We glanced up just as he pushed his long fingers into nothing and parted reality like a curtain. A jagged tear appeared before him, leaking smoke. "Hurry," he urged, waving us forward. "Before either the First Queen or Iron Prince notices we're coming."

Okay, then. Guess it's time. No more running, Keirran. We're coming for you now.

"Let's go," I told Kenzie, Annwyl and Razor, and started toward the Thin Man, through the ranks of fey. Meghan and Ash remained behind for a moment, the Iron Queen putting her hands on his face as she gazed up at him.

"Be careful, Ash," I heard her whisper as I passed. "I can't lose you, and my brother, and my son in the same night."

"I'll watch out for him," Ash returned, taking her hands. "And we'll bring Keirran back. That's a promise, Meghan."

I looked away as they kissed, giving them some privacy. I hadn't thought about that, how much Meghan had to lose tonight. Me, Keirran, Ash, the entire half of her family. No wonder she was worried. Puck and the Wolf fell into step beside us, and Ash joined us at the tear a moment later, his face grim and determined.

"Well," Puck commented, looking around at our odd party, "this is it, huh? I must admit, this is probably one of the stranger things I've had to do, with one of the stranger groups I've had to do it with."

The Wolf snorted. "No stranger than usual, Goodfellow."

"I guess not." Puck sighed, then straightened with a bright grin, rubbing his hands. "Welp, as a certain furball would point out, time's a-wasting. Who's up for saving the Nevernever one more time?"

Kenzie slipped her fingers through mine and squeezed. I took a deep breath, and we stepped through the tear into the Between.

PART III

CHAPTER NINETEEN

REALM OF THE FIRST QUEEN

"Okay," Puck remarked as the curtain of reality closed behind us, trapping us in the Between once more, "that's...cheery."

A cold wind blew against my back, and I shivered. A stark, jagged landscape surrounded us, rocky outcroppings soaring out of the ground at random intervals, spearing into a dull gray sky. Jet-black mountains surrounded a sullen valley, the mist and shadows so thick they were impenetrable. There was no color anywhere. The rocks were gray, the few trees scattered here and there were black with white stripes and patches circling the trunks. A few silvery blades of grass poked up from between rocks, and the shadows were unnaturally long, almost appearing to move. It was like being inside an old negative photograph, and since the color leach hadn't affected the rest of us, we definitely stood out. Puck's red hair and Razor's glowing blue teeth were almost painfully bright, and Wolf nearly blended into the background, his eyes floating green orbs in the dark.

"Yes," the Thin Man agreed, turning in a slow circle, momentarily vanishing from sight. "It seems the First Queen has been very busy," he mused, reappearing once more. "No wonder her army of Forgotten have been able to hide in the Between."

"Yep, getting a definite *Nosferatu* vibe here," Puck went

on, observing the dead gray landscape with his hands on his hips, before giving a tiny shudder. *"Brr,* definitely creepytown. Wonder where all the natives are? And the First Queen?"

Kenzie pointed. "I'm going to guess in there."

I followed her arm. A massive black fortress sat atop a mountain peak, pointed towers silhouetted against the sky. Leading up to the castle was a long, long stone bridge, suspended over a several-hundred-foot drop into utter darkness.

"Oh, that looks safe," Puck remarked, raising an eyebrow. "Can't think of anything that could go wrong there."

"Come on," Ash said, walking forward. "That's where Keirran will be heading. Let's try to catch him before he reaches the First Queen."

We started across the bleak landscape, heading toward the fortress looming in the distance. Ash, Puck and the Thin Man led. I trailed behind with Kenzie and Annwyl, and Wolf brought up the rear, padding silently over the rocks. Except for Razor's low, constant buzzing and the deep, guttural panting from the Wolf, everything was quiet. Even our footsteps seemed muffled, swallowed up by the shadows that clawed at us from every corner. They shifted and wriggled in the corners of my eyes, and more than once, I thought I saw glowing yellow spheres, watching us from the black. But when I jerked up my head to look at them directly, they were always gone.

"Anyone else get the feeling that we're being watched?" I finally said, my voice unnaturally loud in the silence.

Behind us, the Wolf gave a low chuckle.

"Definitely," he growled, making my hairs stand up. "The shadows are full of eyes. I can feel them, even if I cannot smell them. We are not alone."

"Why aren't they attacking us?" Kenzie asked, moving closer to me. Razor gave a worried buzz and hid beneath her hair. "What are they waiting for?"

"I imagine only a few Forgotten have noticed we are here," the Thin Man said. "However, it only takes a few to alert the rest of the army. We should probably move a little faster."

So we did, striding over the bleak, black-and-gray landscape, on alert for anything that could come leaping out of the eternal shadows. As we drew closer to the bridge, more and more yellow eyes appeared in the darkness surrounding us. The Forgotten's numbers were growing.

"Quickly!" Ash said, beckoning us forward. I joined him and saw a long stone staircase cut into the side of the cliff, zigzagging its way up the mountain. We climbed, and the eyes followed us, slithering over the rocks and up the cliff face, turning into a huge swarm. Scrambling up the steps, we finally reached the top and the narrow stone bridge that stretched out over nothing. In the distance, the castle beckoned, a jagged smear of black against the gray.

A Forgotten heaved itself over the side and grabbed at Kenzie with pointed fingers. I yanked her away, slashing at the thing with my sword, and it billowed away into mist. But more shadows appeared, crawling over the railing, surging up the steps, a thousand pairs of yellow eyes coming at us, and we ran.

The fortress loomed overhead, dark and menacing, making me feel tiny beneath its shadow. I felt, rather than heard, the horde of Forgotten at our backs and wondered how we were ever going to confront Keirran while running from an army.

Ash stopped and turned around with a swirl of his cape, drawing his sword. Blue light washed over the bridge as Ash flung out a hand, causing a line of ice spears to grow from the stones, wickedly sharp points aimed back at the Forgotten.

"Ash!"

"Keep going." The dark faery's voice was calm as Puck and the Wolf whirled around and joined him in the center of the bridge. Together, the three formed a barrier between us and

the approaching horde. "We'll hold them here," Ash continued, as Puck drew his daggers and Wolf panted a savage grin.
"You three go on to the castle."

"Are you crazy? We're not leaving you here!"

He ignored me, facing the throng with his sword glowing blue at his side. The Forgotten continued to pile on to
the bridge, slithering over the stones, massing beyond the ice
barrier until the other side was nothing but black. Ash, Puck
and the Wolf stood quietly, waiting for them, three motionless bodies against a flood of shadows and eyes.

"That's an awful lot of Forgotten, ice-boy," Puck mused
as the group reached the barrier and began clawing their way
over it. He twirled his daggers in both hands and stepped
forward, a fierce grin in his voice. "We might not make it
through this one. Exciting, isn't it? Just like old times."

I stepped forward to join them, but a swirl of light and glitter erupted between us, making me flinch back. I squinted
up as the tall, elegant form of the Exile Queen walked out of
the light, copper hair flowing behind her.

"Hello, darlings."

I gaped at the tall faery. "Leanansidhe? What are you doing?
How did you even get here?"

"Darling, please." The Exile Queen waved an airy hand. "It's
the Between. This is still my realm, even if a few interlopers
have moved in." She glared at the Forgotten, blue eyes scary and
cold. "It appears that I'm going to have to kick them out myself."

"Aw, Lea, you mean you didn't come here to see *us*?" Puck
asked, twirling his daggers as he sauntered forward. "I'm hurt.
But, hey, if you're here to help us toss some shadows over the
side of the bridge, I'm not complaining."

"Ethan." Ash didn't turn around as he spoke, but raised his
arm. Glamour swirled, and ice daggers formed in the air over
his head. "This is the best we can do for you," the faery con-

tinued. "Find Keirran. Nothing else matters now. Find him, and bring him home."

The Forgotten drew close. Ash flung out his arm, and the flurry of ice daggers sped through the air into the horde coming across the bridge. Several jerked and writhed, twisting away into nothing, coils of shadow vanishing on the wind. Leanansidhe raised her arms, light and energy crackling around her, and sang out a single piercing note. My ears rang, and I gritted my teeth at the sudden pain in my skull, seeing Kenzie wince and cover her ears. In front of Leanansidhe, the entire first row of Forgotten jerked, hands flying up to cover the sides of their heads, before their skulls exploded into black clouds and dissolved into nothingness.

I cringed as Wolf let out an eager, booming howl that vibrated the stones of the bridge and sprang forward into the recoiling mass of Forgotten. Puck hooted, daggers flashing, as he leaped forward, as well. Ash spared me one last piercing glare.

"Ethan, *go!*"

I whispered a curse and ran, hearing Ash, Puck and Wolf clash with the army of Forgotten, their howls and bursts of glamour ringing out behind us. A few Forgotten crawled up the sides of the bridge and leaped at me, but I cut them down and kept going.

My eyes stung, and I angrily blinked tears away as we retreated across the bridge. I would not think of Ash, Puck and Wolf as a sacrifice. They would *not* be a sacrifice, dammit. If anyone could survive an army of Forgotten, it would be those three. And they had Leanansidhe backing them up. I had to trust them. They were buying us time, keeping the Forgotten off our backs so we could deal with Keirran in peace. I would not let them down.

We reached the castle steps and climbed to the large wooden doors at the top. As we reached them, I wondered, fleetingly, if they would be locked or barred from the inside. We'd kinda be screwed if they were. But the handle turned under my palm when I wrenched on it, and the heavy doors slowly creaked open when I pushed. Peering through the crack, I saw an empty, open courtyard, as bleak and flat as everything else. Overhead, a strangely dull full moon hung from the sky, looking more like a portrait that anything real. Weird statues lined the perimeter wall—statues of faeries I'd never seen before. The Forgotten, perhaps? Before they'd changed into creepy shadow creatures? I didn't know. But the space appeared to be empty; no movement, no yellow eyes gleaming in the darkness, no Forgotten moving through the shadows. I shoved the door open farther and let Kenzie and Annwyl slip through before I followed with the Thin Man, making sure the courtyard really was empty. Turning, I put a shoulder to the wood and pushed it shut, and the hollow boom of the door closing echoed through the castle.

All right. Here we were, in the First Queen's foyer. I wondered if she knew we were here, before deciding that of course she did; this was her kingdom, after all. So if the Lady already knew we were here, that meant Keirran probably did, too.

So, where was he?

"Stay close," I warned the others. Kenzie was gazing around curiously, Razor perched on her shoulder, while Annwyl scanned the yard as if searching for the prince in the shadows. A cold wind billowed across the flagstones as I edged farther inside, and I saw that a section of the high stone wall that surrounded the courtyard had crumbled away. Beyond the gap was darkness, open air and a long, long drop to the bottom of the mountain. I shivered and took a cautious step back. "Be careful," I warned, making sure Kenzie was a safe distance away from the broken wall and lethal plunge. "Keirran and the Lady could be anywhere. We don't want them surprising us."

"That won't be a problem, Uncle."

I jerked. A bright, cloaked form stood on a balcony against the opposite wall, gazing down at us. Even with his black cloak and armor, he shone in the darkness, silver hair and ice-blue eyes a stark contrast to the dreary surroundings.

As soon as we saw him, Keirran waved a hand, and a heavy wooden portcullis dropped over the door we'd just come through, hitting the stones with a boom. Another fell over the archway at the other end of the yard, boxing us in. I drew my swords as my heart began a rapid thud in my chest. This was it. It was just us and Keirran now.

The prince leaped over the balcony railing and dropped through the air to land gracefully on the flagstones. His eyes were already glowing as he rose, wind and glamour beginning to swirl around him, whipping at his hair. His smile was cruel as he stepped forward.

"And here you are." Keirran's voice was flat, his eyes cutting. "Just as the queen said you would be. You are quite predictable, aren't you, Ethan?" His gaze flicked from me to the girls, pressed to either side of me, and narrowed. "You shouldn't have brought Annwyl and Kenzie, though. I have no wish to hurt them. This is between you and me. And *you*..."

He gestured sharply. A blast of wind shrieked through the courtyard, tossing dust and leaves and making Kenzie's and Annwyl's clothes snap, though it wasn't directed at us. But there was a cry, and the Thin Man suddenly slammed into a statue, his body winking into existence before collapsing motionless to the stones. Keirran gestured again, and the statue lurched and tumbled forward, crashing to the stones and pinning the Thin Man beneath it. The prince smiled coldly.

"Fool me once," he murmured, and raised his arm again.

"Keirran, stop!" Annwyl stepped around me, her eyes tearful as she faced down the prince. "Please," she begged, holding out her hands. "If you ever loved me, please, stop this.

It's not too late. You can leave this place, leave the Lady and return home."

Keirran looked at her, his eyes softening. "Annwyl," he said, and for a moment, his voice was almost like the Keirran I used to know. "How can you ask me that?" he whispered. "Everything I've done, everything I've sacrificed, was for you. The Lady, the exiles, the Forgotten—they were all dying, but what I cared about most was saving you."

"I didn't want to be saved," Annwyl returned. "Not when it turned you into this. Not when it cost me everything I loved about you." Her voice grew harsher, almost desperate. "I don't *want* this, Keirran," she said. "I want the old you back, even if I can see him for only a moment. Even if I must die for you to return."

Reaching around her neck, she yanked off the amulet, holding it up so that it swayed and throbbed in the eerie un-light. Keirran went rigid at the sight of it. "This is the cause of everything," she said. "Prolonging my life, at the cost of your soul. It is an evil thing, Keirran, can't you feel that? I want no part of it anymore." She thrust the amulet at him, making it swing and glitter on its cord. "You have to destroy it. I can't do it myself."

"No."

"Keirran—"

"I won't watch you die, Annwyl!" For just a moment, a spark of anger and grief crossed his face. Gritting his teeth, he closed his eyes. "This is my legacy," he whispered. "Death, and betrayal, and destruction. This is destiny, what fate has decided. You are the only good thing I will leave behind. If I...kill you, as well—" he made a weary, hopeless gesture "—if you die, this will all be for nothing. Everyone I've betrayed, all the death I've caused, will be for *nothing*." He raked a hand through his silver bangs, his eyes shadowed. "What do

I care if the Forgotten and exiles are saved," he whispered, "if you're not in the world any longer?"

Kenzie's voice was sympathetic. "You still love her."

"I never stopped," Keirran growled, giving her a cold look. "Maybe it's foolish. Maybe that's the only piece of my soul I still have left. But it doesn't matter. The First Queen's plan is nearly complete. It's too late for me to stop it."

"It's *not* too late for you, Prince," I snapped. "You can still end this. Walk out with us, and go home. Do you really want to keep fighting *everyone*? Your parents, the courts, the entire Nevernever?" I gestured back toward the front gate. "Ash is out there, right now, holding off the Forgotten. If he makes it up here, what are you going to do? Fight your own dad? Are you going to kill your whole family before this is over?"

For just a second, he hesitated. For a heartbeat, I thought we'd gotten through. But then his eyes clouded over, and his face became hard.

"No," he said, his voice resolved. "I can't stop now. Not when we're this close. I've chosen my path, and I won't falter. The prophecy has decided my fate, and I am what they call me—the Destroyer. The Soulless One. So be it." His eyes went icy, that cold apathy settling on him like a mantle. "I will be their villain," he murmured, raising his head, "but I will also change the world with the First Queen. And nothing will stand in our way."

"Keirran, please," Annwyl whispered. "The realm is being torn apart. This war will obliterate everything. Please, you have to destroy the amulet. Just let me go."

The Iron Prince looked at her blankly, all traces of the old Keirran disappearing as the icy stranger took his place. "Do I?" he mused, cocking his head. "Maybe I will. Maybe I will destroy it after all. But not until the Veil has fallen. Even now, the Lady works to weaken it." He glanced at me. "There is only one thing missing, one thing that she needs for it to shatter and never re-form again."

"You tried that once," I growled at him. "It didn't work. What makes you think this time will be any different?"

He gave me a chilling smile and gestured to the courtyard. "Look around you," Keirran said. "Do you know where you are? Does any of this seem familiar?"

"Not even a little bit."

"We saw it once, in passing," Keirran insisted. "Don't you remember? The first time I took you through the Between. It was just a ruin then, but I made note of where it was. A site of great power. A place that exists in both worlds."

As usual, Kenzie got it before I did. "This is an anchor," she guessed, and the prince nodded.

"Just a ruin," he said. "A few stones. But it was enough. Enough for the Lady to build this kingdom and create a safe haven for the Forgotten. Not that it will be needed much longer."

He turned to me, a smile playing across his lips. "We had it wrong before," he almost whispered. "We know now why the Veil re-formed. The sacrifice must be done at the site of *both* worlds, not just the mortal realm." His smile grew wider, more evil. "So, I guess it's fortunate you didn't die in Ireland after all."

Horror flooded me, and Kenzie gasped with the realization. Keirran drew his sword, the raspy screech echoing over the walls. I backed away, shoving the girls behind me, and raised my own weapon. The Iron Prince stepped forward, the air around him turning frigid. "Well, now that you're here, you can fulfill the *true* prophecy, Ethan Chase. You can die, again, and your blood will be the final force that will shatter the Veil for good." He raised his sword, icy glamour beginning to swirl around him. "And this time, there will be no coming back."

CHAPTER TWENTY

BLOOD AND SACRIFICE

He didn't bother with magic this time. No lightning, ice darts, blast of wind, nothing. He just lunged at me, the curved steel blade slicing down at my neck. I leaped back, barely getting my sword up in time, and the screech of metal on metal rocked me and sent a chill racing up my spine.

Kenzie and Annwyl darted back. "Keirran, stop!" Annwyl cried, raising her arm. Glamour swirled around her, but the Iron Prince turned, flinging out a hand toward her. A vicious gust of wind sent her tumbling off her feet and sprawling against the stones with a gasp. Keirran smiled grimly.

"You might be immune to glamour now, but I'm afraid your friends are not," he said, and gestured again, sending Kenzie stumbling back. "And I would like to keep the interference at a minimum this time, so..."

I started toward Kenzie, ignoring the prince, but the shadows around us suddenly came alive. Forgotten emerged from the darkness, yellow eyes gleaming, and slithered toward the girls. Two pounced on Annwyl, dragging her upright by the arms, and another pair seized Kenzie. Razor shrieked and lunged at one with fangs bared but was slapped away and hit a statue with a tiny but sickening crack. He dropped to the stones, moaning and holding his arm, and the Forgotten pulled Kenzie against the wall, ignoring her cries of protest.

Furious, I went for the Forgotten holding Kenzie, but a line of glittering ice spears rose from the ground between us.

"The fight is here, Ethan," Keirran called in a mocking voice. "Unless you're afraid to fight me one-on-one. No Titania to save you this time." I whirled on him, snarling, and he smiled. "No interruptions now. Just you and me."

"Fine," I growled, brandishing my sword. Anger, fury and hate boiled up as I faced my nephew across the flagstones. This was it. The final battle between me and the Iron Prince, and I was ready. No more holding back or trying to talk him down. This had been coming since the day we met. "Come on, then, Prince," I said, curling my lip into a sneer. "If this is the only way to stop the war and save the Nevernever, then I'll just have to kick your ass all the way back to your precious Lady."

He grinned and lunged at me. I met him in the center of the courtyard, the clang of our weapons ringing off the stones. We swung and parried with our blades, barely missing each other, the razor edges coming uncomfortably close. Keirran had only one sword to my two, but his speed and unnatural grace made up for it. Plus he had been trained by Ash, one of the best swordsmen in the Nevernever. I knew it was only a matter of time before the blood started to fly and fleetingly wondered who would draw it first.

I had my answer about five seconds later. Keirran dodged a vicious swat to his head, darted in and stabbed me in the arm with the point of his blade. The cut wasn't very deep, but pain flared across my forearm as blood welled and dripped to the flagstones.

A shiver went through the air as I grimaced and staggered back, and the entire world *rippled* like the surface of a pond. Kenzie gasped, and Keirran lowered his blade, smiling.

"Do you feel that?" he whispered, gazing up at the sky. "It's happening. The Veil is unraveling. Every drop of your blood weakens it a little more. And when you die, it will finally fall. Humans will finally be able to see us, fear us, *believe* in us again."

"Are those really your ideals, Keirran?" Kenzie demanded from the wall, still struggling with her captors. "Or is that the First Queen talking?" When he didn't answer, she pressed on. "I thought so. I don't think you even know what you want, just that you have to follow this path because of some stupid prophecy. Well, that's bullshit! There is always a choice, Keirran!"

"Silence," Keirran growled, gesturing at her, and one of the Forgotten covered her mouth with a hand. "Both of you," he added, and the Forgotten holding Annwyl did the same. "Your constant protests are becoming tiresome, and I've already made my choice. If you don't mind, I would like to kill my uncle in peace."

I lunged at Keirran with a snarl, fury and desperation hot in my veins, and Keirran stepped forward, his eyes murderous. Our swords clanged and screeched in the grim silence, echoing off the walls. We fought viciously, both giving no mercy or quarter. I lashed out and scored a nasty cut across his cheek. He responded with a stinging gash below my ribs. More blood spread across my shirt, warm and sticky, and the world wavered with every drop that hit the ground.

Lunging in, I smacked Keirran's sword away and stabbed deep, hitting him in the shoulder right below his collarbone. Grimacing, Keirran stumbled back, throwing out a hand, and a flurry of ice daggers came at me and veered away. I smiled grimly.

"Still immune to magic, Prince. Or did you forget?"

He glared stonily, holding a hand to the wound. "No," he said. "But that's a very annoying talent you've picked up."

Sneering, I raised my sword. "Aw, what's the matter, Prince? Can't face me in a fair fight? Sad that you actually have to get your hands dirty?"

His glare grew colder. "Don't push me, Ethan," he warned in an icy voice. "I can kill you anytime I want. I thought, for family's sake, I would do it the honorable way. But if you insist, I can be the heartless demon you think I am."

"Really?" I stepped forward. "Then give it your best shot, Keirran."

"As you wish."

He raised his arm, and ice spears formed in the air, pointed and lethal. "Just remember, you pushed me to this," Keirran said, and swept his hand down…

…at Kenzie.

My heart lodged in my throat. I watched, helpless, as the Forgotten holding Kenzie vanished into the wall, a moment before the flurry of ice spears slammed into them. The spears shattered against the rock with the sound of breaking glass, and Kenzie screamed, hands flying up to cover her face, as the razor shards of ice tore at her skin and shredded her clothes.

"Kenzie!" I lunged toward her as she collapsed, bleeding from a dozen small wounds all over her body.

Keirran's voice rang out as I scrambled forward, icy and unmerciful. "You might be immune to glamour, but Kenzie is not!" I ignored him and continued to spring toward Kenzie, as Keirran's voice followed me. "Love is a weakness, Ethan! You might've stood a chance if she had not been here, but now you will die, because you cannot let her go."

Another strong pulse of glamour went through the stones, and I flung myself at my girlfriend. Just as I reached her, the ground erupted, thick roots and vines coiling into the air, sending rock and gravel flying. They snaked around Kenzie, lifting her away, out of my reach. I howled in rage and sank my blade into the trunks, trying to hack them down, but the roots were thick and gnarled, and resisted my efforts. Kenzie was raised high, vines circling her arms and legs until she hung twenty feet in the air. With a creaking and groaning of limbs, the knot of roots twisted, dangling her over the perimeter wall, into empty space.

"No!" I whirled on Keirran, standing calmly with his arm outstretched, his eyes impassive. "Dammit, Keirran, don't you fucking dare! Kenzie was the only one who stood up for you, even to me! She was your friend when I was ready to say *screw it* and walk out. You can't—"

"No?" Keirran's voice was icy. "Why not? What is one human life to me, when thousands of exiles and Forgotten hang in the balance?" His eyes narrowed, hard and expressionless. "You don't know me anymore, Ethan. Or what I'm willing to sacrifice. Don't underestimate what I'm capable of."

"All right!" My voice broke, and I took a ragged breath, meeting his cold gaze. "Don't hurt her," I whispered. "You win. Do what you want with me, just...let her go."

"Ethan." Kenzie's voice echoed somewhere above me, weak and tight with pain. "No. What about your sister and your parents? You can't let him—"

Some of the limbs uncoiled, releasing her so that her legs swung out over the drop. Kenzie gasped, clawing at the vines to keep hold of them, and I nearly choked on panic.

"*Nooooo!*"

A tiny, furious cry rang out, and Razor landed on Keirran's shoulder, beating him with his fists, teeth bared. "No, no, Master stop! Stop stop! No hurt pretty girl!"

"Razor!" Keirran snapped, sounding exasperated. He gestured sharply, and the little gremlin flew away with a blast of wind, tumbling to the ground. Before he could recover, a root snaked down, lifted the hissing, squirming gremlin into the air and tossed him over the wall. Razor wailed as he arched over the stones, a tiny speck of black against the sky, and dropped out of sight. Kenzie screamed his name in horror and outrage.

"*Damn you*, Keirran—"

"I could send her after him," the prince remarked calmly, and several coils loosened, dropping Kenzie a couple feet. She cried out, desperately grabbing the branches, but her fingers slipped, and she plunged downward. Only one vine, wrapped around her wrist, kept her from plummeting to her death. Frantic, I whirled and took a step toward him.

"Keirran, stop! Dammit, you win already! Look!" I threw my swords aside, tossing them to the ground. "I'm done," I choked out as he gazed at me. "I won't fight you. Just kill me, if that's what you want."

My chest felt tight with failure, knowing I'd let everyone down. Meghan, my parents, Guro, my whole damn world. *I'm sorry, Kenzie*, I thought, as Keirran finally lowered his arm and turned away from her. *I never thought he would go this far. But if I can save only one person out of this whole stupid ordeal, it's going to be you every time. I love you. Please, take care of yourself.*

Keirran raised his sword and pointed to the middle of the courtyard. "Here, Ethan," he ordered quietly. "No more fighting. No more delays. We do it right here."

Numbly, I walked to where the Iron Prince pointed, facing him across the stones. He stepped forward, his steel blade glittering in the darkness. "Kneel," he told me.

I dropped to my knees on the flagstones. Small spatters of blood already dotted the ground where I knelt; in a moment, there would be a huge puddle spreading across the stones. *Dead again*, I mused. Only this time, I wasn't coming back, and the Veil would be destroyed for good. *Meghan*, I thought as Keirran stepped in front of me, my skin prickling in the sudden chill. *I hope you can forgive me.*

"I'll make it quick," Keirran said almost gently, and raised his sword. I bowed my head but kept my eyes open, hearing my heart roar in my ears, bracing for the final blow. "You won't feel anything, Ethan, I promise."

Searing light flooded the courtyard.

CHAPTER TWENTY-ONE

ANNWYL'S CHOICE

Keirran jerked, and I looked up as a brilliant light illuminated the darkness, driving back the shadows. It was hot and golden, like sunlight on a blistering summer's day, blinding and intense. We both flinched back, and I shielded my eyes with a hand, squinting at the spot the radiance was coming from.

Annwyl.

Annwyl was glowing, a tiny sun that was almost too bright to look at. Around her, the Forgotten writhed and cringed away, shrinking back from the light, as the Summer girl stepped toward us, her hair floating around her like a halo. Her eyes glowed a savage green as she faced Keirran, who looked stunned.

"Enough, Keirran." Her voice rang out over the courtyard, clear and confident. And pissed. She strode forward, and I scrambled away from her, feeling warmth wash over my skin as she approached. I looked closer and saw tears streaming down her face, even as she held her furious gaze on the prince.

"No more," Annwyl said softly, and her voice was both resolved and incredibly sad. "This has gone far enough."

"Annwyl," Keirran whispered, incredulous. He staggered back and dropped to a knee, bracing himself on the flagstones. "How...? Your magic...you have no glamour anymore."

"No, I don't." Annwyl stepped in front of me, putting herself between me and the prince. "This is *your* magic, Keirran. The amulet binds us together. Your glamour is what kept me alive all this time. I never used it before, because I feared draining you further and hastening your death. For so long, I denied myself magic, barely clinging to existence, because I was worried about you." She breathed deeply, and the light expanded with her, pushing the darkness back. "I love you, Keirran," she whispered, as the prince struggled to his feet. "But this cannot go on. I cannot stand here and watch you destroy everything you once loved. If you are willing to slaughter your own family, then the prince I knew is truly dead. And I…must make this right, for everyone."

"Annwyl…" Keirran looked almost nervous as he backed away, skirting the light. "Stop. Don't make me kill you, too."

The Summer faery shook her head. "I'm already gone, Keirran," she said quietly. "I have been for a long time now. But I plan to take you with me when my essence returns to the Nevernever. And maybe someday, when we're reborn, we'll meet again."

Now Keirran looked angry. He raised his arm, but Annwyl's light flared hotter, brighter. The ground at her feet cracked, and grass began to emerge, crawling over the barren stones and spreading around her. The prince staggered, his color leaching away, as light continued to pour from Annwyl. Where it touched, flowers and ferns appeared, shocking bits of color in the dead gray courtyard.

"Ethan," Annwyl continued, without taking her gaze from Keirran, "go help Kenzie. I will deal with the prince."

"Annwyl—"

"Go, Ethan Chase!" The Summer faery's voice rang with authority, and I went.

"No," Keirran snarled, as I dashed for the wall. I saw him

start after me, but there was a burst of heat from Annwyl, and the prince gave a cry of dismay and rage. I didn't look back. Snatching one of my dropped swords from the ground, I raced to the wall and leaped onto the tangle of roots and vines, climbing my way toward the top.

"Kenzie!"

She looked up at me, dangling over the vast precipice, one arm still tangled in vines. "Hang on," I told her, and sank my blade into one of the vines coiled around her arm. Kenzie clung doggedly as I cleared most of the knot, then reached out an arm. "Here!" I yelled, straining for her. "Kenzie, take my hand."

Gritting her teeth, she lunged for it, clamping on to my wrist. I pulled her from the coil of roots, then carefully lowered her to the courtyard below. Relief stabbed through me as she hit the ground. *Safe.*

But before I could relax, the roots beneath me went nuts, writhing and swaying like something on fire. Startled, I grabbed wildly for a vine, but with a sudden heave, the branch bucked me off, thankfully in the direction of the courtyard. For a few seconds, I was airborne and saw the ground rushing up at me.

I hit grass instead of stone, which was a blessing, though it still clacked my teeth together and sent a flare of pain up my side. Dazed, I looked up to see Keirran and Annwyl in the center of a magical whirlwind, leaves, twigs, rocks and ice shards swirling around them. Keirran had his sword raised, and Annwyl was unarmed, bursts of magic erupting all around them. The Iron Prince looked pale and weak, somehow less of himself, while Annwyl still blazed with her stolen glamour, her hair whipping around her head.

Seeing us, Keirran's eyes narrowed, and he raised his arm, pointing toward Kenzie, making my heart skip. On instinct,

I dived in front of her as a lightning bolt flashed out, curled around me and slammed into the wall, barely missing her. "I will not be defeated, Ethan!" Keirran exclaimed, as I backed in front of Kenzie, shielding her as best I could. "Either you die, or Kenzie dies! The Veil *will* fall—"

"No!" Annwyl thrust her palm toward Keirran, and a savage burst of wind lifted the prince off his feet, slamming him to the ground a few feet away. Stunned, he looked up as Annwyl stepped forward, the storm swirling around her. She raised her hand, and a ball of flame, lightning and pure sunlight formed in her palm as she held it out. Keirran staggered, looking pale and vulnerable as the Summer faery loomed over him.

"Annwyl," he whispered, his voice lost in the gale around them. "Stop. Please. Everything I've done…all of this…it was for you."

As he spoke, there was a shimmer of movement from the corner of my eye. I looked over to see one of my swords had lifted itself off the ground, the point angled at Annwyl's back. Annwyl, facing down Keirran, didn't notice.

"I'm sorry, Keirran," Annwyl said, as I leaped up and sprinted toward her. Her voice was choked with tears as she raised her arm. "I wish it didn't have to be this way."

The sword flew toward her. I slammed into the Summer faery, pushing her aside just as the blade reached us. At the same time, a blaze of agony ripped across my back as the weapon sliced into me, tearing a deep cut across my skin. I cried out and nearly fell, and saw Keirran's eyes widen for a split second, then narrow sharply as he realized.

Not immune to Iron glamour.

He scrambled to his feet, raising his hand. Alone, in pain and unarmed, I could only watch as the air above him flared, and a dozen glittering knives flickered into existence. For a heartbeat, our eyes met. I saw a split-second hesitation cross his face, a heartbeat of regret, before he threw out his hand, and the storm of lethal blades flew at me.

I flinched away and raised my arms, bracing myself to be skewered. I felt one of the knives graze my shoulder, tearing through my sleeve, making me gasp. I heard the solid, sickening thumps of iron hitting flesh, striking home, but felt no pain.

Cautiously, I opened my eyes, and my heart dropped.

Annwyl stood in front of me, arms crossed before her in an X, facing Keirran. For a few seconds, I could only stare, hopeful and horrified. Her back was to me, so I couldn't see the damage, but she didn't appear to be in pain. Maybe Keirran had missed. Maybe he'd redirected the attack at the last second.

And then I saw the blood, dripping in puddles beneath her, as Annwyl gave a breathless gasp and fell backward into my arms. Her body was covered with knives, sunk deep into her chest and stomach, welling with blood. A thin line of red trickled from her mouth as she coughed, her delicate frame shuddering violently in my grasp.

Keirran's sword dropped from his hands with a clang.

"Annwyl." Sickened, I sank to my knees, cradling the Summer faery as gently as I could. Her eyes were glassy with pain as she gazed up at me, struggling to speak. "Hey, don't try to talk," I choked out. "Just hold on, we'll…think of something."

She smiled gently and shook her head. I felt a soft touch on my shoulder and knew Kenzie had come up, that she had seen everything. Even as I held her, Annwyl flickered, becoming almost weightless in my arms. The amulet pulsed against her chest, as if desperately sucking in glamour, trying to save her life. But Annwyl continued to fade, her color slowly leaching away, even as blood soaked her dress and dripped to the ground beneath us.

A shadow fell over me. I didn't have to look up to know it

was Keirran. Would he kill me, here and now? Drive a sword through my heart and let us both bleed out on the stones? But he was motionless, not speaking, adding to the eerie silence around us. The storm had faded, the grass and flowers had already shriveled and were blowing away. The brilliant light surrounding Annwyl had died, and everything was dark again, plunged into shadow. I couldn't look at the prince, but Annwyl's gaze drifted up, and she weakly raised a hand.

"Keirran."

Her voice was barely audible, and Keirran fell to his knees and grasped her hand. I finally looked at him and saw his face.

My stomach twisted. His expression was emotionless, except for the single tear crawling down his face. Easing closer, he reached out, sliding his arms under Annwyl, taking her from me. For a second, I resisted, he had no right. But Annwyl's gaze was only for Keirran, and knowing these were her final moments in the world, I let her go.

Rising, I stepped back with Kenzie, who slid her arms around my waist and pressed close. And together, we watched the Iron Prince and the Summer faery's last exchange. Kenzie sniffed, her tears dampening the front of my shirt, and I held her tight, too emotionally exhausted to wonder where we would be when this was over.

"Annwyl." Keirran's voice was a whisper. His shoulders trembled as he bent over her, one hand hovering over the shards of metal jutting from her chest. Helplessly, he clenched a fist. "I never...meant for this to happen," he breathed. "I..."

The Summer faery shook her head. "No apologies," she murmured, and Keirran instantly fell silent, his gaze tormented. "No empty promises, Keirran. There's not...much time left." She flickered again, her outline fading at the edges. Keirran closed his eyes, and a sob finally tore itself free.

"I wanted to save you," he said in a low, anguished voice.

His hand lifted, trailing down her cheek. "What will I do now, Annwyl? How will I face anything...when you're gone?"

She reached for his hand, placing it over her heart, over the amulet pulsing against her chest. "Take back your soul, Keirran," she whispered. He blinked, gazing down at her, and she smiled. "Please. Before I go, let me see you...as you were. As the prince I fell in love with."

He bowed his head, hesitating for a few heartbeats. When he opened his eyes again, they were glassy with tears, grief, regret...and resignation. Slowly, he nodded.

Raising the amulet, he held it in his palm, and Annwyl's hand came to rest over them both. Keirran's fingers tightened, and the amulet began to glow. It grew hotter and brighter, until the two fey seemed to be holding a pulsing star between them.

Finally, with the sound of breaking glass, the amulet shattered. Keirran jerked, stiffening, as swirls of light flowed from his palm and curled into the air. They spiraled up, casting a brilliant light over the kneeling faery, before turning as one and rushing down on him. Keirran hunched his shoulders as the spears of light slammed into his body and vanished beneath his skin. He shuddered, holding Annwyl close, as he flickered and pulsed like a strobe light, making it hard to look at him.

Finally, the light sputtered and went out, plunging everything into darkness once more. Panting, Keirran straightened slowly and looked down at Annwyl.

My throat tightened, and Kenzie clenched a fist in my shirt. I could barely see the Summer faery. She was so faint, a fading shadow cradled in his arms, growing dimmer by the second. Keirran gazed down at her, tears now streaming unchecked from his eyes, and gently pulled her close. His lips moved, though his voice was too soft to hear. I couldn't really see

Annwyl's face, but I think she smiled at him. Slowly, one transparent hand rose, pressing against his cheek.

And then she was gone.

For a long while after, the three of us didn't move. Kenzie clung to me, weeping softly, her cheek pressed to my shirt. Keirran knelt on the flagstones, head bowed and shoulders hunched. I didn't know what to do, what to say to him. I wasn't even sure that he wouldn't still try to kill me. Yeah, he had gotten his soul back, but that didn't mean he would abandon his plan to destroy the Veil.

"Ethan." Keirran's voice was a whisper, and he didn't move from where he knelt on the flagstones. I tensed and felt Kenzie stiffen, too, holding her breath. Keirran raised his head, but he still didn't look at us. "You should go," he murmured softly, and with those words, he was himself again. The Keirran I knew before all this craziness happened. I didn't know whether to be relieved or if I wanted to march over and punch him in the teeth. "The Lady...will be coming soon," Keirran went on. "She'll know the amulet has been destroyed, and she'll be looking to kill you here, once and for all. Go, Ethan. You have to leave, or the Veil will fall. Take Kenzie and go back to the Nevernever."

I took a deep breath and released it slowly. One breath, to decide what I was going to do. To choose where I stood with him now. "What about you?" I asked.

"I'll stay behind. Try to slow her down a bit." He struggled to his feet, gazing around for his sword. He still didn't look at us, and his next words were choked, barely audible. "It's the least I can do...for everything I caused. I will face the First Queen myself."

Kenzie frowned. "She'll kill you, Keirran."

"I know." He picked up his sword and let it hang at his side.

"But at least I'll know what side I'm supposed to be on." He inhaled, and when he spoke again, his voice was thick with self-loathing. "I can't even begin to apologize, Ethan," he said. "There's nothing I can say that will ever make it right. The other courts will call for my death or exile, and they'll be completely justified. It's better this way." He ran a hand down his face. "Tell...tell my parents that I died fighting the First Queen, and that I'm sorry...for everything."

He shivered. Raising his head, his gaze went to the sky. "She's coming," he whispered. "Go, Ethan. Get out of here."

"No," I growled.

He looked at me, blue eyes widening with wary surprise. Ignoring him, I glanced down at Kenzie, wondering—hoping—that she thought the same. If she wanted to get out of here, I didn't know what I was going to do. But she gave me a tiny smile and a nod, making me slump with relief. Gently, I released her and started toward my forgotten swords. Keirran watched me a moment, then shook his head.

"Ethan, you don't—"

"Keirran, once and for all, get your head out of your ass!" Snatching up one of my blades, I whirled on him, furious. "Do you really think I can go back and tell Meghan that I let you die? When we came all this way to find you? When Annwyl *died* to..." I trailed off. The prince looked like he'd been punched in the stomach and was about to collapse. "We are leaving together," I told him firmly. "Right now. Screw the Lady—the other rulers will take care of her. I didn't come here to fight faery queens. I came for you." I narrowed my gaze and stared the prince down. "And you are going to walk out of here, alive, and you are going to go back to Meghan and *beg* for forgiveness and hope she doesn't kick your ass like you deserve. But I'll be damned if we went through all this hell to bring you back, and you decide to throw yourself at the Lady and get yourself killed!"

"They'll never forgive me."

"Bullshit," Kenzie broke in, sounding angry, too. Keirran blinked at her, and she scowled. "This whole time you've been waging war against the courts, all your parents have thought about was bringing you home. And not just them, either. Puck, Wolf, Grimalkin, the Thin Man, Razor—" Her voice broke on the last name, and she swiped at her eyes. "They've all sacrificed something to bring you back."

"More than you deserve," I added in a cold voice. He didn't contradict me, and I pointed a sword at him. "So, you don't get to play martyr, Keirran. Dying is the easy way out. If you're really sorry, go back to every single person you put through hell and *tell* them. Don't let Annwyl's sacrifice be for nothing."

Keirran closed his eyes. "Annwyl," he finally murmured, and dragged in a shaky breath. "Yes. You're right. I have…a lot of people I need to apologize to. A lot of things to atone for." He opened his eyes, and they were bright with grief and regret, but also that stubborn determination I'd seen all too often. "Someday I'll be worthy of her," he whispered, almost to himself. "Wherever you are, Annwyl, if you can see me now, I swear I'll make it right. Let this be the first step."

Sheathing his sword, he turned to me, his expression solemn. "I'm with you, Ethan," he said. "Let's get out of here, before the Lady arrives."

"Too late, I'm afraid," announced a new voice, somewhere overhead.

CHAPTER TWENTY-TWO

THE FIRST QUEEN

We spun, looking up, and my heart plummeted.

The Lady, the First Queen, hovered in the air about thirty feet off the ground. She was no longer the pale, faded-out faery I'd seen in Ireland, colorless and nearly transparent, with the shattered skeleton of wings behind her back. Now she glowed with power, jet-black hair flowing around her, eyes shifting from green to blue to solid black in the light. Her wings were now full and as dark as a raven's, the feathers giving off faint, metallic shivers as they moved in the breeze. She hovered there like a goddess, an avenging angel, her shifting, multicolored gaze settling on me and Keirran.

"My dear prince," the Lady said, her voice soft, soothing. "I believe you are confused. Did I hear you speak of leaving? Now? When we are so close, one step away from achieving what we had planned?"

"Yes." Keirran's tone was firm as he stepped forward, gazing up at her. "I'm done, my lady," he said. "No more fighting. No more killing. I won't be your instrument of war any longer."

She cocked her head. "The war is nearly done, Prince Keirran. Once the Veil falls and mortals are able to see us, the fighting will be long forgotten. We can start over, a new beginning with new rules. A world in which humans actually fear and believe in us as they should, where the Nevernever will grow strong once more, and faeries will never again Fade into nothingness." Her face softened as she gave Keirran a sympathetic look. "You could have saved your Summer girl, had the boy only gotten here sooner."

Keirran's jaw tightened, his eyes turning dangerous. The First Queen held up a finger. "One more death," she whispered, "that is all I ask of you, Keirran. One death to save thousands, an entire world. Look around you, Prince. Look at what is at stake."

She raised her arms, indicating the courtyard. I glanced up and saw hundreds of yellow eyes peering at me from atop the courtyard walls. A whole army of silent Forgotten, gazing down at us. A chill raced up my back, and I stepped closer to Kenzie, raising my sword. Keirran stared up at the Forgotten, his expression a mix of sorrow and guilt.

"We have come so far," the Lady whispered. "So very far. We have survived being forgotten, a war, having the memory of us purged from the Nevernever. We have clung to existence by a thread, and now the instrument of our salvation is standing *right there*." The long, elegant finger suddenly pointed right at me. "Kill him, Prince," she urged, as I tensed. "Once more. For the future of us all. Your hands are already stained with his blood. It should not matter now." Keirran hesitated, and the Lady's voice grew triumphant. "You cannot escape destiny, Prince," she said. "This is what was prophesied from the beginning. This is what you were always fated to do."

"Fate?"

Keirran looked up at the queen, and a hard smile twisted his lips. "You speak of that so easily, as if I have no choice in the matter," he said. "But you knew about the amulet, and what it was doing to me. I was soulless and empty, and your magic kept me alive even as it filled me with anger toward the courts and everything they had done. I was easy to manipulate, but even then, I knew I had a choice. Even though I believed in your cause and wanted to save the Forgotten, I knew I didn't have to wage war on the other courts. I *chose* to become the enemy. Just as I have a choice right now."

He drew his sword, giving me the briefest of looks before turning back to the Lady. "I have much to answer for," he said in a pained voice, "but I finally know where I stand, and it's with my family. If you want Ethan, or anyone in the Never-never, you'll have to get past me."

The First Queen's eyes shifted completely to black.

"As you wish, Prince Keirran," she said in a deadly calm voice. "I am sorry that it has come to this. But the Veil will fall tonight. And if I must spill your blood as well as his, then so be it. It will be a small price to pay for our salvation."

She swept her wings forward. I felt a blast of wind toss my hair, just as a flurry of black feathers sped toward us like darts. I grabbed Kenzie, shielding her with my body, and Keirran flung out an arm with a burst of Winter glamour. The feathers veered away with a hiss, sticking into the walls and stones, glittering like shards of onyx.

Crap.

"Kenzie," I warned, and she nodded. As Keirran sent a small blizzard of ice daggers toward the queen, she broke away and sprinted toward the wall. To the statue where the barely visible form of the Thin Man still sprawled under the rock.

Good. Get out of sight, Kenzie. This is going to be ugly. I turned back, raising my sword, as the Lady's wings swept down, and Keirran's ice daggers shattered against them. She laughed.

"You are not the only one with multiple glamours, my dear prince," the Lady mocked, rising higher into the air. Around us, the Forgotten were a silent audience, watching the battle with glowing yellow eyes. The queen held up her hands, ice and lightning swirling between her fingers. "Before there was a Summer and Winter court, before Arcadia and Tir Na Nog, *I* ruled the Nevernever! Both Summer and Winter bow to me, as will you all, in the end!"

She flung out her arms, and a maelstrom erupted around us. Tornado winds shrieked, lightning flickered, ice and rock fragments spun madly in a circle, sparking off each other. Half-blinded, I raised my arm, searching for Keirran. Though the wind yanked savagely at my hair and clothes, and I felt the charge of electricity raising the hair on my skin, nothing actually touched me, not even the frozen shards and pebbles swirling through the air. Though Keirran was a different story.

I spotted the prince and lurched toward him, just as a pair of lightning bolts streaked down, catching him in a deadly cross fire. Keirran cried out, arching back in agony, then collapsed to his knees on the flagstones.

I lunged at the prince, managing to put myself between him and a razor chunk of ice spinning toward his head. It zipped past me, close enough to make my ear burn with cold, and went spinning off as I huddled over him.

"Keirran." I reached out and grabbed his shoulder, trying to see the damage. He was panting, smoke curling off his back, his face tight with pain. Wind shrieked around us, lightning flickered, and debris flew everywhere, but it was calmer in the center of the storm. I hunched closer to my nephew, sword drawn to deflect any sharp objects that came at him, trying to protect us both.

"It's no good," he muttered through clenched teeth. "She's too strong. This isn't even half of her power. She was…a queen of Faery, after all." He looked up at me, blue eyes full of pain and regret. "You can still…run, Ethan. Her glamour can't touch you now…but if she orders the Forgotten to attack…"

"Shut up," I told him, and smacked down a rock streaking

for his head. "I'm still breathing, so it's not over yet. We're getting out of here…somehow." Glancing desperately around, I saw that the Forgotten had edged closer, many dropping from the wall to the flagstones below. A black swarm waiting at the edge of the courtyard.

Abruptly, the wind sputtered and died. The lightning flickered out, the ice shards and rocks dropped to the ground with faint clinks, bouncing away or shattering on the rock. I straightened, still standing over Keirran, as the First Queen cocked her head, regarding me with cold black eyes.

"Ethan Chase." Her voice was no longer soft or soothing; now it was merely annoyed. "You are either the luckiest or most stubborn mortal I have met in my long existence. How many times must I kill you for it to take? You just will not die like you should."

I smirked, raising my sword and stepping in front of Keirran. "People keep telling me that. I guess I'm just that cockroach you can't get rid of."

She sent a dozen gleaming thorns at me, foot-long and deadly sharp. I stepped back to protect Keirran, and the barbs curved around us, flying into a couple Forgotten instead. They jerked and writhed away into shadow, and the First Queen scowled.

"Very well, Ethan Chase. I was going to give you a quick death, but you refuse to cooperate. Therefore…" She raised her arms and soared higher into the air. "You can be torn to pieces by my Forgotten. You and the prince both. Kill them!" she shouted at the swarm of fey around us. "Rip them apart! Spill their blood across the stones, and let the Veil finally fall!"

The black mass of Forgotten leaped from the walls, pouring into the courtyard and sliding toward us like ink. I spun as Keirran lurched to his feet and raised his sword. For a moment, standing back to back with the Iron Prince, surrounded by

Forgotten in a place of power, I had a surreal flash of déjà vu. The last time this had happened, Keirran had turned around and run a sword through my middle.

"Ethan." His voice was quiet, just like last time. I tensed and forced a raspy chuckle.

"Keirran, if you're about to stab me, I swear I'm going to claw my way out of the grave and drag you back with me."

"No." A shiver went through him, and he took a deep breath. "Just...thank you. And, I'm sorry. For everything. I just... I wish I could talk to my parents one more time." He shifted back and raised his sword, his voice going hard. "But I'll be proud to die fighting beside you."

I grimaced. "Let's not get ahead of ourselves." But it looked pretty hopeless from where I was standing. There were a ton of Forgotten, in the courtyard, on the walls, with even more sliding into view. Even with Keirran's help, I couldn't fight that many. Though I'd give them a hell of a hard time before I went down.

Kenzie, I thought with a pang of regret. I couldn't see her through the press of Forgotten, but I desperately hoped she was safe. *Go home. Go home, and be safe. Things are going to get crazy after tonight, but I know you'll be okay. You're too smart to let them beat you. And if you see my parents, tell them I'm sorry I couldn't come home.*

The Forgotten crept closer, just a few feet away now. I felt the tension surrounding us, saw the swarm getting ready to lunge, and took a deep, final breath.

"Stop!"

A new voice rang out, clear and strong with authority, making everything freeze. Stunned, I looked toward the corner where the voice originated and saw the Thin Man on his feet, one slender hand braced on Kenzie's shoulder as she stood beside him. His pale eyes swept over the Forgotten and narrowed.

"Stop this!" he hissed again. "All of you! This is madness! This is not what you want!"

"You," muttered the First Queen, as the Forgotten, shockingly and as one, turned to face him. "I know you."

"Yes," the Thin Man agreed. "You know me. You've all seen me before, in Phaed. And I know you." His gaze swept the crowd. "All of you. Even now, when you have been twisted nearly beyond recognition, I know you." He shook his head, his voice sympathetic. "Forgotten, hear me. Is this truly what you want? Going to war, fighting the other courts, killing for her? *Dying* for her? Do you really believe she has your best interests at heart? Look at what she has done to you all. What she has turned you into."

The Forgotten were silent, their whole attention riveted to the Thin Man. A few shuffled uneasily, but the rest just stared at him, unblinking. The Thin Man stepped away from Kenzie and walked a few paces forward, still glaring around at the horde.

"You were happy in Phaed," he said. "Content to know nothing, to return quietly to the Nevernever until you could be reborn again. And then, she awoke and convinced you that her ideals were your own." His voice hardened. "They are not. You were never like that! And now, you are nothing but pawns in her quest for power! She will—"

He jerked, throwing his head back, as a storm of razor feathers slammed into him from behind, ripping through his chest with coils of mist. Kenzie gasped, and the Forgotten straightened as the Thin Man swayed on his feet, mouth open midsentence. Slowly, he came apart, fraying at the edges, and collapsed to his knees, before he finally disintegrated into mist.

A breeze stirred the courtyard, and the coils of what used to be the ancient mayor of Phaed vanished into the wind.

"You were always a thorn in my side," the Lady said into the shocked silence. "You will question me no more." Looking over the still frozen crowd, she smiled. "Your mayor is gone," she called, triumphant. "I am your queen and have always been your queen! Obey me, Forgotten. There is no one left to follow, no one who will lead you to victory but I."

"Yes, there is!"

Keirran's voice made me jump. The Iron Prince stepped forward, raising his voice to the crowd. "Forgotten!" he cried. "Rally to me! You've followed me into battle, obeyed my commands and trusted me with your lives. Follow me now! We can cease this fighting, put an end to this war. I swear, I will not let you Fade away, but destroying the Veil is not the answer. You've been used by the First Queen. She has turned you against your own kind, but if we stand together, we can put a stop to this for good!"

"Silence, traitor!" the First Queen hissed, and sent a flurry of razor feathers at him. I quickly lunged forward, and they went spinning aside. "The Forgotten are mine," the queen spat at Keirran. "You have no claim, Iron Prince! You have not been forgotten by the courts. You are in no danger of Fading away. You do not need the emotions and belief of mortals just to stay alive, to exist! I will lead the Forgotten to a new age, an age where all mortals will fear us, believe in us! An age where the courts are no more, where there is only one queen of the Nevernever, and that will be me! Forgotten!" she cried, sweeping her hand down. "Kill them! The Iron Prince and the mortals! Kill them all!"

I tensed, but the Forgotten didn't move. They stared at her, golden eyes unblinking. The First Queen frowned, gazing around in confusion. Keirran stepped forward again.

"It seems the Forgotten do not share your views after all, my lady," he said in a quiet voice, as the queen's expression shifted to fury. "Perhaps if you had truly listened to them, you would have known what they really wanted. But I am sorry that it has come to this."

The First Queen stiffened, power and glamour beginning to swirl around her, whipping at her hair. "Ingrates!" she raged. "Traitors! Obey my commands, or I will destroy you all, every last one of you!"

The Forgotten still didn't move. The Lady swelled with fury and rose higher into the air, raising her arms. "Very well," she growled, as lightning flickered around her. "If that is your choice, then you will all—"

She faltered, dropping several feet from the sky, her eyes going huge. The wind and lightning sputtered and went out. "What?" she gasped, as Keirran bowed his head, looking pained. "What is...? No. No, how *dare* you! Stop, I order you all to stop!"

Confused, I looked around. The Forgotten were still in the same spots, but their eyes were fixed on the First Queen as she flapped and wobbled overhead, trying desperately to stay airborne. I felt a chill go through the air, a faint, sluggish, pulling sensation, and suddenly realized what was happening.

They were draining her glamour. Sucking away her magic and her essence, as they had done to the exiles and half-breeds long ago. Dazed, I watched as the queen hissed and cursed and threw out lightning and wind and ice shards, but all of these sputtered and died before they reached any of the Forgotten. There were too many of them, I realized, hundreds of yellow eyes staring at the First Queen. Even her tremendous power was no match for the combined stares of the Forgotten.

"Iron Prince!" the First Queen cried, searching frantically for Keirran. I glanced at my nephew and found him watching her calmly, though his expression was grim. "Stop! Tell them to stop! You are making a terrible mistake!" Keirran didn't reply, and the queen dropped lower, just a few feet off the ground now, her wings beating the air desperately. "All I wanted was to be remembered," she whispered. "That's all I longed for. To not be forgotten. And to finally defeat the Fade, for all of us. Is that…so terrible? Is it so terrible to be remembered?"

"No, my lady," Keirran answered, as calm and polite as ever. "But there is wanting, and there is doing whatever it takes to achieve it, at the cost of everything around you." His brow creased. "I didn't understand that until recently. How obsession can rob you of everything, even your soul." His gaze flicked to me very briefly. "Sometimes, holding on too hard is dangerous. You have to know when to let go."

With a final cry, the First Queen collapsed to the flagstones. She was losing color now, wisps of glamour rising off her like smoke. A few feathers broke away, fluttering across the courtyard, and Keirran bowed his head.

"I'm sorry," he murmured. "But I won't allow you to hurt my family anymore."

"You," the queen panted, baring her teeth. Planting her palms on the ground, she pushed herself upright, eyes blazing. The Forgotten continued to stare at her, but she staggered forward, her jaw set in determination. "You are more than a monster, Prince. You turned them against me. You destroyed everything we worked so hard for." She raised her hands, black nails growing from her fingertips, and Keirran took a step back. "I may die here, forgotten by all, but I will take you with me!"

She lunged, clawed hands reaching for Keirran's face. I jumped between them, raising my weapon, and felt a jolt run up my arm as the First Queen slammed into the blade, the point sinking deep into her stomach.

Her eyes bulged, but she turned on me with a hiss, and her hands were suddenly around my throat, squeezing hard. I felt curved claws sink into my neck and cut off my air. Gagging, I tried shoving her off, but she clung to me with the strength of the dying, forcing me to my knees, and my vision started to go black.

There was a cry, as a furious, snarling Kenzie lunged to my side, bringing my other sword slashing down at the queen. The Lady shrieked and reeled away, one pale arm writhing into mist, as Keirran stepped up, his face hard and remorseful at the same time, and drove his blade through the Lady's chest, all the way to the hilt.

The First Queen staggered, her face going slack with shock as she stared at the prince. Keirran met her gaze sadly.

"Goodbye, my lady," he said. "You won't be forgotten, I promise."

He yanked the blade free and stepped away. The Lady shuddered, trembling hands going to her chest, as if she couldn't quite believe she'd been stabbed. Her mouth moved, her gaze again seeking the prince, before she bent forward and collapsed in a pile of bones and feathers. Her color faded, leaking out until she was a pale, nearly transparent ghost. The razor-sharp wing feathers dissolved, leaving behind shattered bones. With a final tremor, the First Queen frayed apart, mist and shadows boiling over the ground from where she lay, and writhed into nothingness on the wind.

Kenzie shivered, clinging to me, as we watched the last traces of mist fade away. "Did we win?" she whispered, as I pulled her close and held her against me, just listening to the sound of her heart against mine. "Is it really over?"

Keirran took a deep breath and let it out slowly. "It's done," he said. "The First Queen is gone. The war is over."

As usual, the Forgotten were silent. No cheers, no shouts, no jumping up and down in celebration. They surrounded us, dark and unmoving, their eyes solely on Keirran. One shadow disentangled from the rest and edged forward, until he was a few feet from the prince.

"Iron Prince," it whispered. "The Lady is gone, and we have no purpose, no home. We have given up everything to follow you. What will become of us now?"

Keirran glanced at me, then swept his gaze over the rest of the Forgotten, waiting on the edges. "I don't know," he admitted softly. "I'm not certain what will happen or what will become of us, but I will promise you one thing. I won't forget you. The Lady's way was wrong, but she was right about one thing—you deserve to be remembered, to not Fade away into oblivion. I'll do my best to make a place for you in the Nevernever, but...I have a lot to answer for, and the courts might not be willing to listen. But I won't abandon you. I'll try my hardest to make them see. That's the best I can offer right now. I hope it will be enough."

"Keirran!"

My heart jumped as a deep, familiar voice rang out through the courtyard. Keirran straightened quickly, a flicker of relief, joy and utter terror going through his eyes before he turned toward the entrance.

Ash, Puck and the Wolf strode through the gate, parting Forgotten before them like birds. Ash's cloak was torn to shreds, and Puck had a bloody gash across one cheek, but other than, that they seemed fine. Like they hadn't fought their way through an entire army to get to us. Leanansidhe was not with them, but I had zero doubts that the self-proclaimed Exile Queen was alive and well. She had probably gone back to her own pocket of reality as soon as the battle was over. Puck and Wolf eyed the Forgotten on either side, the Wolf curling a lip in silent warning as they passed, but Ash's bright, intense stare was only for Keirran.

I glanced at the prince. He stood, rigid, in the center of the courtyard, watching his father approach. I looked closer and saw that his hands were shaking, before he clenched them into fists at his sides. The Forgotten drew back into shadows as Ash walked across the flagstones and stood a few feet in front of Keirran.

"Father." Unable to meet those piercing eyes, Keirran's gaze dropped to the ground. Ash didn't say anything at first, his expression unreadable as he faced his son. "I…"

He faltered, wincing. "There is nothing I can say," he whispered, shaking his head. "Nothing that would ever be acceptable. I know I've disappointed you beyond reason—"

Ash took one step forward, hooked the back of Keirran's neck and pulled him close. Keirran let out a shaky breath and squeezed his eyes shut, collapsing against his father, and the two of them stood like that for a few heartbeats while the Forgotten watched silently from the edges of the courtyard. Kenzie leaned against me, and Puck crossed his arms, the faint smirk on his face failing to cover his relief.

"No matter what you've done," Ash murmured, his low voice barely reaching us in the quiet, "or what you tried to accomplish, you're still my son. Nothing will change that, Keirran." He closed his eyes, bowing his head, as the faintest of smiles crossed his face. "Although, you have no idea of the trouble you're in when we get home."

Keirran gave a shaky laugh and nodded. "I figured," he choked out. Ash released him, briefly pressing a palm to the side of his face, before turning to us.

"Ethan," he said, sounding relieved, as well. "Kenzie. You're safe. Where is the First Queen?"

"She's gone," I replied, not missing the flicker of pain and guilt that went through Keirran's eyes. "For good this time. She won't be coming back."

Ash took a quiet breath and let it out slowly. I thought I could see the tension leave him, some great burden lift from his shoulders as he opened his eyes. "Then it's truly over," he said. "The war is done."

"What happened to Leanansidhe?" Kenzie asked.

"Oh, you know Lea." Puck shrugged. "She went back home when she was done making eardrums explode." He stuck a finger in his own ear, rubbing vigorously. "She *was* going to have a chat with the princeling, here, but ice-boy convinced her to let it go." He wrinkled his nose. "Still, I'd avoid her for a few decades if I were you, princeling. She's not terribly happy with you or your friends right now."

Keirran winced. "I don't imagine anyone is," he muttered, and looked back at the ring of yellow eyes, watching us all. "I just hope the rulers will spare the Forgotten," he whispered. "They're not a threat anymore, and I promised I would take care of them, somehow." Ash narrowed his eyes, and Keirran dropped his gaze. "If...if the courts will allow it. If I'm still around...after they decide what to do with me."

Ash gave a somber nod. "The Forgotten concern will have to be addressed," he said, and looked at Puck, who shrugged. "The courts will have to decide what to do about them. But we'll worry about that later. Right now..." He sighed, sounding tired, relieved and eager all at once. "Let's go home. Meghan will be waiting, for all of us."

That sounded good to me. Taking Kenzie's hand, I laced our fingers together and began following Ash and Keirran out of the courtyard. The Forgotten watched us go, making no move to stop us or intervene. Their faces and expressions were impossible to see, but I noticed their eyes following Keirran as he walked away, and a lump settled in my gut. They thought they were never going to see him again.

"That's funny," Puck muttered. "I feel like I'm forgetting something. What was… Oh, right!" Striding forward, he reached out and smacked Keirran on the back of the head, hard.

"Ow!" Keirran spun around, one hand going to his skull, to face Puck's challenging smirk. The Great Prankster raised an eyebrow, almost daring him to say something, and Keirran winced. "Okay, I guess I deserved that," he muttered.

"Ya think?" Puck shot back, and his eyes were dangerous. "Trust me, kid, I'm only going easy on you because you, my friend, still have to face Meghan when we get back to the Nevernever. So, yeah, good luck with that. Otherwise, I'd probably kick your ass for what you put her through."

At the gate, the Wolf snorted a laugh and heaved himself to his feet. "You're all idiots," he stated, shaking his massive head. "I'll be glad to return to the Deep Wyld. Away from all this drama." He eyed Keirran and Puck and curled a lip. "You all are the most delinquent pack I've ever seen."

I smirked, but Kenzie suddenly slowed and pulled me to a stop. Puzzled, I glanced at her and saw she was looking back at the courtyard, her face tight with sorrow.

"Kenzie?"

Her expression fell. "I thought I heard him," she whispered. "For just a second, I thought…" She sniffed, running a hand across her eyes. "I'm going to miss him," she said. "Dammit. I'm going to miss his shrill little voice."

My throat tightened at the thought of our smallest casualty. "I'm sorry," I told her, because there was nothing else I could say. "Will you be all right?"

She nodded. "Yeah," she muttered, squeezing my hand. "I'll be fine. Just...let's get out of here."

I put my arm around her shoulders, and we turned away from the Lady's castle, starting after Ash, Puck and the rest of them.

"Waaaaiiit!"

This time we both froze. I held my breath, and Kenzie was rigid beside me, listening, as a faint, tiny voice drifted over the breeze. I counted the seconds in my head, praying I had heard correctly, that my ears weren't playing tricks on me.

"Wait!" the voice called again...and then he appeared, huge ears poking over the top of the wall. Kenzie's hands went to her mouth, eyes widening, as the gremlin dragged himself atop the stones with one arm. "Wait!" he panted, glowing eyes huge and frantic as he stared down at us. "No leave! No leave Razor! Razor is here!" And he leaped into Kenzie's arms.

CHAPTER TWENTY-THREE

THE FORGOTTEN KING

The faery camp was silent as we stepped through the tear in the Between, back into the Nevernever one last time. Around us, the earth still bore the marks of the last fierce battle; uprooted trees and snapped limbs lay everywhere, tents had been flung to all corners of the camp, and long gouges had been raked through the dirt like claw marks. Everything was quiet as we slipped through the Veil. A squad of Summer and Winter knights straightened quickly as we came through, but other than the guards, there were no signs of fey.

"Huh," Puck remarked, crossing his arms and gazing around at the destruction. "Well, that's disappointing. No cheering crowd to welcome the heroes home? I'm wounded."

"We took a lot of damage and a lot of casualties," Ash replied grimly. "I imagine they're regrouping and trying to recover from the last battle."

Puck sniffed. "Still, you'd think at least someone would be here to greet us… Oh, well, there ya go."

And the Iron Queen appeared, rising from a stump near the edge of the trees, obviously waiting for us. Striding to the center of the clearing, her gaze flickered over all of us, relieved and grateful, before it settled on Keirran.

Keirran swallowed hard. Ash gave him a warning look that

clearly said *don't go anywhere*, and began walking across the field, his long legs carrying him easily over churned ground and scattered limbs. After a moment, Keirran took a deep breath and followed, trailing his father until both stood before the Iron Queen.

Ash didn't stop or slow down but walked straight into Meghan's arms and kissed her fiercely. It was more relief than passion, though Meghan returned the kiss with equal intensity, clutching him tight. And for the first time, I didn't resent it. I finally understood why Meghan had left, all those years ago. If the situation was reversed, I would do the same for Kenzie.

Ash and Meghan drew back, Meghan briefly pressing a palm to the side of his face, before turning to Keirran. He stood, head bowed, eyes on the ground between them, and didn't look up as the queen stepped forward. I saw Meghan's lips move, though her voice was too soft to be heard, meant only for Keirran, and the prince raised his head. His hands trembled as he replied, again too quiet to hear, and Meghan put both hands on his shoulders. One word, one look, passed between them, and then Keirran let out a quiet sob and fell into her arms.

Kenzie sighed, and I moved close, slipping an arm around her as she leaned against me. Razor snorted, giving me a resigned look before moving to her other shoulder. I barely noticed. Watching Meghan, Keirran and Ash, I felt the last of the tension finally drain away. It was done. I didn't know what was in store for Keirran now, what punishment the courts would demand, but for us, at least, it was over. The Lady was gone, the amulet shattered, and the Iron Prince was home. This half of my family was finally safe.

Though the losses were still stupidly high; my throat still hurt at the thought of Annwyl, giving her life to save the prince she loved, and the Thin Man's final words to the Forgotten. The Nevernever was a mess, the Between danger-ously unstable. Keirran's war had ripped this world apart, and those scars would take a long time to heal. Nothing would ever be the same.

Beside us, Puck gave a very exaggerated sniff and wiped his cheek. "Aw, it's a Hallmark moment," he remarked, while the Wolf snorted and rolled his eyes. "Remind me to never ever ever ever have kids, ever."

The Wolf panted a grin. "I think the entire world would echo that sentiment, Goodfellow."

"See? Never say I'm not a giver." Gazing back toward the trio in the clearing, he winced. "Well, here come the courts. Things are gonna get interesting."

I looked back. The courts had indeed arrived, with Oberon, Titania and Mab at the head, a large crowd of fey trailing be-hind. Quickly, we walked forward to join Meghan, Ash and Keirran, as the armies of Summer, Winter and Iron crowded the clearing, dozens of angry fey eyes fastened on the prince.

Keirran gently freed himself from Meghan's arms, stepped back and lowered himself to a knee, bowing his head, as the rulers of Faery halted a few yards away. I could feel the angry energy swirling in the air, freezing temperatures making my skin prickle and static electricity making my hair stand up.

"Prince Keirran." It was Oberon who spoke, and his voice was not friendly. "You have returned. Where is the First Queen?"

"She's dead, Lord Oberon," Keirran replied, keeping his head bowed. "She will threaten the courts and the Between no more. The war is over. The Forgotten have relinquished this fight..." His voice dropped a little. "As have I."

"How convenient," came Titania's smooth, hateful voice. "Now that the First Queen is gone, you attempt to beg your way back to the court's good graces. But we have not forgot-

ten your crimes, the destruction you brought to the Nevernever, the lives you took, your attempt to destroy the Veil.
The Iron Queen cannot protect you this time, Prince." Titania narrowed her eyes, her lip curled in hate and triumph.
"You are a traitor to Faery, and the law demands you must be
punished. Death or eternal exile from the Nevernever. That is
the reward for treason. And neither Mab nor the Iron Queen
can argue with that. It is the ancient law."

"Screw the law," I broke in, startling everyone, even myself.
Why the hell was I defending him again? I just couldn't stop
myself when it came to family. Keirran deserved punishment,
sure, but I was thinking more community service or maybe
grounding him until he was a hundred. Death or eternal exile
from his world and family seemed a little harsh, even for him.

Besides, I'd be damned if I let the evil Summer bitch queen
have her way here. I might've been pissed at my nephew, but
I couldn't stand Titania. "He killed the First Queen," I went
on, staring the rulers down. "The Lady would have destroyed
the Veil, and Keirran chose to stop her and end the war himself. That should count for something."

"You know nothing of our laws, Ethan Chase." This time,
Mab was the one who spoke, though her voice was not quite as
venomous as Titania's. The Winter Queen almost sounded…
regretful. Almost. "Prince Keirran is a traitor to all of Faery.
He waged war on the courts, trying to bring a usurper to
power. Not only that, he attempted to destroy the Veil and
throw both the mortal realm and the Nevernever into chaos.
He is responsible for the destruction of hundreds of lives and,
had his plan succeeded, thousands more. Any one of those
crimes would be cause for death or exile. We cannot simply
turn a blind eye, even if the Iron Prince is the queen's son.
Even if he is kin to us all." Mab raised her voice, her tone

icy. "The law is clear. He must face the consequences of his actions."

"If the Iron Queen refuses," Titania added, smirking at Meghan, "she faces war from both Summer and Winter. Do not think you can let the prince go free. The whole Never-never will rebel if you do."

"I am well aware of this, Queen Titania," Meghan said tightly. "Have I said anything to the contrary? Keirran will be punished, but perhaps you would allow me to decide my son's fate on my own."

The Summer Queen glared at her. "He deserves death," she hissed, making me tense, and Kenzie stiffened in horror. "Exile is too good for him, not with the destruction he has caused. That boy is a danger to the Nevernever and all of Faery, and we should make certain he will never have the chance to rebel again."

"If any would like to try," came Ash's deep, terrifying voice, and a sheet of frost spread over the ground, "they can step forward right now." Unsurprisingly, no one did.

"What would you have us do, then, Iron Queen?" Oberon asked. "Titania does raise a serious concern. Your son is a prince of Faery, with the glamour of all three courts flowing through him. You have seen firsthand the destruction he is capable of. If we exile him, how do we know he will not someday return with an army of exiles at his back to threaten the Nevernever once more?"

"Oh, come on!" Kenzie exclaimed. "He's right there, on his knees. Does he really look like he's going to try to take over the Nevernever again?" Her voice softened, and she gazed down at the prince in sympathy. "He's lost things, too," she murmured. "More than you would understand. If you just talked to him, you would know that."

"Is that so?" Oberon didn't sound convinced. "Then perhaps he should tell us these things. Speak, then, Iron Prince," he ordered, gazing down at the kneeling faery. "Now is your chance to state your intentions, before we decide your fate. Do you not have anything to say on your behalf?"

"I throw myself on the mercy of the courts," Keirran replied in a flat voice, not looking up. "I have nothing to say in my defense. Do with me what you will. But..." He hesitated, then took a quiet breath. "Please, spare the Forgotten. They were pawns in the Lady's scheme, and she...*we*, used them terribly. They're not a threat to the courts or the Nevernever. They truly just want to survive."

"Not a threat?" Titania mocked, making me want to stab her. "The army that attacked us this very evening, who followed the First Queen and killed for her without fail, are not a threat? They are nearly as dangerous as you, Iron Prince. They must be dealt with, one way or another."

"Do you wish another war, then, Queen Titania?" Meghan challenged. "Or are you simply advising the complete genocide of a whole race of faery? These Forgotten are not as dangerous as the Iron fey when they were under Ferrum and Machina. Surely there is a way the Forgotten can live without being a danger to Faery."

A very loud, bored yawn interrupted what would've been another challenge from Titania. "I believe," said a large gray cat sitting on a rock where nothing had been before, "that you are all missing the obvious solution.

"The Forgotten are huddled in the Between," Grimalkin went on, curling his tail around himself as the entire Summer, Winter and Iron courts turned to stare at him. "They must not become a danger to the Nevernever or the Veil, that is very clear. Who is the only one, besides the First Queen, that can slip between worlds? Who has already carved out a place, an entire kingdom, within the Veil? Whom do the Forgotten already listen to?" With another yawn, the cat shook his head and bent to lick his back toes. "Really, it is a wonder Faery has survived this long," he mused. "I shudder to think of what would happen were I not here to point out the obvious."

Silence fell after Grimalkin's statement. Titania looked like she wanted to say something, but couldn't find the words to argue or protest. Oberon merely looked thoughtful, but Mab had the faintest trace of a smile on her lips. It was gone in the next instant, but it was there.

I looked at Meghan, saw her exchange a glance with Ash. He gave a grim nod, and she closed her eyes.

Straightening her shoulders, she gazed down at Keirran.

"Prince Keirran." Her voice rang with authority, and everything went perfectly still, holding its breath. Keirran was motionless, staring rigidly at the ground, waiting. "You have been found guilty of treason against the Iron, Winter and Summer courts. As monarch of Mag Tuiredh, I hereby sentence you to exile...in the Between. You are no longer welcome in the Nevernever, the trods will be forever closed to you, and you are not to enter Faery through the Veil or by any other path." Her voice trembled for just a moment, before growing strong again. "From this day on, you will be known as the Forgotten King, Guardian of the Veil, and you will make sure your subjects never again threaten the Nevernever. Do you understand?"

"Yes, Your Majesty," Keirran whispered, sounding dazed.

"Then rise, King of the Forgotten," Meghan said. "And return to your subjects." She blinked rapidly as Keirran rose, still in a state of shock. "Go to the Forgotten. They are your responsibility now. Tell them that the war is over, and the courts will leave them in peace if they do the same."

"I will, Your Majesty," Keirran said, and there was a change in his voice now. Determined and grave, that same resolve I'd seen before, but without the stubborn abandon. "I promise, I will make this right. I will earn my title and my redemption, even if it takes me a thousand years."

"It might, Forgotten King," Mab said softly. The Winter Queen did not seem angry or hostile, but her voice was a subtle warning. "We are fey. We do not forget. We do not forgive. And we will remember this day for eternity. If you hope for redemption, I'm afraid you will be waiting a very long time."

Keirran bowed to them all. "Then I had best get started quickly."

"Hold," Meghan said as Keirran took a step back. Facing the other rulers and the army of fey behind them, she raised her voice. "It is done," she stated. "The sentence has been carried out. Keirran will depart the Nevernever momentarily, but before he leaves, I would speak to my son alone."

Oberon nodded. The three rulers turned away, after Titania shot a vicious, disgusted look at Meghan, and the army behind them began to clear out. Soon, it was just me, Kenzie and Puck standing across from Meghan, Ash and Keirran. I looked around and, with a start, saw that Wolf had vanished, slipping back into the unknown where he'd come from, having finally gotten tired of crowds and eternal faery politics. Grimalkin sat on the same rock a few feet away, still washing his fur but probably listening to everything we said. Razor poked his head out of Kenzie's hair, bared his teeth at the cat and ducked back again, muttering "bad kitty" under his breath.

"Well." Puck sighed, lacing his hands behind his skull. "Here we are, one more time. I guess this is See Ya Later, for all of us." He glanced at Keirran, raising an eyebrow. "I hope you don't expect me to call you 'Your Majesty' now, kid. 'Cause that ain't gonna happen."

Keirran gave a sad smile. "Thank you," he whispered, soft enough that no other faery would catch it. "All of you. I know

I don't deserve it but…I'll try to do this right. For the For-gotten. And Annwyl. Ethan?" He swallowed hard, and his gaze rose to mine. "I know I've wronged you the most of all. And you still came back for me. You and Kenzie both." He glanced at the girl beside me, and she smiled, though Razor hissed at Keirran and muttered "Bad master," then turned his back on him. Keirran's eyes clouded with pain and guilt, and he took a second to compose himself.

"I…owe you more than my life," Keirran went on, stum-bling a bit over the words. "And after what I did to you, I can't ever begin to apologize, but—" he raked a hand through his hair "—I just… I wanted to let you know…"

"Oh, shut up." I sighed, and held out a hand. "Apology ac-cepted. Just shake my hand and stop talking before this gets even more awkward."

Keirran smiled. Stepping forward, he grasped my palm, nearly crushing my fingers in relief. I clenched my jaw and endured, gripping his hand in return. "I guess you're going home after this," he said, finally dropping my hand. "Back to the mortal world?" I nodded.

"Yeah. Hopefully for good this time." I thought of my par-ents and how long it had been since they'd seen me last. Back in the real world, my eighteenth birthday had come and gone, and I hadn't been there to celebrate. Thinking about Mom, sitting in the house on my birthday, crying over an unlit cake, made my throat tighten. I, too, had a lot to make up for.

He nodded. "Goodbye, then, Ethan. Maybe I'll see you around someday. Kenzie, you, too."

"Hold on," Kenzie said as he stepped back. "You owe some-one else an apology, Keirran." When he stopped, puzzled, she pointed to the gremlin on her shoulder. "I think you have something to say to Razor, don't you?"

"Ah." Keirran blinked, then smiled sadly. "Yes. I would

have earlier, but gremlins are faeries. They hold a grudge forever. He has every right to be angry with me."

"That's not an excuse! You threw him over a wall, among other things."

"You're right." Keirran held up his hands, then looked at the gremlin. Razor's head was turned away, deliberately not looking at him. "I'm sorry, Razor," the prince said, very solemnly. "I know you're angry, and that's okay. Thank you for taking care of Kenzie."

The gremlin's ears twitched. Slowly, he turned his head, meeting the prince's gaze, and sniffed. "Bad Master," he said, almost a reprimand. "Not care about Razor. Don't hurt pretty girl again. Promise!"

Keirran's eyebrows rose in shock. "Oh," he said, as the gremlin glared at him. "I...I won't. I promise."

Puck laughed, shaking his head at the prince's expression. "Looks like you just got scolded by a gremlin, *Your Majesty*," he chuckled, and crossed his arms. "Ah, can't say I'm not gonna miss you two. We had some fun times, right, princeling? Saddest part is, I won't ever hear ice-boy complain that I'm corrupting you again. But, I guess all good things must come to an end." He sighed, gave Keirran a friendly arm punch and raised his hand. "See ya 'round, kid. Try not to let those Slim Shadys suck out all your fun. Ethan Chase?" Puck winked at me. "I'm sure I'll see you again, whether you like it or not."

"Yeah," I deadpanned. "So looking forward to it."

Puck laughed again. "Don't you forget it. Until the next adventure, kiddos." Sticking his hands into his pockets, the Great Prankster sauntered off, whistling, until he reached the edge of the trees and vanished into the shadows.

Keirran watched him go, then took a breath. "I guess that leaves me," he murmured, staring around at the forest, as if memorizing it. "It's strange. I never thought it would be this hard to leave it behind."

Meghan embraced him once more. "I love you, Keirran," she whispered, as the prince buried his face in her shoulder. "Always. No matter where you are, never forget that."

"I won't," Keirran choked out. "And I'll make you proud. Someday, I'll redeem myself and come home. I promise."

She pulled back and kissed him on the forehead. Ash gripped his shoulder, sharing a brief, knowing look with his son. Then Keirran stepped back, bowed to them both and turned away.

We watched him walk across the clearing, to the place where the Forgotten had poured through the barrier earlier that night. Watched him raise his arm and part the Veil, revealing the darkness of the Between through the tear. Keirran looked back only once, blue eyes and silver hair glowing in the moonlight. For a moment, I was reminded of that first night, the first time I'd met my nephew, perched on a balcony railing in the Iron Palace, bright and carefree with the moonlight blazing down on him. He gave a brief, fleeting smile…

…and vanished into the Between, slipping away like he was never there at all.

Meghan blinked, a tear crawling down her face, before she wiped her eyes and turned to me.

"All right," she said, and though the terrible grief lingered on her face, she tried to smile. "It has been a very, very long night. Let's get the both of you home."

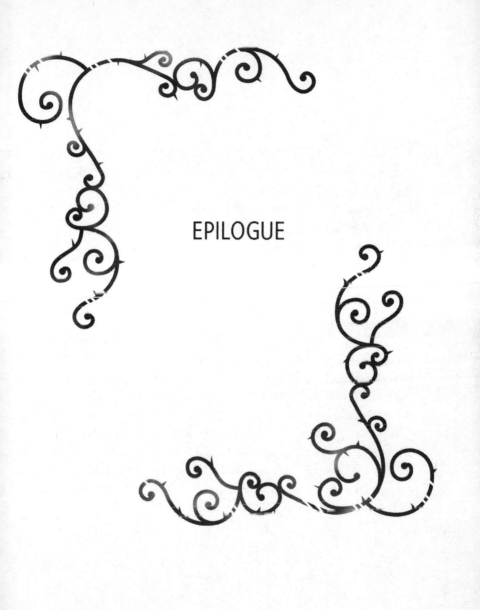

EPILOGUE

Eight months later

I stood in my room, staring at my bed, arms crossed as I scanned the assortment of clothes folded in the open suitcase. Shirts, pants, underwear, socks, toiletries…was I missing anything? Other than the anti-faery items, stuffed into another duffel bag, that is. Not that I needed them much, anymore. Being immune to magic and glamour, I was no fun to torment now, as most faeries soon discovered and left me alone. I wished humans were so easy to sway.

It had been one year since the Veil disappeared, since humans became able to see the fey, and even though it had been for only a few minutes, it had left its mark. Nothing large or obvious, but the world *had* changed in subtle ways. Even in my small corner of reality. At school, the art and music programs had exploded in attendance, and you couldn't go one week without seeing flyers for a poetry jam or a sign-up form for drama class, at least according to Kenzie. Five months ago, I'd received the shock of my life when Todd Wyndham showed up on my doorstep, his memory fully restored, wanting to discuss everything that had happened. He was still human, but he could see the fey again, and we'd spent several long evenings talking about the Hidden World and what he would do now. We weren't exactly close, but Todd was another person who could see the fey, who understood that part of my life and knew what I was going through. When he and his family moved to another state in the summer, I was sorry to see him go.

Todd wasn't the only one affected. Everywhere I went, people seemed...less frantic, I supposed. Less cynical and jaded, and more willing to believe things lurked out there in the dark. The fey world, too, had changed, at least on this side of the Veil. The faeries I glimpsed in the mortal world were brighter now, more...real...than They'd been before the Between went down. I felt that, with just a little more glamour, a little more belief, They just might pierce the Veil and start becoming visible to those who wanted to see Them.

Or maybe I was crazy. Maybe seeing the fey for so long had skewed my perception of reality. But, ever since I'd returned from the Nevernever, I'd noticed that the world around me—both worlds, actually, were a little different than before. I suspected it would be a while before things truly returned to normal, if ever. Maybe that was a good thing.

"Ethan?" Mom tapped on the door of my room. "MacKenzie is here. Should I tell her you're busy?"

I jerked up. "No! Be right out," I called. Closing the suitcase, I zipped it shut, then put it on the floor next to the duffel bag and opened the door.

Kenzie smiled at me over the threshold. "Hey, tough guy," she greeted, as Razor cackled and bounced from her shoulder into my room. Though her smile was cheerful, her eyes were shadowed. "Thought I'd get here a little early, seeing as I'm going to lose you tomorrow."

I drew her into my arms, kissing her deeply. "You're not losing me," I said as we pulled back. "I just... I have to get out of here, Kenzie. You know that. Too many whispers. Too many rumors surrounding me and my family. I need to find a place where nobody knows me, where I can try to start again." Kenzie sighed, and I held her tighter. "I'll be back," I promised. "I'm not leaving you."

She sniffed. "I know."

"Besides," I teased, running my fingers through her hair, "you'll be off to college soon, Ms. Scholarship Girl. And you'll be so busy with parties and classes and sorority clubs that you'll forget all about me."

"I very seriously doubt that," Kenzie said, her gaze flicking to Razor, chewing on one of my pencils on the desk. "Hard to forget what we've been through when there's a gremlin staring you in the face all the time." Her brow furrowed, and she shook her head. "I don't know what's going to happen when I leave for college, because there's no way Razor is staying behind. When I told him to go back to the Iron Realm last week, he nearly short-circuited all the lights in the house with his tantrum. So, looks like I'm stuck with him." She rolled her eyes. "Whatever happens, it's gonna be interesting."

Drawing back, she walked over to my bed and plopped onto the mattress, and I crossed the room to shut the door. "Hey, how are the therapy sessions going?" I asked, rescuing an ink pen from Razor, who gave me an irritated buzz and bounced over to Kenzie. She snorted, absently patting the gremlin's head as he scrambled to her shoulder.

"Okay, I guess. Dad still doesn't like talking about Mom, but this woman is persistent. He actually choked up during the last session." Kenzie shook her head, amazed. "We finally had a sort-of conversation this morning, without any intervention. He doesn't know about my...um...talent with invisible things, but I don't think that will ever be in the cards. Still, I figure by the time I leave for college, he might actually treat me like a daughter and not a very breakable piece of furniture." She sighed. "Though it will be nice to leave the house without hearing all the warnings about drugs and teen pregnancy."

I chuckled. "He still hates my guts, doesn't he?"

"*Hate* is such a strong word." Kenzie grimaced. "It's more of a strong revulsion now. And I've sung your praises, told him you got your GED over the summer, everything I could think of. The man is intractable."

"Yeah." I shoved the thought of Kenzie's father out of my head, determined not to ruin this moment. "Hey, come here a second." She frowned but stood up and walked to where I was leaning against the desk. My heart pounded as I turned, reached into one of the drawers and pulled out a small white box. "I…um…got you something," I said, watching her eyes light up as I turned back. "Sort of a congratulations gift. Six months as of today, you've been in remission. I hope it's for another six years. Longer than that. I hope its forever."

A lump rose to my throat, and I swallowed hard. It might not be forever, I reminded myself. Remission wasn't a cure, it was not a sure thing. Kenzie's illness could come back someday. Who knew how much time we had? But that was the real world; Faery magic couldn't make everything better. You couldn't wave a wand and have all your wishes come true. Real life wasn't a fairy tale.

I was okay with that, though. I didn't need magic to solve everything. However long I had with Kenzie, I wasn't going to waste it.

She blinked, and her eyes went a little glassy. "It's not much," I warned, holding out the box. "Just a reminder that, even though I'll be away from you, I'll always be yours."

Carefully, she opened the box. Inside was a simple necklace with two hearts, one gold and one silver, intertwined in the center. They were engraved, the silver one reading *tough guy*, the other simply saying *forever.*

"Ethan," Kenzie whispered, sounding awed. "It's beautiful."

Gently, I drew it out and fastened it around her neck, and she gazed at me with huge dark eyes, the hint of a smile playing on her lips. "I never thought you could be such a romantic."

I smiled. "Well, then, let me convince you beyond all doubt," I said. Brushing back her hair, I drew closer, gazing into her eyes. "I love you, Kenzie," I said. "You're my partner, and my sanity, and my saving grace. We've gone through so much, more than any normal person could dream of, and you've always been there for me. Someday, when you're ready, it'll be a ring in that box instead of a necklace. I can't think of anyone else I'd rather have at my side. And someday, if Faery calls me back, I want you with me. Fighting dragons and bargaining with faery queens and arguing with talking cats." She was crying now, smiling broadly through the tears, and I brushed her cheek. "So you don't have to worry about losing me tomorrow," I told her. "Because there's no way I'll ever leave you behind."

She kissed me then, and it went on for a long while. Not even Razor's cackles of *kissy-kissy* could distract me from the girl in my arms. Only the sound of the doorbell ringing broke us apart. Curious, I pulled back, listening as it rang again. We didn't have many visitors. Other than Kenzie, who never rang the doorbell, no one really visited the house.

Leaving the room, we wandered hand in hand down the hall, meeting Mom in the kitchen. She looked as puzzled as I felt. Dad was home tonight as well, and was walking across the tile to answer the door. As his hand closed on the knob, Razor let out an excited cry and, abruptly, I knew.

Pulling the door back, Dad stared in surprise as Meghan

smiled at me through the frame. My heart jumped, and Mom gasped.

"Meghan!"

She rushed forward, and Meghan stepped inside to be engulfed in a hug. Stunned, I could only watch as Mom drew back, her face alight with questions. "We didn't know you were coming!" Mom exclaimed, taking her hands. "How have you been? Will you be staying long—"

She stopped, staring at something just outside the door. Meghan took a deep breath and moved aside...

...as Keirran stepped into the room.

I straightened, and beside me, Kenzie's hand went to her mouth. The Forgotten King, dressed in very normal-looking jeans and a T-shirt, smiled and nodded at me across the room. He looked...happy. Content. Though there was a somberness to him now that hadn't been there before, a maturity that went beyond his years. Razor gave a high-pitched, welcoming buzz and waved to his former master, and Keirran grinned at him, as well.

"Mom." Meghan's voice was soft, hesitant, as she turned to Keirran and placed a hand on his shoulder. But her voice and face glowed with pride as she drew him forward, and his brightness seemed to fill the entire room. "I think it's past time you met your grandson."

★ ★ ★ ★ ★

ACKNOWLEDGMENTS

Well, here we are. The end of the Iron Fey series. Hard to believe we've reached the finale, but what a trip it has been.

Back when I first started *The Iron King*, I had no idea the journey I would set out on, or where it would lead. I had no idea it would spawn a massive, magical world filled with characters who have become as familiar to me as my own family. Meghan, Ash, Puck, Ethan, Keirran, Kenzie, Grimalkin… they've become so much more than words on paper. They've become characters with entire histories, past lives, fears, triumphs, failures and legacies. And the world of the Iron Fey has grown beyond all my expectations.

Thank you to all my readers and fans who have taken this journey with me. I wouldn't be here without you.

Thank you to my agent, Laurie, for taking a chance on a shy, unknown writer from Kentucky.

Thank you to my editor, Natashya, who has always, always made my work stronger.

Thank you to the amazing people at Harlequin TEEN. For awesome covers, fabulous support and everything else.

And finally, to my wonderful husband, Nick, who started this adventure with me and has been there every step of the way. Still couldn't have done it without you.

And so, after all these years, we finally close the door on the Iron Fey series. But one thing about doors is this: they can always be opened again. Perhaps someday in the future a door will swing back, and the Nevernever will be glimpsed through the frame once again, urging you to take that first step...into a new adventure.

"It was...quite a ride, wasn't it?"
—*Meghan Chase*

Enter a new world created by
Julie Kagawa—
a world in which dragons walk among
us in human form, hiding in plain sight...
but not for long.

Turn the page to read an excerpt from

book one of The Talon Saga.

Available now.
Only from Julie Kagawa
and Harlequin TEEN!

EMBER

"YOU LOOK TIRED, HATCHLING." Scary Talon Lady eyed me critically across the desk, arms crossed as she looked me up and down. "Did you not get enough sleep? I told your guardians I wanted you here early today."

"It's five-thirty in the morning," I said, knowing how I must look—eyes bloodshot, hair spiky with wind and salt. "The sun isn't even up yet."

"Well, this should perk you right up." My instructor smiled in that way that chilled my blood. "We're doing something a little different this morning. Follow me."

Nervously, I trailed her down to the storage room, then blinked in surprise when she opened the door. The normally vast, empty space was filled wall to wall with crates, pallets, steel drums and ladders. Some were stacked nearly to the ceiling, creating a labyrinth of shadowy aisles, hallways and corridors, a gigantic maze inside the room.

"What's this for?" I asked, just as something small and fast streaked from the darkness and hit me right in the chest. With a yelp, I staggered back, clutching my shoulder. Thick liquid spread over my clothes, and my hand came away smeared with red. "What the hell?" I gasped.

"It's paint," my trainer said calmly, easing my panicked confusion. "But, make no mistake, had that been a real bullet, you would most assuredly be dead." She waved an arm toward the labyrinth of boxes looming before me in the darkness. "There are a dozen 'St. George soldiers' hiding in that maze," she continued, smiling down at me. "All hunting you. All looking to kill you. Welcome to phase two of your training, hatchling. I want you to go in there and survive as long as you can."

I stared into the room, trying to catch glimpses of my attackers, these "soldiers" of St. George. I couldn't see anything, but I was quite certain they could see me and were probably watching us right now. "How long is long enough?" I asked quietly.

"Until I say so."

Of course. With a sigh, I began walking toward the maze, but Scary Talon Lady's voice stopped me before I took three steps.

"What do you think you're doing, hatchling?"

Annoyed, I turned back, wondering what I'd done wrong this time. "I'm doing what you told me to. Go into maze, get shot at, survive. Isn't that what you want?"

My instructor gave me a blatant look of disgust and shook her head. "You're not taking this seriously. If you are trapped in a warehouse with a team of well-trained, heavily armed St. George soldiers, do you really think you are going to survive as a human?"

I stared at her, frowning, before I got what she was really saying. "You...you mean I can do this in my real form?"

She rolled her eyes. "I do hope your brother catches on faster than you. It would be a shame to lose you both to stupidity."

"Yes!" I whispered, clenching my fist. I barely heard the insult. I could finally be a dragon without breaking the rules. That almost made this whole crazy exercise worth it.

My trainer snapped her fingers and pointed to a large stack of crates in the corner.

"If you are concerned about modesty or your clothes, you may change over there," she ordered in a flat voice. "Though

you are eventually going to have to get over that. There will
be no time to find a bathroom if you are being chased by snip-
ers in helicopters."

I hurried over and ducked behind the boxes, then shrugged
out of my clothes as fast as I could. My body rippled as the
dragon burst free again, wings brushing against the wooden
crates as they unfurled for the second time that morning. It
was still liberating, still completely freeing, even after a whole
night of flying around.

My talons clicked over the concrete as I stalked back to the
maze, feeling comfortable and confident in my dragon skin.
Even Scary Talon Lady didn't look quite so scary anymore,
though she eyed my dragon self with as much bored disdain
as she did my human self.

"Hold still," she ordered, and pressed something into my ear
hole, right behind my horns. I snorted and reared back, shaking my head, and she cuffed me under the chin. "Stop that.
It's just an earbud. It will allow me to communicate with you
in the maze, and to hear everything that is going on around
you. So, stop twitching."

I curled my lip, trying not to think about it, even though
it was uncomfortable. My trainer didn't notice. "On my signal," she continued, pulling out her phone, "you have two
minutes to find a good position and prepare for the hunt. If
you are shot, you are 'dead.' Which means you have two minutes to find another position before the hunt starts again, and
I add another fifteen minutes to the overall game. How long
we are here depends on how long you survive, understand?"

Crap. That meant I just would have to avoid getting shot.
No way I was staying here all afternoon, not with Garret wait-
ing for me. Dragon or no, I'd promised him a surf lesson, and
I still wanted to see him. "Yes," I answered.

"I will be observing your progress from up top," she continued, "so do not think you can lie about being killed. We *will* stay here all day if that is what it takes until I am satisfied."

Double crap. How long I would have to stay alive before this unappeasable woman was "satisfied?" Probably much longer than I thought.

"Two minutes," Scary Talon Lady reminded me. "Starting... now."

I spun, claws raking over the cement, and bounded into the maze.

I didn't see any soldiers as I wove my way through the endless corridors, peeking around crates to make sure the aisles were empty. Everything remained very quiet, save for my breathing and the click of my talons on the cement. As I crept farther into the room, no one shot at me, nothing moved in the shadows, no footsteps shuffled over the ground. Where were these so-called soldiers, anyway? Maybe this was an elaborate hoax my trainer had cooked up to make me paranoid. Maybe there was no one here at all...

Something small and oval dropped into the corridor from above, bounced once with a metallic click and came to rest near my claws. As I stared in confusion, there was a sudden deafening hiss, and white smoke erupted from the tiny object, spewing everywhere. I backed away, squinting, but the smoke had completely filled the aisle and I couldn't see where I was going.

Shots erupted overhead, and several blows struck me from all sides. As the smoke cleared, I looked up to see six humans standing atop the aisle, three on either side. They wore heavy tactical gear and ski masks, and carried large, very real-looking guns in their hands. My whole body was covered in red paint, dripping down my scales and spattering to the concrete. I cringed as the realization hit. I'd stood no chance against them. I'd walked right into their ambush, and if these were real St. George soldiers, I'd be blown to bits.

"And you're dead," buzzed a familiar voice in my ear as the figures slipped away and vanished as quickly as they had appeared. "A very dismal start, I'm afraid. Let us hope you can turn this around, or we will be here all day. Two minutes!"

A little daunted now, I hurried down another corridor, attempting to put as much distance between me and the six highly trained soldiers as I could.

SOMETIME LATER I CROUCHED, exhausted, behind a stack of pallets, my sides heaving from the last little scuffle. I'd been running from the soldiers for what seemed like hours, and they always seemed one step ahead of me. I'd slip away from one only to be shot by another hiding atop the crates overhead. I'd enter a corridor to find it blocked by two soldiers, and when I turned to run, two more would appear behind me, boxing me in. I was almost completely covered in paint; it seeped between my scales and dripped to the floor when I moved, looking very much like blood. And each time I was hit, my trainer's bored, smug voice would crackle in my ear, taunting me, telling me I had failed again, that I was dead.

I had no idea how much time had passed from the last time I'd been shot. Minutes? Hours? I didn't think it mattered, not with my sadistic instructor keeping track. Curling my tail around myself, I huddled in the dark corner, breathing as quietly as I could and hoping that maybe the "hide and hope they don't notice you" method would allow me to survive long enough to get out of here.

A small oval object sailed over the stack of crates, hit the wall and bounced toward me with a clink. I hissed and shot out of the corner before it could go off. Most of the projectiles lobbed at me had been smoke grenades, which, while

I didn't have to worry about things like smoke inhalation, made it very difficult to see in the tight corridors. Death by paint usually followed as I thrashed around in confusion. But the last grenade had exploded in a blinding burst of light, and the soldiers had pumped me full of rounds as I'd stood there, stunned. *Not going through that again, thanks.*

I darted for another shadowy corner and ran into a bullet storm. The bastards were lying in wait right outside my hiding spot, and had trapped me inside a funnel of death. Cringing, I closed my eyes and hunkered down as I was bathed in red paint, again.

"Pathetic," sighed a familiar, hated voice when the ambush was done and the soldiers had slipped back into the maze. "Let us pray that you are not ever hunted by the real soldiers of St. George, because your head would be mounted over their fireplace in no time. Two minutes!"

Anger blazed, and my fraying temper finally snapped. With a snarl, I turned and lashed out at a pile of crates, ripping a huge chunk of wood from the boxes with my claws.

All right, enough was enough! Why should I be the hunted? I was a freaking *dragon*. The apex predator, according to Talon. If survival meant not getting shot at all costs, maybe I should be the one doing the hunting.

I crouched, then leaped atop one of the crate piles, landing as quietly as I could. The labyrinth spread out before me, looking much different from up top. *All right, you bastards*, I thought, lowering myself into a stalking position, my belly scales nearly brushing the crates. *We're changing the rules a bit. This time, I'm coming for you.*

I prowled along the top of the maze, keeping my body low and straight and my wings pressed to my back, all senses attuned for the sights, sounds and smell of my prey. Slithering over the narrow aisles, my steps light so my talons wouldn't clack and give me away, I felt a savage, growing excitement. *This* felt natural, easy. The fear I'd had before disappeared, and everything seemed sharper, clearer, now that I was on the hunt. I could sense my enemies, lurking in the shadows and darkness, waiting for me. But now, they were the ones in danger.

I caught a whiff of human ahead of me and froze, one claw suspended above the crates. Holding myself perfectly still, I watched a soldier creep along the top of the maze without seeing me, then drop silently into the narrow aisle below.

Crouching even lower, my chin just a few inches from the wood, I stalked noiselessly to the place the soldier had dropped out of sight and peered over the edge. He stood almost directly below, his gaze and the muzzle of his gun pointed at the end of the corridor, where another two soldiers waited, I saw. None of them had noticed me.

Hello, boys. I grinned, and felt my back haunches wriggle as I tensed to pounce. *Payback's a bitch.*

"Death from above!" I howled, leaping toward my opponents with talons and wings spread. The soldier jerked and looked up, just as I landed on him with a snarl, driving him to the cement. His helmeted head struck the back of a pallet, and he lay there, dazed.

The other two soldiers instantly whipped around and raised their guns. I roared, baring my fangs, and went for them, barely avoiding a paintball to the face as I lunged. Bounding toward the first soldier, I leaped sideways, catapulted off the wall to avoid the spray of bullets and drove my horned head into his chest, flinging him back several feet. He crashed into a stack of crates, which collapsed on top of him, and struggled to rise. The last soldier swiftly backed away as I spun on him, growling, and tensed to pounce.

"Stop!"

The command rang in my ear but also directly in front of

me, and I stumbled to halt a lunge away from the last opponent. Shouldering the gun, the final soldier reached up and pulled off his helmet and mask, revealing Scary Talon Lady's face in the dim light. I blinked in surprise and quickly stepped back.

"Finally." My trainer raked a hand through her hair, long golden strands falling down her back. Her acidic eyes regarded me over the hall. "About time, hatchling. I was wondering if the purpose for this exercise would ever penetrate that thick skull of yours. I was certain we'd be here until midnight, chasing you around the building, before you finally figured it out."

Confused, I shook my head. "You...you *wanted* me to attack," I guessed. "To go on the offensive. That was the whole point, wasn't it?" My trainer raised a mocking eyebrow, and I scowled. "You weren't going to let me quit until I started fighting back, no matter how long I survived down here."

She lowered the gun and nodded. "Exactly. Dragons are never *prey*, hatchling. Dragons are *hunters*. Even to the soldiers of St. George, we are deadly, intelligent, highly adaptable killers. We are not to be taken lightly. If you are ever trapped in a building with a soldier of St. George, his life should be in just as much danger, do you understand? Because you'll be hunting him, as well. And one more thing..."

Faster than thought, she raised the gun and fired it, point-blank, at my chest. The paint bullet exploded in a spray of crimson, making me flinch even though it didn't hurt. My instructor smiled coldly.

"*Never* hesitate to go in for the kill."

From TALON by Julie Kagawa. Available now!

Copyright © 2014 by Julie Kagawa

New York Times Bestselling Author

JULIE KAGAWA

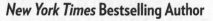

THE IRON FEY

"Julie Kagawa is one killer storyteller." —MTV's *Hollywood Crush* blog

Book 1   Book 2   Book 3   Book 4

Book 5   Book 6   Book 7   Anthology

The Iron Fey
Boxed Set

Available wherever books are sold.

juliekagawa.com

HTIRONFEYTR8

A reckoning is brewing...
Should they retreat to fight another day,
or start an all-out war?

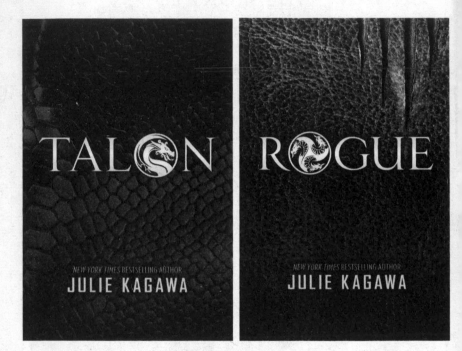

Read books 1 & 2 of the epic *Talon Saga*
by *New York Times* bestselling author
Julie Kagawa!

™ www.HarlequinTEEN.com

juliekagawa.com

HTJKTALONR3

From the *New York Times* bestselling author
of **The Iron Fey** series and **The Talon Saga**

JULIE KAGAWA

BLOOD OF EDEN

AVAILABLE WHEREVER BOOKS ARE SOLD!

IN A FUTURE WORLD, VAMPIRES REIGN.
HUMANS ARE BLOOD CATTLE.
AND ONE GIRL WILL SEARCH FOR THE KEY
TO SAVE HUMANITY.

www.HarlequinTEEN.com

juliekagawa.com

HTBBOETR4

Alexander the Great meets *Games of Thrones*
for teens in Book 1 of the epic new
Blood of Gods and Royals series
by *New York Times* bestselling author

ELEANOR HERMAN

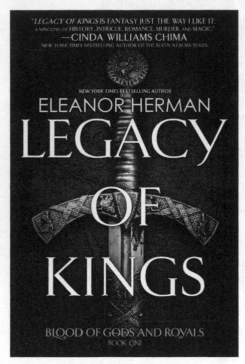

IMAGINE A TIME
WHEN CITIES BURN...
AND IN THEIR ASHES
EMPIRES RISE.

Available Now!

www.HarlequinTEEN.com

HTEHLOKR4

Somewhere between
reality and myth lies...
THE TWIXT

Some things are permanent.
Indelible.

Some things lie beneath
the surface.
Invisible.
With the power to
change everything.

True evil is rarely obvious.
It is quiet, patient.
Insidious.
Awaiting the perfect
moment to strike.

"This exhilarating story of Ink and Joy has marked my heart forever. More!"
—Nancy Holder, *New York Times* bestselling author of *Wicked*

Don't miss a single installment of ***The Twixt***.
Books 1–3 available wherever books are sold!

www.HarlequinTEEN.com

HTINDTR4

FROM *NEW YORK TIMES* BESTSELLING AUTHOR

GENA SHOWALTER

THE WHITE RABBIT CHRONICLES

Book 1   Book 2   Book 3   Book 4

Don't miss a single thrilling installment of
The White Rabbit Chronicles!

The night her entire family dies in a terrible car accident,
Alice Bell finds out the truth—the "monsters" her father
always warned her about are real. They're zombies.
And they're hungry—for her.

www.HarlequinTEEN.com

HTAIZTR5